LODORE

REDISCOVERED CLASSICS

LODORE

MARY SHELLEY

UNION
SQUARE
& CO.

NEW YORK

**UNION
SQUARE
& CO.**

NEW YORK

UNION SQUARE & CO. and the distinctive Union Square & Co.
logo are trademarks of Sterling Publishing Co., Inc.

Union Square & Co., LLC, is a subsidiary
of Sterling Publishing Co., Inc.

This 2022 edition published by Union Square & Co., LLC.

ISBN 978-1-4549-4722-6
ISBN 978-1-4549-4723-3 (e-book)

Library of Congress Control Number: 2022940593

For information about custom editions, special sales, and premium
purchases, please contact specialsales@unionsquareandco.com.

Printed in Canada

2 4 6 8 10 9 7 5 3 1

unionsquareandco.com

Interior design by Gavin Motnyk

Image credit: Happy Art/Shutterstock.com (interior icons)

"In the turmoil of our lives,
Men are like politic states, or troubled seas,
Tossed up and down with several storms and tempests,
Change and variety of wrecks and fortunes;
Till, labouring to the havens of our homes,
We struggle for the calm that crowns our ends."

—FORD

VOLUME I

CHAPTER I

"Absent or dead, still let a friend be dear,
A sigh the absent claims, the dead a tear."

—*Pope*

In the flattest and least agreeable part of the county of Essex, about five miles from the sea, is situated a village or small town, which may be known in these pages by the name of Longfield. Longfield is distant eight miles from any market town, but the simple inhabitants, limiting their desires to their means of satisfying them, are scarcely aware of the kind of desert in which they are placed. Although only fifty miles from London, few among them have ever seen the metropolis. Some claim that distinction from having visited cousins in Lothbury and viewed the lions in the tower. There is a mansion belonging to a wealthy nobleman within four miles, never inhabited, except when a parliamentary election is going forward. No one of any pretension to consequence resided in this secluded nook, except the honourable Mrs. Elizabeth Fitzhenry; she ought to have been the shining star of the place, and she was only its better angel. Benevolent, gentle, and unassuming, this fair sprig of nobility had lived from youth to age in the abode of her forefathers, making a part of this busy world, only through the kindliness of her disposition, and her constant affection for one who was far away.

The mansion of the Fitzhenry family, which looked upon the village green, was wholly incommensurate to our humblest ideas of what belongs to nobility; yet it stood in solitary splendour, the Great House of Longfield. From time immemorial, its possessors had been the magnates of the village; half of it belonged to them, and the whole voted according to their wishes. Cut off from the rest of the world, they claimed here a consideration and a deference, which, with the moderate income of fifteen hundred a-year, they would have vainly sought elsewhere.

There was a family tradition, that a Fitzhenry had sat in parliament; but the time arrived, when they were to rise to greater distinction. The father of the lady, whose name has been already introduced, enjoyed all the privileges attendant on being an only child. Extraordinary efforts were made for his education. He was placed with a clergyman near Harwich, and imbibed in that neighbourhood so passionate a love for sea, that, though tardily and with regret, his parents at last permitted him to pursue a naval career. He became a brave, a clever, and a lucky officer. In a contested election, his father was the means of insuring the success of the government candidate, and the promotion of his son followed. Those were the glorious days of the English navy, towards the close of the American war; and when that war terminated, and the admiral, now advanced considerably beyond middle life, returned to the Sabine farm, of which he had, by course of descent, become proprietor, he returned adorned with the rank of a peer of the realm, and with sufficient wealth to support respectably the dignity of the baronial title.

Yet an obscure fate pursued the house of Fitzhenry, even in its ennobled condition. The new lord was proud of his elevation, as a merited reward; but next to the deck of his ship, he loved the tranquil precincts of his paternal mansion, and here he spent his latter days in peace. Midway in life, he had married the daughter of the rector of Longfield. Various fates had attended the offspring of this union; several died, and at the time of his being created a peer, Lord Lodore found himself a widower, with two children. Elizabeth, who had been born twelve years before, and Henry, whose recent birth had cost the life of his hapless and lamented mother.

But those days were long since passed away; and the first Lord Lodore, with most of his generation, was gathered to his ancestors. To the new-sprung race that filled up the vacant ranks, his daughter Elizabeth appeared a somewhat ancient but most amiable maiden, whose gentle melancholy was not (according to innumerable precedents in the traditions regarding unmarried ladies) attributed to an ill-fated attachment, but to the disasters that had visited her house, and still clouded the fortunes of her family. What these misfortunes originated from, or even in what they consisted, was not exactly known; especially at Longfield, whose inhabitants were no adepts in the gossip of the metropolis. It was believed that Mrs. Elizabeth's brother still lived; that some very strange circumstances had attended his career in life, was known; but conjecture fell lame when it tried to proceed beyond these simple facts: it was whispered, as a wonder and a secret, that though Lord Lodore was far away, no one knew where, his lady (as the *Morning Post* testified in its lists of fashionable arrivals and fashionable parties) was a frequent visitor to London. Once or twice the bolder gossips, male or female, had resolved to sound (as they called it) Mrs. Elizabeth on the subject. But the fair spinster, though innoffensive to a proverb, and gentle beyond the wont of her gentle sex, was yet gifted with a certain dignity of manner, and a quiet reserve, that checked these good people at their very outset.

Henry Fitzhenry was spoken of by a few of the last generation, as having been a fine, bold, handsome boy—generous, proud, and daring; he was remembered, when as a youth he departed for the continent, as riding fearlessly the best hunter in the field, and attracting the admiration of the village maidens at church by his tall elegant figure and dark eyes; or, when he chanced to accost them, by a nameless fascination of manner, joined to a voice whose thrilling silver tones stirred the listener's heart unaware. He left them like a dream, nor appeared again till after his father's death, when he paid his sister a brief visit. There was then something singularly grave and abstracted about him. When he rode, it was not among the hunters, though it was soft February weather, but in the solitary lanes, or with lightning speed over the moors, when the sun was setting and shadows gathered round the landscape.

Again, some years after, he had appeared among them. He was then married, and Lady Lodore accompanied him. They stayed but three days. There was something of fiction in the way in which the appearance of the lady was recorded. An angel bright with celestial hues, breathing heaven, and spreading a halo of calm and light around, as it winged swift way amidst the dusky children of earth: such ideas seemed to appertain to the beautiful apparition, remembered as Lord Lodore's wife. She was so young, that time played with her as a favourite child; so etherial in look, that the language of flowers could alone express the delicate fairness of her skin, or the tints that sat upon her cheek: so light in motion, and so graceful. To talk of eye or lip, of height or form, or even of the colour of her hair, the villagers could not, for they had been dazzled by an assemblage of charms before undreamt of by them. Her voice won adoration, and her smile was as the sudden withdrawing of a curtain displaying paradise upon earth. Her lord's tall, manly figure, was recollected but as a back-ground—a fitting one—and that was all they would allow to him—for this resplendent image. Nor was it remembered that any excessive attachment was exhibited between them. She had appeared indeed but as a vision—a creature from another sphere, hastily gazing on an unknown world, and lost before they could mark more than that void came again, and she was gone.

Since that time, Lord Lodore had been lost to Longfield. Some few months after Mrs. Elizabeth visited London on occasion of a christening, and then after a long interval, it was observed, that she never mentioned her brother, and that the name of his wife acted as a spell, to bring an expression of pain over her sedate features. Much talk circulated, and many blundering rumours went their course through the village, and then faded like smoke in the clear air. Some mystery there was—Lodore was gone—his place vacant: he lived; yet his name, like those of the dead, haunted only the memories of men, and was allied to no act or circumstance of present existence. He was forgotten, and the inhabitants of Longfield, returning to their obscurity, proceeded in their daily course, almost as happy as if they had had their lord among them, to vary the incidents of their quiet existence with the proceedings of the "Great House."

Yet his sister remembered him. In her heart his image was traced indelibly—limned in the colours of life. His form visited her dreams, and was the unseen, yet not mute, companion of her solitary musings. Years stole on, casting their clouding shadows on her cheek, and stealing the colour from her hair, but Henry, but Lodore, was before her in bright youth—her brother—her pride—her hope. To muse on the possibility of his return, to read the few letters that reached her from him, till their brief sentences seemed to imply volumes of meaning, was the employment that made winter nights short, summer days swift in their progress. This dreamy kind of existence, added to the old-fashioned habits which a recluse who lives in a state of singleness is sure to acquire, made her singularly unlike the rest of the world—causing her to be a child in its ways, and inexpert to detect the craftiness of others.

Lodore, in exile and obscurity, was in her eyes, the first of human beings; she looked forward to the hour, when he would blaze upon the world with renewed effulgence, as to a religious promise. How well did she remember, how in grace of person, how in expression of countenance, and dignity of manner, he transcended all those whom she saw during her visit to London, on occasion of the memorable christening: that from year to year this return was deferred, did not tire her patience, nor diminish her regrets. He never grew old to her—never lost the lustre of early manhood; and when the boyish caprice which kept him afar was sobered, so she framed her thoughts, by the wisdom of time, he would return again to bless her and to adorn the world. The lapse of twelve years did not change this notion, nor the fact that, if she had cast up an easy sum in arithmetic, the parish register would have testified, her brother had now reached the mature age of fifty.

• • •

CHAPTER II

"Settled in some secret nest,
In calm leisure let me rest;
And far off the public stage.
Pass away my silent age."

—*Seneca, Marvell's Trans.*

Twelve years previous to the opening of this tale, an English gentleman, advanced to middle age, accompanied by an infant daughter, and her attendant, arrived at a settlement in the district of the Illinois in North America. It was at the time when this part of the country first began to be cleared, and a new comer, with some show of property, was considered a welcome acquisition. Still the settlement was too young, and the people were too busy in securing for themselves the necessaries of life, for much attention to be paid to any thing but the "overt acts" of the stranger—the number of acres which he bought, which were few, the extent of his clearings, and the number of workmen that he employed, both of which were, proportionately to his possession in land, on a far larger scale than that of any of his fellow colonists. Like magic, a commodious house was raised on a small height that embanked the swift river—every vestige of forest disappeared from its immediate vicinity, replaced by agricultural cultivation, and a garden bloomed in the wilderness. His labourers were many, and golden harvests shone in his fields, while the dark forest, or untilled plain, seemed yet to set at defiance the efforts of his fellow settlers; and at the same time comforts of so civilized a description, that the Americans termed them luxuries, appeared in the abode and reigned in the domestic arrangements of the Englishman, although to his eye every thing was regulated by the strictest regard to republican plainness and simplicity.

He did not mingle much in the affairs of the colony, yet his advice was always to be commanded, and his assistance was readily afforded. He superintended the operations carried on on his own land; and it was observed that they differed often both from American and English modes of agriculture. When questioned, he detailed practices in Poland and Hungary, and gave his reasons why he thought them applicable to the soil in question. Many of these experiments of course failed; others were eminently successful. He did not shun labour of any sort. He joined the hunting parties, and made one on expeditions that went out to explore the neighbouring wilds, and the haunts of the native Indians. He gave money for the carrying on any necessary public work, and came forward willingly when called upon for any useful purpose. In any time of difficulty or sorrow—on the overflowing of the stream, or the failure of a crop, he was earnest in his endeavours to aid and to console. But with all this, there was an insurmountable barrier between him and the other inhabitants of the colony. He never made one at their feasts, nor mingled in the familiar communications of daily life; his dwelling, situated at the distance of a full mile from the village, removed him from out of the very hearing of their festivities and assemblies. He might labour in common with others, but his pleasures were all solitary, and he preserved the utmost independence as far as regarded the sacred privacy of his abode, and the silence he kept in all concerns regarding himself alone.

At first the settlement had to struggle with all the difficulties attendant on colonization. It grew rapidly, however, and bid fair to become a busy and large town, when it met with a sudden check. A new spot was discovered, a few miles distant, possessing peculiar advantages for commercial purposes. An active, enterprising man engaged himself in the task of establishing a town there on a larger scale and with greater pretensions. He succeeded, and its predecessor sunk at once into insignificance. It was matter of conjecture among them whether Mr. Fitzhenry (so was named the English stranger) would remove to the vicinity of the more considerable town, but no such idea seemed to have occurred to him. Probably he rejoiced in an accident that tended to render his abode so entirely secluded. At first the former town rapidly declined, and many a log hut fell to ruin; but at last, having sunk into the appearance and name of a village, it continued to exist, bearing few marks of that busy enterprising stir which usually characterizes a new settlement in America. The ambitious and scheming had deserted it—it was left to those who courted tranquillity, and desired the necessaries of life without the hope of great future gain. It acquired an almost old-fashioned appearance. The houses began to look weatherworn, and none with fresh faces sprung up to shame them. Extensive clearings, suddenly checked, gave entrance to the forests, without the appendages of a manufacture or a farm. The sound of the axe was seldom heard, and primeval quiet again took possession of the wild. Meanwhile Mr. Fitzhenry continued to adorn his dwelling with imported conveniences, the result of European art, and to spend much time and labour in making his surrounding land assume somewhat of the appearance of pleasure-ground.

He lived in peace and solitude, and seemed to enjoy the unchanging tenor of his life. It had not always been so. During the first three or four years of his arrival in America, he had evidently been unquiet in his mind, and dissatisfied with the scene around him. He gave directions to his workmen, but did not overlook their execution. He took great pains to secure a horse, whose fiery spirit and beautiful form might satisfy a fastidious connoisseur. Having with much trouble and expense got several animals of English breed together, he was perpetually seen mounted and forcing his way amid the forest land, or galloping over the unincumbered country. Sadness sat on his brow, and dwelt in eyes, whose dark large orbs were peculiarly expressive of tenderness and melancholy,

"Pietosi a riguardare, a mover parchi."

Often, when in conversation on uninteresting topics, some keen sensation would pierce his heart, his voice faltered, and an expression of unspeakable wretchedness was imprinted on his countenance, mastered after a momentary struggle, yet astounding to the person he might be addressing. Generally on such occasions he would seize an immediate opportunity to break away and to remain alone. He had been seen, believing himself unseen, making passionate gestures, and heard uttering some wild exclamations. Once or twice he had wandered away into the woods, and not returned for several days, to the exceeding terror of his little household. He evidently sought loneliness, there to combat unobserved with the fierce enemy that dwelt within his breast. On such occasions, when intruded upon and disturbed, he was irritated to fury. His resentment was expressed in terms ill-adapted to republican equality—and no one could doubt that in his own country he had filled a high station in society, and been educated in habits of command, so that he involuntarily looked upon himself as of a distinct and superior race to the human beings that each day crossed his path. In general, however, this was only shown by a certain loftiness of demeanour and cold abstraction, which might annoy, but could not be resented. Any ebullition of temper he was not backward to atone for by apology, and to compensate by gifts.

There was no tinge of misanthropy in Fitzhenry's disposition. Even while he shrunk from familiar communication with the rude and unlettered, he took an interest in their welfare. His benevolence was active, his compassion readily afforded. It was quickness of feeling, and not apathy, that made him shy and retired. Sensibility checked and crushed, an ardent thirst for sympathy which could not be allayed in the wildernesses of America, begot a certain appearance of coldness, altogether deceptive. He concealed his sufferings—he abhorred that they should be pried into; but this reserve was not natural to him, and it added to the misery which his state of banishment occasioned.

"Quiet to quick bosoms is a hell."

And so was it with him. His passions were powerful, and had been ungoverned. He writhed beneath the dominion of *sameness*; and tranquillity, allied to loneliness, possessed no charms. He groaned beneath the chains that fettered him to the spot, where he was withering in inaction. They caused unutterable throes and paroxysms of despair. Ennui, the daemon, waited at the threshold of his noiseless refuge, and drove away the stirring hopes and enlivening expectations, which form the better part of life. Sensibility in such a situation is a curse: men become "cannibals of their own hearts"; remorse, regret, and restless impatience usurp the place of more wholesome feeling: every thing seems better than that which is; and solitude becomes a sort of tangible enemy, the more dangerous, because it dwells within the citadel itself. Borne down by such emotions, Fitzhenry was often about to yield to the yearnings of his soul, and to fly from repose into action, however accompanied by strife and wretchedness; to leave America, to return to Europe, and to face at once all the evils which he had journeyed so far to escape. He did not—he remained. His motives for flight returned on him with full power after any such paroxysm, and held him back. He despised himself for his hesitation. He had made his choice, and would abide by it. He was not so devoid of manliness as to be destitute of fortitude, or so dependent a wretch as not to have resources in himself.

He would cultivate these, and obtain that peace which it had been his boast that he should experience.

It came at last. Time and custom accomplished their task, and he became reconciled to his present mode of existence. He grew to love his home in the wilderness. It was all his own creation, and the pains and thought he continued to bestow upon it, rendered it doubly his. The murmur of the neighbouring river became the voice of a friend; it welcomed him on his return from any expedition; and he hailed the first echo of it that struck upon his ear from afar, with a thrill of joy.

Peace descended upon his soul. He became enamoured of the independence of solitude, and the sublime operations of surrounding nature. All further attempts at cultivation having ceased in his neighbourhood, from year to year nothing changed, except at the bidding of the months, in obedience to the varying seasons;—nothing changed, except that the moss grew thicker and greener upon the logs that supported his roof, that the plants he cultivated increased in strength and beauty, and that the fruit-trees yielded their sweet produce in greater abundance. The improvements he had set on foot displayed in their progress the taste and ingenuity of their projector; and as the landscape became more familiar, so did a thousand associations twine themselves with its varied appearances, till the forests and glades became as friends and companions.

As he learnt to be contented with his lot, the inequalities of humour, and singularities of conduct, which had at first attended him, died away. He had grown familiar with the persons of his fellow-colonists, and their various fortunes interested him. Though he could find no friend, tempered like him, like him nursed in the delicacies and fastidiousness of the societies of the old world;—though he, a china vase, dreaded too near a collision with the brazen ones around; yet, though he could not give his confidence, or unburthen the treasure of his soul, he could approve of, and even feel affection for several among them. Personal courage, honesty, and frankness, were to be found among the men; simplicity and kindness among the women. He saw instances of love and devotion in members of families, that made him sigh to be one of them; and the strong sense and shrewd observations of many of the elder settlers exercised his understanding. They opened, by their reasonings and conversation, a new source of amusement, and presented him with another opiate for his too busy memory.

Fitzhenry had been a patron of the fine arts; and thus he had loved books, poetry, and the elegant philosophy of the ancients. But he had not been a student. His mind was now in a fit state to find solace in reading, and excitement in the pursuit of knowledge. At first he sent for a few books, such as he wished immediately to consult, from New York, and made slight additions to the small library of classical literature he had originally brought with him on his emigration. But when once the desire to instruct himself was fully aroused in his mind, he became aware how slight and inadequate his present library was, even for the use of one man. Now each quarter brought chests of a commodity he began to deem the most precious upon earth. Beings with human forms and human feelings he had around him; but, as if made of coarser, half-kneaded clay, they wanted the divine spark of mind and the polish of taste. He had pined for these, and now they were presented to him. Books became his friends: they, when rightly questioned, could answer to his thoughts. Plato could elevate, Epictetus calm, his soul. He could revel with Ovid in the imagery presented by a graceful, though voluptuous imagination; and hang enchanted over the majesty and elegance of Virgil. Homer was as a dear and revered friend—Horace a pleasant companion. English, Italian, German, and French, all yielded their stores in turn; and the abstruse sciences were often a relaxation to a mind, whose chief bane was its dwelling too entirely upon one idea. He made a study, also, of the things peculiarly befitting his present situation; and he rose in the estimation of those around, as they became aware of his talents and his knowledge.

Study and occupation restored to his heart self-complacency, which is an ingredient so necessary to the composition of human happiness. He felt himself to be useful, and knew himself to be honoured. He no longer asked himself, "Why do I live?" or looked on the dark, rapid waves, and longed for the repose that was in their gift. The blood flowed equably in his veins; a healthy temperance regulated his hopes and wishes. He could again bless God for the boon of existence, and look forward to future years, if not with eager anticipation, yet with a calm reliance upon the power of good, wholly remote from despair.

• • •

CHAPTER III

Miranda.—Alack! what trouble
　Was I then to you!
Prospero.—O, a cherubim
　Thou wast, that did preserve me!

—*The Tempest*

Such was the Englishman who had taken refuge in the furthest wilds of an almost untenanted portion of the globe. Like a Corinthian column, left single amidst the ruder forms of the forest oaks, standing in alien beauty, a type of civilization and the arts, among the rougher, though perhaps not less valuable, growth of Nature's own. Refined to fastidiousness, sensitive to morbidity, the stranger was respected without being understood, and loved though the intimate of none.

Many circumstances have been mentioned as tending to reconcile Fitzhenry to his lot; and yet one has been omitted, chiefest of all;—the growth and development of his child was an inexhaustible source of delight and occupation. She was scarcely three years old when her parent first came to the Illinois. She was then a plaything and an object of solicitude to him, and nothing more. Much as her father loved her, he had not then learned to discover the germ of the soul just nascent in her infant form; nor to watch the formation, gradual to imperceptibility, of her childish ideas. He would watch over her as she slept, and gaze on her as she sported in the garden, with ardent and unquiet fondness; and, from time to time, instil some portion of knowledge into her opening mind: but this was all done by snatches, and at intervals. His affection for her was the passion of his soul; but her society was not an occupation for his thoughts. He would have knelt to kiss her footsteps as she bounded across the grass, and tears glistened in his eyes as she embraced his knees on his return from any excursion; but her prattle often wearied him, and her very presence was sometimes the source of intense pain.

He did not know himself how much he loved her, till she became old enough to share his excursions and be a companion. This occurred at a far earlier age than would have been the case had she been in England, living in a nursery with other children. There is a peculiarity in the education of a daughter, brought up by a father only, which tends to develop early a thousand of those portions of mind, which are folded up, and often destroyed, under mere feminine tuition. He made her fearless, by making her the associate of his rides; yet his incessant care and watchfulness, the observant tenderness of his manner, almost reverential on many points, springing from the difference of sex, tended to soften her mind, and make her spirit ductile and dependent. He taught her to scorn pain, but to shrink with excessive timidity from any thing that intrenched on the barrier of womanly reserve which he raised about her. Nothing was dreaded, indeed, by her, except his disapprobation; and a word or look from him made her, with all her childish vivacity and thoughtlessness, turn as with a silken string, and bend at once to his will.

There was an affectionateness of disposition kneaded up in the very texture of her soul, which gave it its "very form and pressure." It accompanied every word and action; it revealed itself in her voice, and hung like light over the expression of her countenance.

Her earliest feeling was love of her father. She would sit to watch him, guess at his thoughts, and creep close, or recede away, as she read encouragement, or the contrary, in his eyes and gestures. Except him, her only companion was her servant; and very soon she distinguished between them, and felt proud and elate when she quitted her for her father's side. Soon, she almost never quitted it. Her gentle and docile disposition rendered her unobtrusive, while her inexhaustible spirits were a source of delightful amusement. The goodness of her heart endeared her still more; and when it was called forth by any demand made on it by him, it was attended by such a display of excessive sensibility, as at once caused him to tremble for her future happiness, and love her ten thousand times more. She grew into the image on which his eye doated, and for whose presence his heart perpetually yearned. Was he reading, or otherwise occupied, he was restless, if yet she were not in the room; and she would remain in silence for hours, occupied by some little feminine work, and all the while watching him, catching his first glance towards her, and obeying the expression of his countenance, before he could form his wish into words. When he left her for any of his longer excursions, her little heart would heave, and almost burst with sorrow. On his return, she was always on the watch to see, to fly into his arms, and to load him with infantine caresses.

There was something in her face, that at this early age gave token of truth and affection, and asked for sympathy. Her large brown eyes, such as are called hazel, full of tenderness and sweetness, possessed within their depths an expression and a latent fire, which stirred the heart. It is difficult to describe, or by words to call before another's mind, the picture so palpable to our own. The moulding of her cheek, full just below the eyes, and ending in a soft oval, gave a peculiar expression, at once beseeching and tender, and yet radiant with vivacity and gladness. Frankness and truth were reflected on her brow, like flowers in the clearest pool; the thousand nameless lines and mouldings, which create expression, were replete with beaming innocence and irresistible attraction. Her small chiselled nose, her mouth so delicately curved, gave token of taste. In the whole was harmony, and the upper part of the countenance seemed to reign over the lower and to ennoble it, making her usual placid expression thoughtful and earnest; so that not until she smiled and spoke, did the gaiety of her guileless heart display itself, and the vivacity of her disposition give change and relief to the picture. Her figure was light and airy, tall at an early age, and slender. Her rides and rambles gave elasticity to her limbs, and her step was like that of the antelope, springy and true. She had no fears, no deceit, no untold thought within her. Her matchless sweetness of temper prevented any cloud from ever dimming her pure loveliness: her voice cheered the heart, and her laugh rang so true and joyous on the ear, that it gave token in itself of the sympathizing and buoyant spirit which was her great charm. Nothing with her centred in self; she was always ready to give her soul away: to please her father was the unsleeping law of all her actions, while his approbation imparted a sense of such pure but entire happiness, that every other feeling faded into insignificance in the comparison.

In the first year of exile and despair, Fitzhenry looked forward to the long drawn succession of future years, with an impatience of woe difficult to be borne. He was surprised to find, as he proceeded in the quiet path of life which he had selected, that instead of an increase of unhappiness, a thousand pleasures smiled around him. He had looked on it as a bitter task to forget that he had a name and country, both abandoned for ever; now, the thought of these seldom recurred to his memory. His forest home became all in all to him. Wherever he went, his child was by his side, to cheer and enliven him. When he looked on her, and reflected that within her frame dwelt spotless innocence and filial piety, that within that lovely "bower of flesh," not one thought or feeling resided that was not akin to heaven in its purity and sweetness, he, as by infection, acquired a portion of the calm enjoyment, which she in her taintless youth naturally possessed.

Even when any distant excursion forced him to absent himself, her idea followed him to light him cheerily on his way. He knew that he should find her on his return busied in little preparations for his welcome. In summer time, the bower in the garden would be adorned; in the inclement season of winter the logs would blaze on the hearth, his chair be drawn towards the fire, the stool for Ethel at his feet, with nothing to remind him of the past, save her dear presence, which drew its greatest charm, not from that, but from the present. Fitzhenry forgot the thousand delights of civilization, for which formerly his heart had painfully yearned. He forgot ambition, and the enticements of gay vanity; peace and security appeared the greatest blessings of life, and he had them here.

Ethel herself was happy beyond the knowledge of her own happiness. She regretted nothing in the old country. She grew up among the grandest objects of nature, and they were the sweet influences to excite her to love and to a sense of pleasure. She had come to the Illinois attended by a black woman and her daughter, whom her father had engaged to attend her at New York, and had been sedulously kept away from communication with the settlers—an arrangement which it would have been difficult to bring about elsewhere, but in this secluded and almost deserted spot the usual characteristics of the Americans were scarcely to be found. Most of the inhabitants were emigrants from Scotland, a peaceable, hard-working population.

Ethel lived alone in their lonely dwelling. Had she been of a more advanced age when taken from England, her curiosity might have been excited by the singularity of her position; but we rarely reason about that which has remained unchanged since infancy; taking it as a part of the immutable order of things, we yield without a question to its control. Ethel did not know that she was alone. Her attendants she was attached to, and she idolized her father; his image filled all her little heart. Playmate she had none, save a fawn and a kid, a dog grown old in her service, and a succession of minor favourites of the animal species.

It was Fitzhenry's wish to educate his daughter to all the perfection of which the feminine character is susceptible. As the first step, he cut her off from familiar communication with the unrefined, and, watching over her with the fondest care, kept her far aloof from the very knowledge of what might, by its baseness or folly, contaminate the celestial beauty of her nature. He resolved to make her all that woman can be of generous, soft, and devoted; to purge away every alloy of vanity and petty passion—to fill her with honour, and yet to mould her to the sweetest gentleness: to cultivate her tastes and enlarge her mind, yet so to control her acquirements, as to render her ever pliant to his will. She was to be lifted above every idea of artifice or guile, or the caballing spirit of the worldling—she was to be single-hearted, yet mild. A creature half poetry, half love—one whose pure lips had never been tainted by an untruth—an enthusiastic being, who could give her life away for the sake of another, and yet who honoured herself as a consecrated thing reserved for one worship alone. She was taught that no misfortune should penetrate her soul, except such as visited her affections, or her sense of right; and that, set apart from the vulgar uses of the world, she was connected with the mass only through another—that other, now her father and only friend—hereafter, whosoever her heart might select as her guide and head. Fitzhenry drew his chief ideas from Milton's Eve, and adding to this the romance of chivalry, he satisfied himself that his daughter would be the embodied ideal of all that is adorable and estimable in her sex.

The instructor can scarcely give sensibility where it is essentially wanting, nor talent to the unpercipient block. But he can cultivate and detect the affections of the pupil, who puts forth, as a parasite, tendrils by which to cling, not knowing to what—to a supporter or a destroyer. The careful rearer of the ductile human plant can instil his own religion, and surround the soul by such a moral atmosphere, as shall become to its latest day the air it breathes. Ethel, from her delicate organization and quick parts, was sufficiently plastic in her father's hands. When not with him, she was the playmate of nature. Her birds and pet animals—her untaught but most kind nurse, were her associates: she had her flowers to watch over, her music, her drawings, and her books. Nature, wild, interminable, sublime, was around her. The ceaseless flow of the brawling stream, the wide-spread forest, the changes of the sky, the career of the wide-winged clouds, when the winds drove them athwart the atmosphere, or the repose of the still, and stirless summer air, the stormy war of the elements, and the sense of trust and security amidst their loudest disturbances, were all circumstances to mould her even unconsciously to an admiration of all that is grand and beautiful.

A lofty sense of independence is, in man, the best privilege of his nature. It cannot be doubted, but that it were for the happiness of the other sex that she were taught more to rely on and act for herself. But in the cultivation of this feeling, the education of Fitzhenry was lamentably deficient. Ethel was taught to know herself dependent; the support of another was to be as necessary to her as her daily food. She leant on her father as a prop that could not fail, and she was wholly satisfied with her condition. Her peculiar disposition of course tinged Fitzhenry's theories with colours not always their own, and her entire want of experience in intercourse with her fellow-creatures, gave a more decided tone to her sense of dependence than she could have acquired, if the circumstances of her daily life had brought her into perpetual collision with others. She was habitually cheerful even to gaiety; yet her character was not devoid of petulence, which might become rashness or self-will if left to herself. She had a clear and upright spirit, and suspicion or unkindness roused her to indignation, or sunk her into the depths of sorrow. Place her in danger, and tell her she must encounter it, and she called up all her courage and became a heroine; but on less occasions, difficulties dismayed and annoyed her, and she longed to escape from them into that dreamy existence, for which her solitary mode of life had given her a taste: active in person, in mind she was too often indolent, and apt to think that while she was docile to the injunctions of her parent, all her duties were fulfilled. She seldom thought, and never acted, for herself.

With all this she was so caressingly affectionate, so cheerful and obedient, that she inspired her father with more than a father's fondness. He lived but for her and in her. Away, she was present to his imagination, the loadstone to draw him home, and to fill that home with pleasure. He exalted her in his fancy into angelic perfection, and nothing occurred to blot the fair idea. He in prospect gave up his whole life to the warding off every evil from her dear and sacred head. He knew, or rather believed, that while we possess one real, devoted, and perfect friend, we cannot be truly miserable. He said to himself—though he did not love to dwell on the thought—that of course cares and afflictions might hereafter befal her; but he was to stand the shield to blunt the arrows of sorrow—the shelter in which she might find refuge from every evil ministration. The worst ills of life, penury and desertion, she could never know; and surely he, who would stand so fast by her through all—whose nightly dream and waking thought was for her good, would even, when led to form other connexions in life, so command her affections as to be able to influence her happiness.

Not being able to judge by comparison, Ethel was unaware of the peculiarity of her good fortune in possessing such a father. But she loved him entirely; looked up to him, and saw in him the reward of every exertion, the object of each day's employment. In early youth we have no true notion of what the realities of life are formed, and when we look forward it is without any correct estimate of the chances of existence. Ethel's visionary ideas were all full of peace, seclusion, and her father. America, or rather the little village of the Illinois which she inhabited, was all the world to her; and she had no idea that nearly every thing that connected her to society existed beyond the far Atlantic, in that tiny isle which made so small a show upon her maps. Fitzhenry never mentioned these things to his daughter. She arrived at the age of fifteen without forming a hope that should lead her beyond the pale which had hitherto enclosed her, or having imagined that any train of circumstances might suddenly transplant her from the lonely wilderness to the thronged resorts of mankind.

• • •

CHAPTER IV

"Les deserts sont faits pour les amants,
mais l'amourne se fait pas aux deserts."

—*Le Barbier de Paris*

Twelve years had led Ethel from infancy to childhood; and from child's estate to the blooming season of girlhood. It had brought her father from the prime of a man's life, to the period when it began to decline. Our feelings probably are not less strong at fifty than they were ten or fifteen years before; but they have changed their objects, and dwell on far different prospects. At five-and-thirty a man thinks of what his own existence is; when the maturity of age has grown into its autumn, he is wrapt up in that of others. The loss of wife or child then becomes more deplorable, as being impossible to repair; for no fresh connexion can give us back the companion of our earlier years, nor a "new sprung race" compensate for that, whose career we hoped to see run. Fitzhenry had been a man of violent passions; they had visited his life with hurricane and desolation;—were these dead within him? The complacency that now distinguished his physiognomy seemed to vouch for internal peace. But there was an abstracted melancholy in his dark eyes—a look that went beyond the objects immediately before him, that seemed to say that he often anxiously questioned fate, and meditated with roused fears on the secrets of futurity.

Educating his child, and various other employments, had occupied and diverted him. He had been content; he asked for no change, but he dreaded it. Often when packets arrived from England he hesitated to open them. He could not account for his new-born anxieties. Was change approaching? "How long will you be at peace?" Such warning voice startled him in the solitude of the forests: he looked round, but no human being was near, yet the voice had spoken audibly to his sense; and when a transient air swept the dead leaves near, he shrunk as if a spirit passed, invisible to sight, and yet felt by the subtle atmosphere, as it gave articulation and motion to it.

"How long shall I be at peace?" A thrill ran through his veins. "Am I then *now* at peace? Do love, and hate, and despair, no longer wage their accustomed war in my heart? and is it true that gently flowing as my days have lately been, that during their course I have not felt those mortal throes that once made life so intolerable a burthen? It is so. I *am at peace*; strange state for suffering mortality! And this is not to last? My daughter! there only am I vulnerable; yet have I surrounded her with a sevenfold shield. My own sweet Ethel! how can I avert from your dear head the dark approaching storm?

"But this is folly. These waking dreams are the curse of inaction and solitude. Yesterday I refused to accompany the exploring party. I will go—I am not old; fatigue, as yet, does not seem a burthen; but I shall sink into premature age, if I allow this indolence to overpower me. I will set out on this expedition, and thus I shall no longer be at peace." Fitzhenry smiled as if thus he were cheating destiny.

The proposed journey was one to be made by a party of his fellow-settlers, to trace the route between their town and a large one, two hundred miles off, to discover the best mode of communication. There was nothing very arduous in the undertaking. It was September, and hunting would diversify the tediousness of their way. Fitzhenry left his daughter under the charge of her attendants, to amuse herself with her books, her music, her gardening, her needle, and, more than all, her new and very favourite study of drawing and sketching. Hitherto the pencil had scarcely been one of her occupations; but an accident gave scope to her acquiring in it that improvement for which she found that she had prodigious inclination, and she was assured, no inconsiderable talent.

The occasion that had given rise to this new employment was this. Three or four months before, a traveller arrived for the purpose of settling, who claimed a rather higher intellectual rank than those around him. He was the son of an honest tradesman of the city of London. He displayed early signs of talent, and parental fondness gave him opportunities of cultivating it. The means of his family were small, but some of the boy's drawings having attracted the attention of an artist, he entered upon the profession of a painter, with sanguine hopes of becoming hereafter an ornament to it.

Two obstacles were in the way of his success. He wanted that intense love of his art—that enthusiastic perseverance in labour, which distinguishes the man of genius from the man of talent merely. He regarded it as a means, not an end. Probably therefore he did not feel that capacity in himself for attaining first-rate excellence, which had been attributed to him. He had a taste also for social pleasures and vulgar indulgencies, incompatible with industry and with that refinement of mind which is so necessary an adjunct to the cultivation of the imaginative arts. Whitelock had none of all this; but he was quick, clever, and was looked on among his associates as a spirited, agreeable fellow. The death of his parents left him in possession of their little wealth: depending for the future on the resources which his talent promised him, he dissipated the two or three hundred pounds which formed his inheritance: debt, difficulties, with consequent abstraction from his profession, completed his ruin. He arrived at the Illinois in search of an uncle, on whose kindness he intended to depend, with six dollars in his purse. His uncle had long before disappeared from that part of the country. Whitelock found himself destitute. Neither his person, which was diminutive, nor his constitution, which was delicate, fitted him for manual labour; nor was he acquainted with any mechanic art. What could he do in America? He began to feel very deeply the inroads of despair, when hearing of the superior wealth of Mr. Fitzhenry, and that he was an Englishman, he paid him a visit, feeling secure that he could interest him in his favour.

The emigrant's calculations were just. His distinguished countryman exerted himself to enable the young man to obtain a subsistence. He established him in a school, and gave him his best counsels how to proceed. Whitelock thanked him; commenced the most odious task of initiating the young Americans in the rudiments of knowledge, and sought meanwhile to amuse himself to the best of his power. Fitzhenry's house he first made his resort. He was not to be baffled by the reserved courtesy of his host. The comfort and English appearance of the exile's dwelling were charming to him; and while he could hear himself talk, he fancied that every one about him must be satisfied. Fitzhenry was excessively annoyed. There was an innate vulgarity in his visitant, and an unlicensed familiarity that jarred painfully with the refined habits of his sensitive nature. Still, in America he had been forced to tolerate even worse than this, and he bore Whitelock's intrusions as well as he could, seeking only to put such obstacles in the way of his too frequent visits, as would best serve to curtail them. Whitelock's chief merit was his talent; he had a real eye for the outward forms of nature, for the tints in which she loves to robe herself, and the beauty in which she is for ever invested. He occupied himself by sketching the surrounding scenery, and gave life and interest to many a savage glade and solitary nook, which, till he came, had not been discovered to be picturesque. Ethel regarded his drawings with wonder and delight, and easily obtained permission from her father to take lessons in the captivating art. Fitzhenry thought that of all occupations, that of the pencil, if pursued earnestly and with real taste, most conduced to the student's happiness. Its scope is not personal display, as is the case most usually with music, and yet it has a visible result which satisfies the mind that something has been done. It does not fatigue the attention like the study of languages, yet it suffices to call forth the powers, and to fill the mind with pleasurable sensations. It is a most feminine occupation, well replacing, on a more liberal and rational scale, the tap-estry of our grandmothers. Ethel had already shown a great inclination for design, and her father was glad of so favourable an opportunity for cultivating it. A few difficulties presented themselves. Whitelock had brought his own materials with him, but he possessed no superfluity—and they were not to be procured at the settlement. The artist offered to transfer them all for Ethel's convenience to her own abode, so that he might have free leave to occupy himself there also. Fitzhenry saw all the annoyances consequent on this plan, and it was finally arranged that his daughter should, three or four times a week, visit the school-house, and in a little room, built apart for her especial use, pursue her study.

The habit of seeing and instructing his lovely pupil awoke new ideas in Whitelock's fruitful brain. Who was Mr. Fitzhenry? What did he in the Illinois? Whitelock sounded him carefully, but gathered no information, except that this gentleman showed no intention of ever quitting the settlement. But this was much. He was evidently in easy circumstances—Ethel was his only child. She was here a garden-rose amidst briars, and Whitelock flattered himself that his position was not materially different. Could he succeed in the scheme that all these considerations suggested to him, his fortune was made, or, at least, he should bid adieu for ever to blockhead boys and the dull labours of instruction. As these views opened upon him, he took more pains to ingratiate himself with Fitzhenry. He became humble; he respect-fully sought his advice—and while he contrived a thousand modes of throwing himself in his way, he appeared less intrusive than before—and yet he felt that he did not get on. Fitzhenry was kind to him, as a countryman in need of assistance; he admired his talent as an art-ist, but he shrunk from the smallest approach to intimacy. Whitelock hoped that he was only shy, but he feared that he was proud; he tried to break through the barrier of reserve opposed to him, and he became a considerable annoyance to the recluse. He waylaid him during his walks with his daughter—forced his company upon them, and forging a thousand obliging excuses for entering their dwelling, he destroyed the charm of their quiet evenings, and yet tempered his manners with such shows of humility and gratitude as Fitzhenry could not resist.

Whitelock next tried his battery on the young lady herself. Her passion for her new acquirement afforded scope for his enterprizing disposition. She was really glad to see him whenever he came; questioned him about the pictures which existed in the old world, and, with a mixture of wonder and curiosity, began to think that there was magic in an art, that produced the effects which he described. With all the enthusiasm of youth, she tried to improve herself, and the alacrity with which she welcomed her master, or hurried to his school, looked almost like—Whitelock could not exactly tell what, but here was ground to work upon.

When Fitzhenry went on the expedition already mentioned, Ethel gave up all her time, with renewed ardour, to her favourite pursuit. Early in the morning she was seen tripping down to the school-house, accompanied by her faithful negro woman. The attendant used her distaff and spindle, Ethel her brush, and the hours flew unheeded. Whitelock would have been glad that her eyes had not always been so intently fixed on the paper before her. He proposed sketching from nature. They made studies from trees, and contemplated the changing hues of earth and sky together. While talking of tints, and tones of colour spread over the celestial hemisphere and the earth beneath, were it not an easy transition to speak of those which glistened in a lady's eye, or warmed her cheek? In the solitude of his chamber, thus our adventurer reasoned; and wondered each night why he hesitated to begin. Whitelock was short and ill-made. His face was not of an agreeable cast: it was impossible to see him without being impressed with the idea that he was a man of talent; but he was otherwise decidedly ugly. This disadvantage was counterbalanced by an overweening vanity, which is often to be remarked in those whose personal defects place them a step below their fellows. He knew the value of an appearance of devotion, and the power which an acknowledgment of entire thraldom exercises over the feminine imagination. He had succeeded ill with the father;

but, after all, the surest way was to captivate the daughter: the affection of her parent would induce him to ratify any step necessary to her happiness; and the chance afforded by this parent's absence for putting his plan into execution, might never again occur—why then delay?

It was, perhaps, strange that Fitzhenry, alive to the smallest evil that might approach his darling child, and devoted to her sole guardianship, should have been blind to the sort of danger which she ran during his absence. But the paternal protection is never entirely efficient. A father avenges an insult; but he has seldom watchfulness enough to prevent it. In the present instance, the extreme youth of Ethel might well serve as an excuse. She was scarcely fifteen; and, light-hearted and blithe, none but childish ideas had found place in her unruffled mind. Her father yet regarded her as he had done when she was wont to climb his knee, or to gambol before him: he still looked forward to her womanhood as to a distant event, which would necessitate an entire change in his mode of living, but which need not for several years enter into his calculations. Thus, when he departed, he felt glad to get rid, for a time, of Whitelock's disagreeable society; but it never crossed his imagination that his angelic girl could be annoyed or injured, meanwhile, by the presumptuous advances of a man whom he despised.

Ethel knew nothing of the language of love. She had read of it in her favourite poets; but she was yet too young and guileless to apply any of its feelings to herself. Love had always appeared to her blended with the highest imaginative beauty and heroism, and thus was in her eyes, at once awful and lovely. Nothing had vulgarized it to her. The greatest men were its slaves, and according as their choice fell on the worthy or unworthy, they were elevated or disgraced by passion. It was the part of a woman so to refine and educate her mind, as to be the cause of good alone to him whose fate depended on her smile. There was something of the Orondates' vein in her ideas; but they were too vague and general to influence her actions. Brought up in American solitude, with all the refinement attendant on European society, she was aristocratic, both as regarded rank and sex; but all these were as yet undeveloped feelings—seeds planted by the careful paternal hand, not yet called into life or growth.

Whitelock began his operations, and was obliged to be explicit to be at all understood. He spoke of misery and despair; he urged no plea, sought no favour, except to be allowed to speak of his wretchedness. Ethel listened—Eve listened to the serpent, and since then, her daughters have been accused of an aptitude to give ear to forbidden discourse. He spoke well, too, for he was a man of unquestioned talent. It is a strange feeling for a girl, when first she finds the power put into her hand of influencing the destiny of another to happiness or misery. She is like a magician holding for the first time a fairy wand, not having yet had experience of its potency. Ethel had read of the power of love; but a doubt had often suggested itself, of how far she herself should hereafter exercise the influence which is the attribute of her sex. Whitelock dispelled that doubt. He impressed on her mind the idea that he lived or died through her fiat.

For one instant, vanity awoke in her young heart; and she tripped back to her home with a smile of triumph on her lips. The feeling was short-lived. She entered her father's library; and his image appeared to rise before her, to regulate and purify her thoughts. If he had been there, what could she have said to him—she who never concealed a thought?—or how would he have received the information she had to give? What had happened, had not been the work of a day; Whitelock had for a week or two proceeded in an occult and mysterious manner: but this day he had withdrawn the veil; and she understood much that had appeared strange in him before. The dark, expressive eyes of her father she fancied to be before her, penetrating the depths of her soul, discovering her frivolity, and censuring her lowly vanity; and, even though alone, she felt abashed. Our faults are apt to assume giant and exaggerated forms to our eyes in youth, and Ethel felt degraded and humiliated; and remorse sprung up in her gentle heart, substituting itself for the former pleasurable emotion.

The young are always in extremes. Ethel put away her drawings and paintings. She secluded herself in her home; and arranged so well, that notwithstanding the freedom of American manners, Whitelock contrived to catch but a distant glimpse of her during the one other week that intervened before her father's return. Troubled at this behaviour, he felt his bravery ooze out. To have offended Fitzhenry, was an unwise proceeding, at best; but when he remembered the haughty and reserved demeanour of the man, he recoiled, trembling, from the prospect of encountering him.

Ethel was very concise in the expressions she used, to make her father, on his return, understand what had happened during his absence. Fitzhenry heard her with indignation and bitter self-reproach. The natural impetuosity of his disposition returned on him, like a stream which had been checked in its progress, but which had gathered strength from the delay. On a sudden, the future, with all its difficulties and trials, presented itself to his eyes; and he was determined to go out to meet them, rather than to await their advent in his seclusion. His resolution formed and he put it into immediate execution: he would instantly quit the Illinois. The world was before him; and while he paused on the western shores of the Atlantic, he could decide upon his future path. But he would not remain where he was another season. The present, the calm, placid present, had fled like morning mist before the new risen breeze: all appeared dark and turbid to his heated imagination. Change alone could appease the sense of danger that had risen within him. Change of place, of circumstances,—of all that for the last twelve years had formed his life. "How long am I to remain at peace?"— the prophetic voice heard in the silence of the forests, recurred to his memory, and thrilled through his frame. "Peace! was I ever at peace? Was this unquiet heart ever still, as, one by one, the troubled thoughts which are its essence, have risen and broken against the barriers that embank them? Peace! My own Ethel!—all I have done—all I would do—is to gift thee with that blessing which has for ever fled the thirsting lips of thy unhappy parent." And thus, governed by a fevered fancy and untamed passions, Fitzhenry forgot the tranquil lot which he had learnt to value and enjoy; and quitting the haven he had sought, as if it had never been a place of shelter to him, unthankful for the many happy hours which had blessed him there, he hastened to reach the stormier seas of life, whose breakers and whose winds were ready to visit him with shipwreck and destruction.

• • •

CHAPTER V

"The boy is father of the man."

—*Wordsworth*

Fitzhenry having formed his resolution, acted upon it immediately: and yet, while hastening every preparation for his departure, he felt return upon him that inquietude and intolerable sense of suffering, which of late years had subsided in his soul. Now and then it struck him as madness to quit his house, his garden, the trees of his planting, the quiet abode which he had reared in the wilderness. He gave his orders, but he was unable to command himself to attend to any of the minutiae of circumstance connected with his removal. As when he first arrived, again he sought relief in exercise and the open air. He felt each ministration of nature to be his friend, and man, in every guise, to be his enemy. He was about to plunge among them again. What would be the result?

Yet this was no abode for the opening bloom of Ethel. For her good his beloved and safe seclusion must be sacrificed, and that he was acting for her benefit, and not his own, served to calm his mind. She contemplated their migration with something akin to joy. We could almost believe that we are destined by Providence to an unsettled position on the globe, so invariably is a love of change implanted in the young. It seems as if the eternal Lawgiver intended that, at a certain age, man should leave father, mother, and the dwelling of his infancy, to

seek his fortunes over the wide world. A few natural tears Ethel shed—
they were not many. She, usually so resigned and quiet in her feelings,
was now in a state of excitement: dreamy, shadowy visions floated
before her of what would result from her journey, and curiosity and
hope gave life and a bright colouring to the prospect.

The day came at last. On the previous Sunday she had knelt for
the last time in church on the little hassock which had been her's from
infancy, and walked along the accustomed pathway towards her home
for the last time. During the afternoon, she visited the village to bid
adieu to her few acquaintances. The sensitive refinement of Fitzhenry
had caused him to guard his daughter jealously from familiar intercourse with their fellow settlers, even as a child. But she had been
accustomed to enter the poorer cottages, to assist the distressed, and
now and then to partake of tea drinking with the minister. This personage, however, was not stationary. At one time they had had a venerable old man whom Ethel had begun to love; but latterly, the pastor
had not been a person to engage her liking, and this had loosened her
only tie with her fellow colonists.

The day came. The father and daughter, with three attendants,
entered their carriage, and wound along the scarcely formed road.
One by one they passed, and lost sight of objects, that for many years
had been woven in with the texture of their lives. Fitzhenry was sad.
Ethel wept, unconstrainedly, plentiful showery tears, which cost so
much less to the heart, than the few sorrowful drops which, in after
life, we expend upon our woes. Still as they proceeded the objects that
met their eyes became less familiar and less endeared. They began to
converse, and when they arrived at their lodging for the night, Ethel
was cheerful, and her father, mastering the unquiet feelings which
disturbed him, exerted himself to converse with her on such topics as
would serve to introduce her most pleasantly to the new scenes which
she was about to visit.

There was one object, however, which lay nearest to the emigrant's
heart, to which he had not yet acquired courage to allude; his own

position in the world, his former fortunes, and the circumstances that had driven him from Europe, to seek peace and obscurity in the wilderness. It was a strange tale; replete with such incidents as could scarcely be made intelligible to the nursling of solitude—one difficult for a father to disclose to his daughter; involving besides a consideration of his future conduct, to which he did not desire to make her a party. Thus they talked of the cities they might see, and the strange sights she would behold, and but once did her father refer to their own position. After a long silence, on his part sombre and abstracted—as Prospero asked the ever sweet Miranda, so did Fitzhenry inquire of his daughter, if she had memory of aught preceding their residence in the Illinois? And Ethel, as readily as Miranda, replied in the affirmative.

"And what, my love, do you remember? Gold-laced liveries and spacious apartments?"

Ethel shook her head. "It may be the memory of a dream that haunts me," she replied, "and not a reality; but I have frequently the image before me, of having been kissed and caressed by a beautiful lady, very richly dressed."

Fitzhenry actually started at this reply. "I have often conjectured," continued Ethel, "that that lovely vision was my dear mother; and that when—when you lost her, you despised all the rest of the world, and exiled yourself to America."

Ethel looked inquiringly at her father as she made this leading remark; but he in a sharp and tremulous accent repeated the words, "Lost her!"

"Yes," said Ethel, "I mean, is she not lost—did she not die?"

Fitzhenry sighed heavily, and turning his head towards the window on his side, became absorbed in thought, and Ethel feared to disturb him by continuing the conversation.

It has not been difficult all along for the reader to imagine, that the lamented brother of the honourable Mrs. Elizabeth Fitzhenry and the exile of the Illinois are one; and while father and daughter are proceeding on their way towards New York, it will be necessary, for the interpretation of the ensuing pages, to dilate somewhat on the previous history of the father of our lovely heroine.

It may be remembered, that Henry Fitzhenry was the only son of Admiral Lord Lodore. He was, from infancy, the pride of his father and the idol of his sister; and the lives of both were devoted to exertions for his happiness and well-being. The boy soon became aware of their extravagant fondness, and could not do less in consequence than fancy himself a person of considerable importance. The distinction that Lord Lodore's title and residence bestowed upon Longfield made his son and heir a demigod among the villagers. As he rode through it on his pony, every one smiled on him and bowed to him; and the habit of regarding himself superior to all the world, became too much an habit to afford triumph, though any circumstances that had lessened his consequence in his own eyes would have been matter of astonishment and indignation. His personal beauty was the delight of the women, his agility and hardihood the topic of the men of the village. For although essentially spoiled, he was not pampered in luxury. His father, with all his fondness, would have despised him heartily had he not been inured to hardship, and rendered careless of it. Rousseau might have passed his approbation upon his physical education, while his moral nurture was the most perniciously indulgent. Thus, at the same time, his passions were fostered, and he possessed none of those habits of effeminacy, which sometimes stand in the gap, preventing our young self-indulged aristocracy from rebelling against the restraints of society. Still generous and brave as was his father, benevolent and pious as was his sister, Henry Fitzhenry was naturally led to love their virtues, and to seek their approbation by imitating them. He would not wantonly have inflicted a pang upon a human being; yet he exerted any power he might possess to quell the smallest resistance to his desires; and unless when they were manifested in the most intelligible manner, he scarcely knew that his fellow-creatures had any feelings at all, except pride and gladness in serving him, and gratitude when he showed them kindness. Any poor family visited by rough adversity, any unfortunate child enduring unjust oppression, he assisted earnestly and with all his heart. He was courageous as a lion, and, upon occasion, soft-hearted and pitiful; but once roused to anger by opposition, his eyes darted fire, his little form swelled, his boyish voice grew big, nor could he be pacified except by the most entire submission on the part of his antagonist. Unfortunately for him, submission usually followed any stand made against his authority, for it was always a contest with an inferior, and he was never brought into wholesome struggle with an equal.

At the age of thirteen he went to Eton, and here every thing wore an altered and unpleasing aspect. Here were no servile menials nor humble friends. He stood one among many—equals, superiors, inferiors, all full of a sense of their own rights, their own powers; he desired to lead, and he had no followers; he wished to stand aloof, and his dignity, even his privacy, was perpetually invaded. His schoolfellows soon discovered his weakness—it became a bye-word among them, and was the object of such practical jokes, as seemed to the self-idolizing boy, at once frightful and disgusting. He had no resource. Did he lay his length under some favourite tree to dream of home and independence, his tormentors were at hand with some new invention to rouse and molest him. He fixed his large dark eyes on them, and he curled his lips in scorn, trying to awe them by haughtiness and frowns, and shouts of laughter replied to the concentrated passion of his soul. He poured forth vehement invective, and hootings were the answer. He had one other resource, and that in the end proved successful:—a pitched battle or two elevated him in the eyes of his fellows, and as they began to respect him, so he grew in better humour with them and with himself. His good-nature procured him friends, and the sun once more shone unclouded upon him.

Yet this was not all. He put himself foremost among a troop of wild and uncivilized school-boys; but he was not of them. His tastes, fostered in solitude, were at once more manly and dangerous than theirs. He could not distinguish the nice line drawn by the customs of the place between a pardonable resistance, or rather evasion of authority, and rebellion against it; and above all, he could not submit to practice equivocation and deceit. His first contests were with his schoolfellows, his next were with his masters. He would not stoop to shows of humility, nor tame a nature accustomed to take pride in daring and independence. He resented injustice wherever he encountered or fancied it; he equally spurned it when practiced on himself, or defended others when they were its object—freedom was the watchword of his heart. Freedom from all trammels, except those of which he was wholly unconscious, imposed on him by his passions and pride. His good-nature led him to side with the weak; and he was indignant that his mere fiat did not suffice to raise them to his own level, or that his representations did not serve to open the eyes of all around him to the true merits of any disputed question.

He had a friend at school. A youth whose slender frame, fair, effeminate countenance, and gentle habits, rendered him ridiculous to his fellows, while an unhappy incapacity to learn his allotted tasks made him in perpetual disgrace with his masters. The boy was unlike the rest; he had wild fancies and strange inexplicable ideas. He said he was a mystery to himself—he was at once so wise and foolish. The mere aspect of a grammar inspired him with horror, and a kind of delirious stupidity seized him in the classes; and yet he could discourse with eloquence, and pored with unceasing delight over books of the abstrusest philosophy. He seemed incapable of feeling the motives and impulses of other boys: when they jeered him, he would answer gravely with some story of a ghastly spectre, and tell wild legends of weird beings, who roamed through the dark fields by night, or sat wailing by the banks of streams: was he struck, he smiled and turned away; he would not fag; he never refused to learn, but could not; he was the scoff, and butt, and victim, of the whole school.

Fitzhenry stood forward in his behalf, and the face of things was changed. He insisted that his friend should have the same respect paid him as himself, and the boys left off tormenting him. When they ceased to injure, they began to like him, and he had soon a set of friends whom he solaced with his wild stories and mysterious notions. But his powerful advocate was unable to advance his cause with his masters, and the cruelty exercised on him revolted Fitzhenry's generous soul. One day, he stood forth to expostulate, and to show wherefore Derham should not be punished for a defect, that was not his fault. He was ordered to be silent, and he retorted the command with fierceness. As he saw the slender, bending form of his friend seized to be led to punishment, he sprang forward to rescue him. This open rebellion astounded every one; a kind of consternation, which feared to show the gladness it felt, possessed the boyish subjects of the tyro kingdom. Force conquered; Fitzhenry was led away; and the masters deliberated what sentence to pass on him. He saved them from coming to a conclusion by flight.

He hid himself during the day in Windsor Forest, and at night he entered Eton, and scaling a wall, tapped at the bedroom window of his friend. "Come," said he, "come with me. Leave these tyrants to eat their own hearts with rage—my home shall be your home."

Derham embraced him, but would not consent. "My mother," he said, "I have promised my mother to bear all"; and tears gushed from his large light blue eyes; "but for her, the green grass of this spring were growing on my grave. I dare not pain her."

"Be it so," said Fitzhenry; "nevertheless, before the end of a month, you shall be free. I am leaving this wretched place, where men rule because they are strong, for my father's house. I never yet asked for a thing that I ought to have, that it was not granted me. I am a boy here, there I am a man—and can do as men do. Representations shall be made to your parents; you shall be taken from school; we shall be free and happy together this summer at Longfield. Good night; I have far to walk, for the stage coachmen would be shy of me near Eton; but I shall get to London on foot, and sleep to-morrow in my father's house. Keep up your heart, Derham, be a man—this shall not last long; we shall triumph yet."

• • •

CHAPTER VI

"What is youth? a dancing billow,
Winds behind, and rocks before!"

—*Wordsworth*

This exploit terminated Fitzhenry's career at Eton. A private tutor was engaged, who resided with the family, for the purpose of preparing him for college, and at the age of seventeen he was entered at Oxford. He still continued to cultivate the friendship of Derham. This youth was the younger son of a rich and aristocratic family, whose hopes and cares centred in their heir, and who cared little for the comfort of the younger. Derham had been destined for the sea, and scarcely did his delicate health, and timid, nervous disposition exempt him from the common fate of a boy, whose parents did not know what to do with him. The next idea was to place him in the church; and at last, at his earnest entreaty, he was permitted to go abroad, to study at one of the German universities, so to prepare himself, by a familiarity with modern languages, for diplomacy.

It was singular how well Fitzhenry and his sensitive friend agreed;—the one looked up with unfeigned admiration—the other felt attracted by a mingled compassion and respect, that flattered his vanity, and yet served as excitement and amusement. From Derham, Fitzhenry imbibed in theory much of that contempt of the world's opinion, and carelessness of consequences, which was inherent in the one, but was an extraneous graft on the proud and imperious spirit of the other. Derham looked with calm yet shy superiority on his fellow-creatures. Yet superiority is not the word, since he did not feel himself superior to, but different from—incapable of sympathizing or extracting sympathy, he turned away with a smile, and pursued his lonely path, thronged with visions and fancies—while his friend, when he met check or rebuff, would fire up, his eyes sparkling, his bosom heaving with intolerable indignation.

After two years spent at Oxford, instead of remaining to take his degree, Fitzhenry made an earnest request to be permitted to visit his friend, who was then at Jena. It was but anticipating the period for his travels, and upon his promise to pursue his studies abroad, he won a somewhat reluctant consent from his father. Once on the continent, the mania of travelling seized him. He visited Italy, Poland, and Russia: he bent his wayward steps from north to south, as the whim seized him. He became of age, and his father earnestly desired his return: but again and again he solicited permission to remain, from autumn till spring, and from spring till autumn, until the very flower of his youth seemed destined to be wasted in aimless rambles, and an intercourse with foreigners, that must tend to unnationalize him, and to render him unfit for a career in his own country. Growing accustomed to regulate his own actions, he changed the tone of request into that of announcing his intentions. At length, he was summoned home to attend the death-bed of his father. He paid the last duties to his remains, provided for the comfortable establishment of his sister in the family mansion at Longfield, and then informed her of his determination of returning immediately to Vienna.

During this visit he had appeared to live rather in a dream than in the actual world. He had mourned for his father; he paid the most affectionate attentions to his sister; but this formed, as it were, the surface of things; a mightier impulse ruled his inner mind. His life seemed to depend upon certain letters which he received; and when the day had been occupied by business, he passed the night in writing answers. He was often agitated in the highest degree, almost always abstracted in reverie. The outward man—the case of Lodore was in England—his passionate and undisciplined soul was far away, evidently in the keeping of another.

Elizabeth, sorrowing for the loss of her father, was doubly afflicted when she heard that it was her brother's intention to quit England immediately. She had fondly hoped that he would, adorned by his newly-inherited title, and endowed with the gifts of fortune, step upon the stage of the world, and shine forth the hero of his age and country. Her affections, her future prospects, her ambition, were all centred in him; and it was a bitter pang to feel that the glory of these was to be eclipsed by the obscurity and distant residence which he preferred. Accustomed to obedience, and to regard the resolutions of the men about her, as laws with which she had no right to interfere, she did not remonstrate, she only wept. Moved by her tears, Lord Lodore made the immense sacrifice of one month to gratify her, which he spent in reading and writing letters at Longfield, in pacing the rooms or avenues absorbed in reverie, or in riding over the most solitary districts, with no object apparently in view, except that of avoiding his fellow-creatures. Elizabeth had the happiness of seeing the top of his head as he leant over his desk in the library, from a little hillock in the garden, which she sought for the purpose of beholding that blessed vision. She enjoyed also the pleasure of hearing him pace his room during the greater part of the night. Sometimes he conversed with her, and then how like a god he seemed! His extensive acquaintance with men and things, the novel but choice language in which he clothed his ideas; his vivid descriptions, his melodious voice, and the exquisite grace of his manner, made him rise like the planet of day upon her. Too soon her sun set. If ever she hinted at the prolongation of his stay, he grew moody, and she discovered with tearful anguish that his favourite ride was towards the sea, often to the very shore: "I seem half free when I only look upon the waves," he said; "they remind me that the period of liberty is at hand, when I shall leave this dull land for—"

A sob from his sister checked his speech, and he repented his ingratitude. Yet when the promised month had elapsed, he did not defer his journey a single day: already had he engaged his passage at Harwich. A fair wind favoured his immediate departure. Elizabeth accompanied him on board, almost she wished to be asked to sail with him. No word but that of a kind adieu was uttered by him. She returned to shore, and watched his lessening sail. Wherefore did he leave his native country? Wherefore return to reside in lands, whose language, manners, and religion, were all at variance with his own? These questions occupied the gentle spinster's thoughts; she had little except such meditations to vary the hours, as years stole on unobserved, and she continued to spend her blameless tranquil days in her native village.

The new Lord Lodore was one of those men, not unfrequently met with in the world, whose early youth is replete with mighty promise; who, as they advance in life, continue to excite the expectation, the curiosity, and even the enthusiasm of all around them; but as the sun on a stormy day now and then glimmers forth, giving us hopes of conquering brightness, and yet slips down to its evening eclipse without redeeming the pledge; so do these men present every appearance of one day making a conspicuous figure, and yet to the end, as it were, they only gild the edges of the clouds in which they hide themselves, and arrive at the term of life, the promise of its dawn unfulfilled. Passion, and the consequent engrossing occupations, usurped the place of laudable ambition and useful exertion. He wasted his nobler energies upon pursuits which were mysteries to the world, yet which formed the sum of his existence. It was not that he was destitute of loftier aspirations. Ambition was the darling growth of his soul—but weeds and parasites, an unregulated and unpruned overgrowth, twisted itself around the healthier plant, and threatened its destruction.

Sometimes he appeared among the English in the capital towns of the continent, and was always welcomed with delight. His manners were highly engaging, a little reserved with men, unless they were intimates, attentive to women, and to them a subject of interest, they scarcely knew why. A mysterious fair one was spoken of as the cynosure of his destiny, and some desired to discover his secret, while others would have been glad to break the spell that bound him to this hidden star. Often for months he disappeared altogether, and was spoken of as having secluded himself in some unattainable district of northern Germany, Poland, or Courland. Yet all these erratic movements were certainly governed by one law, and that was love;—love unchangeable and intense, else wherefore was he cold to the attractions of his fair countrywomen? And why, though he gazed with admiration and interest on the families of lovely girls, whose successive visitations on the continent strike the natives with such wonder, why did he not select some distinguished beauty, with blue eyes, and auburn locks, as the object of his exclusive admiration? He had often conversed with such with seeming delight; but he could withdraw from the fascination unharmed and free. Sometimes a very kind and agreeable mamma contrived half to domesticate him; but after lounging, and turning over music-books, and teaching steps for a week, he was gone—a farewell card probably the only token of regret.

Yet he was universally liked, and the ladies were never weary of auguring the time to be not far off, when he would desire to break the chains that bound him;—and then—he must marry. He was so quiet, so domestic, so gentle, that he would make, doubtless, a kind and affectionate husband. Among Englishmen, he had a friend or two, by courtesy so called, who were eager for him to return to his native country, and to enter upon public life. He lent a willing ear to these persuasions, and appeared annoyed at some secret necessity that prevented his yielding to them. Once or twice he had said, that his present mode of life should not last for ever, and that he would

CHAPTER VII

"Men oftentimes prepare a lot,
   Which ere it finds them, is not what
   Suits with their genuine station."

—Shelley

A t the age of thirty-two, Lord Lodore returned to England. It was subject of discussion among his friends, whether this was to be a merely temporary visit, or whether he was about to establish himself finally in his own country. Meanwhile, he became the lion of the day. As the reputed slave of the fair sex, he found favour in their gentle eyes. Even blooming fifteen saw all that was romantic and winning in his subdued and graceful manners, and in the melancholy which dwelt in his dark eyes. The chief fault found with him was, that he was rather taciturn, and that, from whatever cause, woman had apparently ceased to influence his soul to love. He avoided intimacies among them, and seemed to regard them from afar, with observant but passionless eyes. Some spoke of a spent volcano—others of a fertile valley ravaged by storms, and turned into a desert; while many cherished the hope of renewing the flame, or of replanting flowers on the arid soil.

Lord Lodore had just emancipated himself from an influence, which had become the most grievous slavery, from the moment it had ceased to be a voluntary servitude. He had broken the ties that had so long held him; but this had not been done without such difficulties and struggles, as made freedom less delightful, from the languor and regret that accompanied victory. Lodore had formed but one resolve, which was not to entangle himself again in unlawful pursuits, where the better energies of his mind were to be spent in forging deceptions, and tranquillizing the mind of a jealous and unhappy woman. He entertained a vague wish to marry, and to marry one whom his judgment, rather than his love, should select;—an unwise purpose, good in theory, but very defective in practice. Besides this new idea of marrying, which he buried as a profound secret in his own bosom, he wished to accustom himself to the manners and customs of his own country, so as to enable him to enter upon public life. He was fond of the country in England, and entered with zeal upon the pleasures of the chace. He liked the life led at the seats of the great, and endeavoured to do his part in amusing those around him.

Yet he did not feel one of them. Above all, he did not feel within him the charm of life, the glad spirit that looks on each returning day as a blessing; and which, gilding every common object with its own brightness, requires no lustre unborrowed from itself. All things palled upon Lodore. The light laughter and gentle voices of women were vacant of attraction; his sympathy was not excited by the discussions or pursuits of men. After striving for a whole year to awaken in himself an interest for some one person or thing, and finding all to be "vanity,"—towards the close of a season in town, of extreme brilliancy and variety to common eyes—of dulness and sameness to his morbid sense, he suddenly withdrew himself from the haunts of men, and plunging into solitude, tried to renovate his soul by self-communings, and an intercourse with silent, but most eloquent, Nature.

Youth wasted; affections sown on sand, barren of return; wealth and station flung as weeds upon the rocks; a name, whose "gold" was "o'erdusted" by the inertness of its wearer;—such were the retrospections that haunted his troubled mind. He envied the ploughboy, who whistled as he went; and the laborious cottager, who each Saturday bestowed upon his family the hard-won and scanty earnings of the week. He pined for an aim in life—a bourne—a necessity, to give zest to his palled appetite, and excitement to his satiated soul. It seemed to him that he could hail poverty and care as blessings; and that the dearest gifts of fortune—youth, health, rank, and riches—were disguised curses. All these he possessed, and despised. Gnawing discontent; energy, rebuked and tamed into mere disquietude, for want of a proper object, preyed upon his soul. Where could a remedy be found? No "green spot" of delight soothed his memory; no cheering prospect appeared in view; all was arid, gloomy, unsunned upon.

He had wandered into Wales. He was charmed with the scenery and solitude about Rhyaider Gowy, in Radnorshire, which lies amidst romantic mountains, and in immediate vicinity to a cataract of the Wye. He fixed himself for some months in a convenient mansion, which he found to let, at a few miles from that place. Here he was secure from unwelcome visitors, or any communication with the throng he had left. He corresponded with no one, read no newspapers. He passed his day, loitering beside waterfalls, clambering the steep mountains, or making longer excursions on horseback, always directing his course away from high roads or towns. His past life had been sufficiently interesting to afford scope for reverie; and as he watched the sunbeams as they climbed the hills at evening, or the shadows of the clouds as they careered across the valleys, his heart by turns mourned or rejoiced over its freedom, and the change that had come over it and stilled its warring passions.

The only circumstance that in the least entrenched upon his feeling of entire seclusion, was the mention, not unfrequently made to him, by his servants, of the "ladies at the farm." The idea of these "ladies" at first annoyed him; but the humble habitation which they had chosen—humble to poverty—impressed him with the belief that, however the "ladies" might awe-strike the Welsh peasantry, he should find in them nothing that would impress him with the idea of station. Two or three times, at the distant sight of a bonnet, instead of the Welsh hat, he had altered his course to avoid the wearer. Once he had suddenly come on one of these wonders of the mountains: she might have passed for a very civilized kind of abigail; but, of course, she was one of the "ladies."

As Lodore was neither a poet nor a student, he began at last to tire of loneliness. He was a little ashamed when he remembered that he had taken his present abode for a year: however, he satisfied his conscience by a resolve to return to it; and began seriously to plan crossing the country, to visit his sister in Essex. He was, during one of his rides, deliberating on putting this resolve into execution on the very next morning, when suddenly he was overtaken by a storm. The valley, through which his path wound, was narrow, and the gathering clouds over head made it dark as night; the lightning flashed with peculiar brightness; and the thunder, loud and bellowing, was re-echoed by the hills, and reverberated along the sky in terrific pealings. It was more like a continental storm than any which Lodore had ever witnessed in England, and imparted to him a sensation of thrilling pleasure; till, as the rain came down in torrents, he began to think of seeking some shelter, at least for his horse. Looking round for this, he all at once perceived a vision of white muslin beneath a ledge of rock, which could but half protect the gentle wearer: frightened she was, too, as a slight shriek testified, when a bright flash, succeeded instantaneously by a loud peal of thunder, bespoke the presence of something like danger. Lodore's habitual tenderness of nature rendered it no second thought with him to alight and offer his services; and he was fully repaid when he saw her, who hailed with gladness a protector, though too frightened to smile, or scarcely to speak. She was very young, and more beautiful, Lodore was at once assured, than any thing he had ever before beheld. Her fairness, increased by the paleness of terror, was even snowy; her hair, scarcely dark enough for chesnut, too dark for auburn, clustered in rich curls on her brow; her eyes were dark grey, long, and full of expression, as they beamed from beneath their deeply-fringed lids. But such description says little; it was not the form of eye or the brow's arch, correct and beautiful as these were, in this lovely girl, that imparted her peculiar attraction; beyond these, there was a radiance, a softness, an angel look, that rendered her countenance singular in its fascination; an expression of innocence and sweetness; a pleading gentleness that desired protection; a glance that subdued, because it renounced all victory; and this, now animated by fear, quickly excited, in Lodore, the most ardent desire to re-assure and serve her. She leant, as she stood, against the rock—now hiding her face with her hands—now turning her eyes to her stranger companion, as if in appeal or disbelief; while he again and again protested that there was no danger, and strove to guard her from the rain, which still descended with violence. The thunder died away, and the lightning soon ceased to flash, but this continued; and while the colour revisited the young girl's cheek, and her smiles, displaying a thousand dimples, lighted up new charms, a fresh uneasiness sprung up in her of how she could get home. Her *chaussure*, ill-fitted even for the mountains, could not protect her for a moment from the wet. Lodore offered his horse, and pledged himself for its quietness, and his care, if she could contrive to sit in the saddle. He lifted her light form on to it; but the high-bred animal, beginning a little to prance, she threw herself off into the arms of her new friend, in a transport of terror, which Lodore could by no means assuage. What was to be done? He felt, light as she was, that he could carry her the short half-mile to her home; but this could not be offered. The rain was now over; and her only resource was to brave the humid soil in kid slippers. With considerable difficulty, half the journey was accomplished, when they met the "lady" whom Lodore had before seen;—really the maid in attendance, who had come out to seek her young mistress, and to declare that "my lady" was beside herself with anxiety on her account.

Lodore still insisted on conducting his young charge to her home; and the next day it was but matter of politeness to call to express his hope that she had not suffered from her exposure to the weather. He found the lovely girl, fresh as the morning, with looks all light and sweetness, seated beside her mother, a lady whose appearance was not so prepossessing, though adorned with more than the remains of beauty. She at once struck Lodore as disagreeable and forbidding. Still she was cordial in her welcome, grateful for his kindness, and so perfectly engrossed by the thought of, and love for, her child, that Lodore felt his respect and interest awakened.

An acquaintance, thus begun between the noble recluse and the "ladies of the farm," proceeded prosperously. A month ago, would not have believed that he should feel glad at finding two fair off-shoots of London fashion dwelling so near his retreat; but even if solitude had not rendered him tolerant, the loveliness of the daughter might well perform a greater miracle. In the mother, he found good breeding, good nature, and good sense. He soon became almost domesticated in their rustic habitation.

Lady Santerre was of humble birth, the daughter of a solicitor of a country town. She was handsome, and won the heart of Mr. Santerre, then a minor, who was assisted by her father in the laudable endeavour to obtain more money than his father allowed him. The young gentleman saw, loved, and married. His parents were furiously angry, and tried to illegalize the match; but he confirmed it when he came of age, and a reconciliation with his family never took place. Mr. Santerre sold reversions, turned expectations into money, and lived in the world. For six years, his wife bloomed in the gay parterre of fashionable society, when her husband's father died. Prosperity was to dawn on this event: the new Sir John went down to attend his father's funeral; thence to return to town, to be immersed in recoveries, settlements, and law. He never returned. Riding across the country to a neighbour, his horse shyed, reared, and threw him. His head struck against a fragment of stone: a concussion of the brain ensued; and a fortnight afterwards, he was enclosed beside his father, in the ancestral vault.

His widow was the mother of a daughter only; and her hopes and prospects died with her husband. His brother, and heir, might have treated her better in the sequel; but he was excessively irritated by the variety of debts, and incumbrances, and lawsuits, he had to deal with. He chose to consider the wife most to blame, and she and her child were treated as aliens. He allowed them two hundred a year, and called himself generous. This was all (for her father was not rich, and had a large family) that poor Lady Santerre had to depend upon. She struggled on for some little time, trying to keep up her connexions in the gay world; but poverty is a tyrant, whose laws are more terrible than those of Draco. Lady Santerre yielded, retired to Bath, and fixed her hopes on her daughter, whom she resolved should hereafter make a splendid match. Her excessive beauty promised to render this scheme feasible; and now that she was nearly sixteen, her mother began to look forward anxiously. She had retired to Wales this summer, that, by living with yet stricter economy, she might be enabled, during the winter, to put her plans into execution with greater ease.

Lord Lodore became intimate with the mother and daughter, and his imagination speedily painted both in the most attractive colours. Here was the very being his heart had pined for—a girl radiant in innocence and youth, the nursling, so he fancied, of mountains, waterfalls, and solitude; yet endowed with all the softness and refinement of civilized society. Long forgotten emotions awoke in his heart, and he gave himself up to the bewildering feelings that beset him. Every thing was calculated to excite his interest. The desolate situation of the mother, devoted to her daughter only, and that daughter fairer than imagination could paint, young, gentle, blameless, knowing nothing beyond obedience to her parent, and untaught in the guile of mankind. It was impossible to see that intelligent and sweet face, and not feel that to be the first to impress love in the heart which it mirrored, was a destiny which angles might envy. How proud a part was his, to gift her with rank, fortune, and all earthly blessings, and to receive in return, gratitude, tenderness, and unquestioning submission! If love did not, as thus he reasoned, show itself in the tyrant guise it had formerly assumed in the heart of Lodore, it was the more welcome a guest. It spoke not of the miseries of passion, but offered a bright view of lengthened days of peace and contentedness. He was not a slave at the feet of his mistress, but he could watch each gesture and catch each sound of her voice, and say, goodness and beauty are there, and I shall be happy.

He found the lovely girl somewhat ignorant; but white paper to be written upon at will, is a favourite metaphor among those men who have described the ideal of a wife. That she had talent beyond what he had usually found in women, he was delighted to remark. At first she was reserved and shy. Little accustomed to society, she sat beside her mother in something of a company attitude; her eyes cast down, her lips closed. She was never to be found alone, and a *jeune personne* in France could scarcely be more retired and tranquil. This accorded better with Lodore's continental experience, than the ease of English fashionable girls, and he was pleased. He conversed little with Cornelia until he had formed his determination, and solicited her mother's consent to their union. Then they were allowed to walk together, and she gained on him, as their intimacy increased. She was very lively, witty, and full of playful fancy. Aware of her own deficiencies in education, she was the first to laugh at herself, and to make such remarks as showed an understanding worth all the accomplishments in the world. Lodore now really found himself in love, and blessed the day that led him from among the fair daughters of fashion to this child of nature. His wayward feelings were to change no more—his destiny was fixed. At thirty-four to marry, to settle into the father of a family, his hopes and wishes concentrated in a home, adorned by one whose beauty was that of angels, was a prospect that he dwelt upon each day with renewed satisfaction. Nothing in after years could disturb his felicity, and the very security with which he contemplated the future, imparted a calm delight, at once new and grateful to a heart, weary of storms and struggles, and which, in finding peace, believed that it possessed the consummation of human happiness.

• • •

CHAPTER VIII

"Hopes, what are they? beads of morning
Strung on slender blades of grass,
Or a spider's web adorning,
In a strait and treacherous pass."

—*Wordsworth*

he months of July, August, and September had passed away.
Lord Lodore enjoyed, during the two last, a singularly complacent state of mind. He had come to Wales with worn-out spirits, a victim to that darker species of *ennui*, which colours with gloomy
tints the future as well as the present, and is the ministering angel of evil
to the rich and prosperous. He despised himself, contemned his pursuits,
and called all vanity beneath the vivifying sun of heaven. Real misfortunes have worn the guise of blessings to men so afflicted, but he was
withdrawn from this position, by a being who wore the outward sem-
blance of an angel, and from whom he felt assured nothing but good
could flow.

Cornelia Santerre was lovely, vivacious, witty, and good-humoured;
yet strange to say, her new lover was not rendered happy so much by
the presence of these qualities, as by the promise which they gave for
the future. He loved her; he believed that she would be to the end of his
life a blessing and a delight; yet passion was scarcely roused in his heart;
it was "a sober certainty of waking bliss," and a reasonable belief in the

continuance of this state, that made him, while he loved her, regard her rather as a benefactress than a mistress.

Benefactress is a strange word to use, especially as her extreme youth was probably the cause that more intimate sympathies did not unite them, and why passion entered so slightly into their intercourse. It is possible, so great was the discrepancy of their age, and consequently of their feelings and views of life, that Lodore would never have thought of marrying Cornelia, but that Lady Santerre was at hand to direct the machinery of the drama. She inspired him with the wish to gift her angelic child with the worldly advantages which his wife must possess; to play a god-like part, and to lift into prosperity and happiness, one who seemed destined by fortune to struggle with adversity. Lady Santerre was a worldly woman and an oily flatterer; Lodore had been accustomed to feminine control, and he yielded with docility to her silken fetters.

The ninth of October was Cornelia's sixteenth birthday, and on it she became the wife of Lord Lodore. This event took place in the parish church of Rhyaider Gowy, and it was communicated to "the world" in the newspapers. Many discussions then arose as to who Miss Santerre could be. "The only daughter of the late Sir John." The only late Sir John Santerre remembered, was, in fact, the grandfather of the bride, and the hiatus in her genealogy, caused by her father's death before he had been known as a baronet, puzzled every fashionable gossip. The whole affair, however, had been forgotten, when curiosity was again awakened in the ensuing month of March, by an announcement in the *Morning Post*, of the arrival of the noble pair at Mivart's. Lord Lodore had always rented a box at the King's Theatre. It had been newly decorated at the beginning of the season, and on the first Saturday in April all eyes turned towards it as he entered, having the loveliest, fairest, and most sylph-like girl, that ever trod dark earth, leaning on his arm. There was a child-like innocence, a fascinating simplicity, joined to an expression of vivacity and happiness, in Lady Lodore's countenance, which impressed at first sight, as being the completion of feminine beauty.

She looked as if no time could touch, no ill stain her; artless affection and amiable dependence spoke in each graceful gesture. Others might be beautiful, but there was that in her, which seemed allied to celestial loveliness.

Such was the prize Lord Lodore had won. The new-married pair took up their residence in Berkeley Square, and here Lady Santerre joined them, and took possession of the apartments appropriated to her use, under her daughter's roof. All appeared bright on the outside, and each seemed happy in each other. Yet had any one cared to remark, they had perceived that Lodore looked even more abstracted than before his marriage. They had seen, that, in the domestic *coterie*, mother and daughter were familiar friends, sharing each thought and wish, but that Lodore was one apart, banished, or exiling himself from the dearest blessings of friendship and love. There might be no concealment, but also there was no frankness between the pair. Neither practised disguise, but there was no outpouring of the heart—no "touch of nature," which, passing like an electric shock, made their souls one. An insurmountable barrier stood between Lodore and his happiness—between his love and his wife's confidence; that this obstacle was a shadow—undefined—formless—nothing—yet every thing, made it trebly hateful, and rendered it utterly impossible that it should be removed.

The magician who had raised this ominous phantom, was Lady Santerre. She was a clever though uneducated woman: perfectly selfish, soured with the world, yet clinging to it. To make good her second entrance on its stage, she believed it necessary to preserve unlimited sway over the plastic mind of her daughter. If she had acted with integrity, her end had been equally well secured; but unfortunately, she was by nature framed to prefer the zig-zag to the straight line; added to which, she was imperious, and could not bear a rival near her throne. From the first, therefore, she exerted herself to secure her empire over Cornelia; she spared neither flattery nor artifice; and, well acquainted as she was with every habit and turn of her daughter's mind, her task was comparatively easy.

MARY SHELLEY

The fair girl had been brought up (ah! how different from the sentiments which Lodore had thought to find the natural inheritance of the mountain child!) to view society as the glass by which she was to set her feelings, and to which to adapt her conduct. She was ignorant, accustomed to the most frivolous employments, shrinking from any mental exercise, so that although her natural abilities were great, they lay dormant, producing neither bud nor blossom, unless such might be called the elegance of her appearance, and the charm of the softest and most ingenuous manners in the world. When her husband would have educated her mind, and withdrawn her from the dangers of dissipation, she looked on his conduct as tyrannical and cruel. She retreated from his manly guidance, to the pernicious guardianship of Lady Santerre, and she sheltered herself at her side, from any effort Lodore might make for her improvement.

Those who have never experienced a situation of this kind, cannot understand it; the details appear trivial: there seems wanting but one effort to push away the flimsy web, which, after all, is rather an imaginary than real bondage. But the slightest description will bring it home to those who have known it, and groaned beneath a despotism the more intolerable, as it could be less defined. Lord Lodore found that he had no home, no dear single-hearted bosom where he could find sympathy and to which to impart pleasure. When he entered his drawing-room with gaiety of spirit to impart some agreeable tidings, to ask his wife's advice, or to propose some plan, Lady Santerre was ever by her side, with her hard features and canting falsetto voice, checking at once the kindling kindness of his soul, and he felt that all that he should say would be turned from its right road, by some insidious remark, and the words he was about to speak died upon his lips. When he looked forward through the day, and would have given the world to have had his wife to himself, and to have sought, in some drive or excursion, for the pleasant unreserved converse he sighed for, Lady Santerre must be consulted; and though she never opposed him, she always carried her point in opposition to his. His wishes were made light of, and he was left to amuse himself, and to know that his wife was imbibing the lessons of one, whom he had learnt to despise and hate.

Lord Lodore cherished an ideal of what he thought a woman ought to be; but he had no lofty opinion of woman as he had usually found her. He had believed that the germ of all the excellencies which he esteemed was to be found in Cornelia, and he found himself mistaken. He had expected to find truth, clearness of spirit, and complying gentleness, the adorning qualities of the unsophisticated girl, and he found her the willing disciple of one whose selfish and artful character was in direct contradiction to his own. Once or twice at the beginning, he had attempted to withdraw his wife from this sinister influence, but Lady Lodore highly resented any effort of this kind, and saw in it an endeavour to make her neglect her first and dearest duties. Lodore, angry that the wishes of another should be preferred to his, drew back with disappointed pride; he disdained to enforce by authority, that which he thought ought to be yielded to love. The bitter sense of wounded affections was not to be appeased by knowing that, if he chose, he could command that, which was worthless in his eyes, except as a voluntary gift.

And here his error began; he had married one so young, that her education, even if its foundation had been good, required finishing, and who as it was, had every thing to learn. During the days of courtship he had looked forward with pleasure to playing the tutor to his fair mistress: but a tutor can do nothing without authority, either open or concealed—a tutor must sacrifice his own pursuits and immediate pleasures, to study and adapt himself to the disposition of his pupil. As has been said of those who would acquire power in the state—they must in some degree follow, if they would lead, and it is by adapting themselves to the humour of those they would command, that they establish the law of their own will, or of an apparent necessity. But Lodore understood nothing of all this. He had been accustomed to be managed by his mistress; he had been yielding, but it was because she contrived to make his will her own; otherwise he was imperious:

opposition startled and disconcerted him, and he saw heartlessness in the want of accommodation and compliance he met at home. He had expected from Cornelia a girl's clinging fondness, but that was given to her mother; nor did she feel the womanly tenderness, which sees in her husband the safeguard from the ills of life, the shield to stand between her and the world, to ward off its cruelties; a shelter from adversity, a refuge when tempests were abroad. How could she feel this, who, proud in youth and triumphant beauty, knew nothing of, and disbelieved the tales which sages and old women tell of the perils of life? The world looked to her a velvet strewn walk, canopied from every storm—her husband alone, who endeavoured to reveal the reality of things to her, and to disturb her visions, was the source of any sorrow or discomfort. She was buoyed up by the supercilious arrogance of youth; and while inexperience rendered her incapable of entering into the feelings of her husband, she displayed towards him none of that deference, and yielding submission, which might reasonably have been expected from her youth, but that her mother was there to claim them for herself, and to inculcate, as far as she could, that while she was her natural friend, Lodore was her natural enemy.

He, with strong pride and crushed affections, gave himself up for a disappointed man. He disdained to struggle with the sinister influence of his mother-in-law; he did not endeavour to discipline and invigorate the facile disposition of his bride. He had expected devotion, attention, love; and he scorned to complain or to war against the estrangement that grew up between them. If at any time he was impelled by an overflowing heart to seek his fair wife's side, the eternal presence of Lady Santerre chilled him at once; and to withdraw her from this was a task difficult indeed to one who could not forgive the competition admitted between them. At first he made one or two endeavours to separate them; but the reception his efforts met with galled his haughty soul; and while he cherished a deep and passionate hatred for the cause, he grew to despise the victim of her arts. He thought that he perceived duplicity, low-thoughted pride, and coldness of heart, the native growth of the daughter of such a mother. He yielded her up at once to the world and her parent, and resolved to seek, not happiness, but occupation elsewhere. He felt the wound deeply, but he sought no cure; and pride taught him to mask his soreness of spirit by a studied mildness of manner, which, being joined to cold indifference, and frequent contradiction, soon begot a considerable degree of resentment, and even dislike on her part. Her mother's well-applied flatteries and the adulation of her friends were contrasted with his half-disguised contempt. The system of society tended to increase their mutual estrangement. She embarked at once on the stream of fashion; and her whole time was given up to the engagements and amusements that flowed in on her on all sides; while he—one other regret added to many previous ones— one other disappointment in addition to those which already corroded his heart—bade adieu to every hope of domestic felicity, and tried to create new interests for himself, seeking, in public affairs, for food for a mind eager for excitement.

...

CHAPTER IX

"What are fears, but voices airy
Whisp'ring harm, where harm is not?
And deluding the unwary.
Till the fatal bolt is shot?"

—*Wordsworth*

L ord Lodore was disgusted at the very threshold of his new purpose. His long residence abroad prevented his ever acquiring the habit of public speaking; nor had he the respect for human nature, nor the enthusiasm for a party or a cause, which is necessary for one who would make a figure as a statesman. His sensitive disposition, his pride, which, when excited, verged into arrogance; his uncompromising integrity, his disdain of most of his associates, his incapacity of yielding obedience, rendered his short political career one of struggle and mortification. "And this is life!" he said; "abroad, to mingle with the senseless and the vulgar; and at home, to find a—wife, who prefers the admiration of fools, to the love of an honest heart!"

Within a year after her marriage, Lady Lodore gave birth to a daughter. This circumstance, which naturally tends to draw the parents nearer, unfortunately in this instance set them further apart. Lady Santerre had been near, with so many restrictions and so much interference, which though probably necessary, considering Cornelia's extreme youth, yet seemed vexatious and impertinent to Lodore. All things appeared to be permitted, except those which he proposed. A drive, a ride, even a walk with him, was to be considered fatal; while, at the same time, Lady Lodore was spending whole nights in heated rooms, and even dancing. Her confinement was followed by a long illness; the child was nursed by a stranger, secluded in a distant part of the house; and during her slow recovery, the young mother seemed scarcely to remember that it existed. The love for children is a passion often developed most fully in the second stage of life. Lodore idolized his little offspring, and felt hurt and angry when his wife, after it had been in her room a minute or two, on the first approach it made to a squall, ordered it to be taken away. At the time, in truth, she was reduced to the lowest ebb of weakness; but Lodore, as men are apt to do, was slow to discern her physical suffering, while his cheeks burnt with indignation, as she peevishly repeated the command that his child should go.

When she grew better this was not mended. She was ordered into the country for air, at a time when the little girl was suffering from some infantine disorder, and could not be moved. It was left with its nurses, but Lodore remained also, and rather suffered his wife to travel without him, so to demonstrate openly, that he thought her treatment of her baby unmotherly; not that he expressed this sentiment, nor did Lady Lodore guess at it; she saw only his usual spirit of contradiction and neglect, in his desertion of her at this period.

The mother pressed with careless lips the downy cheek of the little cherub, and departed; while Lodore passed most of his time in the child's apartment, or, turning his library into a nursery, it was continually with him there. "Here," he thought, "I have something to live for, something to love. And even though I am not loved in return, my heart's sacrifice will not be repaid with insolence and contempt." But when the infant began to show tokens of recognition and affection, when it smiled and stretched out its little hands on seeing him, and crowed with innocent pleasure; and still more, when the lisped paternal name fell from its roseate lips—the father repeated more emphatically, "Here is something that makes it worth while to have been born—to live!" An illness of the child overwhelmed him with anxiety and despair. She recovered; and he thanked God, with a lively emotion of joy, to which he had long been a stranger.

His affection for his child augmented the annoyance which he derived from his domestic circle. He had been hitherto sullenly yielding on any contest; but whatever whim, or whatever plan, he formed with regard to his daughter, he abided by unmoved, and took pleasure in manifesting his partiality for her. Lodore was by nature a man of violent and dangerous passions, add to which, his temper was susceptible to irritability. He disdained to cope with the undue influence exercised by Lady Santerre over his wife. He beheld in the latter, a frivolous, childish puppet, endowed with the usual feminine infirmities—

"The love of pleasure, and the love of sway";

and destitute of that tact and tenderness of nature which should teach her where to yield and how to reign. He left her therefore to her own devices, resolved only that he would not give up a single point relative to his child, and consequently, according to the weakness of human nature, ever ready to find fault with and prohibit all her wishes on the subject.

Cornelia, accustomed to be guided by her mother's watchful artifices, and to submit to a tyranny which assumed the guise of servitude, felt only with the feelings implanted by her parent. She was not, like Lady Santerre, heartless; but cherished pride, the effect of perpetual misrepresentation, painted her as such. She looked on her husband as a man essentially selfish—one who, worn out by passion, had married her to beguile his hours during a visitation of *ennui*, and incapable of the softness of love or the kindness of friendship. On occasion of his new conduct with regard to her child, her haughty soul was in arms against him, and something almost akin to hatred sprung up within her. She resented his interference; she believed that his object was to deprive her of the consolation of her daughter's love, and that his chief aim was to annoy and insult her. She was jealous of her daughter with her husband, of her husband with her daughter. If by some chance a word or look passed that might have softened the mutual sentiment of distrust, the evil genius of the scene was there to freeze again the genial current; and any approach to kindness, by an inexplicable but certain result, only tended to place them further apart than before.

Three winters had passed since their marriage, and the third spring was merging into summer, while they continued in this state of war-like neutrality. Any slight incident might have destroyed the fictitious barriers erected by ill-will and guile between them; or, so precarious was their state, any new event might change petty disagreements into violent resentment, and prevent their ever entertaining towards each other those feelings which, but for one fatal influence, would naturally have had root between them. The third summer was come. They were spending the commencement of it in London, when circumstances occurred, unanticipated by either, which changed materially the course of their domestic arrangements.

Lord Lodore returned home one evening at a little after eleven, from a dinner-party, and found, as usual, his drawing-room deserted— Lady Lodore had gone to a ball. He had returned in that humour to moralize, which we so often bring from society into solitude; and he paced the empty apartments with impatient step. "Home!—yes, this is my home! I had hoped that gentle peace and smiling love would be its inmates, that returning as now, from those who excite my spleen and contempt, one eye would have lighted up to welcome me, a dear voice have thanked me for my return. Home! a Tartar beneath his tent—a wild Indian in his hut, may speak of home—I have none. Where shall I spend the rest of this dull, deserted evening?"—for it may be supposed that, sharing London habits, eleven o'clock was to him but an evening hour.

He went into his dressing-room, and casting his eyes on the table, a revulsion came over him, a sudden shock—for there lay a vision, which made his breath come thick, and caused the blood to recede to his heart—a like vision has had the same effect on many, though it took but the unobtrusive form of a little note—a note, whose fold, whose seal, whose superscription, were all once so familiar, and now so strange. Time sensibly rolled back; each event of the last few years was broken off, as it were, from his life, leaving it as it had been ten years ago. He seized the note, and then threw it from him. "It is a mere mistake," he said aloud, while he felt, even to the marrow of his bones, the thrill and shudder as of an occurrence beyond the bounds of nature. Yet still the note lay there, and half as if to undeceive himself, and to set witchcraft at nought, he again took it up—this time in a less agitated mood, so that when the well-known impression of a little foreign coronet on the seal met his eye, he became aware that however unexpected such a sight might be, it was in the moral course of things, and he hastily tore open the epistle: it was written in French, and was very concise. "I arrived in town last night," the writer said; "I and my son are about to join my husband in Paris. I hear that you are married; I hope to see you and your lady before I leave London."

After reading these few lines, Lord Lodore remained for a considerable time lost in thought. He tried to consider what he should do, but his ideas wandered, as they sadly traced the past, and pictured to him the present. Never did life appear so vain, so contemptible, so odious a thing as now, that he was reminded of the passions and sufferings of former days, which, strewed at his feet like broken glass, might still wound him, though their charm and their delight could never be renewed. He did not go out that night; indeed it seemed as if but a minute had passed, when, lo! morning was pouring her golden summer beams into his room—when Lady Lodore's carriage drove up; and early sounds in the streets told him that night was gone and the morrow come.

That same day Lord Lodore requested Cornelia to call with him on a Polish lady of rank, with whom he had formerly been acquainted, to whom he was under obligations. They went. And what Lodore felt when he stood with his lovely wife before her, who for many by-gone years had commanded his fate, had wound him to her will, through the force of love and woman's wiles—who he knew could read every latent sentiment of his soul, and yet towards whom he was resolved now, and for ever in future, to adopt the reserved manners of a mere acquaintance—what of tremor or pain all this brought to Lodore's bosom was veiled, at least beyond Cornelia's penetration, who seldom truly observed him, and who was now occupied by her new acquaintance.

The lady had passed the bloom of youth, and even mid life; she was verging on fifty, but she had every appearance of having been transcendently beautiful. Her dark full oriental eyes still gleamed from beneath her finely-arched brows, and her black hair, untinged by any grizzly change, was gathered round her head in such tresses as bespoke an admirable profusion. Her person was tall and commanding: her manners were singular, for she mingled so strangely, stateliness and affability, disdain and sweetness, that she seemed like a princess dispensing the favour of her smile, or the terror of her frown on her submissive subjects; her sweetest smiles were for Cornelia, who yet turned from her to another object, who attracted her more peculiar attention. It was her son; a youth inheriting all his mother's beauty, added to the fascination of early manhood, and a frank and ingenuous address, which his parent could never have possessed.

The party separated, apparently well pleased with each other. Lady Lodore offered her services, which were frankly accepted; and after an hour spent together, they appointed to meet again the next day, when the ladies should drive out together to shop and see sights.

They became not exactly intimate, yet upon familiar terms. There was a dignity and even a constraint in the Countess Lyzinski's manner that was a bar to cordiality; but they met daily, and Lady Lodore introduced her new friend everywhere. The Countess said that motives of curiosity had induced her to take this country in her way to Paris. Her wealth was immense, and her rank among the first in her own country. The Russian ambassador treated her with distinction, so that she gained facile and agreeable entrance into the highest society. The young

Count Casimir was an universal favourite, but his dearest pleasure was to attend upon Lady Lodore, who readily offered to school him on his entrance into the English world. They were pretty exactly the same age; Casimir was somewhat the junior, yet he looked the elder, while the lady, accustomed to greater independence, took the lead in their intercourse, and acted the monitress to her docile scholar.

Lord Lodore looked on, or took a part, in what was passing around him, with a caprice perfectly unintelligible. With the Countess he was always gentle and obliging, but reserved. While she treated him with a coldness resembling disdain, yet whose chiefest demonstration was silence. Lodore never altered towards her; it was with regard to her son that he displayed his susceptible temper. He took pains to procure for him every proper acquaintance; he was forward in directing him; he watched over his mode of passing his time, he appeared to be interested in every thing he did, and yet to hate him. His demeanour towards him was morose, almost insulting. Lodore, usually so forbearing and courteous, would contradict and silence him, as if he had been a child or a menial. It required all Casimir's deference for one considerably his senior, to prevent him from resenting openly this style of treatment; it required all the fascination of Lady Lodore to persuade him to encounter it a second time. Once he had complained to her, and she remonstrated with her husband. His answer was to reprimand her for listening to the impertinence of the stripling. She coloured angrily, but did not reply. Cold and polite to each other, the noble pair were not in the habit of disputing. Lady Santerre guarded against that. Any thing as familiar as a quarrel might have produced a reconciliation, and with that a better understanding of each other's real disposition. The disdain that rose in Cornelia's bosom on this taunt, fostered by conscious innocence, and a sense of injustice, displayed itself in a scornful smile, and by an augmentation of kindness towards Casimir. He was now almost domesticated at her house; he attended her in the morning, hovered round her during the evening; and she, given up to the desire of pleasing, did not regard, did not even see, the painful earnestness with which Lord Lodore regarded them. His apparent jealousy, if she at all remarked it, was but a new form of selfishness, to which she was not disposed to give quarter. Yet any unconcerned spectator might have started to observe how, from an obscure corner of the room, Lodore watched every step they took, every change of expression of face during their conversation; and then approaching and interrupting them, endeavoured to carry Count Casimir away with him; and when thwarted in this, dart glances of such indignation on the youth, and of scorn upon his wife, as might have awoke a sense of danger, had either chanced to see the fierce, lightning-like passions written in those moments on his countenance, as letters of fire and menace traced upon the prophetic wall.

The Countess appeared to observe him indeed, and sometimes it seemed as if she regarded the angry workings of his heart with malicious pleasure. Once or twice she had drawn near, and said a few words in her native language, on which he endeavoured to stifle each appearance of passion, answering with a smile, in a low calm voice, and retiring, left, as it were, the field to her. Lady Santerre also had remarked his glances of suspicion or fury; they were interpreted into new sins against her daughter, and made with her the subject of ridicule or bitter reproach.

Lord Lodore was entirely alone. To no one human being could he speak a word that in the least expressed the violence of his feelings. Perhaps the only person with whom he felt the least inclined to overflow in confidence, was the Countess Lyzinski. But he feared her: he feared the knowledge she possessed of his character, and the power she had once exercised to rule him absolutely; the barrier between them must be insuperable, or the worst results would follow: he redoubled his own cautious reserve, and bore patiently the proud contempt which she exhibited, resolved not to yield one inch in the war he waged with his own heart, with regard to her. But he was alone, and the solitude of sympathy in which he lived, gave force and keenness to all his feelings. Had they evaporated in words, half their power to wound had been lost; as it was, there was danger in his meditations, and each one in collision with him had occasion to dread that any sudden overflow of stormy rage would be the more violent for having been repressed so long.

One day the whole party, with the exception of Lady Santerre, dined at the house of the Russian ambassador. As Lord and Lady Lodore proceeded towards their destination, he, with pointed sarcasm of manner, requested her to be less marked in her attentions to Count Casimir. The unfounded suspicions of a lover may please as a proof of love, but those of a husband, who thus claims affections which he has ceased to endeavour to win, are never received except as an impertinence and an insult. Those of Lord Lodore appeared to his haughty wife but a new form of cold-hearted despotism, checking her pleasures whencesoever they might arise. She replied by a bitter smile, and afterwards still more insultingly, by the display of kindness and partiality towards the object of her husband's dislike. Her complete sense of innocence, roused to indignation, by the injury she deemed offered to it, led her thus to sport with feelings, which, had she deigned to remark, she might have seen working with volcano-power in the breast of Lodore.

The ladies retired after dinner. They gathered together in groups in the drawing-room, while Lady Lodore, strange to say, sat apart from all. She placed herself on a distant sopha, apparently occupied by examining various specimens of bijouterie, nic-nacs of all kinds, which she took up one after the other, from the table near her. One hand shaded her eyes as she continued thus to amuse herself. She was not apt to be so abstracted; as now, that intent on self-examination, or self-reproach, or on thoughts that wandered to another, she forgot where she was, and by whom surrounded. She did not observe the early entrance of several gentlemen from the dining-room, nor remark a kind of embarrassment which sat upon their features, spreading a sort of uncomfortable wonder among the guests. The first words that roused her, were addressed to her by her husband: "Your carriage waits, Cornelia; will you come?"

"So early?" she asked.

"I particularly wish it," he replied.

"You can go, and send them back for me—and yet it is not worth while, we shall see most of the people here at Lady C——'s to night."

She glanced round the room, Casimir was not there; as she passed the Countess Lyzinski, she was about to ask her whether they should meet again that evening, when she caught the lady's eye fixed on her husband, meeting and returning a look of his. Alarm and disdain were painted on her face, and added to this, a trace of feeling so peculiar, so full of mutual understanding, that Lady Lodore was filled with no agreeable emotion of surprise. She entered the carriage, and the reiterated "Home!" of Lord Lodore, prevented her intended directions. Both were silent during their short drive. She sat absorbed in a variety of thoughts, not one of which led her to enter into conversation with her companion; they were rather fixed on her mother, on the observations she should make to, and the conjectures she should share with, her. She became anxious to reach home, and resolved at once to seek Lady Santerre's advice and directions by which to regulate her conduct on this occasion.

• • •

CHAPTER X

"Who then to frail mortality shall trust,
But limns the water, or but writes in dust."

—*Bacon*

T hey arrived in Berkeley Square. Lady Lodore alighted, and
perceived with something of a beating heart, that her husband followed her, as she passed on to the inner drawing-
room. Lady Santerre was not there. Taking a letter from the table, so
to give herself the appearance of an excuse for having entered a room
she was about immediately to quit, she was going, when Lodore, who
stood hesitating, evidently desirous of addressing her, and yet uncertain how to begin, stopped her by speaking her name, "Cornelia!"

She turned—she was annoyed; her conscience whispered what
was in all probability the subject to which her attention was to be
called. Her meditations in the drawing-room of the Russian Ambassador, convinced her that she had, to use the phrase of the day, flirted
too much with Count Casimir, and she had inwardly resolved to do so
no more. It was particularly disagreeable therefore, that her husband
should use authority, as she feared that he was about to do, and exact
from his wife's obedience, what she was willing to concede to her own
sense of propriety. She was resolved to hear as little as she could on
the subject, and stood as if in haste to go. His faltering voice betrayed
how much he felt, and once or twice it refused to frame the words he

desired to utter: how different was their import from that expected by his impatient auditress!

"Cornelia," said he, at length, "can you immediately, and at once—this very night—prepare to quit England?"

"Quit England! Why?—whither?" she exclaimed.

"I scarcely know," replied Lodore, "nor is it of the slightest import. The world is wide, a shelter, a refuge can be purchased any where—and that is all I seek."

The gaming table, the turf, loss of fortune, were the ideas naturally conveyed into the lady's mind by this reply. "Is all—every thing gone—lost?" she asked.

"My honour is," he answered, with an effort, "and the rest is of little worth."

He paused, and then continued in a low but distinct voice, as if every word cost him a struggle, yet as if he wished each one to be fraught with its entire meaning to his hearer; "I cannot well explain to you the motives of my sudden determination, nor will I complain of the part you have had in bringing on this catastrophe. It is over now. No power on earth—no heavenly power can erase the past, nor change one iota of what, but an hour ago, did not exist, but which now exists; altering all things to both of us for ever; I am a dishonoured man."

"Speak without more comment," cried Lady Lodore; "for Heaven's sake explain—I must know what you mean."

"I have insulted a gentleman," replied her husband, "and I will yield no reparation. I have disgraced a nobleman by a blow, and I will offer no apology, could one be accepted—and it could not; nor will I give satisfaction."

Lady Lodore remained silent. Her thoughts speedily ran over the dire objects which her husband's speech presented. A quarrel—she too readily guessed with whom—a blow, a duel; her cheek blanched—yet not so; for Lodore refused to fight. In spite of the terror with which an anticipated rencontre had filled her, the idea of cowardice in her husband, or the mere accusation of it, brought the colour back to her face.

She felt that her heedlessness had given rise to all this harm; but again she felt insulted that doubts of her sentiments or conduct should be the occasion of a scene of violence. Both remained silent. Lodore stood leaning on the mantelpiece, his cheek flushed, agitation betraying itself in each gesture, mixed with a resolve to command himself. Cornelia had advanced from the door to the middle of the room; she stood irresolute, too indignant and too fearful to ask further explanation, yet anxious to receive it. Still he hesitated. He was desirous of finding some form of words which might convey all the information that it was necessary she should receive, and yet conceal all that he desired should remain untold.

At last he spoke. "It is unnecessary to allude to the irretrievable past. The future is not less unalterable for me. I will not fight with, nor apologize to, the boy I have insulted I must therefore fly—fly my country and the face of man; go where the name of Lodore will not be synonymous with infamy—to an island in the east—to the desert wilds of America—it matters not whither. The simple question is, whether you are prepared on a sudden to accompany me? I would not ask this of your generosity, but that, married as we are, our destinies are linked, far beyond any power we possess to sunder them. Miserable as my future fortunes will be, far other than those which I invited you but four years ago to share, you are better off incurring the worst with me, than you could be, struggling alone for a separate existence."

"Pardon me, Lodore," said Cornelia, somewhat subdued by the magnitude of the crisis brought about, she believed, however involuntarily by herself, and by the sadness that, as he spoke, filled the dark eyes of her companion with an expression more melancholy than tears; "pardon me, if I seek for further explanation. Your antagonist" (they neither of them ventured to speak a name, which hung on the lips of both) "is a mere boy. Your refusal to fight with him results of course from this consideration; while angry, and if I must allude to so distasteful a falsehood, while unjust suspicion prevent your making him fitting and most due concessions. Were the occasion less terrible, I might disdain to assert my own innocence; but as it is, I do most solemnly declare, that Count Casimir—"

"I ask no question on that point, but simply wish to know whether you will accompany me," interrupted Lodore, hastily; "the rest I am sorry for—but it is over. You, my poor girl, though in some measure the occasion, and altogether the victim, of this disaster, can exercise no control over it. No foreign noble would accept the most humiliating submissions as compensation for a blow, and this urchin shall never receive from me the shadow of any."

"Is there no other way?" asked Cornelia.

"Not any," replied Lodore, while his agitation increased, and his voice grew tremulous; "No consideration on earth could arm me against his life. One other mode there is. I might present myself as a mark for his vengeance, with a design of not returning his fire, but I am shut out even from this resource. And this," continued Lodore, losing as he spoke, all self-command, carried away by the ungovernable passions he had hitherto suppressed, and regardless, as he strode up and down the room, of Cornelia, who half terrified had sunk into a chair; "this—these are the result of my crimes—such, from their consequences, I now term, what by courtesy I have hitherto named my follies—this is the end! Bringing into frightful collision those who are bound by sacred ties—changing natural love into unnatural, deep-rooted, unspeakable hate—arming blood against kindred blood—and making the innocent a parricide. O Theodora, what have you not to answer for!"

Lady Lodore started. The image he presented was too detestable. She repressed her emotions, and assuming that air of disdain, which we are so apt to adopt to colour more painful feelings, she said, "This sounds very like a German tragedy, being at once disagreeable and inexplicable."

"It is a tragedy," he replied; "a tragedy brought now to its last dark catastrophe. Casimir is my son. We may neither of us murder the other; nor will I, if again brought into contact with him, do other than chastise the insolent boy. The tiger is roused within me. You have a part in this."

A flash of anger glanced from Cornelia's eyes. She did not reply—she rose—she quitted the room—she passed on with apparent composure, till reaching the door of her mother's chamber, she rushed impetuously in. Overcome with indignation, panting, choked, she threw herself into her arms, saying, "Save me!" A violent fit of hysterics followed.

At first Lady Lodore could only speak of the injury and insult she had herself suffered; and Lady Santerre, who by no means wished to encourage feelings, which might lead to violence in action, tried to soothe her irritation. But when allusions to Lodore's intention of quitting England and the civilized world for ever, mingled with Cornelia's exclamations, the affair assumed a new aspect in the wary lady's eyes. The barbarity of such an idea excited her utmost resentment. At once she saw the full extent of the intended mischief, and the risk she incurred of losing the reward of years of suffering and labour. When an instantaneous departure was mentioned, an endless, desolate journey, which it was doubtful whether she should be admitted to share, to be commenced that very night, she perceived that her measures to prevent it must be promptly adopted. The chariot was still waiting which was to have conveyed Lord and Lady Lodore to their assembly; dressed as she was for this, without preparation, she hurried her daughter into the carriage, and bade the coachman drive to a villa they rented at Twickenham; leaving, in explanation, these few lines addressed to her son-in-law.

> The scene of this evening has had an alarming effect upon Cornelia. Time will soften the violence of her feelings, but some immediate step was necessary to save, I verily believe, her life. I take her to Twickenham, and will endeavour to calm her: until I shall have in some measure succeeded, I think you had better not follow us; but let us hear from you; for although my attention is so painfully

engrossed by my daughter's sufferings, I am distressed on your account also, and shall continue very uneasy until I hear from you.

Friday Evening.

Lady Santerre and her daughter reached Twickenham. Lady Lodore went to bed, and assisted by a strong composing draught, administered by her mother, her wrongs and her anger were soon hushed in profound sleep. Night, or rather morning, was far spent before this occurred, so that it was late in the afternoon of the ensuing day before she awoke, and recalled to her memory the various conflicting sentiments which had occupied her previous to her repose.

During the morning, Lady Santerre had despatched a servant to Berkeley Square, to summon her daughter's peculiar attendants. He now brought back the intelligence that Lord Lodore had departed for the continent, about three hours after his wife had quitted his house. But to this he added tidings of another circumstance, for which both ladies were totally unprepared. Cornelia had entered the carriage the preceding night, without spending one thought on the sleeping cherub in the nursery. What was her surprise and indignation, when she heard that her child and its attendant formed a part of his lordship's travelling suite. The mother's first impulse was to follow her offspring; but this was speedily exchanged for a bitter sense of wrong, aversion to her husband, and a resolve not to yield one point, in the open warfare thus declared by him.

•••

CHAPTER XI

"Amid two seas, on one small point of land,
Wearied, uncertain, and amazed, we stand;
On either side our thoughts incessant turn,
Forward we dread, and looking back we mourn."

—*Prior*

Accustomed to obey the more obvious laws of necessity, those whose situation in life obliges them to earn their daily bread, are already broken in to the yoke of fate. But the rich and great are vanquished more slowly. Their time is their own; as fancy bids them, they can go east, west, north, or south; they wish, and accomplish their wishes; and cloyed by the too easy attainment of the necessaries, and even of the pleasures of life, they fly to the tortures of passion, and to the labour of overcoming the obstacles that stand in the way of their forbidden desires, as resources against ennui and satiety. Reason is lost in the appetite for excitement, and a kind of unnatural pleasure springs from their severest pains, because thus alone are they roused to a full sense of their faculties; thus alone is existence and its purposes brought home to them.

In the midst of this, their thoughtless career, the eternal law which links ill to ill, is at hand to rebuke and tame the rebel spirit; and such a tissue of pain and evil is woven from their holiday pastime, as checks them midcourse, and makes them feel that they are slaves. The young are scarcely aware of this; they delight to contend with Fate, and laugh as she clanks their chains. But there is a period—sooner or later comes to all—when the links envelop them, the bolts are shot, the rivets fixed, the iron enters the flesh, the soul is subdued, and they fly to religion or proud philosophy, to seek for an alleviation, which the crushed spirit can no longer draw from its own resources.

This hour! this fatal hour! How many can point to the shadow on the dial, and say, "Then it was that I felt the whole weight of my humanity, and knew myself to be the subject of an unvanquishable power!" This dark moment had arrived for Lodore. He had spent his youth in passion, and exhausted his better nature in a struggle for, and in the enjoyment of, pleasure. He found disappointment, and desired change. It came at his beck. He married. He was not satisfied; but still he felt that it was because he did not rouse himself, that the bonds sate so heavily upon him. He was enervated. He sickened at the idea of the struggle it would require to cast off his fetters, and he preferred adapting his nature to endure their weight. But he believed that it was only because he did not raise his hand, nor determine on one true effort, that he was thus enslaved. And now his hand was raised—the effort made; but no change ensued; and he felt that there was no escape from the inextricable bonds that fastened him to misery.

He had believed that he did right in introducing his wife to the Countess Lyzinski. He felt that he could not neglect this lady; and such was her rank, that any affectation of a separate acquaintance would invite those observations which he deprecated. It was, after all, matter of trivial import that he should be the person to bring them acquainted. Moving in the same circles, they must meet—they might clash: it was better that they should be on friendly terms. He did not foresee the intimacy that ensued; and still less, that his own violent passions would be called into action. That they were so, was, to the end, a mystery even to himself. He no longer loved the Countess; and, in the solitude of his chamber, he often felt his heart yearn towards the noble youth, her son; but when they met—when Cornelia spent her

blandest smiles upon him, and when the exquisitely beautiful countenance of Casimir became lighted up with gladness and gratitude, a fire
of rage was kindled in his heart, and he could no more command himself, than can the soaring flames of a conflagration bend earthward. He
felt ashamed; but new fury sprung from this very sensation. For worlds,
he would not have his frenzy pried into by another; and yet he had
no power to control its manifestation. His wife expostulated with him
concerning Casimir, and laughed his rebuke to scorn. But she did not
read the tumult of unutterable jealousy and hate, that slept within his
breast, like an earthquake beneath the soil, the day before a city falls.

All tended to add fuel to this unnatural flame. His own exertions
to subdue its fierceness but kindled it anew. Often he entered the same
room with the young Count, believing that he had given his suspicions to the winds—that he could love him as a son, and rejoice with
a father's pride in the graces of his figure and the noble qualities of his
mind. For a few seconds the fiction endured: he felt a pang—it was
nothing—gone; it would not return again:—another! was he for ever
to be thus tortured? And then a word a look, an appearance of slight-
ing him on the part of Casimir, an indiscreet smile on Cornelia's lips,
would at once set a-light the whole devastating blaze. The Countess
alone had any power over him; but though he yielded to her influence,
he was the more enraged that she should behold his weakness; and
that while he succeeded in maintaining an elevated impassibility with
regard to herself, his heart, with all its flaws and poverty of purpose,
should, through the ill-timed interference of this boy, be placed once
more naked in her hand.

Such a state of feeling, where passion combated passion, while reason was forgotten in the strife, was necessarily pregnant with ruin. The
only safety was in flight;—and Lodore would have flown—he would
have absented himself until the cause of his sufferings had departed—
but that, more and more, jealousy entered into his feelings—a jealousy,
wound up by the peculiarity of his situation, into a sensitiveness that
bordered on insanity, which saw guilt in a smile, and overwhelming,

hopeless ruin, in the simplest expression of kindness. Cornelia herself was disinclined to quit London, and tenacious pride rendered him averse to proposing it, since he could frame no plausible pretext for his change of purpose, and it had been previously arranged that they should remain till the end of July. The presence of the Countess Lyzinski was a tie to keep her; and to have pleaded his feelings with regard to Casimir, could he have brought himself so to do, would probably have roused her at once into rebellion. There was no resource; he must bear, and also he must forbear;—but the last was beyond his power, and his attempt at the first brought with it destruction. In the last instance, at the Russian Ambassador's, irritated by Cornelia's tone of defiance, and subsequent levity, he levelled a scornful remark at the guiltless and unconscious offender. Casimir had endured his arrogance and injustice long. He knew of no tie, no respect due, beyond that which youth owes to maturer years; yet the natural sweetness of his disposition inclined him to forbearance, until now, that surrounded by his own countrymen and by Russians, it became necessary that he should assert himself. He replied with haughtiness; Lodore rejoined with added insult;—and when again Casimir retorted, he struck him. The young noble's eyes flashed fire: several gentlemen interposed between them;—and yielding to the expediency of the moment, the Pole, with admirable temper, withdrew.

Humiliated and dismayed, but still burning with fury, Lodore saw at once the consequences of his angry transport. With all the impetuosity of his fiery spirit, he resolved to quit at once the scene in which he had played his part so ill. There was no other alternative. The most frightful crimes blocked up every other outlet: this was his sole escape, and he must seize on it without delay. Lady Lodore had not even deigned to answer his request that she should accompany him; and her mother's note appeared the very refinement of insolence. They abandoned him. They left the roof from which he was about to exile himself, even before he had quitted it, as if in fear of contamination during his brief delay. Thus he construed their retreat; and worked up, as he was, almost to madness, he considered their departure as the commencement of that universal ban, which for ever, hereafter, was to accompany his name. It opened anew the wound his honour had sustained; and he poured forth a vow never more to ally himself in bonds of love or amity with one among his kind.

His purpose was settled, and he did not postpone its execution. Post-horses were ordered, and hasty preparations made, for his departure. Alone, abandoned, disgraced, in another hour he was to quit his home, his wife, all that endears existence, for ever: yet the short interval that preceded his departure hung like a long-drawn day upon him; and time seemed to make a full stop, at a period when he would have rejoiced had it leaped many years to come. The heart's prayer in agony did not avail: he was still kept lingering, when a knocking at the door announced a visitor, who, at that late hour, could come for one purpose only. Lord Lodore ordered himself to be denied, and Count Casimir's second departed to seek him elsewhere. Cold dew-drops stood on Lodore's brow as he heard this gentleman parley in a foreign accent with the servant; trying, doubtless, to make out where it was likely that he should meet with him: the door closed at last, and he listened to the departing steps of his visitor, who could scarcely have left the square, before his travelling chariot drove up. And now, while final arrangements were making, with a heart heavy from bitter self-condemnation, he visited the couch of his sleeping daughter, once more to gaze on her sweet face, and for the last time to bestow a father's blessing on her. The early summer morning was abroad in the sky; and as he opened her curtains, the first sun-beam played upon her features. He stooped to kiss her little rosy lips:—"And I leave this spotless being to the blighting influence of that woman!" His murmurs disturbed the child's slumbers: she woke, and smiled to see her father; and then insisted upon rising, as he was up, and it was day.

"But I am come to say good-bye, sweet," he said; "I am going on a long journey."

"O take me with you!" cried the little girl, springing up, and fastening her arms round his neck. He felt her soft cheek prest to his;

her hands trying to hold fast, and to resist his endeavours to disengage them. His heart warmed within him. "For a short distance I may indulge myself," he said, and he thought how her prattle would solace his darker cares, during his road to Southampton. So, causing her attendant to make speedy preparation, he took her in the carriage with him; and her infantine delight so occupied him, that he scarcely remembered his situation, or what exactly he was doing, as he drove for the last time through the lightsome and deserted streets of the metropolis.

And now he had quitted these; and the country, in all its summer beauty, opened around him—meadows and fields with their hedgerows, tufted groves crowning the uplands, and "the blue sky bent over all." "From these they cannot banish me," he thought; "in spite of dishonour and infamy, the loveliness of nature, and the freedom of my will, still are mine:—and is this all?"—his child had sunk to sleep, nestled close in his arms; "Ah! what will these be to me, when I have lost this treasure, dearest of all?—yet why lose her?" This question, when it first presented itself to him, he put aside as one that answered itself—to deprive a mother of her child were barbarity beyond that of savages;—but again and again it came across him, and he began to reason with it, and to convince himself that he should be unjust towards himself in relinquishing this last remaining blessing. His arguments were false, his conclusions rash and selfish; but of this he was not aware. Our several minds, in reflecting to our judgments the occurrences of life, are like mirrors of various shapes and hues, so that we none of us perceive passing objects with exactly similar optics; and while all pretend to regulate themselves by the quadrant of justice, the deceptive medium through which the reality is viewed, causes our ideas of it to be at once various and false. This is the case in immaterial points; how much more so, when self-love magnifies, and passion obscures, the glass through which we look upon others and ourselves. The chief task of the philosopher is to purify and correct the intellectual prism;—but Lodore was the reverse of a philosopher; and the more he gazed and considered, the more imperfect and distorted became his perception.

To act justly by ourselves and others, is the aim of every well-conditioned mind: for the sight of pain in our fellow-creatures, and the sense of self-condemnation within ourselves, is fraught with a pang from which we would willingly escape; and every heart not formed of the coarsest materials is keenly alive to such emotions. Lodore resolved to judge calmly, and he reviewed coolly, and weighed (he believed) impartially, the various merits of the question. He thought of Lady Santerre's worldliness, her vulgar ambition, her low-born contempt for all that is noble and elevating in human nature. He thought of Cornelia's docility to her mother's lessons, her careless disregard of the nobler duties of life, of her frivolity and unfeeling nature:—then, almost against his will, his own many excellencies rose before him;—his lofty aspirations, his self-sacrifice for the good of others, the affectionateness of his disposition, his mildness, his desire to be just and kind to all, his willingness to devote every hour of the day, and every thought of his mind, to the well-bringing-up of his daughter: a person must be strangely blind who did not perceive that, as far as the child was concerned, she would be far better off with him.

And then, in another point of view: Lady Lodore had her mother—and she had the world. She had not only beauty, rank, and wealth; but she had a taste for enjoying the advantages yielded by these on the common soil of daily life. He cared for nothing in the wide world—he loved nothing but this little child. He would willingly exchange for her the far greater portion of his fortune, which Lady Lodore should enjoy; reserving for himself such a pittance merely as would suffice for his own and his daughter's support. He had neither home, nor friends, nor youth, nor taintless reputation; nor any of all the blessings of life, of which Cornelia possessed a superabundance. Her child was as nothing in the midst of these. She had left her without a sigh, even without a thought; while but to imagine the moment of parting was a dagger to her father's heart. What a fool he had been to hesitate so long—to hesitate at all! There she was, this angel of comfort; her little form was cradled in his arms, he felt her soft breath upon his hand, and the regular heaving of her bosom responded to the beatings of his own heart; her golden, glossy hair, her crimsoned cheek, her soft, round limbs;—all this matchless "bower of flesh," that held in the budding soul, and already expanding affections of this earthly cherub, was with him. And had he imagined that he could part with her? Rather would he return to Lady Lodore, to dishonour, to scenes of hate and of the world's contempt, so that thus he preserved her: it could not be required of him; but if Cornelia's heart was animated by a tithe of the fondness that warmed his, she would not hesitate in her choice; but, discarding every unworthy feeling, follow her child into the distant and solitary abode he was about to select.

Thus pacifying his conscience, Lodore came to the conclusion of making his daughter the partner of his exile. Soon after mid-day, they arrived at Southampton; a small vessel was on the point of sailing for Havre, and on board this he hurried. Before he went he gave one hasty retrospective view to those he was leaving behind—his wife, his sister, the filial antagonist from whom he was flying; he could readily address himself to the first of these, when landed on the opposite coast; but as he wished to keep his destination a secret from the latter, and to prevent, if possible, his being followed and defied by him, an event still to be feared, he employed the few remaining minutes, before quitting his country for ever, in writing a brief letter to the Countess Lyzinski, which he gave in charge to a servant whom he dismissed, and sent back to town. And thus he now addressed her, who, in his early life, had been as the moon to raise the tide of passion, incapable, alas! of controlling its waves when at the full.

It is all over: I have fulfilled my part—the rest remains with you. To prevent the ruin which my folly has brought down, from crushing any but myself, I quit country, home, good name—all that is dear to man. I do not complain, nor will I repine. But let the evil, I entreat you, stop here. Casimir must not follow me; he must not know whither I am gone; and while he brands his antagonist with the name of coward, he must not guess that for his sake I endure this stain. I leave it to your prudence and sagacity to calm or to mislead him, to prevent his suspecting the truth, or rashly seeking my life. I sacrifice more, far more, than my heart's blood on his account—let that satisfy even your vengeance.

I would not write harshly. The dream of life has long been over for me; it matters not how or where the last sands flow out. I do not blame you even for this ill-omened journey to England, which could avail you nothing. Once before we parted for ever, Theodora; but that separation was as the pastime of children in comparison with the tragic scene we now enact. A thousand dangers yawn between us, and we shall neither dare to repass the gulf that divides us. Forget me;—be happy, and forget me! May Casimir be a blessing to you, and while you glory in his perfections and prosperity, cast into oblivion every thought of him, who now bids you an eternal adieu.

• • •

CHAPTER XII

"Her virtue, like our own, was built
Too much on that indignant fuss,
Hypocrite pride stirs up in us,
To bully out another's guilt."

—Shelley

The fifth day after Lord Lodore's departure brought Cornelia a letter from him. She had spent the interval at Twickenham, surrendering her sorrows and their consolation to her mother's care; and inspired by her with deep resentment and angry disdain. The letter she received was dated Havre: the substance of it was as follows.

Believe me I am actuated by no selfish considerations, when I ask you once again to reflect before the Atlantic divides us—probably for ever. It is for your own sake, your own happiness only, that I ask you to hesitate. I will not urge your duty to me; the dishonour that has fallen on me I am most ready to bear alone; mine towards you, as far as present circumstances permit, I am desirous to fulfil, and this feeling dictates my present address.

Consider the solitary years you will pass alone, even though in a crowd, divided from your husband and your child—your home desolate—calumny and ill-nature at watch around you—not one protecting arm stretched over you. Your mother's presence, it is true, will suffice to prevent your position from being in the least equivocal; but the time will soon come when you will discover your mistake in her, and find how unworthy she is of your exclusive affection. I will not urge the temptations and dangers that will beset you; your pride will, I doubt not, preserve you from these, yet they will be near you in their worst shape: you will feel their approaches; you will shudder at their menaces, you will desire my death, and the faith pledged to me at the altar will become a chain and a torture to you.

I can only offer such affection as your sacrifice will deserve to adorn a lonely and obscure home; rank, society, flatterers, the luxuries of civilization—all these blessings you must forego. Your lot will be cast in solitude. The wide forest, the uninhabited plain, will shelter us. Your husband, your child; in us alone you must view the sum and aim of your life. I will not use the language of persuasion, but in inviting you to share my privations, I renew, yet more solemnly, the vows we once interchanged; and it shall be my care to endeavour to fulfil mine with more satisfaction to both of us than has until now been the case.

It is useless to attempt to veil the truth, that hitherto our hearts have been alienated from each other. The cause is not in ourselves, and must never again be permitted to influence either of us. If amidst the avocations of society, the presence of a third person has been sufficient to place division between us;—if, on the flowery path of our prosperous life, one fatal interference has strewn thorns and burning ashes beneath our feet, how much more keenly would this intervention be felt in the retirement in which we are hereafter to spend our days.—In the lonely spot to which it will be necessary to contract all our thoughts and hopes, love must alone reign; or hell itself would be but pastime in comparison to our ever-renewing and sleepless torments. The spirit of worldliness, of discord, of paltry pride, must not enter the paling which is to surround our simple dwelling. Come, attended by affection, by open-hearted confidence;—come to me—to your child!—you will find with us peace and mutual love, the true secret of life. All that can make your mother happy in England, shall be provided with no niggard hand:—but come alone, Cornelia, my wife!—come, to take possession of the hearts that are truly yours, and to learn a new lesson, in a new world, from him who will dedicate himself entirely to you.

Alas! I fear that I speak an unknown language, and one that you will never deign to understand. Still I again implore you to reflect before you decide. On one point I am firm—I feel that I am in the right—that every thing depends upon it. Our daughter's guileless heart shall never be tainted by all that I abhor and despise. For her sake, for yours, more than for my own, I am as rock upon one question. Do not strive to move me—it will be useless! Come alone! and ten thousand welcomes and blessings shall hail your arrival!

A vessel, in which I have engaged a passage, sails for New York, from this place, in five days time. You must not delay your decision; but hasten, if such be your gracious resolve, to join me here.

If you decide to sacrifice yourself to one who will never repay that sacrifice, and to the world,—that dreary, pain-haunted jungle,— at least you shall receive from me all that can render your situation there prosperous. You shall not complain of want of generosity on my part. I shall, in my new course of life, require little myself; the remainder of my fortune shall be at your disposal.

I need not recommend secrecy to you as to the real motive of my exile—your own sense of delicacy will dictate reserve and silence. This letter will be delivered to you by Fenton: he will attend you back here, or bring me your negative—the seal, I feel assured, of your future misery. God grant that you choose wisely and well! Adieu.

The heart of Lady Lodore burnt within her bosom as she read these lines. Haughty and proud, was she to be dictated to thus? and to follow, an obedient slave, the master that deigned to recall her to his presence, after he had (so she termed his abrupt departure) deserted her? Her mother sate by, looking at her with an anxious and inquiring glance, as she read the letter. She saw the changes of her countenance, as it expressed anger, scorn, and bitter indignation. She finished—she was still silent; —how could she show this insulting address to her parent? Again she seemed to study its contents—to ponder.

Lady Santerre rose—gently she was taking the paper from Cornelia's hand. "You must not read it," she cried;— "and yet you must;—and thus one other wrong is heaped upon the many."

Lady Santerre read the letter; silently she perused it—folded it—placed it on the table. Cornelia looked up at her. "I do not fear your decision," she said; "you will not abandon a parent, who has devoted herself to you from your cradle—who lives but for you."

The unhappy girl, unable to resist her mother's appeal, threw herself into her arms. Even the cold Lady Santerre was moved—tears flowed from her eyes:— "My dear child!" she exclaimed.

"My dear child!"—the words found an echo in Lady Lodore's bosom;— "I am never to see my child more!"

"Such is his threat," said her mother, "knowing thus the power he has over you; but do not fear that it will be accomplished. Lord Lodore's conduct is guided by no principle—by no deference to the opinion of the world—by no just or sober motives. He is as full of passion as a madman, and more vacillating. This is his fancy now—to quit England for the wilderness, and to torture you into following him. You are as lost as he, if you yield. A little patience, and all will be right again. He will soon grow tired of playing the tragic hero on a stage surrounded by no spectators; he will discover the folly of his conduct; he will return, and plead for forgiveness, and feel that he is too fortunate in a wife, who has preserved her own conduct free from censure and remark, while he has made himself a laughing stock to all. Do not permit yourself, dear Cornelia, to be baffled in this war of passion with reason; of jealousy, selfishness, and tyranny, with natural affection, a child's duty, and the respect you owe to yourself. Even if he remain away, he will quickly become weary of being accompanied by an infant and its nurse, and too glad to find that you will still be willing to act the mother towards his child. Firmness and discretion are the arms you must use against folly and violence. Yield, and you are the victim of a despotism without parallel, the slave of a task-master, whose first commands are gentle, soft, and easy injunctions to desert your mother: to exile yourself from your country, and to bury yourself alive in some unheard-of desert, whose name even he does not deign to communicate. All this would be only too silly and too wild, were it not too wicked and too cruel. Believe me, my love, trust yourself to my guidance, and all will be well; Lodore himself will thank, if such thanks be of value, the prudence and generosity you will display."

Cornelia listened, and was persuaded. Above all, Lady Santerre tried to impress upon her mind, that Lodore, finding her firm, would give up his rash schemes, and remain in Europe; that even he had, probably, never really contemplated crossing the Atlantic. At all events, that she must not be guided by the resolves, changeable as the moon, of a man governed by no sane purpose; but that, by showing herself determined, he would be brought to bend to her will. In this spirit Lady Lodore replied to her husband's letter. Fenton, Lord Lodore's valet, who had been the bearer, had left it, and proceeded to London. He returned the day following, to receive his lady's orders. Cornelia saw him and questioned him. She heard that Lord Lodore was to dismiss him and all his English servants before embarking for America, with the exception of the child's nurse, whom he had promised to send back on his arrival at New York. He had engaged his passage, and fitted up cabins for his convenience, so that there could be no doubt of his having finally resolved to emigrate. This was all he knew; Cornelia gave him her letter, and he departed on the instant for Southampton.

In giving his wife so short an interval in which to form her determination, Lodore conceived that her first impulse would be to join her child, that she would act upon it, and at least come as far as Havre, though perhaps her mother would accompany her, to claim her daughter, even if she did not besides foster a hope of changing his resolves. Lodore had an unacknowledged reserve in his own mind, that if she would give up her mother, and for a time the world, he would leave the choice of their exile to her, and relinquish the dreary scheme of emigrating to America. With these thoughts in his mind, he anxiously awaited each day the arrival of the packets from England. Each day he hoped to see Cornelia disembark from one of them; and even though accompanied by Lady Santerre, he felt that his heart would welcome her. During this interval, his thoughts had recurred to his home; and imagination had already begun to paint the memory of that home, in brighter colours than the reality. Lady Lodore had not been all coldness and alienation; in spite of dissension, she had been his; her form, graceful as a nymph's, had met his eyes each morning; her smile, her voice, her light cheering laugh, had animated and embellished, how many hours during the long days, grown vacant without her. Cherishing a hope of seeing her again, he forgot her petulance— her self-will—her love of pleasure; and remembering only her beauty and her grace, he began, in a lover-like fashion, to impart to this charming image, a soul in accordance to his wishes, rather than to the reality. Each day he attended less carefully to the preparations of his long voyage. Each day he expected her; a chill came over his heart at each evening's still recurring disappointment, till hope awoke on the ensuing morning. More than once he had been on the eve of sailing to England to meet and escort her; a thousand times he reproached himself for not having made Southampton the place of meeting, and he was withheld from proceeding thither only by the fear of missing her. Giving way to these sentiments, the tide of affection, swelling into passion, rose in his breast. He doubted not that, ere long, she would arrive, and taxed himself for modes to show his gratitude and love.

The American vessel was on the point of sailing—it might have gone without him, he cared not; when on the sixth day Fenton arrived, and put into his hand Cornelia's letter. This then was the end of his expectation, this little paper coldly closed in the destruction of his hopes; yet might it not merely contain a request for delay? There was something in the servant's manner, that looked not like that; but still, as soon as the idea crossed him, he tore open the seal. The words were few, they were conceived in all the spirit of resentment.

"You add insult to cruelty," it said,

"but I scorn to complain. The very condition you make displays the hollowness and deceit of your proceeding. You well know that I cannot, that I will not, desert my mother; but by calling on me for this dereliction of all duty and virtuous affection, you contrive to throw on me the odium of refusing to accompany you; this is a worthy design, and it is successful.

"I demand my child—restore her to me. It is cruelty beyond compare, to separate one so young from maternal tenderness and fosterage. By what right—through what plea, do you rob me of her? The tyranny and dark jealousy of your vindictive nature display themselves in this act of unprincipled violence, as well as in your insulting treatment of my mother. You alone must reign, be feared, be thought of; all others are to be sacrificed, living victims, at the shrine of your self-love. What have you done to merit so much devotion? Ask your heart—if it be not turned to stone, ask it what you have done to compare with the long years of affection, kindness, and never-ceasing care that my beloved parent has bestowed on me. I am your wife, Lodore; I bear your name; I will be true to the vows I have made you, nor will I number the tears you force me to shed; but my mother's are sacred, and not one falls in vain for me.

"Give me my child—let the rest be yours—depart in peace! If Heaven have blessings for the coldly egotistical, the unfeeling despot, may these blessings be yours; but do not dare to interfere with emotions too pure, too disinterested for you ever to understand. Give me my child, and fear neither my interference nor resentment. I am content to be as dead to you—quite content never to see you more."

• • •

CHAPTER XIII

"And so farewell; for we will henceforth be
As we had never seen, ne'er more shall see."

—*Heywood*

❧

Lodore had passed many days upon the sea, on his voyage to America, before he could in the least calm the bitter emotions to which Cornelia's violent letter had given birth. He was on the wide Atlantic; the turbid ocean swelled and roared around him, and heaven, the mansion of the winds, showed on its horizon an extent of water only. He was cut off from England, from Europe, for ever; and the vast continents he quitted dwindled into a span; but still the images of those he left behind dwelt in his soul, engrossing and filling it. They could no longer personally taunt nor injure him; but the thought of them, of all that they might say or do, haunted his mind; it was like an unreal strife of gigantic shadows beneath dark night, which, when you approach, dwindles into thin air, but which, contemplated at a distance, fills the hemisphere with star-reaching heads, and steps that scale mountains. There was a sleepless tumult in Lodore's heart; it was a waking dream of the most painful description. Again and again Cornelia assailed him with reproaches, and Lady Santerre poured out curses upon him; his fancy lent them words and looks full of menace, hate, and violence. Sometimes the sighing of the breeze in the shrouds assumed a tone that mocked their voices; his sleep was disturbed by dreams more painful than his daylight fancies; and the sense which they imparted of suffering and oppression, was prolonged throughout the day.

He occasionally felt that he might become mad, and at such moments, the presence of his child brought consolation and calm; her caresses, her lisped expressions of affection, her playfulness, her smiles, were spells to drive away the fantastic reveries that tortured him. He looked upon her cherub face, and the world, late so full of wretchedness and ill, assumed brighter hues; the storm was allayed, the dark clouds fled, sunshine poured forth its beams; by degrees, tender and gentle sensations crept over his heart; he forgot the angry contentions in which, in imagination, he had been engaged, and he felt, that alone on the sea, with this earthly angel of peace near him, he was divided from every evil, to dwell with tranquillity and love.

To part with her had become impossible. She was all that rendered him human—that plucked the thorn from his pillow, and poured one mitigating drop into the bitter draught administered to him.

Cornelia, Casimir, Theodora, his mother-in-law, these were all various names and shapes of the spirit of evil, sent upon earth to torture him: but this heavenly sprite could set at nought their machinations and restore him to the calm and hopes of childhood. Extreme in all things, Lodore began more than ever to doat upon her and to bind up his life in her. Yet sometimes his heart softened at the recollection of his wife, of her extreme youth, and of the natural pang she must feel at being deprived of her daughter. He figured her pining, and in tears— he remembered that he had vowed to protect and love her for ever; and that deprived of him, never more could the soft attentions and sweet language of love soothe her heart or meet her ear, unattended with a sense of guilt and degradation. He knew that hereafter she might feel this—hereafter, when passion might be roused, and he could afford no remedy. Influenced by such ideas, he wrote to her; many letters he wrote during his voyage, destroying them one after another, dictated by the varying feelings that alternately ruled him. Reason and persuasion, authority and tenderness, reigned by turns in these epistles; they were written with all the fervour of his ardent soul, and breathed irresistible power. Had some of these papers met Cornelia's eye, she had assuredly been vanquished; but fate ordained it otherwise: fate that blindly weaves our web of life, culling her materials at will, and often wholly refusing to make use of our own desires and intentions, as forming a part of our destiny.

Lodore arrived at New York, and found, by some chance, letters already waiting for him there. He had concluded one to his wife full of affection and kindness, when a letter with the superscription written by Lady Santerre was delivered to him. It spoke of law proceedings, of eternal separation, and announced her daughter's resolve to receive no communication, to read no address, that was not prefaced by the restoration of her child; it referred him to a solicitor as the medium of future intercourse. With a bitter laugh Lodore tore to pieces the eloquent and heart-felt appeal he had been on the point of sending; he gave up his thoughts to business only; he wrote to his agent, he arranged for his intended journey; in less than a month he was on his road to the Illinois.

Thus ended all hope of reconciliation, and Lady Santerre won the day. She had worked on the least amiable of her daughter's feelings, and exalted anger into hatred, disapprobation into contempt and aversion. Soon after Cornelia had dismissed the servant, she felt that she had acted with too little reflection. Her heart died within her at the idea, that too truly Lodore might sail away with her child, and leave her widowed and solitary for ever. Her proud heart knew, on this account, no relenting towards her husband, the author of these painful feelings, but she formed the resolve not to lose all without a struggle. She announced her intention of proceeding to Havre to obtain her daughter. Lady Santerre could not oppose so natural a proceeding, especially as her companionship was solicited as in the highest degree necessary. They arrived at Southampton; the day was tempestuous, the wind contrary. Lady Santerre was afraid of the water, and their voyage was deferred.

On the evening of the following day, Fenton arrived from Havre. Lord Lodore had sailed, the stormy waves of the Atlantic were between him and the shores of England; pursuit were vain; it would be an acknowledgment of defeat to follow him to America. Cornelia returned to Twickenham, maternal sorrow contending in her heart with mortified pride, and a keen resentful sense of injury.

Lady Lodore was nineteen; an age when youth is most arrogant, and most heedless of the feelings of others. Her beauty and the admiration it acquired, sate her on the throne of the world, and, to her own imagination, she looked down like an eastern princess, upon slaves only: her sway she had believed to be absolute; it was happiness for others to obey. Exalted by adulation, it was natural that all that lowered her elevation in her own eyes, should appear impertinent and hateful. She had not learned to feel with or for others. To act in contradiction to her wishes was a crime beyond compare, and her soul was in arms to resent the insolence which thus assailed her majesty of will. The act of Lodore, stepping beyond common-place opposition into injury and wrong, found no mitigating excuses in her heart. No gentle return of love, no compassion for the unhappy exile—no generous desire to diminish the sufferings of one, who was the victim of the wildest and most tormenting passions, softened her bosom. She was injured, insulted, despised, and her swelling soul was incapable of any second emotion to the scorn and hate with which she visited the author of her degradation. She was to become the theme of the world's discourse, of its ill-natured censure or mortifying pity. In whatever light she viewed her present position, it was full of annoyance and humiliation; her path was traced through a maze of pointed angles, that pained her at every turn, and her reflections magnifying the imprudence of which she accused herself, suggested no excuse for her husband, but caused her wounds to fester and burn. Cornelia was not of a lachrymose disposition; she was a woman who in Sparta had formed an heroine; who in periods of war and revolution, would unflinchingly have met calamity, sustaining and leading her own sex. But through the bad education she had received, and her extreme youth, elevation of feeling degenerated into mere personal pride, and heroism was turned into obstinacy; she had been capable of the most admirable self-sacrifice, had she been taught the right shrine at which to devote herself; but her mind was narrowed by the mode of her bringing up, and her loftiest ideas were centered in worldly advantages the most worthless and pitiable. To defraud her of these, was to deprive her of all that rendered life worth preserving.

Lady Santerre soothed, flattered, and directed her. She poured the balm of gratified vanity upon injured pride. She bade her expect speedy repentance from her husband, and impressed her with the idea, that if she were firm, he must yield. His present blustering prognosticated a speedy calm, when he would regret all that he had done, and seek, by entire submission, to win back his wife. Any appearance of concession on her part would spoil all. Cornelia's eyes flashed fire at the word. Concession! and to whom? To him who had wronged and insulted her? She readily gave into her mother's hands the management of all future intercourse with him, reserving alone, for her own satisfaction, an absolute resolve never to forgive.

The correspondence that ensued, carried on across the Atlantic, and soon with many miles of continent added to the space, only produced an interchange of letters written with cool insolence on one side, with heart-burning and impatience on the other. Each served to widen the breach. When Cornelia was not awakened to resent for herself, she took up arms on her mother's account. When Lodore blamed her for being the puppet of one incapable of any generous feeling, one dedicated to the vulgar worship of Mammon, she repelled the taunt, and denied the servitude of soul of which she was accused; she declared that every virtue was enlisted on her mother's side, and that she would abide by her for ever. In truth, she loved her the more for Lodore's hatred, and Lady Santerre spared no pains to impress her with the belief, that she was wholly devoted to her.

Thus years passed away. At first Lady Lodore had lived in some degree of retirement, but persuaded again to emerge, she soon entered into the very thickest maze of society. Her fortune was sufficient to command a respectable station, her beauty gained her partisans, her untainted reputation secured her position in the world. Attractive as she was, she was so entirely and proudly correct, that even the women were not afraid of her. All her intimate associates were people whose rank gave weight and brilliancy to her situation, but who were conspicuous for their domestic virtues. She was looked upon as an injured and deserted wife, whose propriety of conduct was the more admirable from the difficulties with which she was surrounded; she became more than ever the fashion, and years glided on, as from season to season she shone a bright star among many luminaries, improving in charms and grace, as knowledge of the world and the desire of pleasing were added to her natural attractions.

The stories at first in circulation on Lodore's departure, all sufficiently wide from the truth, were half forgotten, and served merely as an obscure substratum for Cornelia's bright reputation. He was gone: he could no longer injure nor benefit any, and was therefore no longer an object of fear or love. The most charitable construction put upon his conduct was, that he was mad, and it was piously observed, that his removal from this world would be a blessing. Lady Santerre triumphed. Withering away in unhonoured age, still she appeared in the halls of the great, and played the part of Cerberus in her daughter's drawing-room. Lady Lodore, beautiful and admired, intoxicated with this sort of prosperity, untouched by passion, unharmed by the temptations that surrounded her, believed that life was spent most worthily in following the routine observed by those about her, and securing the privilege of being exclusive. She was the glass of fashion—the imitated by a vast sect of imitators. The deprivation of her child was the sole cloud that came between her and the sun. In despite of herself, she never saw a little cherub with rosy cheeks and golden hair, but her heart was visited by a pang; and in her dreams she often beheld, instead of the image of the gay saloons in which she spent her evenings, a desert wild—a solitary home—and tiny footsteps on the dewy grass, guiding her to

CHAPTER XIV

"Time and Change together take their flight."

—*L. E. L.*

🌹

Fitzhenry and his daughter travelled for many days in rain and sunshine, across the vast plains of America. Conversation beguiled the way, and Ethel, delighted by the novelty and variety of all she saw, often felt as if springing from her seat with a new sense of excitement and gladness. So much do the young love change, that we have often thought it the dispensation of the Creator, to show that we are formed, at a certain age, to quit the parental roof, like the patriarch, to seek some new abode where to pitch our tents, and pasture our flocks. The clear soft eyes of the fair girl glistened with pleasure at each picturesque view, each change of earth and sky, each new aspect of civilization and its results, as they were presented to her.

Fitzhenry—or as he approaches the old world, so long deserted by him, he may resume his title—Lord Lodore had quitted his abode in the Illinois upon the spur of the moment; he had left his peaceful dwelling impatiently, and in haste, giving himself no time for second thoughts—scarcely for recollection. As the fever of his mind subsided, he saw no cause to repent his proceeding, and yet he began to look forward with an anxious and foreboding mind. He had become aware that the village of the Illinois was not the scene fitted for the development of his daughter's first social feelings, and that he ought to take her among the educated and refined, to give her a chance for happiness. A Gertrude or an Haidée, brought up in the wilds, innocent and free, and bestowing the treasure of their hearts on some accomplished stranger, brought on purpose to realize the ideal of their dreamy existences, is a picture of beauty, that requires a miracle to change into an actual event in life; and that one so pure, so guileless, and so inexperienced as Ethel, should, in sheer ignorance, give her affections away unworthily, was a danger to be avoided beyond all others. Whitelock had performed the part of the wandering stranger, but he was ill-fitted for it; and Lodore's first idea was to hurry his daughter away before she should invest him, or any other, with attributes of glory, drawn from her own imagination and sensibility, wholly beyond his merits.

This was done. Father and daughter were on their way to New York, having bid an eternal adieu to the savannas and forests of the west. For a time, Lodore's thoughts were haunted by the image of the home they had left. The murmuring of its stream was in his ears, the shape of each distant hill, the grouping of the trees, surrounding the wide-spread prairie, the winding pathway and trellised arbour were before his eyes, and he thought of the changes that the seasons would operate around, and of his future plans unfulfilled, as any home-bred farmer might, when his lease was out, and he was forced to remove to another county.

As their steps drew near the city which was their destination, these recollections became fainter, and, except in discourse with Ethel, when their talk usually recurred to the prairie, and their late home, he began to anticipate the future, and to reflect upon the results of his present journey.

Whither was he about to go? To England? What reception should he there meet? and under what auspices introduce his child to her native country? There was a stain upon his reputation that no future conduct could efface. The name of Lodore was a by-word and a mark for scorn; it was introduced with a sneer, followed by calumny and rebuke. It could not even be forgotten. His wife had remained to keep alive the censure or derision attached to it. He, it is true, might have ceased to live in the memories of any. He did not imagine that his idea ever recurred to the thoughtless throng, whose very name and identity were changed by the lapse of twelve years. But when it was mentioned, when he should awaken the forgotten sound by his presence, the echo of shame linked to it would awaken also; the love of a sensation so rife among the wealthy and idle, must swell the sound, and Ethel would be led on the world's stage by one who was the object of its opprobrium.

What then should he do? Solicit Lady Lodore to receive and bring out her daughter? Deprive himself of her society; and after having guarded her unassailed infancy, desert her side at the moment when dangers grew thick, and her mother's example would operate most detrimentally on her? He thought of his sister, with whom he kept up a regular though infrequent correspondence. She was ill fitted to guide a young beauty on a path which she had never trod. He thought of France, Italy, and Germany, and how he might travel about with her during the two or three succeeding years, enlarging and storing her mind, and protracting the happy light-hearted years of youth. His own experience on the continent would facilitate this plan; and though it presented, even on this very account, a variety of objections, it was that to which he felt most attracted.

There was yet another—another image and another prospect to which he turned with a kind of gasping sensation, which was now a shrinking aversion to—now an ardent desire for, its fulfilment. This was the project of a reconciliation with Cornelia, and that they should henceforth unite in their labours to render each other and their child happy.

Twelve years had passed since their separation: twelve years, which had led him from the prime of life to its decline—which forced Cornelia to number, instead of nineteen, more than thirty years—bringing her from crude youth to fullest maturity. What changes might not time have operated in her mind! Latterly no intercourse had passed between them, they were as dead to each other; and yet the fact of the existence of either was a paramount law with both, ruling their actions and preventing them from forming any new tie. Cornelia might be tired of independence, have discovered the hollowness of her mother's system, and desire, but that pride prevented her, a reunion with her long-exiled husband. Her understanding was good; intercourse with the world had probably operated to cultivate and enlarge it—maternal love might reign in full force, causing her heart to yearn towards the blooming Ethel, and a thousand untold sorrows might make her regard the affection of her child's father, as the prop, the shelter, the haven, where to find peace, if not happiness.

And yet Cornelia was still young, still beautiful, still admired: he was on the wane—a healthy life had preserved the uprightness of his form and the spring of his limbs; but his countenance, how changed from the Lodore who pledged his faith to her in the rustic church at Rhyaider Gowy! The melting softness of his dark eyes was altered to mere sadness—his brow, from which the hair had retreated, was delved by a thousand lines; grey sprinkled his black hair,—a wintry morning stealing drearily upon night—each year had left its trace, and with no Praxitelean hand, engraven lines upon the rounded cheek, and sunk and diminished the full eye. Twelve years had scarcely operated so great a change as here described; but thus he painted it to himself, exaggerating and deforming the image his mirror presented—and where others had only marked the indications of a thoughtful mind, and the traces of over-wrought sensibility, he beheld careful furrows and age-worn wrinkles.

And was he thus to claim the beautiful, the courted—she who still reigned supreme on Love's own throne? and to whom, so had he been told, time had brought increased charms as its gift, strewing roses and fragrance on her lovely head, so proving that neither grief nor passion had disturbed the proud serenity of her heart.

Lodore had lived many years the life of a recluse, having given up ambition, hope, almost life itself, inasmuch as that existence is scarcely to be termed life, which does not bring us into intimate connexion with our fellow-creatures, nor develope in its progress some plan of present action or anticipation for the future. He was roused from his lethargy as he approached peopled cities; a desire to mingle again in human affairs was awakened, together with an impatience under the obscurity to which he had condemned himself. He grew at last to despise his supineness, which had prevented him from struggling with and vanquishing his adverse fortunes. He resolved no longer to be weighed down by the fear of obloquy, while he was conscious of the bravery and determination of his soul, and with what lofty indignation he was prepared to sweep away the stigma attached to him, and to assert the brightness of his honour. This, for his daughter's sake, as well as for his own, he determined to do.

He had no wish, however, to enter upon the task in America. His native country must be the scene of his exertions, as to re-assert himself among his countrymen was their object. He felt, also, that, from the beginning, he must take no false step; and it behoved him fully to understand the state of things in England as regarded him, before he presented himself. He delayed his voyage, therefore, till he had exchanged letters with Europe. He wrote to his sister, immediately on arriving at New York, asking for intelligence concerning Lady Lodore; and communicating his intention to return immediately, and, if possible, to effect a reconciliation with his estranged wife. He besought an immediate reply, as he did not wish to defer his voyage beyond the spring months.

Having sent this letter, he gave himself up to the society of his daughter. He occupied himself by endeavouring to form her for the new scenes on which she was about to enter, and to divest her of the first raw astonishment excited by the contrast formed by the busy, commercial eastern, with the majestic tranquillity of the western portion of the new world. He wished to accustom her to mingle with her fellow-creatures with ease and dignity; and he sought to enlarge her mind, and to excite her curiosity, by introducing her to the effects of civilization. He would willingly have formed acquaintances for her sake, but that such a circumstance might interfere with the incognito he meant to preserve while away from his native country. We can never divest ourselves of our identity and consciousness, and are apt to fancy that others are equally alive to our peculiar individuality. It was not probable that the name of Lodore, or of Fitzhenry, should be known in New York; but as the title had been bestowed as a reward for victories obtained over the Americans, he who bore it was less to be blamed for fancying that they had heard with pleasure the story of his disgrace, and would be ready to visit his fault with malignant severity.

An accident, however, brought him into contact with an English lady, and he gladly availed himself of this opportunity to bring Ethel into the society of her country people. One day he received an elegant little note, such as are written in London by the fashionable and the fair, which, with many apologies, contained a request. The writer had heard that he was about to return to England with his daughter. Would he refuse to take under his charge a young lady, who was desirous of returning thither? The distance from their native land drew English people together, and usually made them kindly disposed towards each other. The circumstances under which this request was made were peculiar; and if he would call to hear them explained, his interest would be excited, and he would not refuse a favour which would lay the writer under the deepest obligation.

Lodore answered this application in person. He found an English family residing in one of the best streets of New York, and was introduced to the lady who had addressed him. Her story, the occasion of her request, was detailed without reserve. Her husband's family had formerly been American royalists, refugees in England, where they had lived poor and forgotten. A brother of his father had remained behind in the new country, and acquired a large fortune. He had lived to extreme old age; and dying childless, left his wealth to his English nephew, upon condition that he settled in America. This had caused their emigration. While in England, they had lived at Bath, and been intimate with a clergyman, who resided near. This clergyman was a singular man—a recluse, and a student—a man of ardent soul, held down by a timid, nervous disposition. He was an outcast from his family, which was wealthy and of good station, on account of having formed a mes-alliance. How indeed he could have married his unequal partner was matter of excessive wonder. She was illiterate and vulgar—coarse-minded, though good-natured. This ill-matched pair had two daughters;—one, the younger, now about fourteen years old, was the person whom it was desired to commit to Lodore's protection.

The lady continued:—She had a large family of boys, and but one girl, of the age of Fanny Derham;—they had been for some years companions and friends. When about to emigrate, she believed that she should benefit equally her daughter and her friend, if she made the latter a companion in their emigration. With great reluctance, Mr. Derham had consented to part with his child: he had thought it for her good, and he had let her go. Fanny obeyed her father. She manifested no disinclination to the plan; and it seemed as if the benevolent wishes of Mrs. Greville were fulfilled for the benefit of all. They had been in America nearly a year, and now Fanny was to return. She herself had borne her absence from her father with fortitude: yet it required an exertion of fortitude to bear it, which was destroying the natural vivacity of her disposition. Gloom gathered over her mind; she fled society; she sought solitude; and spent day after day in reverie. Mrs. Greville strove to rouse her, and Fanny lent herself with good grace to any exertion demanded of her; yet it was plain, that even when she gave herself most up to her desire to please her hostess, her thoughts were far away, her eye was tracing the invisible outline of objects divided from her by the ocean; and her inmost sense was absorbed by the recollection of one far distant; while her ear and voice were abstractedly lent to those immediately around her. Mrs. Greville endeavoured vainly to amuse and distract her thoughts. The only pleasure which attracted her young mind was study—a deep and unremitted application to those profound acquirements, to the knowledge of which her father had introduced her.

"When you know my young friend," continued Mrs. Greville, "you will understand the force of character which renders her unlike every other child. Fanny never was a child. Mrs. Derham and her daughter Sarah bustled through the business of life—of the farm and the house; while it devolved on Fanny to attend to, to wait upon, her father. She was his pupil—he her care. The relation of parent and child subsisted between them, on a different footing than in ordinary cases. Fanny nursed her father, watched over his health and humours, with the tenderness and indulgence of a mother; while he instructed her in the dead languages, and other sorts of abstruse learning, which seldom make a part of a girl's education. Fanny, to use her own singular language, loves philosophy, and pants after knowledge, and indulges in a thousand Platonic dreams, which I know nothing about; and this mysterious and fanciful learning she has dwelt upon with tenfold fervour since her arrival in America.

"The contrast," continued Mrs. Greville, "between this wonderful, but strange girl, and her parent, is apparent in nothing more than the incident that made me have recourse to your kindness. Fanny pined for home, and her father. The very air of America was distasteful to her—we were not congenial companions. But she never expressed discontent. As much as she could, she shut herself up in the world of her own mind; but outwardly, she was cheerful and uncomplaining. A week ago we had letters from her parents, requesting her immediate return. Mr. Derham wasted away without her; his health was seriously injured by what, in feminine dialect, is called fretting; and both he and her mother have implored me to send her back to them without delay."

Lord Lodore listened with breathless interest, asking now and then such questions as drew on Mrs. Greville to further explanation. He soon became convinced that he was called upon to do this act of kindness for the daughter of his former school-fellow—for Francis Derham, whom he had not known nor seen since they had exchanged the visions of boyhood for the disappointing realities of maturer age. And this was Derham's fate!—poor, mis-matched, destroyed by a morbid sensibility, an object of pity to his own young child, yet adored by her as the gentlest and wisest of men. How different—and yet how similar—the destinies of both! It warmed the heart of Lodore to think that he should renew his boyish intimacy. Derham would not reject him—would not participate in the world's blind scorn: in his bosom no harsh nor unjust feeling could have place; his simple, warm heart would yearn towards him as of yore; and the school-fellows become again all the world to each other.

After this explanation, Mrs. Greville introduced her young friend. Her resemblance to her father was at first sight remarkable, and awoke with greater keenness the roused sensibility of Lodore. She was pale and fair; her light, golden hair clustered in short ringlets over her small, well-formed head, leaving unshaded a high forehead, clear as opening day. Her blue eyes were remarkably light and penetrating, with defined and straight brows. Intelligence, or rather understanding, reigned in every feature; independence of thought, and firmness, spoke in every gesture. She was a mere child in form and mien—even in her expressions; but within her was discernible an embryo of power, and a grandeur of soul, not to be mistaken. Simplicity and equability of temper were her characteristics: these smoothed the ruggedness which the singularity of her character might otherwise have engendered.

Lodore rejoiced in the strange accident that gave such a companion to his daughter. Nothing could be in stronger contrast than these two girls;—the fairy form, the romantic and yielding sweetness of Ethel, whose clinging affections formed her whole world,—with the studious and abstracted disciple of ancient learning. Notwithstanding this want of similarity, they soon became mutually attached. Lodore was a link between them. He excited Ethel to admire the concentrated and independent spirit of her new friend; and entered into conversation with Fanny on ancient philosophy, which was unintelligible and mysterious to Ethel. The three became inseparable: they prolonged their excursions in the neighbouring country; while each enjoyed peculiar pleasures in the friendship and sympathy of their companions.

This addition to their society, and an intimacy cultivated with Mrs. Greville, whose husband was absent at Washington, formed, as it were, a weaning time for Lodore, from the seclusion of the Illinois. There he had lived, cut off from the past and the future, existing in the present only. He had been happy there; cured of the wounds which had penetrated his heart so deeply, through the ministration of all-healing nature. He felt the gliding of the hours as a blessing; and the occupations of each day were replete with calm enjoyment. He thought of England, as a seaman newly saved from a wreck would of the tempestuous ocean, with fear and loathing, and with heart-felt gladness that he was no longer the sport of its waves. He cultivated such a philosophic turn of mind as often brought a smile of self-pity on his lips, at the recollection of scenes which, during their passage, had provoked bitter and burning sensations. What was all this strife of passion, this eager struggle for something, he knew not what, to him now? The healthy labours of his farm, the tranquillity of his library, the endearing caresses of his child, were worth all the vanities of life.

Thus he had felt in the Illinois; and now again he looked back to his undisturbed life there, wondering how he had endured its monotonous loneliness. A desire for action, for mingling with his fellow-men, had arisen in his heart. He felt like a strong swimmer, who longs to battle with the waves. He desired to feel and to exert his powers, to fill a space in the eyes of others, to re-assert himself in their esteem, or to resent their scorn. He could no longer regard the past with imperturbability. Again his passions were roused, as he thought of his mother-in-law, of his wife, and of the strange scenes which had preceded and caused his flight from England. These ideas had long occupied his mind, without occasioning any emotion. But now again they were full of interest; and pain and struggle again resulted from the recollection. At such times he was glad that Ethel had a companion, that he might leave her and wander alone. He became a préy to the same violence of passion, the same sense of injury and stinging hurry of thought, which for twelve years had ceased to torture him. But no tincture of cowardice entered into his sensations. His soul was set upon victory over the evil fortune to which he had so long submitted. When he thought of returning to England, from which he had fled with dishonour, his cheek tingled as a thousand images of insult and contumely passed rapidly through his mind, as likely to visit him. His heart swelled within him—his very soul grew faint; but instead of desiring to fly the anticipated opprobrium, he longed to meet it and to wash out shame, if need were, with his life's blood; and, by resolution and daring, to silence his enemies, and redeem his name from obloquy.

One day, occupied by such thoughts, he stood watching that vast and celebrated cataract, whose everlasting and impetuous flow mirrored the dauntless but rash energy of his own soul. A vague desire of plunging into the whirl of waters agitated him. His existence appeared to be a blot in the creation; his hopes, and fears, and resolves, a worthless web of ill-assorted ideas, best swept away at once from the creation. Suddenly his eye caught the little figure of Fanny Derham, standing on a rock not far distant, her meaning eyes fixed on him. The thunder of the waters prevented speech; but as he drew near her, he saw that she had a paper in her hand. She held it out to him; a blush mantled over her usually pale countenance as he took it; and she sprung away up the rocky pathway.

Lodore cast his eyes on the open letter, and his own name, half forgotten by him, presented itself on the written page. The letter was from Fanny's father—from Derham, his friend and school-fellow. His heart beat fast as he read the words traced by one formerly so dear. "The beloved name of Fitzhenry"—thus Derham had written—

awakens a strange conjecture. Is not your kind protector, the friend and companion of my boyish days? Is it not the long absent Lodore, who has stretched out a paternal hand to my darling child, and who is about to add to his former generous acts, the dearer one of restoring my Fanny to me? Ask him this question;—extract this secret from him. Tell him how my chilled heart warms with pleasure at the prospect of a renewal of our friendship. He was a god-like boy; daring, generous, and brave. The remembrance of him has been the bright spot which, except yourself, is all of cheering that has chequered my gloomy existence. Ask him whether he remembers him whose life he saved—whom he rescued from oppression and misery. I am an old man now, weighed down by sorrow and infirmity. Adversity has also visited him; but he will have withstood the shocks of fate, as gallantly as a mighty ship stems the waves of ocean: while I, a weather-worn skiff, am battered and wrecked by the tempest. From all you say, he must be Lodore. Mark him, Fanny: if you see one lofty in his mien, yet gracious in all his acts; his person adorned by the noblest attributes of rank; full of dignity, yet devoid of pride; impatient of all that is base and insolent, but with a heart open as a woman's to compassion;—one whose slightest word possesses a charm to attract and enchain the affections:—if such be your new friend, put this letter into his hand; he will remember Francis Derham, and love you for my sake, as well as for your own.

• • •

CHAPTER XV

"It is our will
That thus enchains us to permitted ill."

—Shelley

This was a new inducement to bring back Lodore from the wilds of America, to the remembrance of former days. The flattering expressions in Derham's letter soothed his wounded pride, and inspired a desire of associating once more with men who could appreciate his worth, and sympathize with his feelings. His spirits became exhilarated; he talked of Europe and his return thither, with all the animation of sanguine youth. It is one of the necessary attributes of our nature, always to love what we have once loved; and though new objects and change in former ones may chill our affections for a time, we are filled with renewed fervour after every fresh disappointment, and feel an impatient longing to return to the cherishing warmth of our early attachments; happy if we do not find emptiness and desolation, where we left life and hope.

Ethel had never been as happy as at the present time, and her affection for her father gathered strength from the confidence which existed between them. He was the passion of her soul, the engrossing attachment of her loving heart. When she saw a cloud on his brow, she would stand by him with silent but pleading tenderness, as if to ask whether any exertion of hers could dissipate his inquietude. She hung upon his discourse as a heavenly oracle, and welcomed him with gladdened looks of love, when he returned after any short absence. Her heart was bent upon pleasing him, she had no thought or pursuit which was not linked with his participation.

There is perhaps in the list of human sensations, no one so pure, so perfect, and yet so impassioned, as the affection of a child for its parent, during that brief interval when they are leaving childhood, and have not yet felt love. There is something so awful in a father. His words are laws, and to obey them happiness. Reverence and a desire to serve, are mingled with gratitude; and duty, without a flaw or question, so second the instinct of the heart, as to render it impera-tive. Afterwards we may love, in spite of the faults of the object of our attachment; but during the interval alluded to, we have not yet learnt to tolerate, but also, we have not learned to detect faults. All that a parent does, appears an emanation from a diviner world; while we fear to offend, we believe we have no right to be offended; eager to please, we seek in return approval only, and are too humble to demand a reciprocity of attention; it is enough that we are permitted to dem-onstrate our devotion. Ethel's heart overflowed with love, reverence, worship of her father. He had stood in the wilds of America a solitary specimen of all that is graceful, cultivated, and wise among men; she knew of nothing that might compare to him; and the world without him, was what the earth might be uninformed by light: he was its sun, its ruling luminary. All this intensity of feeling existed in her, without her being aware scarcely of its existence, without her questioning the cause, or reasoning on the effect. To love her father was the first law of nature, the chief duty of a child, and she fulfilled it unconsciously, but more completely than she could have done had she been associated with others, who might have shared and weakened the concentrated sensibility of her nature.

At length the packet arrived which brought letters from England. Before his eyes lay the closed letter pregnant with fate. He was not of a disposition to recoil from certainty; and yet for a few moments he hesitated to break the seals—appalled by the magnitude of the crisis which he believed to be at hand.

Latterly the idea of a reconciliation with Cornelia had been a favourite in his thoughts. The world was a painful and hard-tasking school. She must have suffered various disappointments, and endured much disgust, and so be prepared to lend a willing ear to his overture. She was so very young when they parted, and since then, had lived entirely under the influence of Lady Santerre. But what had at one time proved injurious, might, in course of years, have opened her eyes to the vanity of the course which she was pursuing. Lodore felt persuaded, that there were better things to be expected from his wife, than a love of fashion and an adherence to the prejudices of society. He had failed to bring her good qualities to light, but time and events might have played the tutor better, and it merely required perhaps a seasonable interference, a fortunate circumstance, to prove the truth of his opinion, and to show Lady Lodore as generous, magnanimous, and devoted, as before she had appeared proud, selfish, and cold.

How few there are possessed of any sensibility, who mingle with, and are crushed by the jostling interests of the world, who do not ever and anon exclaim with the Psalmist, "O for the wings of a dove, that I might flee away and be at rest!" If such an aspiration was ever breathed by Cornelia, how gladly, how fondly would her husband welcome the weary flutterer, open his bosom for her refuge, and study to make her forget all the disquietudes and follies of headstrong youth!

This was a mere dream. Lodore sighed to think that his position would not permit him to afford her a shelter from the poisoned arrows of the world. She must come to him prepared to suffer much. It required not only the absence of the vulgar worldliness of Lady Santerre, but great strength of mind to forgive the past, and strong affection to endure the present. He could only invite her to share the lot of a dishonoured man, to become a partner in the struggle which he was prepared to enter upon, to regain his lost reputation. This was no cheering prospect. Pride and generosity equally forbad his endeavouring to persuade his wife to quit a course of life she liked, to enter upon a scene of trials and sorrows with one for whom she did not care.

All these conjectures had long occupied him, but here was certainty—the letter in his hand. It was sealed with black, and a tremulous shudder ran through his frame as he tore it open. He soon satisfied himself—Cornelia lived: he breathed freely again, and proceeded more calmly to make himself master of the intelligence which the paper he held contained.

Cornelia lived; but his sister announced a death which he believed would change the colour of his life. Lady Santerre was no more!

Yes, Cornelia was alive; the bride that had stood beside him at the altar—whose hand he had held while he pronounced his vows—with whom he had domesticated for years—the mother of his child still lived. The cold consuming grave did not wrap her lovely form. The idea of her death, which the appearance of the black seal conveyed suddenly to his imagination, had been appalling beyond words. For the last few weeks his mind had been filled with her image; his thoughts had fed upon the hope that they should meet once more. Had she died while he was living in inactive seclusion in the Illinois, he might have been less moved; his vivid fancy, his passionate heart, could not spare her now, without a pang of agony. It passed away, and his mind reverted to the actual situation in which they were placed by the death of his mother-in-law. Reconciliation had become easy by the removal of that fatal barrier. He felt assured that he could acquire Cornelia's confidence, win her love, and administer to her happiness; he determined to leave nothing untried to bring about so desirable a conclusion to their long and dreary alienation. The one insuperable obstacle was gone; their daughter, that loveliest link, that soft silken tie remained: Cornelia must welcome with maternal delight this better portion of herself.

He glanced over his sister Elizabeth's letter, announcing the death of Lady Santerre, and then read the one enclosed from Lady Lodore to her sister-in-law. It was cold, but very decisive. She thanked her first for the inquiries she had made, and then proceeded to say, that she took this opportunity, the only one likely to present itself, of expressing what her own feelings were on this melancholy occasion. "I am afraid," she said, "that your brother will look on the death of my dearest mother as opening the door to our re-union. Some words in your letter seem indeed to intimate this, or I should have hoped that I was entirely forgotten. I trust that I am mistaken. My earnest desire is, that my natural grief, and the tranquillity which I try to secure for myself, may not be disturbed by fruitless endeavours to bring about what can never be. My determination may be supposed to arise from pride and implacable resentment: perhaps it does, but I feel it impossible that we should ever be any thing but strangers to each other. I will not complain, and I wish to avoid harsh allusions, but respect for her I have lost, and a sense of undeserved wrong, are paramount with me. I shall never intrude upon him. Persuade him that it will be unmanly cruelty to force himself, even by a letter, on me."

From this violent declaration of an unforgiving heart, Lodore turned to Elizabeth's letter. This excellent lady, to whom the names of dissipation and the metropolis were synonymous, and who knew as much of the world as Parson Adams, assured her brother, that Cornelia, far from feeling deeply the blow of her mother's death, was pursuing her giddy course with greater pertinacity than ever. Surrounded by flatterers, given up to pleasure, she naturally shrunk from being reminded of her exiled husband and her forgotten child. Her letter showed how ill she deserved the tenderness and interest which Lodore had expressed. She was a second Lady Santerre, without being gifted with that maternal affection, which had in some degree dignified that person's character.

Elizabeth lamented that his wife's hardness of heart might prevent his proposed visit to England. She did not like to urge it—it might seem selfish: hitherto she had let herself and her sorrows go for nothing; could she think of her own gratification, while her brother was suffering so much calamity? She was growing old—indeed she was old—she had no kin around her—early friends were dead or lost to her—she had nothing to live on but the recollection of her brother; she should think herself blest could she see him once more before she died.

"O my dear brother Henry," continued the kind-hearted lady, "if you would but say the word—the sea is nothing; people older than I—and I am not at all infirm—make the voyage. Let me come to America—let me embrace my niece, and see you once again—let me share your dear home in the Illinois, which I see every night in my dreams. I should grieve to be a burthen to you, but it would be my endeavour to prove a comfort and a help."

Lodore read both of these letters, one after the other, again and again. He resolved on going to England immediately. Either Cornelia was entirely callous and worthless, and so to be discarded from his heart for ever, or after her first bitter feelings on her mother's death were over, she would soften towards her child, or there was some dread secret feeling that influenced her, and he must save her from calamity and wretchedness. One of those changes of feeling to which the character of Lodore was peculiarly subject, came over him. Lady Santerre was dead—Cornelia was alone. A thousand dangers surrounded her. It appeared to him that his first imperious duty was to offer himself to guard and watch over her. He resolved to leave nothing untried to make her happy. He would give up Ethel to her—he would gratify every wish she could frame—pour out benefits lavishly before her—force her to see in him a benefactor and a friend; and at last, his heart whispered, induce her to assume again the duties of a wife.

•••

CHAPTER XVI

"What is peace? When life is over,
And love ceases to rebel,
Let the last faint sigh discover,
Which precedes the passing knell."

—*Wordsworth*

Lodore was henceforth animated by a new spirit of hope. His projects and resolves gave him something to live for. He looked forward with pleasure; feeling, on his expected return to his native country, as the fabled voyager, who knew that he ought to be contented in the fair island where chance had thrown him, and yet who hailed with rapture the approach of the sail that was to bear him back to the miseries of social life. He reflected that he had in all probability many years before him, and he was earnest that the decline of his life should, by a display of prudence and virtuous exertion, cause the errors of his earlier manhood to be forgotten.

This inspiriting tone of mind was very congenial to Ethel. The prospects that occupied her father had a definite horizon: all was vague and misty to her eyes, yet beautiful and alluring. Lodore gave no outline of his plans: he never named her mother. Uncertain himself, he was unwilling to excite feelings in Ethel's mind, to be afterwards checked and disappointed. He painted the future in gay colours, but left it in all the dimness most favourable for an ardent imagination to exercise itself upon.

In a very few days they were to sail for England. Their passage was engaged. Lodore had written to his sister to announce his return. He spoke of Longfield, and of her kind and gentle aunt to Ethel, and she, who, like Miranda, had known no relative or intimate except her father, warmed with pleasure to find new ties bind her to her fellow-creatures. She questioned her father, and he, excited by his own newly-awakened emotions, dilated eloquently on the joys of his young days, and pleased Fanny, as well as his own daughter, by a detail of boyish pranks and adventures which his favourite school-fellow shared. The freedom he enjoyed in his paternal home, the worship that waited on him there, the large space which in early youth he appeared to fill in all men's eyes, the buoyancy and innocence associated with those unshadowed days, painted them to his memory cloudless and bright. It would be to renew them to see Longfield again,—to clasp once more the hand of Francis Derham.

A kind of holiday and festal feeling was diffused through Ethel's mind by the vivid descriptions and frank communications of her father. She felt as if about to enter Paradise. America grew dim and sombre in her eyes; its forests, lakes, and wilds, were empty and silent, while England swarmed with a thousand lovely forms of pleasure. Her father strewed a downy velvet path for her, which she trod with light, girlish steps, happy in the present hour, happier in the anticipated future.

A few days before the party were to sail, Lodore and his daughter dined with Mrs. Greville. As if they held the reins, and could curb the course of, fate, each and all were filled with hilarity. Lodore had forgotten Theodora and her son—had cast from his recollection the long train of misery, injury, and final ruin, which for so long had occupied his whole thoughts. He was in his own eyes no longer the branded exile. A strange distortion of vision blinded this unfortunate man to the truth, which experience so perpetually teaches us, that the consequences of our actions *never die*: that repentance and time may paint them to us in different shapes; but though we shut our eyes, they are still beside us, helping the inexorable destinies to spin the fatal thread, and sharpening the implement which is to cut it asunder.

Lodore lived the morning of that day, (it was the first of May, realizing by its brilliancy and sweets, the favourite months of the poets,) as if many a morning throughout the changeful seasons was to be his. Some time he spent on board the vessel in which he was to sail; seeing that all the arrangements which he had ordered for Ethel and Fanny's comfort were perfected; then father and daughter rode out together. Often did Ethel try to remember every word of the conversation held during that ride. It concerned the fair fields of England, the splendours of Italy, the refinements and pleasures of Europe. "When we are in London,"—"When we shall visit Naples,"—such phrases perpetually occurred. It was Lodore's plan to induce Cornelia to travel with him, and to invite Mr. Derham and Fanny to be their companions; a warmer climate would benefit his friend's health. "And for worlds," he said, "I would not lose Derham. It is the joy of my life to think that by my return to my native country I secure to myself the society of this excellent and oppressed man."

At six o'clock Lodore and Ethel repaired to Mrs. Greville's house. It had been intended that no other persons should be invited, but the unexpected arrival of some friends from Washington, about to sail to England, had obliged the lady to alter this arrangement. The new guests consisted of an English gentleman and his wife, and one other, an American, who had filled a diplomatic situation in London. Annoyed by the sight of strangers, Lodore kept apart, conversing with Ethel and Fanny.

At dinner he sat opposite to the American. There was something in this man's physiognomy peculiarly disagreeable to him. He was not a pleasing-looking man, but that was not all. Lodore fancied that he must have seen him before under very painful circumstances. He felt inclined to quarrel with him—he knew not why; and was disturbed and dissatisfied with himself and every body. The first words which the man spoke were as an electric shock to him. Twelve long years rolled back—the past became the present once again. This very American had sat opposite to him at the memorable dinner at the Russian Ambassador's. At the moment when he had been hurried away by the fury of his passion against Casimir, he remembered to have seen a sarcastic sneer on his face, as the republican marked the arrogance of the English noble. Lodore had been ready then to turn the fire of his resentment on the insolent observer; but when the occasion passed away he had entirely forgotten him, till now he rose like a ghost to remind him of former pains and crimes.

The lapse of years had scarcely altered this person. His hair was grizzled, but it crowned his head in the same rough abundance as formerly. His face, which looked as if carved out of wood, strongly and deeply lined, showed no tokens of a more advanced age. He was then elderly-looking for a middle-aged man; he was now young-looking for an elderly man. Nature had disdained to change an aspect which showed so little of her divinity, and which no wrinkles nor withering could mar. Lodore, turning from this apparition, caught the reflection of himself in an opposite mirror. Association of ideas had made him unconsciously expect to behold the jealous husband of Cornelia. How changed, how passion-worn and tarnished was the countenance that met his eyes. He recovered his self-possession as he became persuaded that this chance visitant, who had seen him but once, would be totally unable to recognize him.

This unwelcome guest had been attached to the American embassy in England, and had but lately returned to New York. He was full of dislike of the English. Contempt for them, and pride in his countrymen, being the cherished feelings of his mind; the latter he held up to admiration from prejudiced views; a natural propensity to envy and depreciation led him to detract from the former. He was, in short, a most disagreeable person; and his insulting observations on his country moved Lodore's spleen, while his mind was shaken from its balance by the sight of one who reminded him of his past errors and ruin. He was fast advancing to a state of irritability, when he should lose all command over himself. He felt this, and tried to subdue the impetuous rush of bitterness which agitated him; he remembered that he must expect many trials like this, and that, rightly considered, this was a good school wherein he might tutor himself to self-possession and firmness. He went to another extreme, and addressing himself to, and arguing with, the object of his dislike, endeavoured to gloss over to himself the rising violence of his impassioned temper.

The ladies retired, and the gentlemen entered upon a political discussion on some event passing in Europe. The English guest took his departure early, and Lodore and the other continued to converse. Some mention was made of newspapers newly arrived, and the American proposed that they should repair to the coffee-house to see them. Lodore agreed: he thought that this would be a good opportunity to shake off his distasteful companion.

The coffee-room contained nearly twenty persons. They were in loud discussion upon a question of European politics, and reviling England and her manners in the most contemptuous terms. This was not balm for Lodore's sore feelings. His heart swelled indignantly at the sarcasms which these strangers levelled against his native country; he felt as if he was acting a coward's part while he listened tamely. His companion soon entered with vehemence into the conversation; and the noble, who was longing to quarrel with him, now drew himself up with forced composure, fixing his full meaning eyes upon the speaker, hoping by his quiescence to entice him into expressions which he would insist on being retracted. His temper by this time entirely mastered him. In a calmer moment he would have despised himself for being influenced by such a man, to any sentiment except contempt; but the tempest was abroad, and all sobriety of feeling was swept away like chaff before the wind.

Mr. Hatfield,—such was the American's name,—perceiving that he was listened to, entered with great delight on his favourite topic, a furious and insolent philippic against England, in mass and in detail. Lodore still listened; there was a dry sneer in the tones of the speaker's voice, that thrilled him with hate and rage. At length, by some chance reverting to the successful struggle America had made for her independence, and ridiculing the resistance of the English on the occasion, Hatfield named Lodore.

"Lodore!" cried one of the by-standers; "Fitzhenry was the name of the man who took the Oronooko."

"Aye, Fitzhenry it was," said Hatfield, "Lodore is his nickname. King George's bit of gilt gingerbread, which mightily pleased the sapient mariner. An Englishman thinks himself honoured when he changes one name for another. Admiral Fitzhenry was the scum of the earth—Lord Lodore a pillar of state. Pity that infamy should so soon have blackened the glorious title!"

Lodore's pale cheek suddenly flushed at these words, and then blanched again, as with compressed lips he resolved to hear yet more, till the insult should no longer be equivocal. The word "infamy" was echoed from various lips. Hatfield found that he had insured a hearing, and, glad of an audience, he went on to relate his story—it was of the dinner at the Russian Ambassador's—of the intemperate violence of Lodore—and the youthful Lyzinski's wrongs. "I saw the blow given," continued the narrator, "and I would have caned the fellow on the spot, had I not thought that a bullet would do his business better. But when it came to that, London was regaled by an event which could not have happened here, for we have no such cowards among us. My lord was not to be found—he had absconded—sneaked off like a mean-spirited, pitiful scoundrel!"

The words were still on the man's lips when a blow, sudden and unexpected, extended him on the floor. After this swiftly-executed act of retaliation, Lodore folded his arms, and as his antagonist rose, foaming with rage, said, "You, at least, shall have no cause to complain of not receiving satisfaction for your injuries at my hands. I am ready to give it, even in this room. I am Lord Lodore!"

Duels, that sad relic of feudal barbarism, were more frequent then than now in America; at all times they are more fatal and more openly carried on there than in this country. The nature of the quarrel in the present instance admitted of no delay; and it was resolved, that the antagonists should immediately repair to an open place near the city, to terminate, by the death of one, the insults they had mutually inflicted.

Lodore saw himself surrounded by Americans, all strangers to him; nor was he acquainted with one person in New York whom he could ask to be his second. This was matter of slight import: the idea of vindicating his reputation, and of avenging the bitter mortifications received from society, filled him with unnatural gladness; and he was hastening to the meeting, totally regardless of any arrangement for his security.

There was a gentleman, seated at a distant part of the coffee-room, who had been occupied by reading; nor seemed at all to give ear to what was going on, till the name of Lodore occurred: he then rose, and when the blow was given, drew nearer the group; though he still stood aloof, while, with raised and angry voices, they assailed Lodore, and he, replying in his deep, subdued voice, agreed to the meeting which they tumultuously demanded. Now, as they were hastening away, and Lodore was following them, confessedly unbefriended, this gentleman approached, and putting his card into the nobleman's hand, said, "I am an Englishman, and should be very glad if you would accept my services on this painful occasion."

Lodore looked at the card, on which was simply engraved the name of "Mr. Edward Villiers," and then at him who addressed him. He was a young man—certainly not more than three-and-twenty. An air of London fashion, to which Lodore had been so long unused, was combined with a most prepossessing countenance. He was light-haired and blue-eyed; ingenuousness and sincerity marked his physiognomy. The few words he had spoken were enforced by a graceful cordiality of manner, and a silver-toned voice, that won the heart. Lodore was struck by his prepossessing exterior, and replied with warm thanks; adding, that his services would be most acceptable on certain conditions,—which were merely that he should put no obstacle to the immediate termination of the quarrel, in any mode, however desperate, which his adversary might propose. "Otherwise," Lodore added, "I must entirely decline your interference. All this is to me matter of far higher import than mere life and death, and I can submit to no control."

"Then my services must be limited to securing fair play for you," said Mr. Villiers.

During this brief parley, they were in the street, proceeding towards the place of meeting. Day had declined, and the crescent moon was high in the heavens: each instant its beams grew more refulgent, as twilight yielded to night.

"We shall have no difficulty in seeing each other," said Lodore, in a cheerful voice. He felt cheerful: a burthen was lifted from his heart. How much must a brave man suffer under the accusation of cowardice, and how joyous when an opportunity is granted of proving his courage! Lodore was brave to rashness: at this crisis he felt as if about to be born again to all the earthly blessings of which he had been deprived so long. He did not think of the dread baptism of blood which was to occasion his regeneration—still less of personal danger; he thought only of good name restored—of his reputation for courage vindicated—of the insolence of this ill-spoken fellow signally chastised.

"Have you weapons?" asked his companion.

"They will procure pistols, I suppose," replied Lodore: "we should lose much time by going to the hotel for mine."

"We are passing that where I am," said Mr. Villiers. "If you will wait one moment I will fetch mine;—or will you go up with me?"

They entered the house, and the apartments of Mr. Villiers. At such moments slight causes operate changes on the human heart; and as various impulses sweep like winds over its chords, that subtle instrument gives forth various tones. A moment ago, Lodore seemed to raise his proud head to the stars: he felt as if escaping from a dim, intricate cavern, into the blessed light of day. The strong excitement permitted no second thought—no second image. With a lighter step than Mr. Villiers, he followed that gentleman up-stairs. For a moment, as he went into an inner apartment for the pistols, Lodore was alone: a desk was open on the table; and paper, unwritten on, upon the desk. Scarcely knowing what he did, Lodore took the pen, and wrote—"Ethel, my child! my life's dearest blessing! be virtuous, be useful, be happy!—farewell, for ever!"—and under this he wrote Mrs. Greville's address. The first words were written with a firm hand; but the recollection of all that might occur, made his fingers tremble as he continued, and the direction was nearly illegible. "If any thing happens to me," said he to Mr. Villiers, "you will add to your kindness immeasurably by going there,"—pointing to the address,—"and taking precaution that my daughter may hear of her disaster in as tender a manner as possible."

"Is there any thing else?" asked his companion. "Command me freely, I beseech you; I will obey your injunctions to the letter."

"It is too late now," replied the noble; "and we must not keep these gentlemen waiting. The little I have to say we will talk of as we walk."

"I feel," continued Lodore, after they were again in the street, "that if this meeting end fatally, I have no power to enforce my wishes and designs beyond the grave. The providence which has so strangely conducted the drama of my life, will proceed in its own way after the final catastrophe. I commit my daughter to a higher power than mine, secure that so much innocence and goodness must receive blessings, even in this ill-grained state of existence. You will see Mrs. Greville: she is a kind-hearted, humane woman, and will exert herself to console my child. Ethel—Miss Fitzhenry, I mean—must, as soon as is practicable, return to England. She will be received there by my sister, and remain with her till—till her fate be otherwise decided. We were on the point of sailing;—I have fitted up a cabin for her;—she might make the voyage in that very vessel. You, perhaps, will consult—though what claim have I on you?"

"A claim most paramount," interrupted Villiers eagerly,—"that of a countryman in a foreign land—of a gentleman vindicating his honour at the probable expense of life."

"Thank you!" replied Lodore;—"my heart thanks you—for my own sake, and for my daughter's—if indeed you will kindly render her such services as her sudden loss may make sadly necessary."

"Depend upon me;—though God grant she need them not!"

"For her sake, I say Amen!" said Lodore; "for my own—life is a worn-out garment—few tears will be shed upon my grave, except by Ethel."

"There is yet another," said Villiers with visible hesitation: "pardon me, if I appear impertinent; but at such a moment, may I not name Lady Lodore?"

"For her, indeed," answered the peer, "the event of this evening, if fatal to me, will prove fortunate: she will be delivered from a heavy chain. May she be happy in another choice! Are you acquainted with her?"

"I am, slightly—that is, not very intimately."

"If you meet her on your return to England," continued the noble;—"if you ever see Lady Lodore, tell her that I invoked a blessing on her with my latest breath—that I forgive her, and ask her forgiveness. But we are arrived. Remember Ethel."

"Yet one moment," cried Villiers;—"one moment of reflection, of calm! Is there no way of preventing this encounter?"

"None!—fail me not, I entreat you, in this one thing;—interpose no obstacle—be as eager and as firm as I myself am. Our friends have chosen a rising ground: we shall be excellent marks for one another. Pray do not lose time."

The American and his second stood in dark relief against the moon-lit sky. As the rays fell upon the English noble, Hatfield observed to his companion, that he now perfectly recognized him, and wondered at his previous blindness. Perhaps he felt some compunction for the insult he had offered; but he said nothing, and no attempt was made on either side at amicable explanation. They proceeded at once, with a kind of savage indifference, to execute the murderous designs which caused them to disturb the still and lovely night.

It was indeed a night, that love, and hope, and all the softer emotions of the soul, would have felt congenial to them. A balmy, western breeze lifted the hair lightly from Lodore's brow, and played upon his cheek; the trees were bathed in yellow moonshine; a glow-worm stealing along the grass scarce showed its light; and sweet odours were wafted from grove and field. Lodore stood, with folded arms, gazing upon the scene in silence, while the seconds were arranging preliminaries, and loading the firearms. None can tell what thoughts then passed through his mind. Did he rejoice in his honour redeemed, or grieve for the human being at whose breast he was about to aim?—or were his last thoughts spent upon the account he might so speedily be called on to render before his Creator's throne? When at last he took his weapon from the hand of Villiers, his countenance was serene, though solemn; and his voice firm and calm. "Remember me to Ethel," he said; "and tell her to thank you;—I cannot sufficiently; yet I do so from my heart. If I live—then more of this."

The antagonists were placed: they were both perfectly self-possessed—bent, with hardness and cruelty of purpose, on fulfilling the tragic act. As they stood face to face—a few brief paces only intervening—on the moon-lit hill—neither had ever been more alive, more full of conscious power, of moral and physical energy, than at that moment. Villiers saw them standing beneath the silver moonbeams, each in the pride of life, of strength, of resolution. A ray glanced from

CHAPTER XVII

"En cor gentil, amor per mort no passa."

—*Ausias March, troubadour*

We return to Longfield and to Mrs. Elizabeth Fitzhenry. The glory of summer invested the world with light, cheerfulness, and beauty, when the sorrowing sister of Lodore visited London, to receive her orphan niece from the hands of the friend of Mrs. Greville, under whose protection she had made the voyage. The good lady folded poor Ethel in her arms, overcome by the likeness she saw to her beloved brother Henry, in his youthful days, before passion had worn and misfortune saddened him. Her soft, brown, lamp-like eyes, beamed with the same sensibility. Yet when she examined her more closely, Mrs Elizabeth lost somewhat of the likeness; for the lower part of her face resembled her mother: her hair was lighter and her complexion much fairer than Lodore; besides that the expression of her countenance was peculiar to herself, and possessed that individuality which is so sweet to behold, but impossible to describe.

They lingered but a few days in London. Fanny Derham, who accompanied her on her voyage, had already returned to her father, and there was nothing to detain them from Longfield. Ethel had no adieus to make that touched her heart. Her aunt was more to her than any other living being, and her strongest desire now was, to visit the scenes once hallowed by her father's presence. The future was a chaos of dark regret and loneliness; her whole life, she thought, would be composed of one long memory.

One memory, and one fatal image. Ethel had not only consecrated her heart to her father, but his society was a habit with her, and, until now, she had never even thought how she could endure existence without the supporting influence of his affection. His conversation, so full of a kind penetration into her thoughts, was calculated to develop and adorn them; his manly sense and paternal solicitude, had all fostered a filial love, the most tender and strong. Add to this, his sudden and awful death. Already had they schemed their future life in a world new to Ethel: he had excited her enthusiasm by descriptions of the wonders of art in the old countries, and raised her curiosity while promising to satisfy it; and she had eagerly looked forward to the time when she should see the magical works of man, and mingle with a system of society, of which, except by books, he alone presented any ensample to her. Their voyage was fixed, and on the other side of their watery way she had figured a very Elysium of wonders and pleasures. The late change in their mode of life had served to endear him doubly to her. It had been the occupation of her life to think of her father, to communicate all her thoughts to him, and in the unreflecting confidence of youth, she had looked forward to no termination of a state of existence, that had began from her cradle. He propped her entire world; the foundations must moulder and crumble away without him—and he was gone— where then was she?

Mr. Villiers had, as soon as he was able, hurried to Mrs. Greville's house. By some strange chance, the fatal tidings had preceded him, and he found the daughter of the unfortunate Lodore bewildered and maddened by her frightful calamity. Her first desire was to see all that was left of her parent—she could not believe that he was indeed dead— she was certain that care and skill might revive him—she insisted on being led to his side; her friends strove to restrain her, but she rushed into the street, she knew not whither, to ask for, to find her father.

The timidity of her temper was overborne by the wild expectation of yet being able to recall him from among the dead. Villiers followed her, and, yielding to her wishes, guided her towards the hotel whither the remains of Lodore had been carried. He judged that the exertion of walking thither, and the time that must elapse before she arrived, would calm and subdue her. He talked to her of her father as they went along—he endeavoured to awaken the source of tears—but she was silent—absorbed—brooding darkly on her hopes. Pity for herself had not yet arisen, nor the frightful certainty of bereavement. To see those dear lineaments—to touch his hand—the very hand that had so often caressed her, clay-cold and incapable of motion! Could it be!

She did not answer Villiers, she only hurried forward; she feared obstruction to her wishes; her soul was set on one thought only. Had Villiers endeavoured to deceive her, it would have been in vain. Arrived at the hotel, as by instinct, she sprung up the stairs, and reached the door of the room. It was darkened, in useless but decent respect for the death within; there lay a figure covered by a sheet, and already chilling the atmosphere around it. The imagination is slow to act upon the feelings in comparison with the quick operation of the senses. Ethel now knew that her father was dead. Mortal strength could support no more—the energy of hope deserting her, she sunk lifeless on the ground.

For a long time she was passive in the hands of others. A violent illness confined her to her bed, and physical suffering subdued the excess of mental agony. Villiers left her among kind friends. It was resolved that she and Fanny Derham should proceed to England, under the protection of the friends of Mrs. Greville about to return thither; he was himself obliged to return to England without delay.

Ethel's destiny was as yet quite uncertain. It was decided by the opening of her father's will. This had been made twelve years before on his first arrival at New York, and breathed the spirit of resentment, and even revenge, against his wife. Lodore had indeed not much wealth to leave. His income chiefly consisted in a grant from the crown, entailed on heirs male, which in default of these, reverted back, and in a sinecure which expired with him. His paternal estate at Longfield, and a sum under twenty thousand pounds, the savings of twelve years, formed all his possessions. The income arising from the former was absorbed by Lady Lodore's jointure of a thousand a year, and five hundred a year settled on his sister, together with permission to occupy the family mansion during her life. The remaining sum was disposed of in a way most singular. Without referring to the amount of what he could leave, he bequeathed the additional sum of six hundred a year to Lady Lodore, on the express condition, that she should not interfere with, nor even see, her child; upon her failing in this condition, this sum was to be left to accumulate till Ethel was of age. Ethel was ultimately to inherit every thing; but while her mother and aunt lived, her fortune consisted of little more than five thousand pounds; and even in this, she was limited to the use of the interest only until she was of age; a previous marriage would have no influence on the disposition of her property. Mrs. Elizabeth was left her guardian.

This will was in absolute contradiction to the wishes and feelings in which Lord Lodore died; so true had his prognostic been, that he had no power beyond the grave. He had probably forgotten the existence of this will, or imagined that it had been destroyed: he had determined to make a new one on his arrival in England. Meanwhile it was safely deposited with his solicitor in London, and Mrs. Elizabeth, with mistaken zeal, hastened to put it into force, and showed herself eager to obey her brother's wishes with scrupulous exactitude. The contents of it were communicated to Lady Lodore. She made no comment—returned no answer. She was suddenly reduced from comparative affluence (for her husband's allowance had consisted of several thousands) to a bare sixteen hundred a year. Whether she would be willing to diminish this her scanty income one third, and take on herself, besides, the care of her daughter, was not known. She remained inactive and silent, and Ethel was placed at once under the guardianship of her aunt.

These two ladies left London in the old lumbering chariot which had belonged to the Admiral. Now, indeed, Ethel found herself in a new country, with new friends around her, speaking a new language, and each change of scene made more manifest the complete revolution of her fortunes. She looked on all with languid eyes, and a heart dead to every pleasure. Her aunt, who bore a slight resemblance of her father, won some degree of interest; and the sole consolation offered her, was to trace a similarity of voice and feature, and thus to bring the lost Lodore more vividly before her. The journey to Longfield was therefore not wholly without a melancholy charm. Mrs. Elizabeth longed to obtain more minute information concerning her brother, her pride and her delight, than had been contained in his short and infrequent letters. She hazarded a few questions. Grief loves to feed upon itself, and to surround itself with multiplications of its own image; like a bee, it will find sweets in the poison flower, and nestle within its own creations, although they pierce the heart that cherishes them. Ethel felt a fascination in dwelling for ever on the past. She asked for nothing better than to live her life over again, while narrating its simple details, and to bring her father back from his grave to dwell with her, by discoursing perpetually concerning him. She was unwearied in her descriptions, her anecdotes, her praises. The Illinois rose before the eyes of her aunt, like a taintless paradise, inhabited by an angel. Love and good dwelt together there in blameless union; the sky was brighter; the earth fairer, fresher, younger, more magnificent, and more wonderful, than in the old world. The good lady called to mind, with surprise, the melancholy and despairing letters she had received from her brother, while inhabiting this Eden. It was matter of mortification to his mourning daughter to hear, as from himself, as it were, that any sorrows had visited his heart while with her. When we love one to whom we have devoted our lives with undivided affection, the idea that the beloved object suffered any grief while with us, jars with our sacred sorrow. We delight to make the difference between the possession of their society, and our subsequent bereavement, entire in its contrasted happiness and misery;

from all heart-felt communication with her fellow-creatures, but the presence of Ethel fulfilled her soul's desire; she found sympathy, and an auditress, into whose ever-attentive ear she could pour those reveries which she had so long nourished in secret. Whoso had heard the good lady talk of endless tears and mourning for the loss of Lodore, of life not worth having when he was gone, of the sad desolation of their position, and looked at her face, beaming with satisfaction, with only so much sensibility painted there as to render it expressive of all that is kind and compassionate, good-humour in her frequent smile, and sleek content in her plump person, might have laughed at the contrast; and yet have pondered on the strange riddle we human beings present, and how contradictions accord in our singular machinery. This good aunt was incapable of affectation, and all was true and real that she said. She lived upon the idea of her brother; he was all in all to her, but they had been divided so long, that his death scarcely increased the separation; and she could talk of meeting him in heaven, with as firm and cheerful a faith, as a few months before she had anticipated his return to England. Though sincere in her regret for his death, habit had turned lamentation into a healthy nutriment, so that she throve upon the tears she shed, and grew fat and cheerful upon her sighs. She would lead the agonized girl to the vault which contained the remains of her brother, and hover near it, as a Catholic beside the shrine of a favourite saint— the visible image giving substance and form to her reverie; for hitherto, her dreamy life had wanted the touch of reality, which the presence of her niece, and the sad memorial of her lost brother, afforded.

The home-felt sensations of the mourning orphan, were in entire contrast to this holiday woe. While her aunt brooded over her sorrow "to keep it warm," it wrapped Ethel's soul as with a fiery torture. Every cheerful thought lay buried with her father, and the tears she shed near his grave were accompanied by a wrenching of her being, and a consequent exhaustion, that destroyed the elasticity of the spirit of youth. The memory of Lodore, which soothed his sister, haunted his child like a sad beckoning, yet fatal vision; she yearned to reach the shore where his pale ghost perpetually wandered—the earth seemed a dark prison, and liberty and light dwelt with the dead beyond the grave. Eternally conversant with the image of death, she was brought into too near communion with the grim enemy of life. She wasted and grew pale: nor did any voice speak to her of the unreasonableness of her grief; her father was not near to teach her fortitude, and there appeared a virtue and a filial piety in the excess of her regret, which blinded her aunt to the fatal consequences of its indulgence.

While summer lasted, and the late autumn protracted its serenity almost into winter, Ethel wandered in the lanes and fields; and in spite of wasting grief, the free air of heaven, which swept her cheek, preserved its healthy hue and braced her limbs. But when dreary inclement winter arrived, and the dull fireside of aunt Bessy became the order of the day, without occupation to amuse, or society to distract her thoughts, given up to grief, and growing into a monument of woe, it became evident that the springs of life were becoming poisoned, and that health and existence itself were giving way before the destructive influences at work within. Appetite first, then sleep, deserted her. A slight cold became a cough, and then changed into a preying fever. She grew so thin that her large eyes, shining with unnatural lustre, appeared to occupy too much of her face, and her brow was streaked with ghastly hues. Poor Mrs. Elizabeth, when she found that neither arrow-root nor chicken-broth restored her, grew frightened—the village practitioner exhausted his skill without avail. Ethel herself firmly believed that she was going to die, and fondly cherished the hope of rejoining her father. She was in love with death, which alone could reunite her to the being, apart from whom she believed it impossible to exist.

But limits were now placed to Mrs. Elizabeth's romance. The danger of Ethel was a frightful reality that awoke every natural feeling. Ethel, the representative of her brother, the last of their nearly extinct race, the sole relation she possessed, the only creature whom she could entirely love, was dear to her beyond expression; and the dread of losing her gave activity to her slothful resolves. Having seldom, during the whole course of her life, been called upon to put any plan or wish of her's into actual execution, what another would have immediately and easily done, was an event to call forth all her energies, and to require all her courage; luckily she possessed sufficient to meet the present exigency. She wrote up to London to her single correspondent there, her brother's solicitor. A house was taken, and the first warm days of spring found the ladies established in the metropolis. A physician had been called in, and he pronounced the mind only to be sick. "Amuse her," he said, "occupy her—prevent her from dwelling on those thoughts which have preyed upon her health; let her see new faces, new places, every thing new—and youth, and a good constitution, will do the rest."

There seemed so much truth in this advice, that all dangerous symptoms disappeared from the moment of Ethel's leaving Essex. Her strength returned—her face resumed its former loveliness; and aunt Bessy, overjoyed at the change, occupied herself earnestly in discovering amusements for her niece in the numerous, wide-spread, and very busy congregation of human beings, which forms the western portion of London.

• • •

CHAPTER XVIII

"You are now
In London, that great sea, whose ebb and flow,
At once is deaf and loud."

—*Shelley*

There is no uninhabited desart so dreary as the peopled streets of London, to those who have no ties with its inhabitants, nor any pursuits in common with its busy crowds. A drop of water in the ocean is no symbol of the situation of an isolated individual thrown upon the stream of metropolitan life; that amalgamates with its kindred element; but the solitary being finds no pole of attraction to cause a union with its fellows, and bastilled by the laws of society, it is condemned to incommunicative solitude.

Ethel was thrown completely upon her aunt, and her aunt was a cypher in the world. She had not a single acquaintance in London, and was wholly inexperienced in its ways. She dragged Ethel about to see sights, and Ethel was amused for a time. The playhouses were a great source of entertainment to her, and all kinds of exhibitions, panoramas, and shows, served to fill up her day. Still the great want of all shed an air of dulness over every thing—the absence of human intercourse, and of the conversation and sympathy of her species. Ethel, as she drove through the mazy streets, and mingled with the equipages in the park, could not help thinking what pleasant people might be found among without a wish to draw near to afford protection and support; and the soft expression of her full eyes added to the charm. Her deep mourning dress, the simplicity of her appearance, her face so prettily shaded by her bright ringlets, often caused her to be remarked, and people asked one another who she was. None knew; and the old-fashioned appearance of Mrs. Elizabeth Fitzhenry, and the want of style which characterized all her arrangements, prevented our very aristocratic gentry from paying as much attention to her as they otherwise would.

One day, this gentle, solitary pair attended a morning concert. Ethel had not been to the Opera, and now heard Pasta for the first time. Her father had cultivated her taste for Italian music; for without cultivation—without in some degree understanding and being familiar with an art, it is rare that we admire even the most perfect specimens of it. Ethel listened with wrapt attention; her heart beat quick, and her eyes became suffused with tears which she could not suppress;—so she leant forward, shading her face as much as she could with her veil, and trying to forget the throng of strangers about her. They were in the pit; and having come in late, sat at the end of one of the forms. Pasta's air was concluded; and she still turned aside, being too much agitated to wish to speak, when she heard her aunt addressing some one as an old acquaintance. She called her friend "Captain Markham," expressed infinite pleasure at seeing him, and whispered her niece that here was an old friend of her father's. Ethel turned and beheld Mr. Villiers. His face lighted up with pleasure, and he expressed his joy at the chance which had produced the meeting; but the poor girl was unable to reply. All colour deserted her cheeks; marble pale and cold, her voice failed, and her heart seemed to die within her. The room where last she saw the lifeless remains of her father rose before her; and the appearance of Mr. Villiers was as a vision from another world, speaking of the dead. Mrs. Elizabeth, considerably surprised, asked her how she came to know Captain Markham. Ethel would have said, "Let us go!" but her voice died away, and she felt that tears would follow any attempt at explanation. Ashamed of the very possibility of occasioning a scene, and yet too disturbed to know well what she was about, she suddenly rose, and though the commencement of a new air was commanding silence and attention; she hastily quitted the room, and found herself alone, outside the door, before her aunt was well aware that she was gone. She claimed Captain Markham's assistance to follow the fugitive; and, attended by him, at length discovered her chariot, to which Ethel had been led by the servant, and in which she was sitting, weeping bitterly. Mrs. Elizabeth felt inclined to ask her whether she was mad; but she also was struck dumb; for her Captain Markham had said—"I am very sorry to have distressed Miss Fitzhenry. My name is Villiers. I cannot wonder at her agitation; but it would give me much pleasure if she would permit me to call on her, when she can see me with more composure."

With these words, he assisted the good lady into the carriage, bowed, and disappeared. He was not Captain Markham! How could she have been so stupid as to imagine that he was? He looked, upon the whole, rather younger than Captain Markham had done, when she formed acquaintance with him, during her expedition to London on the occasion of Ethel's christening. He was taller, too, and not quite so stout; yet he was so like—the same frank, open countenance, the same ingenuous manner, and the same clear blue eyes. Certainly Captain Markham was not so handsome;—and what a fool Mr. Villiers must think her, for having mistaken him for a person who resembled him sixteen years ago; quite forgetting that Mr. Villiers was ignorant who her former friend was, and when she had seen him. All these perplexing thoughts passed through Mrs. Fitzhenry's brain, tinging her aged cheek with a blush of shame; while Ethel, having recovered herself, was shocked to remember how foolishly and rudely she had behaved; and longed to apologize, yet knew not how; and fancied that it was very unlikely that she should ever see Mr. Villiers again. Her aunt, engaged by her own distress, quite forgot the intention he had expressed of calling, and could only exclaim and lament over her folly. The rest of the day was spent with great discomfort to both; for the sight of Mr. Villiers renewed all Ethel's sorrows; and again and again she bestowed the tribute of showers of tears to her dear father's memory.

The following day, much to Ethel's delight, and the annoyance of Mrs. Elizabeth, who could not get over her sense of shame, Mr. Villiers presented himself in their drawing-room. Villiers, however, was a man speedily to overcome even any prejudice formed against him; far more easily, therefore, could he obviate the good aunt's confusion, and put her at her ease. His was one of those sunny countenances that spoke a heart ready to give itself away in kindness;—a cheering voice, whose tones echoed the frankness and cordiality of his nature. Blest with a buoyant, and even careless spirit, as far as regarded himself, he had a softness, a delicacy, and a gentleness, with respect to others, which animated his manners with irresistible fascination. His heart was open to pity—his soul the noblest and clearest ever fashioned by nature in her happiest mood. He had been educated in the world—he lived for the world, for he had not genius to raise himself above the habits and pursuits of his countrymen: yet he took only the better part of their practices; and shed a grace over them, so alien to their essence, that any one might have been deceived, and have fancied that he proceeded on a system and principles of his own.

He had travelled a good deal, and was somewhat inclined, when pleased with his company, to narrate his adventures and experiences. Ethel was naturally rather taciturn; and Mrs. Elizabeth was too much absorbed in the pleasure of listening, to interrupt their visitor. He felt himself peculiarly happy and satisfied between the two, and his visit was excessively long; nor did he go away before he had appointed to call the next day, and opened a long vista of future visits for himself, assisted by the catalogue of all that the ladies had not seen, and all that they desired to see, in London.

Villiers had been animated while with them, but he left the house full of thought. The name of Fitzhenry, or rather that of Lodore, was familiar to him; and the strange chance that had caused him to act as second to the lamented noble who bore this title, and which brought him in contact with his orphan and solitary daughter, appeared to him like the enchantment of fairy land. From the presence of Ethel, he proceeded to Lady Lodore's house, which was still shut up; yet he knocked, and inquired of the servant whether she had returned to England. She was still at Baden, he was told, and not expected for a month or two; and this answer involved him in deeper thought than before.

• • •

VOLUME II

CHAPTER I

"Excellent creature! whose perfections make
Even sorrow lovely!"

—*Beaumont and Fletcher*

Mr. Villiers now became the constant visitor of Mrs. Elizabeth and her niece; and all discontent, all sadness, all listlessness, vanished in his presence. There was in his mind a constant spring of vivacity, which did not display itself in mere gaiety, but in being perfectly alive at every moment, and continually ready to lend himself to the comfort and solace of his companions. Sitting in their dingy London house, the spirit of dulness had drawn a curtain between them and the sun; and neither thought nor event had penetrated the fortification of silence and neglect which environed them. Edward Villiers came; and as mist flies before the wind, so did all Ethel's depression disappear when his voice only met her ear: his step on the stairs announced happiness; and when he was indeed before her, light and day displaced every remnant of cheerless obscurity.

The abstracted, wounded, yet lofty spirit of Lodore was totally dissimilar to the airy brightness of Villiers' disposition. Lodore had outlived a storm, and shown himself majestic in ruin. No ill had tarnished the nature of Villiers: he enjoyed life, he was in good-humour with the world, and thought well of mankind. Lodore had endangered his peace from the violence of passion, and reaped misery from the

pride of his soul. Villiers was imprudent from his belief in the goodness of his fellow-creatures, and imparted happiness from the store that
his warm heart insured to himself. The one had never been a boy—the
other had not yet learned to be a man.

Ethel's heart had been filled by her father; and all affection, all interest, borrowed their force from his memory. She did not think of love;
and while Villiers was growing into a part of her life, becoming knit to
her existence by daily habit, and a thousand thoughts expended on him,
she entertained his idea chiefly as having been the friend of Lodore. "He
is certainly the kindest-hearted creature in the world." This was the third
time that, when laying her gentle head on the pillow, this feeling came
like a blessing to her closing eyes. She heard his voice in the silence of
night, even more distinctly than when it was addressed to her outward
sense during the day. For the first time after the lapse of months, she
found one to whom she could spontaneously utter every thought, as it
rose in her mind. A fond, elder brother, if such ever existed, cherishing
the confidence and tenderness of a beloved sister, might fill the place
which her new friend assumed for Ethel. She thought of him with
overflowing affection; and the name of "Mr. Villiers" sometimes fell
from her lips in solitude, and hung upon her ear like sweetest music.
In early life there is a moment—perhaps of all the enchantments of
love it is the one which is never renewed—when passion, unacknowledged to ourselves, imparts greater delight than any after-stage of that
ever-progressive sentiment. We neither wish nor expect. A new joy has
risen, like the sun, upon our lives; and we rejoice in the radiance of
morning, without adverting to the noon and twilight that is to follow.
Ethel stood on the threshold of womanhood: the door of life had been
closed before her;—again it was thrown open—and the sudden splendour that manifested itself blinded her to the forms of the objects of
menace or injury, which a more experienced eye would have discerned
within the brightness of her new-found day.

Ethel expressed a wish to visit Eton. In talking of the past, Lord
Lodore had never adverted to any events except those which had

occurred during his boyish days. His youthful pleasures and exploits had often made a part of their conversation. He had traced for her a plan of Eton college, and the surrounding scenery; spoken of the trembling delight he had felt in escaping from bounds; and told how he and Derham had passed happy hours beside the clear streams, and beneath the copses, of that rural country. There was one fountain which he delighted to celebrate; and the ivied ruins of an old monastery, now become a part of a farm-yard, which had been to these friends the bodily image of many imaginary scenes. Among the sketches of Whitelock, were several taken in the vicinity of Windsor; and there were, in his portfolio, studies of trees, cottages, and also of this same abbey, which Lodore instantly recognized. To many he had some appending anecdote, some school-boy association. He had purchased the whole collection from Whitelock. Ethel had copied a few; and these, together with various sketches made in the Illinois, formed her dearest treasure, more precious in her eyes than diamonds and rubies.

We are most jealous of what sits nearest to our hearts; and we must love fondly before we can let another into the secret of those trivial, but cherished emotions, which form the dearest portion of our solitary meditations. Ethel had several times been on the point of proposing a visit to Eton, to her aunt; but there was an awful sacredness in the very name, which acted like a spell upon her imagination. When first it fell from her lips, the word seemed echoed by unearthly whisperings, and she fled from the idea of going thither,—as it is the feminine disposition often to do, from the full accomplishment of its wishes, as if disaster must necessarily be linked to the consummation of their desires. But a word was enough for Villiers: he eagerly solicited permission to escort them thither, as, being an Etonian himself, his guidance would be of great advantage. Ethel faltered her consent; and the struggle of delight and sensibility made that project appear painful, which was indeed the darling of her thoughts.

On a bright day in the first week of May, they made this excursion. They repaired to one of the inns at Salt Hill, and prolonged their walks and drives about the country. In some of the former, where old walls were to be scrambled up, and rivulets overleaped, Mrs. Elizabeth remained at the hotel, and Ethel and Villiers pursued their rambles together. Ethel's whole soul was given up to the deep filial love that had induced the journey. Every green field was a stage on which her father had played a part; each majestic tree, or humble streamlet, was hallowed by being associated with his image. The pleasant, verdant beauty of the landscape, clad in all the brightness of early summer; the sunny, balmy day—the clouds which pranked the heavens with bright and floating shapes—each hedgerow and each cottage, with its trim garden—each embowered nook—had a voice which was music to her soul. From the college of Eton, they sought the dame's house where Lodore and Derham had lived; then crossing the bridge, they entered Windsor, and prolonged their walk into the forest. Ethel knew even the rustic names of the spots she most desired to visit, and to these Villiers led her in succession. Day declined before they got home, and found Mrs. Elizabeth, and their repast, waiting them; and the evening was enlivened by many a tale of boyish pranks, achieved by Villiers, in these scenes. The following morning they set forth again; and three days were spent in these delightful wanderings. Ethel would willingly never have quitted this spot: it appeared to her as if, seeing all, still much remained to be seen—as if she could never exhaust the variety of sentiments and deep interest which endeared every foot of this to her so holy ground. Nor were her emotions silent, and the softness of her voice, and the flowing eloquence with which she expressed herself, formed a new charm for her companion.

Sometimes her heart was too full to admit of expression, and grief for her father's loss was renewed in all its pristine bitterness. One day, on feeling herself thus overcome, she quitted her companions, and sought the shady walks of the garden of the hotel, to indulge in a gush of sorrow which she could not repress. There was something in her gesture and manner as she left them, that reminded Villiers of Lady Lodore. It was one of those mysterious family resemblances, which are so striking and powerful, and yet which it is impossible to point out to a stranger. A *bligh* (as this indescribable resemblance is called in some parts of England) of her mother struck Villiers forcibly, and he suddenly asked Mrs. Elizabeth, "If Miss Fitzhenry had never expressed a desire to see Lady Lodore."

"God forbid!" exclaimed the old lady; "it was my brother's dying wish, that she should never hear Lady Lodore's name, and I have religiously observed it. Ethel only knows that she was the cause of her father's misfortunes, that she deserted every duty, and is unworthy of the name she bears."

Villiers was astonished at this tirade falling from the lips of the unusually placid maiden, whose heightened colour bespoke implacable resentment. "Do not mention that woman's name, Mr. Villiers," she continued, "I am convinced that I should die on the spot if I saw her; she is as much a murderess, as if she had stabbed her husband to the heart with a dagger. Her letter to me that I sent to my poor brother in America, was more the cause of his death, I am sure, than all the duels in the world. Lady Lodore! I often wonder a thunderbolt from heaven does not fall on and kill her!"

Mrs. Elizabeth's violence was checked by seeing Ethel cross the road to return. "Promise not to mention her name to my niece," she cried.

"For the present be assured that I will not," Villiers answered. He had been struck most painfully by some of Mrs. Elizabeth's expressions, they implied so much more of misconduct on Lady Lodore's part, than he had ever suspected—but she must know best; and it seemed to him, indeed, the probable interpretation of the mystery that enveloped her separation from her husband. The account spread by Lady Santerre, and current in the world, appeared inadequate and improbable; Lodore would not have dared to take her child from her, but on heavier grounds; it was then true, that a dark and disgraceful secret was hidden in her heart, and that her propriety, her good reputation, her seeming pride of innocence, were but the mask to cover the reality that divided her from her daughter for ever.

Villiers was well acquainted with Lady Lodore; circumstances had caused him to take a deep interest in her—these were now at an end: but the singular coincidences that had brought him in contact with her daughter, renewed many forgotten images, and caused him to dwell on the past with mixed curiosity and uneasiness. Mrs. Elizabeth's expressions added to the perplexity of his ideas; their chief effect was to tarnish to his mind the name of Lady Lodore, and to make him rejoice at the termination that had been put to their more intimate connexion.

• • •

CHAPTER II

"One, within whose subtle being,
As light and wind within some delicate cloud,
That fades amid the blue noon's burning sky.
Genius and youth contended."

—*Shelley*

The party returned to town, and on the following evening they went to the Italian Opera. For the first time since her father's death, Ethel threw aside her mourning attire: for the first time also, she made one of the audience at the King's Theatre. She went to hear the music, and to spend the evening with the only person in the world who was drawn towards her by feelings of kindness and sympathy—the only person—but that sufficed. His being near her, was the occasion of more delight than if she had been made the associate of regal splendour. Yet it was no defined or disturbing sentiment, that sat so lightly on her bosom and shone in her eyes. Hers was the first gentle opening of a girl's heart, who does not busy herself with the future, and reposes on the serene present with unquestioning confidence. She looked round on the gay world assembled, and thought, "All are as happy as I am." She listened to the music with a subdued but charmed spirit, and turned now and then to her companions with a glad smile, expressive of her delight. Fewer words were spoken in their little box, probably than in any in the house; but in none were congregated three hearts so guileless, and so perfectly satisfied with the portion allotted to them.

At length both opera and ballet were over, and, leaning on the arm of Villiers, the ladies entered the round-room. The house had been very full and the crowd was great. A seat was obtained for Aunt Bessy on one of the sofas near the door, which opened on the principal stair-case. Villiers and Ethel stood near her. When the crowd had thinned a little, Villiers went to look for the servant, and Ethel remained sur-veying the moving numbers with curiosity, wondering at her own fate, that while every one seemed familiar one to the other, she knew, and was known by, none. She did not repine at this; Villiers had dissipated the sense of desertion which before haunted her, and she was much entertained, as she heard the remarks and interchange of compliments going on about her. Her attention was particularly attracted by a very beautiful woman, or rather girl she seemed, standing on the other side of the room, conversing with a very tall personage, to whom she, being not above the middle size, looked up as she talked; which action, per-haps, added to her youthful appearance. There was an ease in her man-ners that bespoke a matron as to station. She was dressed very simply in white, without any ornament; her cloak hung carelessly from her shoulders, and gave to view her round symmetrical figure; her silky, chestnut-coloured hair, fell in thick ringlets round her face, and was gathered with inimitable elegance in large knots on the top of her head. There was something bewitching in her animated smile, and sensibil-ity beamed from her long and dark grey eyes; her simple gesture as she placed her little hand on her cloak, her attitude as she stood, were wholly unpretending, but graceful beyond measure. Ethel watched her unob-served, with admiration and interest, so that she almost forgot where she was, until the voice of Villiers recalled her. "Your carriage is up—will you come?" The lady turned as he spoke, and recognized him with a cordial and most sweet smile. They moved on, while Ethel turned back to look again, as her carriage was loudly called, and Mrs. Elizabeth seizing her arm, whispered out of breath, "O my dear, do make haste!" She hurried on, therefore, and her glance was momentary; but she saw with wonder, that the lady was looking with eagerness at the party; she caught Ethel's eye, blushed and turned away, while the folding doors closed, and with a kind of nervous trepidation her companions descended the stairs. In a moment the ladies were in their carriage, which drove off, while Mrs. Elizabeth exclaimed in the tone of one aghast, "Thank God, we got away! O, Ethel, that was Lady Lodore!"

"My mother!—impossible!"

"O, that we had never come to town," continued her aunt. "Long have I prayed that I might never see her again;—and she looking as if nothing had happened, and that Lodore had not died through her means! Wicked, wicked woman! I will not stay in London a day longer!"

Ethel did not interrupt her ravings: she remembered Captain Markham, and could not believe but that her aunt laboured under some similar mistake; it was ridiculous to imagine, that this girlish-looking, lovely being, had been the wife of her father, whom she remembered with his high forehead rather bare of hair, his deep marked countenance, his look that bespoke more than mature age. Her aunt was mistaken, she felt sure; and yet when she closed her eyes, the beautiful figure she had seen stole, according to the Arabian image, beneath her lids, and smiled sweetly, and again started forward to look after her. This little act seemed to confirm what Mrs. Elizabeth said; and yet, again, it was impossible! "Had she been named my sister, there were something in it—but my mother,—impossible!"

Yet strange as it seemed, it was so; in this instance, Mrs. Elizabeth had not deceived herself; and thus it was that two so near of kin as mother and daughter, met, it might be said, for the first time. Villiers was inexpressibly shocked; and believing that Lady Lodore must suffer keenly from so strange and unnatural an incident, his first kindly impulse was to seek to see her on the following morning. During her absence, the violent attack of her sister-in-law had weighed with him, but her look at once dissipated his uneasy doubts. There was that in this lady, which no man could resist; she had joined to her beauty, the charm of engaging manners, made up of natural grace, vivacity, intuitive tact, and soft sensibility, which infused a kind of idolatry into the admiration with which she was universally regarded. But it was not the beauty and fashion of Lady Lodore which caused Villiers to take a deep interest in her. His intercourse with her had been of long standing, and the object of his very voyage to America was intimately connected with her.

Edward Villiers was the son of a man of fortune. His father had been left a widower young in life, with this only child, who, thus single and solitary in his paternal home, became almost adopted into the family of his mother's brother, Viscount Maristow. This nobleman being rich, married, and blessed with a numerous progeny, the presence of little Edward was not felt as a burthen, and he was brought up with his cousins like one of them. Among these it would have been hard if Villiers could not have found an especial friend: this was not the elder son, who, much his senior, looked down upon him with friendly regard; it was the second, who was likewise several years older. Horatio Saville was a being fashioned for every virtue and distinguished by every excellence; to know that a thing was right to be done, was enough to impel Horatio to go through fire and water to do it; he was one of those who seem not to belong to this world, yet who adorn it most; conscientious, upright, and often cold in seeming, because he could always master his passions; good over-much, he might be called, but that there was no pedantry nor harshness in his nature. Resolute, aspiring, and true, his noble purposes and studious soul, demanded a frame of iron, and he had one of the frailest mechanism. It was not that he was not tall, well-shaped, with earnest eyes, a brow built up high to receive and entertain a capacious mind; but he was thin and shadowy, a hectic flushed his cheek, and his voice was broken and mournful. At school he held the topmost place, at college he was distinguished by the energy with which he pursued his studies; and these, so opposite from what might have been expected to be the pursuits of his ardent mind, were abstruse metaphysics—the highest and most theoretical mathematics, and cross-grained argument, based upon hair-fine logic; to these he addicted himself. His desire was knowledge; his passion truth; his eager and never-sleeping endeavour was to inform and to satisfy his understanding. Villiers waited on him, as an inferior spirit may attend on an archangel, and gathered from him the crumbs of his knowledge, with gladness and content. He could not force his boyish mind to similar exertions, nor feel that keen thirst for knowledge that kept alive his cousin's application, though he could admire and love these with fervour, when exhibited in another. It was indeed a singular fact, that this constant contemplation of so superior a being, added to his careless turn of mind. Not to be like Horatio was to be nothing— to be like him was impossible. So he was content to remain one of the half-ignorant, uninformed creatures most men are, and to found his pride upon his affection for his cousin, who, being several years older, might well be advanced even beyond his emulation. Horatio himself did not desire to be imitated by the light-hearted Edward; he was too familiar with the exhaustion, the sadness, the disappointment of his pursuits; he could not be otherwise himself, but he thought all that he aspired after, was well exchanged for the sparkling eyes, exhaustless spirits, and buoyant step of Villiers. We none of us wish to exchange our identity for that of another; yet we are never satisfied with our-selves. The unknown has always a charm, and unless blinded by mis-erable vanity, we know ourselves too well to appreciate our especial characteristics at a very high rate. When Horace, after deep midnight study, felt his brain still working like a thousand millwheels, that can-not be stopped; when sleep fled from him, and yet his exhausted mind could no longer continue its labours—he envied the light slumbers of his cousin, which followed exercise and amusement. Villiers loved and revered him; and he felt drawn closer to him than towards any of his brothers, and strove to refine his taste and regulate his conduct through his admonitions and example, while he abstained from following him in the steep and thorny path he had selected.

Horatio quitted college; he was no longer a youth, and his manhood became as studious as his younger days. He had no desire but for knowledge, no thought but for the nobler creations of the soul, and the discernment of the sublime laws of God and nature. He nourished the ambition of showing to these latter days what scholars of old had been, though this feeling was subservient to his instinctive love of learning, and his wish to adorn his mind with the indefeasible attributes of truth. He was universally respected and loved, though little understood. His young cousin Edward only was aware of the earnestness of his affections, and the sensibility that nestled itself in his warm heart. He was outwardly mild, placid, and forbearing, and thus obtained the reputation of being cold—though those who study human nature ought to make it their first maxim, that those who are tolerant of the follies of their fellows—who sympathize with, and assist their wishes, and who apparently forget their own desires, as they devote themselves to the accomplishment of those of their friends, must have the quickest feelings to make them enter into and understand those of others, and the warmest affections to be able to conquer their wayward humours, so that they can divest themselves of selfishness, and incorporate in their own being the pleasures and pains of those around them.

The sparkling eye, the languid step, and flushed cheek of Horatio Saville, were all tokens that there burnt within him a spirit too strong for his frame; but he never complained; or if he ever poured out his pent-up emotions, it was in the ear of Edward only; who but partly understood him, but who loved him entirely. What that thirst for knowledge was that preyed on him, and for ever urged him to drink of the purest streams of wisdom, and yet which ever left him unsatisfied, fevered, and mournful, the gay spirit of Edward Villiers could not guess: often he besought his cousin to close his musty books, to mount a rapid horse, to give his studies to the winds, and deliver his soul to nature. But Horace pointed to some unexplained passage in Plato the divine, or some undiscovered problem in the higher sciences, and turned his eyes from the sun; or if indeed he yielded, and accompanied his youthful friend, some appearance of earth or air would awaken his curiosity, rouze his slumbering mind again to inquire, and making his study of the wide cope of heaven, he gave himself up to abstruse meditation, while nominally seeking for relaxation from his heavier toils.

Horatio Saville was nine-and-twenty when he first met Lady Lodore, who was nearly the same age. He had begun to feel that his health was shaken, and he tried to forget for a time his devouring avocations. He changed the scene, and went on a visit to a friend, who had a country house not far from Hastings. Lady Lodore was expected as a guest, together with her mother. She was much talked of, having become an object of interest or curiosity to the many. A mystery hung over her fate; but her reputation was cloudless, and she was warmly supported by the leaders of fashion. Saville heard of her beauty and her sufferings; the injustice with which she had been treated—of her magnanimity and desolate condition; he heard of her talents, her powers of conversation, her fashion. He figured to himself (as we are apt to incarnate to our imagination the various qualities of a human being, of whom we hear much) a woman, brilliant, but rather masculine, majestic in figure, with wild dark eyes, and a very determined manner. Lady Lodore came: she entered the room where he was sitting, and the fabric of his fancy was at once destroyed. He saw a sweet-looking woman; serene, fair, and with a countenance expressive of contented happiness. He found that her manners were winning, from their softness; her conversation was delightful, from its total want of pretension or impertinence.

What the power was that from the first moment they met, drew Horatio Saville and Lady Lodore together is one of those natural secrets which it is impossible to explain. Though a student, Saville was a gentleman, with the manners and appearance of the better specimens of our aristocracy. There might be something in his look of ill health, which demanded sympathy; something in his superiority to the rest of the persons about her, in the genius that sat on his brow, and the eloquence that flowed from his lips; something in the contrast he presented to every one else she had ever seen—neither entering into their gossiping slanders, nor understanding their empty self-sufficiency, that possessed a charm for one satiated with the world's common scene. It was less of wonder that Cornelia pleased the student. There were no rough corners, no harshness about her; she won her way into any heart by her cheerful smiles and kind tones; and she listened to Saville when he talked of what other women would have lent a languid ear to, with such an air of interest, that he found no pleasure so great as that of talking on.

Saville was accustomed to find the men of his acquaintance ignorant. All the knowledge of worldlings was as a point in comparison with his vast acquirements. He did not seek Lady Lodore's society either to learn or to teach, but to forget thought, and to feel himself occupied and diverted from the sense of listlessness that haunted him in society, without having recourse to the, to him dangerous, attraction of his books.

Lady Lodore had, in the very brightness of her earliest youth, selected a proud and independent position. She had refused to bend to her husband's will, or to submit to the tyranny, as she named it, which he had attempted to exercise. Youth is bold and fearless. The forked tongue of scandal, the thousand ills with which woman is threatened in society, without a guide or a protector—all the worldly considerations which might lead her to unite herself again to her husband, she had rejected with unbounded disdain. Her mother was there to stand between her and the shafts of envy and calumny, and she conceived no mistrust of herself; she believed that she could hold her course with taintless feelings and security of soul, through a thousand dangers. At first she had been somewhat annoyed by ill-natured observations, but Lady Santerre poured the balm of flattery on her wounds, and a few tears shed in her presence dissipated the gathering cloud.

Cornelia had every motive a woman could have for guarding her conduct from reproach. She lived in the midst of polished society, and was thoroughly imbued with its maxims and laws. She witnessed the downfall of several, as young and lovely as herself, and heard the sarcasms and beheld the sneers which were heaped as a tomb above their buried fame. She had vowed to herself never to become one of these. She was applauded for her pride, and held up as a pattern. No one feared her. She was no coquette, though she strove universally to please. She formed no intimate friendships, though every man felt honoured by her notice. She had no prudery on her lips, but her conduct was as open and as fair as day. Here lay her defence against her husband; and she preserved even the outposts of such bulwarks with scrupulous yet unobtrusive exactitude.

Her spirits, as well as her spirit, held her up through many a year. More than ten years had passed since her separation from Lodore—a long time to tell of; but it had glided away, she scarcely knew how— taking little from her loveliness, adding to the elegance of her appearance, and the grace of her manners. Season after season came, and went, and she had no motive for counting them anxiously. She was sought after and admired; it was a holiday life for her, and she wondered what people meant when they spoke of the delusions of this world, and the dangers of our own hearts. She saw a gay reality about her, and felt the existence of no internal enemy. Nothing ever moved her to sorrow, except the reflection that now and then came across, that she had a child—divorced for ever from her maternal bosom. The sight of a baby cradled in its mother's arms, or stretching out its little hands to her, had not unoften caused her to turn abruptly away, to hide her tears; and once or twice she had been obliged to quit a theatre to conceal her emotion, when such sentiments were brought too vividly before her. But when her eyes were drowned in tears, and her bosom heaved with sad emotion, pride came to check the torrent, and hatred of her oppressor gave a new impulse to her swelling heart.

She had rather avoided female friendships, and had been warned from them by the treachery of one, and the misconduct of another, of her more intimate acquaintances. Lady Lodore renounced friendship, but the world began to grow a little dull. The frivolity of one, the hard-heartedness of another, disgusted. She saw each occupied by themselves and their families, and she was alone. Balls and assemblies palled upon her—country pleasures were stupid—she had began to think all things "stale and unprofitable," when she became acquainted with Horatio Saville. She was glad again to feel animated with a sense of living enjoyment; she congratulated herself on the idea that she could take interest in some one thing or person among the empty shapes that surrounded her; and without a thought beyond the amusement of the present moment, most of her hours were spent in his company.

• • •

CHAPTER III

"Ah now, ye gentle pair,—now think awhile,
Now, while ye still can think and still can smile.

So did they think
Only with graver thoughts, and smiles reduced."

—*Leigh Hunt*

A month stole away as if it had been a day, and Lady Lodore was engaged to pass some weeks with another friend in a distant county. It was easily contrived, without contrivance, by Saville, that he should visit a relation who lived within a morning's ride of her new abode. The restriction placed upon their intercourse while residing under different roofs contrasted painfully with the perfect freedom they had enjoyed while inhabiting the same. Their attachment was too young and too unacknowledged to need the zest of difficulty. It required indeed the facility of an unobstructed path for it to proceed to the accustomed bourne; and a straw thrown across was sufficient to check its course for ever.

The impatience and restlessness which Cornelia experienced during her journey; the rush of transport that thrilled through her when she heard of Saville's arrival at a neighbouring mansion, awoke her in an instant to a knowledge of the true state of her heart. Her pride was, happily for herself, united to presence of mind and fortitude. She felt the invasion of the enemy, and she lost not a moment in repelling the dangers that menaced her. She resolved to be true to the line of conduct she had marked out for herself—she determined not to love. She did not alter her manner nor her actions. She met Horatio with the same sweet smile—she conversed with the same kind interest; but she did not indulge in one dream, one thought—one reverie (sweet food of love) during his absence, and guarded over herself that no indication of any sentiment less general than the friendship of society might appear. Though she was invariably kind, yet his feelings told him that she was changed, without his being able to discover where the alteration lay; the line of demarcation, which she took care never to pass, was too finely traced, for any but feminine tact to discern, though it obstructed him as if it had been as high and massive as a city wall. Now and then his speaking eye rested on her with a pleading glance, while she answered his look with a frank smile, that spoke a heart at ease, and perfect self-possession. Indeed, while they remained near each other, in despite of all her self-denying resolves, Cornelia was happy. She felt that there was one being in the world who took a deep and present interest in her, whose thoughts hovered round her and whose mind she could influence to the conception of any act or feeling she might desire. That tranquillity yet animation of spirit—that gratitude on closing her eyes at night—that glad anticipation of the morrow's sun—that absence of every harsh and jarring emotion, which is the disposition of the human soul the nearest that we can conceive to perfect happiness, and which now and then visits sad humanity, to teach us of what unmeasured and pure joy our fragile nature is capable, attended her existence, and made each hour of the day a new-born blessing.

This state of things could not last. An accident revealed to Saville the true state of his heart; he became aware that he loved Cornelia, deeply and fervently, and from that moment he resolved to exile himself for ever from her dear presence. Misery is the child of love when happiness is not; this Horatio felt, but he did not shrink from the endurance. All abstracted and lofty as his speculations were, still his place had been in the hot-bed of patrician society, and he was familiar with the repetition of domestic revolutions, too frequent there. For worlds he would not have Cornelia's name become a byeword and mark for scandal—that name which she had so long kept bright and unreachable. His natural modesty prevented him from entertaining the idea that he could indeed destroy her peace; but he knew how many and easy are the paths which lead to the loss of honour in the world's eyes. That it could be observed and surmised that one man had approached Lady Lodore with any but sentiments of reverence, was an evil to be avoided at any cost. Saville was firm as rock in his resolves—he neither doubted nor procrastinated. He left the neighbourhood where she resided, and, returning to his father's house, tried to acquire strength to bear the severe pain which he could not master.

His gentle and generous nature, ever thoughtful for others, and prodigal of self, was not however satisfied with this mere negative act of justice towards one who honoured him, he felt conscious, with her friendship and kindest thoughts. He was miserable in the idea that he could not further serve her. He revolved a thousand plans in his mind, tending to her advantage. In fancy he entered the solitude of her meditations, and tried to divine what her sorrows or desires were, that he might minister to their solace or accomplishment. Their previous intercourse had been very unreserved, and though Cornelia spoke but distantly and coldly of Lodore, she frequently mentioned her child, and lamented, with much emotion, the deprivation of all those joys which maternal love bestows. Often had Saville said, "Why not appeal more strongly to Lord Lodore? or, if he be inflexible, why calmly endure an outrage shocking to humanity? The laws of your country may assist you."

"They would not," said Cornelia, "for his reply would be so fraught with seeming justice, that the blame would fall back on me. He asks but the trivial sacrifice of my duty to my mother—my poor mother! who, since I was born, has lived with me and for me, and who has no existence except through me. I am to tear away, and to trample upon the first of human ties, to render myself worthy of the guardianship of my child! I cannot do it—I should hold myself a parricide. Do not let us talk more of these things; endurance is the fate of woman, and if I have more than my share, let us hope that some other poor creature, less able to bear, has her portion lightened in consequence. I should be glad if once indeed I were permitted to see my cherub girl, though it were only while she slept; but an ocean rolls between us, and patience must be my comforter."

The soft sweetness of her look and voice, the angelic grace that animated every tone and glance, rendered these maternal complaints mournful, yet enchanting music to the ear of Saville. He could have listened for ever. But when exiled from her, they assumed another form. He began to think whether it were not possible to convince Lord Lodore of the inexcusable cruelty of his conduct; and again and again, he imaged the exultation of heart he should feel, if he could succeed in placing her lost babe in the mother's arms.

Saville was the frankest of human beings. Finding his cousin Edward on a visit at Maristow castle, he imparted his project to him, of making a voyage to America, seeking out Lord Lodore, and using every argument and persuasion to induce him to restore her daughter to his wife. Villiers was startled at the mention of this chivalrous intent. What could have roused the studious Horace to such sudden energy? By one of those strange caprices of the human mind, which bring forth discord instead of harmony, Edward had never liked Lady Lodore—he held her to be false and dangerous. Circumstances had brought him more in contact with her mother than herself, and the two were associated and confounded in his mind, till he heard Lady Santerre's falsetto voice in the sweet one of Cornelia, and saw her deceitful vulgar devices in the engaging manners of her daughter. He was struck with horror when he discovered that Saville loved, nay, idolized this beauteous piece of mischief, as he would have named her. He saw madness and folly in his Quixotic expedition, and argued against it with all his might. It would not do; Horatio was resolved to dedicate himself to the happiness of her he loved; and since this must be done in absence and distance, what better plan than to restore to her the precious treasure of which she had been robbed?

Saville resolved to cross the Atlantic, and, though opposed to his scheme, Villiers offered to accompany him. A voyage to America was but a trip to an active and unoccupied young man; the society of his cousin would render the journey delightful; he preferred it at all times to the commoner pleasures of life, and besides, on this occasion, he was animated with the hope of being useful to him. There was nothing effeminate in Saville. His energy of purpose and depth of thought forbade the idea. Still there was something that appeared to require kindness and support. His delicate health, of which he took no care, demanded feminine attentions; his careless reliance upon the uprightness of others, and total self-oblivion, often hurried him to the brink of dangers; and though fearlessness and integrity were at hand to extricate him, Edward, who knew his keen sensibility and repressed quickness of temper, was not without fear, that on so delicate a mission his ardent feelings might carry him beyond the mark, and that, in endeavouring to serve a woman whom he loved with enthusiastic adoration, he might rouze the angry passions of her husband.

With such feelings the cousins crossed the Atlantic and arrived at New York. Thence they proceeded to the west of America, and passing and his daughter on the road without knowing it, arrived at the Illinois after their departure. They were astonished to find that Mr. Fitzhenry, as he was named to them, had broken up his establishment, sold his farm, and departed with the intention of returning to Europe. What this change might portend they could not guess. Whether it were the result of any communication with Lady Lodore—whether a reconciliation was under discussion, or whether it were occasioned by caprice merely they could not tell; at any rate, it seemed to put an end to Saville's mediation. If Lodore returned to England, it was probable that Cornelia would herself make an exertion to have her child restored to her. Whether he could be of any use was problematical, but untimely interference was to be deprecated; events must be left to take their own course: Saville was scarcely himself aware how glad he was to escape any kind of intercourse with the husband of Cornelia.

This feeling, however unacknowledged, became paramount with him. Now that Lodore was about to leave America, he wished to linger in it; he planned a long tour through the various states, he studied their laws and customs, he endeavoured to form a just estimate of the institutions of the New World, and their influence on those governed by them.

Edward had little sympathy in these pursuits; he was eager to return to London, and felt more inclined to take his gun and shoot in the forests, than to mingle in the society of the various towns. This difference of taste caused the cousins at various times to separate. Saville was at Washington when Villiers made a journey to the borders of Canada, to the falls of the Niagara, and returned by New York; a portion of the United States which his cousin avoided visiting, until Lodore should have quitted it.

Thus it was that a strange combination of circumstances brought Villiers into contact with this unfortunate nobleman, and made him a witness of and a participator in the closing scene of his disastrous and wasted life. Villiers did not sympathize in his cousin's admiration of Cornelia, and was easily won to take a deep interest in the fortunes of her husband. The very aspect of Lodore commanded attention; his voice entered the soul: ill-starred, and struck by calamity, he rose majestically from the ruin around him, and seemed to defy fate. The first thought that struck Villiers was, how could Lady Lodore desert such a man; how pitifully degraded must she be, who preferred the throng of fools to the society of so matchless a being! The gallantry with which he rushed to his fate, his exultation in the prospect of redeeming his honour, his melting tenderness towards his daughter, filled Villiers with respect and compassion. It was all over now. Lodore was dead: his passions, his wrongs, his errors slept with him in the grave. He had departed from the busy stage, never to be forgotten—yet to be seen no more.

Lodore was dead, and Cornelia was free. Her husband had alluded to the gladness with which she would welcome liberty; and Villiers knew that there was another, also, whose heart would rejoice, and open itself at once to the charming visitation of permitted love. Villiers sighed to think that Saville would marry the beautiful widow; but he did not doubt that this event would take place.

Having seen that Ethel was in kind hands, and learnt the satisfactory arrangements made for her return to England, he hastened to join his cousin, and to convey the astounding intelligence. Saville's generous disposition prevented exultation, and subdued joy. Still the prospect of future happiness became familiar to him, shadowed only by the fear of not obtaining the affections of her he so fervently loved. For, strange to say, Saville was diffident to a fault: he could not imagine any qualities in himself to attract a beautiful and fashionable woman. His hopes were slight; his thoughts timid: the pain of eternal division was replaced by the gentler anxieties of love; and he returned to England, scarcely daring to expect that crown to his desires, which seemed too high an honour, too dear a blessing, for earthly love to merit.

• • •

CHAPTER IV

"Ma la fede degli Amanti
È come l'Araba fenice;
Che vi sia, ciaschun' lo dice.
Ma dove sia, nessun lo sa."

—*Metastasio*

Meanwhile Lady Lodore had been enduring the worst miseries of ill-fated love. The illness of Lady Santerre, preceding her death, had demanded all her time; and she nursed her with exemplary patience and kindness. During her midnight watchings and solitary days, she had full time to feel how deep a wound her heart had received. The figure and countenance of her absent friend haunted her in spite of every effort; and when death hovered over the pillow of her mother, she clung, with mad desperation, to the thought, that there was still one, when this parent should be gone, to love her, even though she never saw him more.

Lady Santerre died. After the first burst of natural grief, Cornelia began to reflect that Lord Lodore might now imagine that every obstacle to their reconciliation was removed. She had looked upon her husband as her enemy and injurer; she had regarded him with indignation and fear;—but now she hated him. Strong aversion had sprung up, during the struggles of passion, in her bosom. She hated him as the eternal barrier between her and one who loved her with rare disinterestedness. The human heart must desire happiness;—in spite of every effort at resignation, it must aspire to the fulfilment of its wish. Lord Lodore was the cause why she was cut off from it for ever. He had foreseen that this feeling, this combat, this misery, would be her doom, in the deserted situation she chose for herself: she had laughed his fears to scorn. Now she abhorred him the more for having divined her destiny. While she banished the pleasant thoughts of love, she indulged in the poisoned ones of hate; and while she resisted each softer emotion as a crime, she opened her heart to the bitterest resentment, as a permitted solace; nor was she aware that thus she redoubled all her woes. It was under the influence of these feelings, that she had written to Mrs. Elizabeth Fitzhenry that harsh, decided letter, which Lodore received at New York. The intelligence of his violent death came as an answer to her expressions of implacable resentment. A pang of remorse stung her, when she thought how she had emptied the vials of her wrath on a head which had so soon after been laid low for ever.

The double loss of husband and mother caused Lady Lodore to seclude herself, not in absolute solitude, but in the agreeable retreat of friendly society. She was residing near Brighton, when Saville returned from America, and, with a heart beating high with its own desires, again beheld the mistress of his affections. His delicate nature caused him to respect the weeds she wore, even though they might be termed a mockery: they were the type of her freedom and his hopes; yet, as the tokens of death, they were to be respected. He saw her more beautiful than ever, more courted, more waited on; and he half despaired. How could he, the abstracted student, the man of dreams, the sensitive and timid invalid, ensnare the fancy of one formed to adorn the circles of wealth and fashion?

Thus it was that Saville and Cornelia were further off than ever, when they imagined themselves most near. Neither of them could afterwards comprehend what divided them; or why, when each would have died for the other's sake, cobweb barriers should have proved inextricable; and wherefore, after weathering every more stormy peril, they should perish beneath the influence of a summer breeze.

The pride of Cornelia's heart, hid by the artificial courtesies of society, was a sentiment resolved, confirmed, active, and far beyond her own control. The smallest opposition appeared rebellion to her majesty of will; while her own caprices, her own desires, were sacred decrees. She was too haughty to admit of discussion—too firmly intrenched in a sense of what was due to her, not to start indignantly from remonstrance. It is true, all this was but a painted veil. She was tremblingly alive to censure, and wholly devoted to the object of her attachment; but Saville was unable to understand these contradictions. His modesty led him to believe, that he, of all men, was least calculated to excite love in a woman's bosom. He saw in Cornelia a beautiful creation, to admire and adore; but he was slow to perceive the tenderness of soul, which her disposition made her anxious to conceal, and he was conscious of no qualities in himself that could entitle him to a place in her affections. Except that he loved her, what merit had he? And the interests of his affection he was willing to sacrifice at the altar of her wishes, though his life should be the oblation necessary to insure their accomplishment.

This is not the description of true love on either side; for, to be perfect, that sentiment ought to exist through the entireness of mutual sympathy and trust: but not the less did their passionate attachment engross the minds of both. All might have been well, indeed, had the lovers been left to themselves; but friends and relations interfered to mar and to destroy. The sisters of Saville accused Lady Lodore of encouraging, and intending to marry, the Marquess of C——. Saville instantly resolved to be no obstacle in the way of her ambition. Cornelia was fired with treble indignation to perceive that he at once conceded the place to his rival. One word or look of gentleness would have changed this; but she resolved to vanquish by other arms, and to force him to show some outward sign of jealousy and resentment. Saville had a natural dignity of mind, founded on simplicity of heart and directness of purpose. Cornelia knew that he loved her;—on that his claim rested: all that might be done to embellish and elevate her existence, he would study to achieve; but he could not enter into, nor understand, the puerile fancies of a spoiled Beauty: and while she was exerting all her powers, and succeeded in fascinating a crowd of flatterers, she saw Saville apart, abstracted from such vanities, pursuing a silent course; ready to approach her when her attention was disengaged, but at no time making one among her ostentatious admirers.

There was no moment of her life in which Cornelia did not fully appreciate her lover's value, and her own good fortune in having inspired him with a serious and faithful attachment. But she imagined that this must be known and acknowledged; and that to ask any demonstration of gratitude, was ungenerous and tyrannical. An untaught girl could not have acted with more levity and wilfulness. It was worse when she found that she was accused of encouraging a wealthier and more illustrious rival. She disdained to exculpate herself from the charge of such low ambition, but rather furnished new grounds for accusation; and, in the arrogance of conscious power, smiled at the pettiness of the attempts made to destroy her influence. Proud in the belief that she could in an instant dispel the clouds she had conjured athwart her heaven, she cared not how ominously the thunder muttered, nor how dark and portentous lowered the threatening storm. It came when she least expected it: convinced of the fallacy of his confidence, made miserable by her caprices, agonized by the idea that he only lingered to add another trophy to his rival's triumph, Saville, who was always impetuous and precipitate, suddenly quitted England.

This was a severe blow at first; but soon Cornelia smiled at it. He would return—he must. The sincerity of their mutual preference would overcome the petty obstacles of time and distance. She never felt more sure of his devotion than now; and she looked so happy, and spoke so gaily, that those who were more ready to discern indifference, than love, in her sentiments, assured the absent Saville, that Lady Lodore rejoiced at his absence, as having shaken off a burthen, and got rid of an impediment, which, in spite of herself, was a clog to her brilliant career. The trusting love that painted her face in smiles was a traitor to itself and while she rose each day in the belief that the one was near at hand which would bring her lover before her, dearer and more attached than ever, she was in reality at work in defacing the whole web of life, and substituting dark, blank, and sad disappointment, for the images of light and joy with which her fancy painted it.

Saville had been gone five months. It was strange that he did not return; and she began to ponder upon how she must unbend, and what demonstration she must make, to attract him again to her side. The Marquess of C—— was dismissed; and she visited the daughters of Lord Maristow, to learn what latest news they had received of their brother. "Do you know, Lady Lodore," said Sophia Saville, "that this is Horatio's wedding-day? It is too true: we regret it, because he weds a foreigner—but there is no help now. He is married."

Had sudden disease seized on the frame-work of her body, and dissolved and scattered with poisonous influence and unutterable pains, the atoms that composed it, Lady Lodore would have been less agonized, less terrified. A thousand daggers were at once planted in her bosom. Saville was false! married! divided from her for ever! She was stunned:—scarcely understanding the meaning of the phrases addressed to her, and, unable to conceal her perturbation, she replied at random, and hastened to shorten her visit.

But no interval of doubt or hope was afforded. The words she had heard were concise, true to their meaning and all-sufficing. Her heart died within her. What had she done? Was she the cause? She longed to learn all the circumstances that led to this hasty marriage, and whether inconstancy or resentment had impelled him to the fatal act. Yet wherefore ask these things? It was over; the scene was closed. It were little worth to analyze the poison she had imbibed, since she was past all mortal cure.

Her first resolve was to forget—never, never to think of the false one more. But her thoughts never wandered from his image, and she was eternally busied in retrospection and conjecture. She was tempted at one time to disbelieve the intelligence, and to consider it as a piece of malice on the part of Miss Saville; then the common newspaper told her, that at the Ambassador's house at Naples, the Honourable Horatio Saville had married Clorinda, daughter of the Principe Villamarina, a Neapolitan nobleman of the highest rank.

It was true therefore—and how was it true? Did he love his bride? why else marry?—had he forgotten his tenderness towards her? Alas! it needed not forgetting; it was a portion of past time, fleeting as time itself; it had been borne away with the hours as they passed, and remembered as a thing which had been, and was no more. The reveries of love which for months had formed all her occupation, were a blank; or rather to be replaced by the agonies of despair. Her native haughtiness forsook her. She was alone and desolate—hedged in on all sides by insuperable barriers, which shut out every glimpse of hope. She was humbled in her own eyes, through her want of success, and heartily despised herself, and all her caprices and vanities, which had led her to this desart, and then left her to pine. She detested her position in society, her mechanism of being, and every circumstance, self-inherent, or adventitious, that attended her existence. All seemed to her sick fancy so constructed as to ensure disgrace, desertion, and contempt. She lay down each night feeling as if she could never endure to raise her head on the morrow.

The unkindness and cruelty of her lover's conduct next presented themselves to her contemplation. She had suffered much during the past years, more than she had ever acknowledged, even to herself; she had suffered of regret and sorrow, while she brooded over her solitary position, and the privation of every object on whom she might bestow affection. She had had nothing to hope. Saville had changed all this; he had banished her cares, and implanted hope in her heart. Now again his voice recalled the evils, his hand crushed the new-born expectation of happiness. He was the cause of every ill; and the adversity which she had endured proudly and with fortitude while it seemed the work of fate, grew more bitter and heavy when she felt that it arose through the agency of one, whose kind affection and guardianship she had fondly believed would hereafter prove a blessing sent as from Heaven itself, be to the star of her life.

This fit passed off; with struggles and relapses she wore down the first gush of sorrow, and her disposition again assumed force over her. She had found it difficult to persuade herself, in spite of facts, that she was not loved; but it was easy, once convinced of the infidelity of her lover, to regard him with indifference. She now regretted lost happiness—but Saville was no longer regretted. She wept over the vanished forms of delight, lately so dear to her; but she remembered that he who had called them into life had driven them away; and she smiled in proud scorn of his fleeting and unworthy passion. It was not to this love that she had made so tender and lavish a return. She had loved his constancy, his devotion, his generous solicitude for her welfare—for the happiness which she bestowed on him, and for the sympathy that so dearly united them. These were fled; and it were vain to consecrate herself to an empty and deformed mockery of so beautiful a truth.

Then she tried to hate him—to despise and to lessen him in her own estimation. The attempt recoiled on herself. The recollection of his worth stole across her memory, to frustrate her vain endeavours: his voice haunted—his expressive eyes beamed on her. It were better to forget. Indifference was her only refuge, and to attain this she must wholly banish his image from her mind. Cornelia was possessed of wonderful firmness of purpose. It had carried her on so long unharmed, and now that danger was at hand, it served effectually to defend her. She rose calm and free, above unmerited disaster. She grew proud of the power she found that she possessed of conquering the most tyrannical of passions. Peace entered her soul, and she hailed it as a blessing.

The clause in her husband's will which deprived her of the guardianship of her daughter had been forgotten during this crisis. Before, under the supposition that she should marry, she had deferred taking any step to claim her. The idea of a struggle to be made, unassisted, unadvised, and unshielded, was terrible. She had not courage to encounter all the annoyances that might ensue. To get rid for a time of the necessity of action and reflection, she went abroad. She changed the scene—she travelled from place to place. She gave herself up in the solitude of continental journies to the whole force of contending passions; now overcome by despair, and again repressing regret, asserting to herself the lofty pride of her nature.

By degrees she recovered a healthier tone of mind—a distant and faint, yet genuine sense of duty dawned upon her; and she began to think on what her future existence was to depend, and how she could best secure some portion of happiness. Her heart once again warmed towards the image of her daughter—and she felt that in watching the development of her mind, and leading her to love and depend on her, a new interest and real pleasure might spring up in life. She reproached herself for having so long, by silence and passive submission, given scope to the belief that she was willing to be a party against herself, in the injustice of Lodore; and she returned to England with the intention of instantly enforcing her rights over her child, and taking to her bosom and to her fondest care the little being, whose affection and gratitude was to paint her future life with smiles.

She called to mind Lady Santerre's worldly maxims, and her own experience. She knew that the first step to success is the appearance of prosperity and power. To command the good wishes and aid of her friends she must appear independent of them. She was earnest therefore to hide the wounds her heart had received, and the real loathing with which she regarded all things. She arrayed herself in smiles, and banished, far below into the invisible recesses of her bosom, the contempt and disgust with which she viewed the scene around her.

She returned to England. She appeared at the height of the season, in the midst of society, as beautiful, as charming, as happy in look and manner, as in her days of light-hearted enjoyment. She paused yet a moment longer, to reflect on what step she had better take on first enforcing her claim; but her mind was full of its intention, and set upon the fulfilment.

CHAPTER V

"And as good lost is seld or never found."

—*Shakespeare*

❦

Lady Lodore and Villiers met for the first time since Horatio Saville's marriage. Neither were exactly aware of what the other knew or thought. Cornelia was ignorant how far her attachment to his cousin was known to him; whether he shared the general belief in her worldly coquetry, or what part he might have had in occasioning their unhappy separation. She could not indeed see him without emotion. He had been Lodore's second, and received the last dying breath of him who had, in her brightest youth, selected her from the world, to share his fortunes. Those days were long past; yet as she grew older, disappointed, and devoid of pleasurable interest in the present, she often turned her thoughts backward, and wondered at the part she had acted.

Similar feelings were in Edward's mind. He was prejudiced against her in every way. He despised her worldly calculations, as reported to him, and rejoiced in their failure. He believed these reports, and despised her; yet he could not see her without being moved at once with admiration and pity. The moon-lit hill, and tragic scene, in which he had played his part, came vividly before his eyes. He had been struck by the nobleness of Lodore's appearance— the sensibility that sat on his countenance—his gentle, yet dignified manners. Ethel's idolatry of her father had confirmed the favourable prepossession. He could not help compassionating Cornelia for the loss of her husband, forgetting, for the moment, their separation. Then again recurred to him the eloquent appeals of Saville; his eulogiums; his fervent, reverential affection. She had lost him also. Could she hold up her head after such miserable events? The evidence of the senses, and the ideas of our own minds, are more forcibly present, than any notion we can form of the feelings of others. In spite, therefore, of his belief in her heartlessness, Villiers had pictured Cornelia attired in dismal weeds, the victim of grief. He saw her, beaming in beauty, at the opera;—he now beheld her, radiant in sweet smiles, in her own home. Nothing touched—nothing harmed her; and the glossy surface, he doubted not, imaged well the insensible, unimpressive soul within.

Lady Lodore would have despised herself for ever had she betrayed the tremor that shook her frame when Villiers entered. Her pride of sex was in arms to enable her to convince him, that no regret, no pining, shadowed her days. The reality was abhorrent, and should never be confessed. Thus then they met—each with a whole epic of woe and death alive in their memory; but both wearing the outward appearance of frivolity and thoughtlessness. He saw her as lovely as ever, and as kind. Her softest and sweetest welcome was extended to him. It was this frequent show of frank cordiality which gained her "golden opinions" from the many. Her haughtiness was all of the mind;—a desire to please, and constant association with others, had smoothed the surface, and painted it in the colours most agreeable to every eye.

They addressed each other as if they had met but the day before. At first, a few questions and answers passed,—as to where she had been on the continent, how she liked Baden, &c.;—and then Lady Lodore said—"Although I have not seen her for several years, I instantly recognized a relative of mine with you yesterday evening. Does Miss Fitzhenry make any stay in town?"

The idea of Ethel was uppermost in Villiers's mind, and struck by the manner in which the woman of fashion spoke of her daughter, he replied, "During the season, I believe; I scarcely know. Miss Fitzhenry came up for her health; that consideration, I suppose, will regulate her movements."

"She looked very well last night—perhaps she intends to remain till she gets ill, and country air is ordered?" observed Lady Lodore.

"That were nothing new at least," replied Villiers, trying to hide the disgust he felt at her mode of speaking; "the young and blooming too often protract their first season, till the roses are exchanged for lilies."

"If Miss Fitzhenry's roses still bloom," said the lady, "they must be perennial ones; they have surely grown more fit for a herbal than a vase."

Villiers now perceived his mistake, and replied, "You are speaking of Mrs. Elizabeth Fitzhenry, as the good lady styles herself—I spoke of—her niece—"

"Has Ethel been ill?" Lady Lodore's hurried question, and the use of the christian name, as most familiar to her thoughts, brought home to Villiers's heart the feeling of their near relationship. There was something more than grating; it was deeply painful to speak to a mother of a child who had been torn from her—who did not know—who had even been taught to hate her. He wished himself a hundred miles off, but there was no help, he must reply. "You might have seen last night that she is perfectly recovered."

Lady Lodore's imagination refused to image her child in the tall, elegant, full-formed girl she had seen, and she said, "Was Ethel with you? I did not see her—probably she went home before the opera was over, and I only perceived your party in the crush-room—you appear already intimate."

"It is impossible to see Miss Fitzhenry and not to wish to be intimate," replied Villiers with his usual frankness. "I, at least, cannot help being deeply interested in every thing that relates to her."

"You are very good to take concern in my little girl. I should have imagined that you were too young yourself to like children."

"Children!" repeated Villiers, much amazed; "Miss Fitzhenry!—she is not a child."

Lady Lodore scarcely heard him; a sudden pang had shot across her heart, to think how strangers—how every one might draw near her daughter, and be interested for her, while she could not, without making herself the tale of the town, the subject, through the medium of news-papers, for every gossip's tea-table in England—where her sentiments would be scanned, and her conduct criticized—and this through the revengeful feelings of her husband, prolonged beyond the grave. Tears had been gathering in her eyes during the last moments; she turned her head to hide them, and a quick shower fell on her silken dress. Quite ashamed of this self-betrayal, she exerted herself to overcome her emotion. Villiers felt awkwardly situated; his first impulse had been to rise to take her hand, to soothe her; but before he could do more than the first of these acts, as Lady Lodore fancied for the purpose of taking his leave, she said, "It is foolish to feel as I do; yet perhaps more foolish to attempt to conceal from one, as well acquainted as you are with every thing, that I do feel pained at the unnatural separation between me and Ethel, especially when I think of the publicity I must incur by asserting a mother's claims. I am ashamed of intruding this subject on you; but she is no longer the baby cherub I could cradle in my arms, and you have seen her lately, and can tell me whether she has been well brought up—whether she seems tractable—if she promises to be pretty?"

"Did you not think her lovely?" cried Villiers with animation; "you saw her last night, taking my arm."

"Ethel!" cried the lady. "Could that be Ethel? True, she is now sixteen—I had indeed forgot"—her cheeks became suffused with a deep blush as she remembered all the solicisms she had been committing. "She is sixteen," she continued, "and a woman—while I fancied a little girl in a white frock and blue sash: this alters every thing. We have been indeed divided, and must now remain so for evermore. I will not injure her, at her age, by making her the public talk—besides, many, many other considerations would render me fearful of making myself responsible for her future destiny."

"At least," said Villiers, "she ought to wait on you."

"That were beyond Lord Lodore's bond," said the lady; "and why should she wait on me? Were she impelled by affection, it were well. But this is talking very simply—we could only be acquaintance, and I would rather be nothing. I confess, that I repined bitterly, that I was not permitted to have my little girl, as I termed her, for my plaything and companion—but my ideas are now changed: a dear little tractable child would have been delightful—but she is a woman, with a will of her own—prejudiced against me—brought up in that vulgar America, with all kinds of strange notions and ways. Lord Lodore was quite right, I believe—he fashioned her for himself and—Bessy. The worst thing that can happen to a girl, is to have her prejudices and principles unhinged; no new ones can flourish like those that have grown with her growth; and mine, I fear, would differ greatly from those in which she has been educated. A few years hence, she may feel the want of a friend, who understands the world, and who could guide her prudently through its intricacies; then she shall find that friend in me. Now, I feel convinced that I should do more harm than good."

A loud knock at the street door interrupted the conversation. "One thing only I cannot endure," said the lady hastily, "to present a domestic tragedy or farce to the Opera House—we must not meet in public. I shall shut up my house and return to Paris."

Mere written words express little. Lady Lodore's expressions were nothing; but her countenance denoted a change of feeling, a violence of emotion, of which Villiers hardly believed her capable; but before he could reply, the servant threw open the door, and her brow immediately clearing, serenity descended on her face. With her blandest smile she extended her hand to her new visitor. Villiers was too much discomposed to imitate her, so with a silent salutation he departed, and cantered round the park to collect his thoughts before he called in Seymour Street.

The ladies there were not less agitated than Lady Lodore, and displayed their feelings with the artlessness of recluses. The first words that Mrs. Elizabeth had addressed to her niece, at the break-fast table, were an awkwardly expressed intimation, that she meant instantly to return to Longfield. Ethel looked up with a face of alarm: her aunt continued; "I do not want to speak ill of Lady Lodore, my dear—God forgive her—that is all I can say. What your dear father thought of her, his last will testifies. I suppose you do not mean to disobey him."

"His slightest word was ever a law with me," said Ethel; "and now that he is gone, I would observe his injunctions more religiously than ever. But—"

"Then, my dear, there is but one thing to be done: Lady Lodore will assuredly force herself upon us, meet us at every turn, oblige you to pay her your duty; nor could you avoid it. No, my dear Ethel, there is but one escape—your health, thank God, is restored, and Longfield is now in all its beauty; we will return to-morrow."

Ethel did not reply; she looked very disconsolate—she did not know what to say; at last, "Mr. Villiers will think it so odd," dropped from her lips.

"Mr. Villiers is nothing to us, my dear," said aunt Bessy—"not the most distant relation; he is an agreeable, good-hearted young gentleman—but there are so many in the world."

Ethel left her breakfast untasted and went out of the room: she felt that she could no longer restrain her tears. "My father!" she exclaimed, while a passionate burst of weeping choked her utterance, "my only friend! why, why did you leave me? Why, most cruel, desert your poor orphan child? Gracious God! to what am I reserved! I must not see my mother—a name so dear, so sweet, is for me a curse and a misery! O my father, why did you desert me!"

Her calm reflections were not less bitter; she did not suffer her thoughts to wander to Villiers, or rather the loss of her father was still so much the first grief of her heart, that on any new sorrow, it was to this she recurred with agony. The form of her youthful mother also flitted before her; and she asked herself, "Can she be so wicked?" Lord Lodore had never uttered her name; it was not until his death had put the fatal seal on all things, that she heard a garbled exaggerated statement from her aunt, over whose benevolent features a kind of sacred horror mantled, whenever she was mentioned. The will of Lord Lodore, and the stern injunction it contained, that the mother and daughter should never meet, satisfied Ethel of the truth of all that her aunt said; so that educated to obedience and deep reverence for the only parent she had ever known, she recoiled with terror from transgressing his commands, and holding communication with the cause of all his ills. Still it was hard, and very, very sad; nor did she cease from lamenting her fate, till Villiers's horse was heard in the street, and his knock at the door; then she tried to compose herself. "He will surely come to us at Longfield," she thought; "Longfield will be so very stupid after London."

After London! Poor Ethel! she had lived in London as in a desert; but lately it had appeared to her a city of bliss, and all places else the abode of gloom and melancholy. Villiers was shocked at the appearance of sorrow which shadowed her face; and, for a moment, thought that the rencounter with her mother was the sole occasion of the tears, whose traces he plainly discerned. His address was full of sympathetic kindness;—but when she said, "We return to-morrow to Essex—will you come to see us at Longfield?"—his soothing tones were exchanged for those of surprise and vexation.

"Longfield!—impossible! Why?"

"My aunt has determined on it. She thinks me recovered; and so, indeed, I am."

"But are you to be entombed at Longfield, except when dying? If so, do, pray, be ill again directly! But this must not be. Dear Mrs. Fitzhenry," he continued, as she came in, "I will not hear of your going to Long-field. Look; the very idea has already thrown Miss Fitzhenry into a consumption;—you will kill her. Indeed you must not think of it."

"We shall all die, if we stay in town," said Mrs. Elizabeth, with perplexity at her niece's evident suffering.

"Then why stay in town?" asked Villiers.

"You just now said, that we ought not to return to Longfield," answered the lady; "and I am sure if Ethel is to look so ill and wretched, I don't know what I am to do."

"But there are many places in the world besides either London or Longfield. You were charmed with Richmond the other day: there are plenty of houses to be had there; nothing can be prettier or more quiet."

"Well, I don't know," said Aunt Bessy, "I never thought of that, to be sure; and I have business which makes our going to Longfield very inconvenient. I expect Mr. Humphries, our solicitor, next week; and I have not seen him yet. You really think, Mr. Villiers, that we could get a house to suit us at Richmond?"

"Let us drive there to-day," said Villiers; "we can dine at the Star and Garter. You can go in the britzska—I on horseback. The days are long: we can see every thing; and take your house at once."

This plan sounded very romantic and wild to the sober spinster; but Ethel's face, lighted up with vivid pleasure, said more in its favour, than what the good lady called prudence could allege against it. "Silly people you women are," said Villiers: "you can do nothing by yourselves: and are always running against posts, unless guided by others. This will make every thing easy—dispel every difficulty." His thoughts recurred to Lady Lodore, and her intended journey to Paris, as he said this: and again they flew to a charming little villa on the river's side, whither he could ride every day, and find Ethel among her flowers, alone and happy.

The excursion of this morning was prosperous. The day was warm yet fresh; and as they quitted town, and got surrounded by fields, and hedges, and trees, nature reassumed her rights, and awakened transport in Ethel's heart. The boyish spirits of Villiers communicated themselves to her; and Mrs. Elizabeth smiled, also, with the most exquisite complacency. A few inquiries conducted them to a pretty rural box, surrounded by a small, but well laid-out shrubbery; and this they engaged. The dinner at the inn, the twilight walk in its garden;—the fair prospect of the rich and cultivated country, with its silvery, meandering river at their feet; and the aspect of the cloudless heavens, where one or two stars silently struggled into sight amidst the pathless wastes of sky, were objects most beautiful to look on, and prodigal of the sweetest emotions. The wide, dark lake, the endless forests, and distant mountains, of the Illinois, were not here; but night bestowed that appearance of solitude, which habit rendered dear to Ethel; and imagination could transform wooded parks and well-trimmed meadows into bowery seclusions, sacred from the foot of man, and fresh fields, untouched by his hand.

A few days found Ethel and her aunt installed at their little villa, and delighted to be away from London. Education made loneliness congenial to both: they might seek transient amusements in towns, or visit them for business; but happiness, the agreeable tenor of unvaried daily life, was to be found in the quiet of the country only;—and Richmond was the country to them; for, cut off from all habits of intercourse with their species, they had but to find trees and meadows near them, at once to feel transported, from the thick of human life, into the most noiseless solitude.

Ethel was very happy. She rose in the morning with a glad and grateful heart, and gazed from her chamber window, watching the early sunbeams as they crept over the various parts of the landscape, visiting with light and warmth each open field or embowered nook. Her bosom overflowed with the kindest feelings, and her charmed senses answered the tremulous beating of her pure heart, bidding it enjoy. How beautiful did earth appear to her! There was a delight and a sympathy in the very action of the shadows, as they pranked the sunshiny ground with their dark and fluctuating forms. The leafy boughs of the tall trees waved gracefully, and each wind of heaven wafted a thousand sweets. A magic spell of beauty and bliss held in one bright chain the whole harmonious universe; and the soul of the enchantment was love—simple, girlish, unacknowledged love;—the love of the young, feminine heart, which feels itself placed, all bleakly and dangerously, in a world, scarce formed to be its home, and which plumes itself with Love to fly to the covert and natural shelter of another's protecting care.

Ethel did not know—did not fancy—that she was in love; nor did any of the throes of passion disturb the serenity of her mind. She only felt that she was very, very happy; and that Villiers was the kindest of human beings. She did not give herself up to idleness and reverie. The first law of her education had been to be constantly employed. Her studies were various: they, perhaps, did not sufficiently tend to invigorate her understanding, but they sufficed to prevent every incursion of listlessness. Meanwhile, during each, the thought of Villiers strayed through her mind, like a heavenly visitant, to gild all things with sunny delight. Some time, during the day, he was nearly sure to come; or, at least, she was certain of seeing him on the morrow; and when he came, their boatings and their rides were prolonged; while each moment added to the strength of the ties that bound her to him. She relied on his friendship; and his society was as necessary to her life, as the air she breathed. She so implicitly trusted to his truth, that she was unaware that she trusted at all—never making a doubt about it. That chance, or time, should injure or break off the tie, was a possibility that never suggested itself to her mind. As the silver Thames traversed in silence and beauty the landscape at her feet, so did love flow through her soul in one even and unruffled stream—the great law and emperor of her thoughts; yet more felt from its influence, than from any direct exertion of its power. It was the result and the type of her sensibility, of her constancy, of the gentle, yet lively sympathy, it was her nature to bestow, with guileless confidence. Those around her might be ignorant that her soul was imbued with it, because, being a part of her soul, there was small outward demonstration. None, indeed, near her thought any thing about it: Aunt Bessy was a tyro in such matters; and Villiers—he had resolved, when he perceived love on her side, to retreat for ever: till then he might enjoy the dear delight that her society afforded him.

• • •

CHAPTER VI

"Alas! he knows
The laws of Spain appoint me for his heir;
That all must come to me, if I outlive him,
Which sure I must do, by the course of nature."

—Beaumont and Fletcher

Edward Villiers was the only child of a man of considerable fortune, who had early in life become a widower. From the period of this event, Colonel Villiers (for his youth had been passed in the army, where he obtained promotion) had led the care-less life of a single man. His son's home was at Maristow Castle, when not at school; and the father seldom remembered him except as an incumbrance; for his estate was strictly entailed, so that he could only consider himself possessed of a life interest in a property, which would devolve, without restriction, on his more fortunate son.

Edward was brought up in all the magnificence of his uncle's lordly abode. Luxury and profusion were the elements of the air he breathed. To be without any desired object that could be purchased, appeared baseness and lowest penury. He, also, was considered the favoured one of fortune in the family circle. The elder brother among the Savilles rose above, but the younger fell infinitely below, the undoubted heir of eight thousand a year, and one of the most delightful seats in England. He was brought up to look upon himself as a rich man, and to act as such; and meanwhile, until his father's death, he had nothing to depend on, except any allowance he might make him.

Colonel Villiers was a man of fashion, addicted to all the extravagances and even vices of the times. He set no bounds to his expenses. Gambling consumed his nights, and his days were spent at horse-races, or any other occupation that at once excited and impoverished him. His income was as a drop of water in the mighty stream of his expenditure. Involvement followed involvement, until he had not a shilling that he could properly call his own.

Poor Edward heard of these things, but did not mark them. He indulged in no blameworthy pursuits, nor spent more than beseemed a man in his rank of life. The idea of debt was familiar to him: every one—even Lord Maristow—was in debt, far beyond his power of immediate payment. He followed the universal example, and suffered no inconvenience, while his wants were obligingly supplied by the fashionable tradesmen. He regarded the period of his coming of age as a time when he should become disembarrassed, and enter upon life with ample means, and still more brilliant prospects.

The day arrived. It was celebrated with splendour at Maristow Castle. Colonel Villiers was abroad; but Lord Maristow wrote to him to remind him of this event, which otherwise he might have forgotten. A kind letter of congratulation was, in consequence, received from him by Edward; to which was appended a postscript, saying, that on his return, at the end of a few weeks, he would consult concerning some arrangements he wished to make with regard to his future income.

His return was deferred; and Edward began to experience some of the annoyances of debt. Still no real pain was associated with his feelings; though he looked forward with eagerness to the hour of liberation. Colonel Villiers came at last. He spoke largely of his intended generosity, which was shown, meanwhile, by his persuading Edward to join in a mortgage for the sake of raising an immediate sum. Edward scarcely knew what he was about. He was delighted to be of service to his father; and without thought or idea of having made a sacrifice, agreed to all that was asked of him. He was promised an allowance of six hundred a year.

The few years that had passed since then were full of painful experience and bitter initiation. His light and airy spirit was slow to conceive ill, or to resent wrong. When his annuity remained unpaid, he listened to his father's excuses with implicit credence, and deplored his poverty. One day, he received a note from him, written, as usual, in haste and confusion, but breathing anxiety and regret on his account, and promising to pay over to him the first money he could obtain. On the evening of that day, Edward was led by a friend into the gambling room of a celebrated club. The first man on whom his eyes fell, was his father, who was risking and losing rouleaus and notes in abundance. At one moment, while making over a large sum, he suddenly perceived his son. He grew pale, and then a deep blush spread itself over his countenance. Edward withdrew. His young heart was pierced to the core. The consciousness of a father's falsehood and guilt acted on him as the sudden intelligence of some fatal disaster would have done. He breathed thick—the objects swam round him—he hurried into the streets—he traversed them one after the other. It was not this scene alone—this single act; the veil was withdrawn from a whole series of others similar; and he became aware that his parent had stepped beyond the line of mere extravagance; that he had lost honourable feeling; that lies were common in his mouth; and every other—even his only child—was sacrificed to his own selfish and bad passions.

Edward never again asked his father for money. The immediate result of the meeting in the gambling-room, had been his receiving a portion of what was due to him; but his annuity was always in arrear, and paid so irregularly, that it became worse than nothing in his eyes; especially, as the little that he received was immediately paid over to creditors, and to defray the interest of borrowed money.

He never applied again to Colonel Villiers. He would have considered himself guilty of a crime, had he forced his father to forge fresh subterfuges, and to lie to his own son. Brought up in the midst of the wealthy, he had early imbibed a horror of pecuniary obligation; and this fastidiousness grew more sensitive and peremptory with each added day of his life. Yet with all this, he had not learnt to set a right value upon money; and he squandered whatever he obtained with thoughtless profusion. He had no friend to whose counsel he could recur. Lord Maristow railed against Colonel Villiers; and when he heard of Edward's difficulties, offered to remonstrate and force his brother-in-law to extricate him: but here ended his assistance, which was earnestly rejected. Horatio's means were exceedingly limited; but on a word from his cousin, he eagerly besought him to have recourse to his purse. To avoid his kindness, and his uncle's interference, Edward became reserved: he had recourse to money-lenders; and appeared at ease, while he was involving himself in countless and still increasing embarrassments.

Edward was naturally extravagant; or, to speak more correctly, his education and position implanted and fostered habits of expense and prodigality, while his careless disposition was unapt to calculate consequences: his very attempts at economy frequently cost him more than his most expensive whims. He was not, like his father, a gambler; nor did he enter into any very reprehensible pleasures: but he had little to spend, and was thoughtless and confiding; and being always in arrear, was forced, in a certain way, to continue a system which perpetually led him further into the maze, and rendered his return impossible. He had no hope of becoming independent, except through his father's death: Colonel Villiers, meanwhile, had no idea of dying. He was not fifty years of age; and considering his own a better life than his son's, involuntarily speculated on what he should do if he should chance to survive him. He was a handsome and a fashionable man: he often meditated a second marriage, if he could render it advantageous; and repined at his inability to make settlements, which was an insuperable impediment to his project. Edward's death would overcome this difficulty. Such were the speculations of father and son; and the portion of filial and paternal affection which their relative position but too usually inspires.

Until he was twenty-one, Edward had never spent a thought upon his scanty resources. Three years had past since then—three brief years, which had a little taught him of what homely stuff the world is made; yet care and even reflection had not yet disturbed his repose. Days, months sped on, and nothing reminded him of his relative wealth or poverty in a way to annoy him, till he knew Ethel. He had been interested for her in America—he had seen her, young and lovely, drowned in grief—sorrowing with the heart's first prodigal sorrow for her adored father. He had left her, and thought of her no more—except, as a passing reflection, that in the natural course of things, she was now to become the pupil of Lady Lodore, and consequently, that her unsophisticated feelings and affectionate heart would speedily be tarnished and hardened under her influence. He anticipated meeting her hereafter in ball-rooms and assemblies, changed into a flirting, giddy, yet worldly-minded girl, intent upon a good establishment, and a fashionable partner.

He encountered her under the sober and primitive guardianship of Mrs. Fitzhenry, unchanged and unharmed. The same radiant innocence beamed from her face; her sweet voice was still true and heart-reaching in its tones; her manner mirrored the purity and lustre of a mind incapable of guile, and adorned with every generous and gentle sentiment. He drew near her with respect and admiration, and soon no other object showed fair in his eyes except Ethel. She was the star of the world, and he felt happy only when the light of her presence shone upon him. Her voice and smile visited his dreams, and spoke peace and delight to his heart. She was to him as a jewel (yet sweeter and lovelier than any gem) shut up in a casket, of which he alone possessed the key—as a pearl, of whose existence an Indian diver is aware beneath the waves of ocean, deep buried from every other eye.

There was all in Ethel that could excite and keep alive imaginative and tender love. In characterizing a race of women, a delightful writer has described her individually. "She was in her nature a superior being. Her majestic forehead, her dark, thoughtful eye, assured you that she had communed with herself. She could bear to be left in solitude—yet what a look was her's if animated by mirth or love! She was poetical, if not a poet; and her imagination was high and chivalrous." The elevated tone of feeling fostered by her father, her worship of his virtues, and the loneliness of her life in the Illinois, combined to render her dissimilar to any girl Villiers had ever before known or admired. When unobserved, he watched her countenance, and marked the varying tracery of high thoughts and deep emotions pass over it; her dark eye looked out from itself on vacancy, but read there a meaning only to be discerned by vivid imagination. And then when that eye, so full of soul, turned on him, and affection and pleasure at once animated and softened its glances—when her sweet lips, so delicate in their shape, so balmy and soft in their repose, were wreathed into a smile—he felt that his whole being was penetrated with enthusiastic admiration, and that his nature had bent to a law, from which it could never again be liberated.

That she should mingle with the world—enter into its contaminating pursuits—be talked of in it with that spirit of depreciation and impertinence, which is its essence, was odious to him, and he was overjoyed to have her safe at Richmond—secure from Lady Lodore—shut up apart from all things, except nature—her unsophisticated aunt, and his own admiration—a bird of beauty, brooding in its own fair nest, unendangered by the fowler. These were his feelings; but by degrees other reflections forced themselves on him; and love which, when it has knocked and been admitted, *will* be a tyrant, obliged him to entertain regrets and fears which agonized him. His hourly aspiration was to make her his own. Would that dear heart open to receive into its recesses his image, and thenceforward dedicate itself to him only? Might he become her lover, guardian, husband—and they tread together the jungle of life, aiding each other to thread its mazes, and to ward off every danger that might impend over them.

Bitter worldly considerations came to mar the dainty colours of this fair picture. He could not conceal from himself the poverty that must attend him during his father's life. Lord Lodore's singular will

CHAPTER VII

"The world is too much with us."

—*Wordsworth*

Mrs. Elizabeth Fitzhenry's morning task was to read the newspapers—the only intercourse she held with the world, and all her knowledge of it, was derived from these daily sheets. Ethel never looked at them—her thoughts held no communion with the vulgar routine of life, and she was too much occupied by her studies and reveries to spend any time upon topics so uninteresting as the state of the nation, or the scandal of the day.

One morning, while she was painting, her aunt observed, in her usual tone of voice, scarce lifting her eyes from the paper, "Mr. Villiers did not tell us this—he is going to be married; I wonder who to!"

"Married!" repeated Ethel.

"Yes, my dear, here it is. 'We hear from good authority that Mr. Villiers, of Chiverton Park, is about to lead to the hymeneal altar a young and lovely bride, the only child of a gentleman, said to be the richest commoner in England.'—Who can it be?"

Ethel did not reply, and the elder lady went on to other parts of the newspaper. The poor girl, on whom she had dealt all unaware this chance mortal blow, put down her brush, and hurried into the shrubbery to conceal her agitation. Why did she feel these sharp pangs? Why did a bitter deluge of anguish overflow and seem to choke her breathing, and torture her heart?—she could scarcely tell. "Married!—then I shall never see him more!" And a passion of tears, not refreshing, but forced out by agony, and causing her to feel as if her heart was bursting, shook her delicate frame. At that moment the well-known sound, the galloping of Villiers's horse up the lane, met her ear. "Does he come here to tell us at last of his wedding-day?" The horse came on—it stopped—the bell was rung. Little acts these, which she had watched for, and listened to, for two months, with such placid and innocent delight, now they seemed the notes of preparation for a scene of despair. She wished to retreat to her own room to compose herself; but it was too late; he was already in that through which she must pass—she heard his voice speaking to her aunt. "Now is he telling her," she thought. No idea of reproach, or of accusation of unkindness in him, dawned on her heart. No word of love had passed between them—even yet she was unaware that she loved herself; it was the instinctive result of this despot sentiment, which exerted its sway over her, without her being conscious of the cause of her sufferings.

The first words of Mrs. Fitzhenry had been to speak of the paragraph in the newspaper, and to show it her visitor. Villiers read it, and considered it curiously. He saw at once, that however blunderingly worded, his father was its hero; and he wondered what foundation there might be for the rumour. "Singular enough!" he said, carelessly, as he put the paper down.

"You have kept your secret well," said Mrs. Elizabeth.

"My secret! I did not even know that I had one."

"I, at least, never heard that you were going to be married."

"I!—married! Where is Miss Fitzhenry?"

The concatenation of ideas presented by these words fell unremarked on the blunt senses of the good lady, and she replied, "In the shrubbery, I believe, or upstairs: she left me but a moment ago."

Villiers hastened to the garden and soon discerned the tearful girl, who was bending down to pluck and arrange some flowers, so to hide her disturbed countenance.

Could we, at the moment of trial, summon our reason and our foregone resolves—could we put the impression of the present moment at a distance, which, on the contrary, presses on us with a power as omnipotent over our soul, as a pointed sword piercing the flesh over our life, we might become all that we are not—angels or demigods, or any other being that is not human. As it is, the current of the blood and the texture of the brain are the machinery by which the soul acts, and their mechanism is by no means tractable or easily worked; once put in motion, we can seldom control their operations; but our serener feelings are whirled into the vortex they create. Thus Edward Villiers had a thousand times in his reveries thought over the possibility of a scene occurring, such as the one he was called upon to act in now—and had planned a line of conduct, but, like mist before the wind, this gossamer of the mind was swept away by an immediate appeal to his heart through his outward sensations. There stood before him, in all her loveliness, the creature whose image had lived with him by day and by night, for several long months; and the gaze of her soft tearful eyes, and the faultering tone of her voice, were the laws to which his sense of prudence, of right, was immediately subjected.

A few confused sentences interchanged, revealed to him that she participated in her aunt's mistake, and her simple question, "Why did you conceal this from me?" spoke the guilelessness of her thoughts, while the anguish which her countenance expressed, betrayed that the concealment was not the only source of her grief.

This young pair were ignorant how dear they were to each other. Ethel's affection was that generous giving away of a young heart which is unaware of the value of the gift it makes—she had asked for and thought of no return, though her feeling was the result of a reciprocal one on his side; it was the instinctive love of the dawn of womanhood, subdued and refined by her gentle nature and imaginative mind. Edward was more alive to the nature of his own sentiments—but his knowledge stood him in no stead to fortify him against the power of Ethel's tears. In a moment they understood each other—one second sufficed to cause the before impervious veil to fall at their feet: they had stept beyond this common-place world, and stood beside each other in the new and mysterious region of which Love is emperor.

"Dearest Ethel," said Villiers, "I have much to tell you. Do arrange that we should ride together. I have very much to tell you. You shall know every thing, and judge for us both, though you should condemn me."

She looked up in his face with innocent surprise; but no words could destroy the sunshine that brightened her soul: to know that she was loved sufficed then to fill her being to overflowing with happiness, so that there was no room for a second emotion.

The lovers rode out together, and thus secured the tête-à-tête which Villiers especially yearned for. Although she was country-bred, Mrs. Fitzhenry was too timid to mount on horseback, yet she could not feel fear for her niece who, under her father's guidance, sat her steed with an ease and perfect command of the animal, which long habit rendered second nature to her. As they rode on, considerably in advance of the groom, they were at first silent—the deep sweet silence which is so eloquent of emotion—till with an effort, slackening his pace, and bringing his horse nearer, Villiers began. He spoke of debt, of difficulties, of poverty—of his unconquerable aversion to the making any demands on his father—fruitless demands, for he knew how involved Colonel Villiers was, and how incapable even of paying the allowance he nominally made his son. He declared his reluctance to drag Ethel into the sea of cares and discomforts that he felt must surround his youth. He besought her forgiveness for having loved her—for having linked her heart to his. He could not willingly resign her, while he believed that he, all unworthy, was of any worth in her eyes; but would she not discard him for ever, now that she knew that he was a beggar? and that all to which he could aspire, was an engagement to be fulfilled at some far distant day—a day that might never come—when fortune should smile on him. Ethel listened with exquisite complacency. Every word Villiers spoke was fraught with tenderness; his eye beamed adoration and sincerest love. Consciousness chained her tongue, and her faltering voice refused to frame any echo to the busy instigations of her virgin heart. Yet it seemed to her as if she must speak; as if she were called upon to avow how light and trivial were all worldly considerations in her eyes. With bashful confusion she at length said, "You cannot think that I care for fortune—I was happy in the Illinois."

Her simplicity of feeling was at this moment infectious. It appeared the excess of selfishness to think of any thing but love in a desart—while she had no desire beyond. Indeed, in England or America, she lived in a desart, as far as society was concerned, and felt not one of those tenacious though cobweb-seeming ties, that held sway over Villiers. All his explanations therefore went for nothing. They only felt that this discourse concerning him had drawn them nearer to each other, and had laid the first stone of an edifice of friendship, henceforth to be raised beside the already established one of love. A sudden shower forced them also to return home with speed, and so interrupted any further discussion.

In the evening Villiers left them; and Ethel sought, as speedily as she might, the solitude of her own chamber. She had no idea of hiding any circumstance from Mrs. Fitzhenry; but confidence is, more than any other thing, a matter of interchange, and cannot be bestowed unless the giver is certain of its being received. They had too little sympathy of taste or idea, and were too little in the habit of communicating their inmost thoughts, to make Ethel recur to her aunt. Besides, young love is ever cradled in mystery;—to reveal it to the vulgar eye, appears at once to deprive it of its celestial loveliness, and to marry it to the clod-like earth. But alone—alone—she could think over the past day—recall its minutest incident; and as she imaged to herself the speaking fondness of her lover's eyes, her own closed, and a thrilling sense of delight swept through her frame. What a different world was this to what it had been the day before! The whole creation was invested by a purer atmosphere, balmy as paradise, which no disquieting thought could penetrate. She called upon her father's spirit to approve her attachment; and when she reflected that Edward's hand had supported his dying head—that to Edward Villiers's care his latest words had intrusted her,—she felt as if she were a legacy bequeathed to him, and that she fulfilled Lodore's last behests in giving herself to him. So sweetly and fondly did her gentle heart strive to make a duty of her wishes; and the idea of her father's approbation set the seal of perfect satisfaction on her dream of bliss.

It was somewhat otherwise with Villiers. Things went on as before, and he came nearly every day to Richmond; but while Ethel rested satisfied with seeing him, and receiving slight, cherished tokens of his unabated regard,—as his voice assumed a more familiar tone, and his attentions became more affectionate;—while these were enough for Ethel, he thought of the future, and saw it each day dressed in gloomier colours. In Ethel's presence, indeed, he forgot all but her. He loved her fervently, and beheld in her all that he most admired in woman: her clearness of spirit, her singleness of heart, her unsuspicious and ingenuous disposition, were irresistibly fascinating;—and why not spend their lives thus in solitude?— his—their mutual fortune might afford this:—why not for ever thus—the happy—the beloved?—his life might pass like a dream of joy; and that paradise might be realized on earth, the impossibility of which philosophers have demonstrated, and worldlings scoffed at.

Thus he thought while in the same room with Ethel;—while on his evening ride back to town, her form glided before him, and her voice sounded in his ears, it seemed that where Ethel was, no one earthly bliss could be wanting; where she was not, a void must exist, dark and dreary as a starless night. But his progress onward took him out of the magic circle her presence drew; a portion of his elevated feeling deserted him at each step; it fell off, like the bark pealing from a tree, in successive coats, till he was left with scarce a vestige of its brightness;—as the hue and the scent deserts the flower, when deprived of light,—so, when away from Ethel, her lover lost half the excellence which her presence bestowed.

Edward Villiers was eminently sociable in his disposition. He had been brought up in the thick of life, and knew not how to live apart from it. His frank and cordial heart danced within his bosom, when he was among those who sympathized with, and liked him. He was much courted in society, and had many favourites: and how Ethel would like these, and be liked by them, was a question he perpetually asked himself. He knew the worldliness of many,—their defective moral feeling, and their narrow views; but he believed that they were attached to him, and no man was ever less a misanthrope than he. He wished, if married to Ethel, to see her a favourite in his own circle; but he revolted from the idea of presenting her, except under favourable auspices, surrounded by the decorations of rank and wealth. To give up the world, the English world, formed no portion of his picture of bliss; and to occupy a subordinate, degraded, permitted place in it, was, to one initiated in its supercilious and insolent assumptions, not to be endured.

The picture had also a darker side, which was too often turned towards him. If he felt hesitation when he regarded its brighter aspect, as soon as this was dimmed, the whole current of his feelings turned the other way; and he called himself villain, for dreaming of allying Ethel, not to poverty alone, but to its worst consequences and disgrace, in the shape of debt. "I am a beggar," he thought; "one of many wants, and unable to provide for any;—the most poverty-stricken of beggars, who has pledged away even his liberty, were it claimed of him. I look forward to the course of years with disgust. I cannot calculate the ills that may occur, or with how tremendous a weight the impending ruin may fall. I can bear it alone; but did I see *her* humiliated, whom I would gladly place on a throne,—by heavens! I could not endure life on such terms! and a pistol, or some other dreadful means, would put an end to an existence become intolerable."

As these thoughts fermented within him, he longed to pour them out before Ethel; to unload his mind of its care, to express the sincere affection that led him to her side, and yet urged him to exile himself for ever. He rode over each day to Richmond, intent on such a design; but as he proceeded, the fogs and clouds that thickened round his soul grew lighter. At first his pace was regulated; as he drew nearer, he pressed his horse's flank with impatient heel, and bounded forward. Each turn in the road was a step nearer the sunshine. Now the bridge, the open field, the winding lane, were passed; the walls of her abode, and its embowered windows, presented themselves;—they met; and the glad look that welcomed him drove far away every thought of banishment, and dispelled at once every remnant of doubt and despondency.

This state of things might have gone on much longer,—already had it been protracted for two months,—but for an accidental conversation between Lady Lodore and Villiers. Since the morning after the opera, they had scarcely seen each other. Edward's heart was too much occupied to permit him to join in the throng of a ball-room; and they had no chance of meeting, except in general society. One evening, at the opera, the lady who accompanied Lady Lodore, asked a gentleman, who had just come into their box, "What had become of Edward Villiers?—he was never to be seen?"

"He is going to be married," was the reply: "he is in constant attendance on the fair lady at Richmond."

"I had not heard of this," observed Lady Lodore, who, for Horatio's sake, felt an interest for his favourite cousin.

"It is very little known. The *fiancée* lives out of the world, and no one can tell any thing about her. I did hear her name. Young Craycroft has seen them riding together perpetually in Richmond Park and on Wimbledon Common, he told me. Miss Fitzroy—no;—Miss Fitz-something it is;—Fitzgeorge?—no;—Fitzhenry?—yes; Miss Fitzhenry is the name."

Cornelia reddened, and asked no more questions. She controlled her agitation; and at first, indeed, she was scarcely aware how much she felt: but while the whole house was listening to a favourite air, and her thoughts had leisure to rally, they came on her painfully, and involuntary tears filled her eyes. It was sad, indeed, to hear of her child as of a stranger; and to be made to feel sensibly how wide the gulf was that separated them. "My sweet girl—my own Ethel!—are you, indeed, so lost to me?" As her heart breathed this ejaculation, she felt the downy cheek of her babe close to hers, and its little fingers press her bosom. A moment's recollection brought another image:—Ethel, grown up to womanhood, educated in hatred of her, negligent and unfilial;—this was not the little cherub whose loss she lamented. Let her look round the crowd then about her; and among the fair girls she saw, any one was as near her in affection and duty, as the child so early torn from her, to be for ever estranged and lost.

The baleful part of Cornelia's character was roused by these reflections; her pride, her selfwill, her spirit of resistance. "And for this she has been taken from me," she thought, "to marry, while yet a child, a ruined man—to be wedded to care and indigence. Thus would it not have been had she been entrusted to me. O, how hereafter she may regret the injuries of her mother, when she feels the effects of them in her own adversity! It is not for me to prevent this ill-judged union. The aunt and niece would see in my opposition a motive to hasten it: wise as they fancy themselves—wise and good—what I, the reviled, reprobated, they would therefore pursue with more eagerness. Be it so—my day will yet come!"

A glance of triumph shot across her face as she indulged in this emotion of revenge; the most deceitful and reprehensible of human feelings—revenge against a child—how sad at best—how sure to bring with it its recompense of bitterness of spirit and remorse! But Cornelia's heart had been rudely crushed, and in the ruin of her best affections, her mother had substituted noxious passions of many kinds—pride chief of all.

While thus excited and indignant, she saw Edward Villiers. He came into her box; the lady with her was totally unaware of what had been passing in her thoughts, nor reverted to the name mentioned as having any connexion with her. She asked Villiers if it were true that he was going to be married? Lady heard the question; she turned on him her eyes full of significant meaning, and with a smile of scorn answered for him, "O yes, Mr. Villiers is going to be married. His bride is young, beautiful, and portionless; but he has the tastes of a hermit—he means to emigrate to America—his simple and inexpensive habits are admirably suited to the wilderness."

This was said as if in jest, and answered in the same tone. The third in the trio joined in, quite unaware of the secret meaning of the conversation. Several bitter allusions were made by Lady Lodore, and the truth of all she said sent her words home to Edward's heart. She drew, as if playfully, a representation of highbred indigence, that made his blood curdle. As if she could read his thoughts, she echoed their worst suggestions, and unrolled the page of futurity, such as he had often depicted it to himself, presenting in sketchy, yet forcible colours, a picture from which his soul recoiled. He would have escaped, but there was a fascination in the topic, and in the very bitterness of spirit which she awakened. He rather encouraged her to proceed, while he abhorred her for so doing, acknowledging the while the justice of all she said. Lady Lodore was angry, and she felt pleasure in the pain she inflicted; her wit became keener, her sarcasm more pointed, yet stopping short with care of any thing that should betray her to their companion, and avoiding, with inimitable tact, any expression that should convey to one not in the secret, that she meant any thing more than raillery or good-humoured quizzing, as it is called.

At length Villiers took his leave. "Were I," he said, "the unfortunate man you represent me to be, you would have to answer for my life this night. But re-assure yourself—it is all a dream. I have no thoughts of marrying; and the fair girl, whose fate as my wife Lady Lodore so kindly compassionates, is safe from every danger of becoming the victim of my selfishness and poverty."

This was said laughing, yet an expressive intonation of voice conveyed his full meaning to Cornelia. "I have done a good deed if I have prevented this marriage," she thought; "yet a thankless one. After all, he is a gentleman, and under sister Bessy's guardianship, poor Ethel might fall into worse hands."

While Lady Lodore thus dismissed her anger and all thought of its cause, Villiers felt more resentment than had ever before entered his kind heart. The truths which the lady had spoken were unpalatable, and the mode in which they were uttered was still more disagreeable. He hated her for having discovered them, and for presenting them so vividly to his sight. At one moment he resolved never to see Ethel more; while he felt that he loved her with tenfold tenderness, and would have given worlds to become the source of all happiness to her—wishing this the more ardently, because her mother had pictured him as being the cause to her of every ill.

Edward's nature was very impetuous, but perfectly generous. The tempest of anger allayed, he considered all that Lady Lodore had said impartially; and while he felt that she had only repeated what he had told himself a thousand times, he resolved not to permit resentment to control him, and to turn him from the right path. He felt also, that he ought no longer to delay acting on his good resolutions. His intercourse with Miss Fitzhenry had begun to attract attention, and must therefore cease. Once again he would ride over to Richmond—once again see her—say farewell, and then stoically banish every pleasant dream—every heart-enthralling hope—willingly sacrificing his dearest wishes at the shrine of her welfare.

•••

CHAPTER VIII

"She to a window came, that opened west,
   Towards which coast her love his way addrest,
There looking forth, she in her heart did find
   Many vain fancies working her unrest,
And sent her winged thoughts more swift than wind
To bear unto her love the message of her mind."

—*Spenser*, The Faerie Queen

Ethel, happy in her seclusion, was wholly unaware of her mother's interference and its effects. She had not the remotest suspicion that it would be considered as conducive to her welfare to banish the only friend that she had in the world. In her solitary position, life was a blank without Edward; and while she congratulated herself on her good fortune in the concurrence of circumstances that had brought them together, and, as she believed, established her happiness on the dearest and most secure foundations, she was far from imagining that he was perpetually revolving the necessity of bidding her adieu for ever. If she had been told two years before, that all intercourse between her and her father were to cease, it would scarcely have seemed more unnatural or impossible, than that such a decree should be issued to divide her from one to whom her young heart was entirely given. She relied on him as the support of her life—her guide and protector—she loved him as the giver of good to her—she almost worshipped him for the many virtues, which he either really possessed, or with which her fondness bounteously gifted him.

Meanwhile the unacute observations of Mrs. Fitzhenry began to be awakened. She gave herself great credit for discovering that there was something singular in the constant attendance of Edward, and yet, in fact, she owed her illumination on this point to her man of law. Mr. Humphries, whom she had seen on business the day before, finding how regular a visitor Villiers was, and their only one, first elevated his eyebrows and then relaxed into a smile, as he said, "I suppose I am soon to wish Miss Fitzhenry joy." This same day Edward had ridden down to them; a violent storm prevented his return to town; he slept at the inn and breakfasted with the ladies in the morning. There was something familiar and home-felt in his appearance at the breakfast-table, that filled Ethel with delight. "Women," says the accomplished author of Paul Clifford, "think that they must always love a man whom they have seen in his nightcap." There is deep philosophy in this observation, and it was a portion of that feeling which made Ethel feel so sweetly complacent, when Villiers, unbidden, rang the bell, and gave his orders to the servant, as if he had been at home.

Aunt Bessy started a little; and while the young people were strolling in the shrubbery and renewing the flowers in the vases, she was pondering on the impropriety of their position, and wondering how she could break off an intimacy she had hitherto encouraged. But one way presented itself to her plain imagination, the old resource, a return to Longfield. With light heart and glad looks, Ethel bounded up stairs to dress for dinner, and she was twining her ringlets round her taper fingers before the glass, when her aunt entered with a look of serious import. "My dear Ethel, I have something important to say to you."

Ethel stopped in her occupation and turned inquiring eyes on her aunt; "My dear," continued Mrs. Fitzhenry, "we have been a long time away; if you please, we will return to Longfield."

This time Ethel did not grow pale; she turned again to the mirror, saying with a smile that lighted her whole countenance, "Dear aunt, that is impossible—I would rather not."

No negative could have been more imposing on the good lady than this; she did not know how to reply, how to urge her wish. "Dearest aunt," continued her niece, "you are losing time—dinner will be announced, and you are not dressed. We will talk of Longfield tomorrow—we must not keep Mr. Villiers waiting."

It was often the custom of Aunt Bessy, like the father of Hamlet, to sleep after dinner, she did not betake herself to her orchard, but her arm-chair, for a few minutes' gentle doze. Ethel and Villiers meanwhile walked out, and, descending to the river side, they were enticed by the beauty of the evening to go upon the water. Ethel was passionately fond of every natural amusement; boating was a pleasure that she enjoyed almost more than any other, and one with which she was seldom indulged; for her spinster aunt had so many fears and objections, and considered every event but sitting still in her drawing-room, or a quiet drive with her old horses, as so fraught with danger and difficulty, that it required an absolute battle ever to obtain her consent for her niece to go on the river—she would have died before she could have entered a boat herself, and, walking at the water's edge, she always insisted that Ethel should keep close to the bank, while, by the repetition of expressions of alarm and entreaties to return, she destroyed every possibility of enjoyment.

The river sped swiftly on, calm and free. There is always life in a stream, of which a lake is frequently deprived, when sleeping beneath a windless sky. A river pursues for ever its course, accomplishing the task its Creator has imposed, and its waters are for ever changing while they seem the same. It was a balmy summer evening; the air seemed to brood over the earth, warming and nourishing it. All nature reposed, and yet not as a lifeless thing, but with the same enjoyment of rest as gladdened the hearts of the two beings, who, with gratitude and love, drank in the influence of this softest hour of day. The equal splash of the oar, or its dripping when suspended, the clear reflection of tree and lawn in the river, the very colour of the stream, stolen as it was from heaven itself, the plash of the wings of the waterfowl who skimmed the waves towards their rushy nests,—every sound and every appearance was beautiful, harmonious, and soothing. Ethel's soul was at peace; grateful to Heaven, and satisfied with every thing around her, a tenderness beamed from her eyes, and was diffused over her attitude, and attuned her voice, which acted as a spell to make Edward forget every thing but herself.

They had both been silent for some time, a sweet silence more eloquent than any words, when Ethel observed, "My aunt wishes to return to Longfield."

Villiers started as if he had trodden upon a serpent, exclaiming, "To Longfield! O yes! that were far best—when shall you go?"

"Why is it best? Why should we go?" asked Ethel with surprise.

"Because," replied Villiers impetuously, "it had been better that you had never left it—that we had never met! It is not thus that I can fulfil my promise to your father to guard and be kind to his child. I am practising on your ignorance, taking advantage of your loneliness, and doing you an injury, for which I should call any other a villain, were he guilty."

It was the very delight that Edward had been a moment before enjoying, the very beauty and calmness of nature, and the serenity and kindness of the sweet face turned towards him, which stirred such bitterness; checking himself, however, he continued after a pause, in a more subsided tone.

"Are there any words by which I can lay bare my heart to you, Ethel?—None! To speak of my true and entire attachment, is almost an insult; and to tell you, that I tear myself from you for your own sake, sounds like impertinence. Yet all this is true; and it is the reverence that I have for your excellence, the idolatry which your singleness of heart and sincere nature inspires, which prompts me to speak the truth, though that be different from the usual language of gallantry, or what is called love.

"Will you hate me or pity me most, when I speak of my determination never to see you more? You cannot guess how absolutely I am a ruined man—how I am one of those despicable hangers-on of the rich and noble, who cover my rags with mere gilding. I am a beggar—I have not a shilling that I can call my own, and it is only by shifts and meannesses that I can go on from day to day, while each one menaces me with a prison or flight to a foreign country.

"I shall go—and you will regret me, Ethel, or you will despise me. It were best of all that you forgot me. I am not worthy of you—no man could be; that I have known you and loved you—and for your sake, banished myself from you, will be the solitary ray of comfort that will shed some faint glow over my chilled and darkened existence. Will you say even now one word of comfort to me?"

Ethel looked up; the pure affectionateness of her heart prevented her from feeling for herself, she thought only of her lover. "Would that I could comfort you," she said. "You will do what you think right, and that will be your best consolation. Do not speak of hatred, or contempt, or indifference. I shall not change though we part for ever: how is it possible that I should ever cease to feel regard for one who has ever been kind, considerate, and generous to me? Go, if you think it right—I am a foolish girl, and know nothing of the world; and I will not doubt that you decide for the best."

Villiers took her hand and held it in his; his heart was penetrated by her disinterested self-forgetfulness and confidence. He felt that he was loved, and that he was about to part from her for ever. The pain and pleasure of these thoughts mingled strangely—he had no words to express them, he felt that it would be easier to die than to give her up.

Aunt Bessy, on the river's bank imploring their return, recalled them from the fairy region to which their spirits had wandered. For one moment they had been united in sentiment; one kindred emotion of perfect affection had, as it were, married their souls one to the other; at the alien sound of poor Bessy's voice the spell fled away on airy wings, leaving them disenchanted. The rudder was turned, the boat reached the shore, and unable to endure frivolous talk about any subject except the one so near his heart, Villiers departed and rode back to town, miserable yet most happy—despairing yet full of joy; to such a riddle, love, which finds its completion in sympathy, and knows no desire beyond, is the only solution.

The feelings of Ethel were even more unalloyed. She had no doubts about the future, the present embraced the world. She did not attempt to unravel the dreamy confusion of her thoughts, or to clear up the golden mist that hung before, curtaining most gloriously the reality beyond. Her step was buoyant, her eyes sparkling and joyous. Love and gladness sat lightly on her bosom, and gratitude to Heaven for bestowing so deep a sense of happiness was the only sentiment that mingled with these. Villiers, on leaving them, had promised to return the next day; and on the morrow she rose, animated with such a spirit as may be kindled within the bosom of an Enchantress, when she pronounces the spell which is to control the movements of the planetary orbs. She was more than queen of the world, for she was empress of Edward's heart, and ruling there, she reigned over the course of destiny, and bent to her will the conflicting elements of life.

He did not come. It was strange. Now hope, now fear, were interchanged one for the other, till night and certain disappointment arrived. Yet it was not much—the morrow's sun would light him on his way to her. To cheat the lagging hours of the morrow, she occupied herself with her painting and music, tasking herself to give so many hours to her employments, thus to add speed to the dilatory walk of time. The long day was passed in fruitless expectation—another and another succeeded. Was he ill? What strange mutation in the course of nature had occurred to occasion so inexplicable an absence?

A week went by, and even a second was nearly spent. She had not anticipated this estrangement. Day by day she went over in her mind their last conversation, and Edward's expressions gathered decision and a gloomy reality as she pondered on them. The idea of an heroic sacrifice on his part, and submission to his will on hers, at first soothed her—but never to see him more, was an alternative that tasked her fortitude too high; and while her heart felt all the tumults of despair, she found herself asking what his love could be, that could submit to lose her? Love in a cottage is the dream of many a high-born girl, who is not allowed to dance with a younger brother at Almack's; but a secluded, an obscure, an almost cottage life, was all that Ethel had ever known, and all that she coveted. Villiers rejected this—not for her sake, that could not be, but for the sake of a world, which he called frivolous and vain, and yet to whose tyranny he bowed. To disentwine the tangled skein of thought which was thus presented, was her task by day and night. She awoke in the morning, and her first thought was, "Will he come?" She retired at night, and sleep visited her eyes, while she was asking herself, "Why has he not been?" During the day, these questions, in every variety, forced her attention. To escape from her aunt, to seek solitude, to listen to each sound that might be his horse, and to feel her heart sicken at the still renewed disappointment, became, in spite of herself, all her occupation: she might bend over her drawing, or escape from her aunt's conversation to the piano; but these were no longer employments, but rather means adopted to deliver herself up more entirely to her reveries.

The third, the fourth week came, and the silence of death was between Ethel and her friend. O but for one word, one look to break the spell! Was she indeed never to see him more? Was all, all over?—was the harmony their two hearts made, jarred into discord?—was she again the orphan, alone in the world?—and was the fearless reliance she had placed upon fate and Edward's fidelity, mere folly or insanity?—and was desecration and forgetfulness to come over and to destroy the worship she had so fondly cherished? Nothing had she to turn to—nothing to console her. Her life became one thought, it twined round her soul like a serpent, and compressed and crushed every other emotion with its folds. "I could bear all," she thought, "were I permitted to see him only once again."

She and Mrs. Fitzhenry were invited by Mrs. Humphries to dine with her. They were asked to the awful ceremony of spending a long day, which, in the innocence of her heart, Mrs. Fitzhenry fancied the most delightful thing in the world. She thought that kindness and friendship demanded of her that she should be in Montague Square by ten in the morning. Notwithstanding every exertion, she could not get there till two, and then, when luncheon was over, she wondered why the gap of time till seven appeared so formidable. This was to be got over by a drive in Hyde Park. Ethel had shown peculiar pleasure in the idea of visiting London; she had looked bright and happy during their journey to town, but anxiety and agitation clouded her face, at the thought of the park, of the crisis about to arrive, at the doubt and hope she entertained of finding Villiers there.

The park became crowded, but he was not in the drive; at length he entered in the midst of a bevy of fair cousins, whom Ethel did not know as such. He entered on horseback, flanked on either side by pretty equestrians, looking as gay and light-hearted, as she would have done, had she been one, the chosen one among his companions. Twice he passed. The first time his head was averted—he saw nothing, she even did not see his face: the next time, his eye caught the aspect of the well-known chariot—he glanced eagerly at those it contained, kissed his hand, and went on. Ethel's heart died within her. It was all over. She was the neglected, the forgotten; but while she turned her face to the other window of the carriage, so to hide its saddened expression from her companion, a voice, the dearest, sweetest voice she had ever heard, the soft harmonious voice, whose accents were more melodious than music, asked, "Are you in town? have you left Richmond?" In spite of herself, a smile mantled over her countenance, dimpling it into gladness, and she turned to see the beloved speaker who had not deserted her—who was there; she turned, but there was no answering glance of pleasure in the face of Villiers—he looked grave, and bowed, as if in this act of courtesy he fulfilled all of friendly interchange that was expected of him, and rode off. He was gone—and seen no more.

•••

CHAPTER IX

"Sure, when the separation has been tried.
That we, who part in love, shall meet again."

—Wordsworth

🌹

This little event roused Ethel to the necessity of struggling with the sentiment to which hitherto she had permitted unquestioned power. There had been a kind of pleasure mingled with her pain, while she believed that she suffered for her lover's sake, and in obedience to his will. To love in solitude and absence, was, she well knew, the lot of many of her sex, and all that is imaginative and tender lends poetry to the emotion. But to love without return, her father had taught her was shame and folly—a dangerous and undignified sentiment that leads many women into acts of humiliation and misery. He spoke the more warmly on this subject, because he desired to guard his daughter by every possible means from a fate too common. He knew the sensibility and constancy of her nature. He dreaded to think that these should be played upon, and that her angelic sweetness should be sacrificed at the altar of hopeless passion. That all the powers he might gift her with, all the fortitude and all the pride that he strove to instil, might be insufficient to prevent this one grand evil, he too well knew; but all that could should be done, and his own high-souled Ethel should rise uninjured from the toils of the snarer, the heartless game of the unfaithful lover.

She steeled her heart against every softer thought, she tasked herself each day to devote her entire attention to some absorbing employment; to languages and the composition of music, as occupations that would not permit her thoughts to stray. She felt a pain deep-seated in her inmost heart; but she refused to acknowledge it. When a thought, too sweet and bitter, took perforce possession of the chambers of her brain, she drove it out with stern and unshaken resolve. She pondered on the best means to subdue every rebel idea. She rose with the sun, and passed much time in the open air, that when night came, bodily fatigue might overpower mental regrets. She conversed with her aunt again about her dear lost father; that, by renewing images, so long the only ones dear to her, every subsequent idea might be driven from the place it had usurped. Always she was rewarded by the sense of doing right, often by really mitigating the anguish which rose and went to rest with her, and awakening her in the morning, stung her to renew her endeavours, while it whispered too audibly, "I am here." She grew pale and thin, and her eyes again resumed that lustre which spoke a quick and agitated life within. Her endeavours, by being unremitting, gave too much intensity to every feeling, and made her live each moment of her existence a sensitive, conscious life, wearing out her frame, and threatening, while it accelerated the pulses, to exhaust betimes the animal functions.

She felt this; and she roused herself to contend afresh with her own heart. As a last resource she determined to quit Richmond. Her struggles, and the energy called into action by her fortitude, gave a tone of superiority to her mind, which her aunt felt and submitted to. Now when a change of residence was determined upon, she at once negatived the idea of returning to Longfield—yet whither else betake themselves? Ethel no longer concealed from herself that she and the worthy spinster were solitary wanderers on earth, cut off from human intercourse. A bitter sense of desolation had crept over her from the moment that she knew herself to be deserted by Villiers. All that was bright in her position darkened into shadow. She shrunk into herself when she reflected, that should the ground at her feet open and swallow her, not one among her fellow-creatures would be sensible that the whole universe of thought and feeling, which emanated from her breathing spirit, as water from a living spring, was shrunk up and strangled in a narrow, voiceless grave. A short time before she had regarded death without terror, for her father had been its prey, and his image was often shadowed forth in her fancy, beckoning her to join him. Now it had become more difficult to die. Nature and love were wedded in her mind, and it was a bitter pang for one so young to bid adieu to both for ever. Turning her thoughts from Villiers, she would have been glad to discover any link that might enchain her to the mass. She reverted to her mother. Her inexperience, her youth, and the timidity of her disposition, prevented her from making any endeavour to break through the wall of unnatural separation raised between them. She could only lament. One sign, one word from Lady Lodore, would have been balm to her poor heart, and she would have met it with fervent gratitude. But she feared to offend. She had no hope that any advance would have been met by other than a disdainful repulse; and she shrunk from intruding herself on her unwilling parent. She often wept to think that there was none near to support and comfort her, and yet that at the distance of but a few miles her mother lived—whose very name was the source of the dearest, sweetest, and most cruel emotions. She thought, therefore, of her surviving parent only to despair, and to shrink with terror from the mere possibility of an accidental meeting.

She earnestly desired to leave England, which had treated her with but a step-mother's welcome, and to travel away, she knew not whither. Yet most she wished to go to Italy. Her father had often talked of taking her to that country, and it was painted in her eyes with the hues of paradise. She spoke of her desire to her aunt, who thought her mad, and believed that it was as easy to adventure to the moon, as for two solitary women to brave alps and earthquakes, banditti and volcanoes, a savage people and an unknown land. Still, even while she trembled at the mere notion, she felt that Ethel might lead her thither if she pleased. It is one of the most beneficent dispensations of the Creator, that there is nothing so attractive and attaching as affection. The smile of an infant may command absolutely, because its source is in dependent love, and the human heart for ever yearns for such demonstration from another. What would this strange world be without that "touch of nature?" It is to the immaterial universe, what light is to the visible creation, scent to the flower, hue to the rainbow; hope, joy, succour, and self-forgetfulness, where otherwise all would be swallowed up in vacant and obscure egotism.

No one could approach Ethel without feeling that she possessed an irresistible charm. The overflowing and trusting affectionateness of her nature was a loadstone to draw all hearts. Each one felt, even without knowing wherefore, that it was happiness to obey, to gratify her. Thus while a journey to Italy filled Mrs. Elizabeth with alarm, a consent hovered on her lips, because she felt that any risk was preferable to disappointing a wish of her gentle niece.

And yet even then Ethel paused. She began to repent her desire of leaving the country inhabited by her dearest friend. She felt that she should have an uncongenial companion in her aunt—the child of the wilderness and the good lady of Longfield, were like a living and dead body in conjunction—the one inquiring, eager, enthusiastic even in her contemplativeness, sensitively awake to every passing object; while the other dozed her hours away, and fancied that pitfalls and wild beasts menaced her, if she dared step one inch from the beaten way.

At this moment, while embarrassed by the very yielding to her desires, and experiencing a lingering sad regret for all that she was about to leave behind, Ethel received a letter from Villiers. Her heart beat, and her fingers trembled, when first she saw, as now she held a paper, which might be every thing, yet might be nothing to her; she opened it at last, and forced herself to consider and understand its contents. It was as follows:—

Dear Miss Fitzhenry,

Will your aunt receive me with her wonted kindness when I call to-morrow? I fear to have offended by an appearance of neglect, while my heart has never been absent from Richmond. Plead my cause, I entreat you. I leave it in your hands.

Ever and ever yours.
Edward Villiers.

Grosvenor Square, Saturday.

Dearest Ethel, have you guessed at my sufferings? Shall you hail with half the joy that I do, a change which enables you to revoke the decree of absence so galling at least to one of us? If indeed you have not forgotten me, I shall be rewarded for the wretchedness of these last weeks.

Ethel kissed the letter and placed it near her heart. A calm joy diffused itself over her mind; and that she could indeed trust and believe in him she loved, was the source of a grateful delight, more medicinal than all the balmy winds of Italy and its promised pleasures.

When Villiers had last quitted Richmond, he had resolved not to expose himself again to the influence of Ethel. It was necessary that they should be divided—how far better that they should never meet again! He was not worthy of her. Another, more fortunate, would replace him, if he sacrificed his own selfish feelings, and determinately absented himself from her. As if to confirm his view of their mutual interest, his elder cousin, Mr. Saville, had just offered his hand to the daughter of a wealthy Earl, and had been accepted. Villiers took refuge from his anxious thoughts among his pretty cousins, sisters of the bridegroom, and with them the discussion of estates, settlements, princely mansions, and equipages, was the order of the day. Edward sickened to reflect how opposite would be the prospect, if his marriage with Ethel were in contemplation. It was not that a noble establishment would be exchanged for a modest, humble dwelling—he loved with sufficient truth to feel that happiness with Ethel transcended the wealth of the world. It was the absolute penury, the debt, the care, that haunted him and made such miserable contrast with the tens and hundreds of thousands that were the subject of discussion on the present occasion. His resolution not to entangle Ethel in this wilderness of ills, gained strength by every chance word that fell from the lips of those around him; and the image, before so vivid, of her home at Richmond, which he might at each hour enter, of her dear face, which at any minute might again bless his sight, faded into a far-off vision of paradise, from which he was banished for ever.

For a time he persevered in his purpose, if not with ease, yet with less of struggle than he himself anticipated. That he could at any hour break the self-enacted law, and behold Ethel, enabled him day after day to continue to obey it, and to submit to the decree of banishment he had passed upon himself. He loved his pretty cousins, and their kindness and friendship soothed him; he spent his days with them, and the familiar, sisterly intercourse, hallowed by long association, and made tender by the grace and sweetness of these good girls, compensated somewhat for the absence of deeper interest. They talked of Horatio also, and that was a more touching string than all. The almost worship, joined to pity and fear for him, with which Edward regarded his cousin, made him cling fondly to those so closely related to him, and who sympathized with, and shared, his enthusiastic affection.

This state of half indifference did not last long. His meeting with Ethel in Hyde Park operated an entire change. He had seen her face but a moment—her dear face, animated with pleasure at beholding him, and adorned with more than her usual loveliness. He hurried away, but the image still pursued him. All at once the world around grew dark and blank; at every instant his heart asked for Ethel. He thirsted for the sweet delight of gazing on her soft lustrous eyes, touching her hand, listening to her voice, whose tones were so familiar and beloved. He avoided his cousins to hide his regrets; he sought solitude, to commune with memory; and the intense desire kindled within him to return to her, was all but irresistible. He had received a letter from Horace Saville entreating him to join him at Naples; he had contemplated complying, as a means of obtaining forgetfulness. Should he not, on the contrary, make this visit with Ethel for his companion? It was a picture of happiness most enticing; and then he recollected with a pang, that it was impossible for him to quit England; that it was only by being on the spot, that he obtained the supplies necessary for his existence. With bitterness of spirit he recognized once again his state of beggary, and the hopelessness that attended on all his wishes.

All at once he was surprised by a message from his father, through Lord Maristow. He was told of Colonel Villiers's intended marriage with the only daughter of a wealthy commoner, which yet could not be arranged without the concurrence of Edward, or rather without sacrifices on his part for the making of settlements. The entire payment of his debts, and the promise of fifteen hundred a year for the future, were the bribes offered to induce him to consent. Edward at once notified his compliance. He saw the hour of freedom at hand, and the present was too full of interest, too pregnant with misery or happiness, to allow the injury done to his future prospects to weigh with him for a moment. Thus he might purchase his union with Ethel—claim her for his own. With the thought, a whole tide of tenderness and joy poured quick and warm into his heart, and it seemed as if he had never loved so devotedly as now. How false an illusion had blinded him! he fancied that he had banished hope, while indeed his soul was wedded to her image, and the very struggle to free himself, had served to make the thought of her more peremptory and indelible.

With these thoughts, he again presented himself at Richmond. He asked Mrs. Fitzhenry's consent to address her niece, and became the accepted lover of Ethel. The meeting of their two young hearts in the security of an avowed attachment, after so many hours wasted in despondency and painful struggles, did not visit the fair girl with emotions of burning transport: she felt it rather like a return to a natural state of things, after unnatural deprivation. As if, a young nestling, she had been driven from her mother's side, and was now restored to the dear fosterage of her care. She delivered herself up to a calm reliance upon the future, and saw in the interweaving of duty and affection, the ful-filment of her destiny, and the confirmation of her earthly happiness. They were to be joined never to part more! While each breathed the breath of life, no power could sever them; health or sickness, prosperity or adversity—these became mere words; her health and her riches were garnered in his heart, and while she bestowed the treasures of her affection upon him, could he be poor? It was not therefore to be her odious part to crush the first and single attach-ment of her soul—to tear at once the "painted veil of life," delivering herself up to cheerless realities—to know that, to do right, she must banish from her recollection those inward-spoken vows which she should deem herself of a base inconstant disposition ever to forget. It was not reserved for her to pass joyless years of solitude, reconciling herself to the necessity of divorcing her dearest thoughts from their wedded image. The serene and fair-showing home she coveted was open before her—she might pass within its threshold, and listen to the closing of the doors behind, as they shut out the world from her, with pure and unalloyed delight.

Ethel was very young, yet in youth such feelings are warmer in our hearts than in after years. We do not know then that we can ever change; or that, snake-like, casting the skin of an old, care-worn habit, a new one will come fresh and bright in seeming, as the one before had been, at the hour of its birth. We fancy then, that if our present and first hope is disappointed, our lives are a mere blank, not worth a "pin's fee"; the singleness of our hearts has not been split into the million hair-like differences, which, woven by time into one texture, clothes us in prudence as with a garment. We are as if exposed naked to the action of passions and events, and receive their influence with keen and fearful sensitiveness. Ethel scarcely heard, and did not listen to nor understand, the change of circumstances that brought Villiers back to her—she only knew, that he was confirmed her own. Satisfied with this delightful conclusion to her sufferings, she placed her destiny in his hands, without fear or question.

Mrs. Elizabeth thought her niece very young to marry; but Villiers, who had, while hesitating, done his best to hide his sweet Ethel away from every inquisitive eye, now that she was to be his own, hastened to introduce Lord Maristow (Lady Maristow had died two years before) to her, and to bring her among his cousins, whom he regarded as sisters. The change was complete and overwhelming to the fair recluses. Where before they lived in perpetual tête-à-tête, or separated but to be alone, they were now plunged into what appeared to them a crowd. Sophia, Harriet, and Lucy Saville, were high-born, high-bred, and elegant girls, accustomed to what they called the quiet of domestic life, amidst a thousand relations and ten thousand acquaintances. No female relative had stepped into their mother's place, and they were peculiarly independent and high-spirited; they had always lived in what they called the world, and knew nothing but what that world contained. Their manners were easy, their tempers equable and affectionate. If their dispositions were not all exactly alike, they had a family resemblance that drew them habitually near each other. They received Ethel among their number with cordiality, bestowing on her every attention which politeness and kindness dictated. Yet Ethel felt somewhat as a wild antelope among tame ones. Their language, the topics of their discourse, their very occupations, were all new to her. She lent herself to their customs with smiles and sweetness, but her eye brightened when Edward came, and she often unconsciously retreated to his side as a shelter and a refuge. Edward's avocations had been as worldly perhaps as those of his pretty cousins; but a man is more thrown upon the reality of life, while girls live altogether in a factitious state. He had travelled much, and seen all sorts of people. Besides, between him and Ethel, there was that mute language which will make those of opposite sexes intelligible to one another, even when literally not understanding each other's dialect. Villiers found no deficiency of intelligence or sympathy in Ethel, while the fashionable girls to whom he had introduced her felt a little at a loss how to entertain the stranger.

Lord Maristow and his family had been detained in town till after Mr. Saville's marriage, and were now very eager to leave it. They remained out of compliment to Edward, and looked forward impatiently to his wedding as the event that would set them free. London was empty, the shooting season had begun; yet still he was delayed by his father. He wished to sign the necessary papers, and free himself from all business, that he and his bride might immediately join Horatio at Naples. Yet still Colonel Villiers's marriage was delayed; till at last he intimated to his son, that it was postponed for the present, and begged that he would not remain in England on his account.

Edward was somewhat staggered by this intelligence. Yet as the letter that communicated it contained a considerable remittance, he quieted himself. To give up Ethel now was a thought that did not for a moment enter his mind; it was but the reflection of the difficulties that would surround them, if his prospects failed, that for a few seconds clouded his brow with care. But it was his nature usually to hope the best, and to trust to fortune. He had never been so prudent as with regard to his marriage with Ethel; but that was for her sake. This consideration could not again enter; for, like her, he would, under the near hope of making her his, have preferred the wilds of the Illinois, with her for his wife, than the position of the richest English nobleman, deprived of such a companion. His heart, delivered up to love, was complete in its devotion and tenderness. He was already wedded to her in soul, and would sooner have severed his right arm from his body, than voluntarily have divided himself from this dearer part of himself. This "other half," towards whom he felt as if literally he had, to give her being,

"Lent
Out of his side to her, nearest his heart;
Substantial life, to have her by his side,
Henceforth an individual solace dear."

With these feelings, an early day was urged and named; and, drawing near, Ethel was soon to become a bride. On first making his offer, Villiers had written to Lady Lodore; and Mrs. Fitzhenry, much against her will, by the advice of her solicitor, did the same. Lady Lodore was in Scotland. No answer came. The promised day approached; but still she preserved this silence: it became necessary to proceed without her consent. Banns were published; and Ethel became the wife of Villiers on the 25th of October. Lord Maristow hastened down to his Castle to kill pheasants: while, on her part, Mrs. Fitzhenry took her solitary way to Longfield, half consoled for separating from Ethel, by this return to the habits of more than sixty years. In vain had London or Richmond wooed her stay; in vain was she pressed to pay a visit to Maristow Castle: to return to her home was a more enticing prospect. Her good old heart danced within her when she first perceived the village steeple; the chimneys of her own house made tears spring into her eyes; and when, indeed, she found herself by the familiar hearth, in the accustomed arm-chair, and her attentive housekeeper came to ask if she would not take any thing after her journey, it seemed to her as if all the delights of life were summed up in this welcome return to monotony and silence.

•••

CHAPTER X

"Let me
Awake your love to my uncomforted brother."

—*Old play*

Meanwhile Villiers and his bride proceeded on their way to Naples. It mattered little to Ethel whither they were going, or to whom. Edward was all in all to her; and the vehicle that bore them along in their journey was a complete and perfect world, containing all that her heart desired. They avoided large towns, and every place where there was any chance of meeting an acquaintance. They passed up the Rhine, and Ethel often imaged forth, in her fancy, a dear home in a secluded nook; and longed to remain there, cut off from the world, for ever. She had no thought but for her husband, and gratitude to Heaven for the happiness showered on her. Her soul might have been laid bare, each faculty examined, each idea sifted, and one spirit, one sentiment, one love, would have been found pervading and uniting them all. The heart of a man is seldom as single and devoted as that of a woman. In the present instance, it was natural that Edward should not be so absolutely given up to one thought as was his bride. Ethel's affections had never been called forth except by her father, and by him who was now her husband. When it has been said, that she thought of heaven to hallow and bless her happiness, it must be understood that the dead made a part of that heaven, to which she turned her eyes with such sweet thankfulness. She was constant to the first affection of her heart. She might be said to live perpetually in thought beside her father's grave. Before she had wept and sorrowed near it; now she placed the home of her happy married life close to the sacred earth, and fancied that its mute inhabitant was the guardian angel to watch over and preserve her.

Villiers had lived among many friends, and was warmly attached to several. His cousin Horatio was dearer to him than any thing had ever been, till he knew Ethel. Even now he revered him more, and felt a kind of duteous attachment drawing him towards him. He wanted Horatio to see and approve of Ethel:—not that he doubted what his opinion of her would be; but the delight which his own adoration of her excellence imparted to him would be doubled, when he saw it shared and confirmed by his friend. Besides this, he was anxious to see Horace on his own account. He wished to know whether he was happy in his marriage; whether Clorinda were worthy of him; and if Lady Lodore were entirely forgotten. As they advanced on their journey, his desire to see his cousin became more and more present to his mind; and he talked of him to Ethel, and imparted to her a portion of his fervent and affectionate feelings.

Entering Switzerland, they came into a world of snow. Here and there, on the southern side of a mountain, a lawny upland might disclose itself in summer verdure; and the brawling torrents, increased by the rains, were not yet made silent by frost. Edward had visited these scenes before; and he could act the guide to his enraptured Ethel, who remembered her father's glowing descriptions; and while she gazed with breathless admiration, saw his step among the hills, and thought that his eye had rested on the wonders she now beheld. Soon the mountains, the sky-seeking "palaces of nature," were passed, and they entered fair, joyous Italy. At each step they left winter far behind. Ethel would willingly have lingered in Florence and Rome; but once south of the Appenines, Edward was eager to reach Naples; and the letters he got from Saville spurred him on to yet greater speed.

Before leaving England, Lucy Saville had said to Ethel,—"You are now taking our other comfort from us; and what we are to do without either Horatio or Edward, I am unable to conjecture. We shall be like a house without its props. Divided, they are not either of them half what they were joined. Horace is so prudent, so wise, so considerate, so sympathizing; Edward so active and so kind-hearted. In any difficulty, we always asked Horace what we ought to do; and Edward did the thing which he pointed out.

"Horatio's marriage was a sad blow to us all. You will bring Edward back, and we shall be the happier for your being with him; but shall we ever see our brother again?—or shall we only see him to lament the change? Not that he can ever really alter; his heart, his understanding, his goodness, are as firm as rock; but there is that about him which makes him too much the slave of those he is in immediate contact with. He abhors strife; the slightest disunion is mortal to him. He is not of this world. Pure-minded as a woman, honourable as a knight of old, he is more like a being we read of, and his match is not to be found upon earth. Horatio never loved but once, and his attachment was unfortunate. He loved Lady ——" Here recollection dyed Miss Saville's cheeks with crimson: she had forgotten that Lady Lodore was the mother of Ethel. After a moment's hesitation she continued:—"I have no right to betray the secrets of others. Horace was a discarded lover; and he was forced to despise the lady whom he had imagined possessed of every excellence. For the first time he was absorbed in what may be termed a selfish sentiment. He could not bear to see any of us: he fled even from Edward, and wandering away, we heard at last that he was at Naples, whither he had gone quite unconscious of the spot of earth to which he was bending his steps. The first letter we got from him was dated from that place. His letter was to me; for I am his favourite sister; and God knows my devoted affection, my worship of him, deserves this preference. You shall read it; it is the most perfect specimen of enthusiastic and heart-moving eloquence ever penned. He had been as in a trance, and awoke again to life as he looked down from Pausilippo on the Bay of Naples. The attachment to one earthly object, which preyed on his being, was suddenly merged in one universal love and adoration. He saw that the "creation was good"; he purged his heart at once of the black spot which had blotted and marred its beauty; and opened his whole soul to pure, elevated, heavenly love. I tamely quote his burning and transparent expressions, through which you may discern, as in a glass, the glorious excellence of his soul."

"But, alas! this state of holy excitement could not endure; something human will still creep in to mingle with and sully our noblest aspirations. Horatio was taken by an acquaintance to see a beautiful girl at a convent; in a fatal moment an English lady said to him, 'Come, and I will show you what perfect beauty is:' and those words decided my poor brother's destiny. Of course I only know our new sister through his letters. He told us that Clorinda was shut up in this convent through the heartless vanity of her mother, who dreaded her as a rival, to wait there till her parents should find some suitable match, which she must instantly accept, or be doomed to seclusion for ever. In his younger days Horace had said, 'I am in love with an idea, and therefore women have no power over me.' But the time came when his heart was to be the dupe of his imagination—so was it with his first love—so now, I fear, did he deceive himself with regard to Clorinda. He declared indeed that his love for her was not an absorbing passion like his first, but a mingling of pity, admiration, and that tenderness which his warm heart was ever ready to bestow. He described her as full of genius and sensibility, a creature of fire and power, but dimmed by sorrow, and struggling with her chains. He visited her again; he tried to comfort, he offered to serve her. It was the first time that a manly, generous spirit had ever presented itself to the desponding girl. The high-souled Englishman appeared as a god beside her sordid countrymen; indeed, Horatio would have seemed such compared with any of his sex; his fascination is irresistible—Clorinda felt it; she loved him with Italian fervour, and the first word of kindness from him elicited a whole torrent of gratitude and passion. Horace had no wish to marry;

his old wound was by no means healed, but rather opened, and bled afresh, when he was called upon to answer the enthusiastic ardour of the Italian girl. He felt at once the difference of his feeling for her, and the engrossing sentiment of which he had been nearly the victim. But he could rescue her from an unworthy fate, and make her happy. He acted with his usual determination and precipitancy, and within a month she became his wife. Here ends my story; his letters were more concise after his marriage. At first I attributed this to his having a new and dearer friend, but latterly when he has written he has spoken with such yearning fondness for home, that I fear—And then when I offered to visit him, he negatived my proposition. How unlike Horatio! it can only mean that his wife was averse to my coming. I have questioned slightly any travellers from Italy. Mrs. Saville seldom appears in English society except at balls, and then she is always surrounded by Italians. She is decidedly correct in her conduct, but more I cannot tell. Her letters to us are beautifully written, and of her talents, even her genius, I do not entertain a doubt. Perhaps I am prejudiced, but I fear a Neapolitan, or rather, I should say, I fear a convent education; and that taste which leads her to associate with her own demonstrative, unrefined countrymen, instead of trying to link herself to her husband's friends. I may be wrong—I shall be glad to be found so. Will you tell me whether I am? I rather ask you than Edward, because your feminine eyes will discern the truth of these things quicker than he. Happy girl! you are going to see Horatio—to find a new, gifted, fond friend; one as superior to his fellow-creatures, as perfection is superior to frailty."

This account, remembered with more interest now that she approached the subject of it, excited Ethel's curiosity, and she began, as they went on their way from Rome to Naples, in a great degree to participate in Edward's eagerness to see his cousin.

• • •

CHAPTER XI

"Sad and troubled?
How brave her anger shows! How it sets off
Her natural beauty! Under what happy star
Was Virolet born, to be beloved and sought
By two incomparable women?"

—Fletcher

It was the month of December when the travellers arrived at this "piece of heaven dropt upon earth," as the natives themselves name it. The moon hung a glowing orb in the heavens, and lighted up the sea to beauty. A blood-red flash shot up now and then from Vesuvius; a summer softness was in the atmosphere, while a thousand tokens presented themselves of a climate more friendly, more joyous, and more redundant than that of the northern Isle from which they came. It was very late at night when they reached their hotel, and they were heartily fatigued, so that it was not till the next morning, that immediately after breakfast, Villiers left Ethel, and went out to seek the abode of his cousin.

He had been gone some little time, when a waiter of the hotel, throwing open Ethel's drawing-room door, announced "Signor Orazio." Quite new to Italy, Ethel was ignorant of the custom in that country, of designating people by their christian names; and that Horatio Saville, being a resident in Naples, and married to a Neapolitan, was known everywhere by the appellation which the servant now used. Ethel was not in the least aware that it was Lucy's brother who presented himself to her. She saw a gentleman, tall, very slight in person, with a face denoting habitual thoughtfulness, and stamped by an individuality which she could not tell whether to think plain, and yet it was certainly open and kind. An appearance of extreme shyness, almost amounting to awkwardness, was diffused over him, and his words came hesitatingly; he spoke English, and was an Englishman—so much Ethel discovered by his first words, which were, "Villiers is not at home?" and then he began to ask her about her journey, and how she liked the view of the bay of Naples, which she beheld from her windows. They were in this kind of trivial conversation when Edward came bounding up-stairs, and with exclamations of delight greeted his cousin. Ethel, infinitely surprised, examined her guest with more care. In a few minutes she began to wonder how she came to think him plain. His deep-set, dark-grey eyes struck her as expressive, if not handsome. His features were delicately moulded, and his fine forehead betokened depth of intellect; but the charm of his face was a kind of fitful, beamy, inconstant smile, which diffused incomparable sweetness over his physiognomy. His usual look was cold and abstracted—his eye speculated with an inward thoughtfulness—a chilling seriousness sat on his features, but this glancing and varying half-smile came to dispel gloom, and to invite and please those with whom he conversed. His voice was modulated by feeling, his language was fluent, graceful in its turns of expression, and original in the thoughts which it expressed. His manners were marked by high breeding, yet they were peculiar. They were formed by his individual disposition, and under the dominion of sensibility. Hence they were often abrupt and reserved. He forgot the world around him, and gave token, by absence of mind, of the absorbing nature of his contemplations. But at a touch this vanished, and a sweet earnestness, and a beaming kindliness of spirit, at once displaced his abstraction, rendering him attentive, cordial, and gay.

Never had Horatio Saville appeared to so little advantage as during his short tête-à-tête with his new relative. At all times, when quiescent, he had a retiring manner, and an appearance, whose want of pretension did not at first allure, and yet which afterwards formed his greatest attraction. He was always unembarrassed, and Ethel could not guess that towards her alone he felt as timid and shy as a girl. It was with considerable effect that Horatio had commanded himself to appear before the daughter of Lady Lodore. There was something incongruous and inconceivable in the idea of the child of Cornelia a woman, married to his cousin. He feared to see in her an image of the being who had subdued his heart of hearts, and laid prostrate his whole soul; he trembled to catch the sound of her voice, lest it might echo tones which could disturb to their depths his inmost thoughts. Ethel was so unlike her mother, that by degrees he became reassured; her eyes, her hair, her stature, and tall slender shape, were the reverse of Lady Lodore; so that in a little while he ventured to raise his eyes to her face, and to listen to her, without being preoccupied by a painful sensation, which, in its violence, resembled terror. It is true that by degrees this dissimilarity to her mother became less; she had gestures, smiles, and tones, that were all Lady Lodore, and which, when discerned, struck his heart with a pang, stealing away his voice, and causing him to stand suspended in the act he was about, like one acted upon by magic.

While this mute and curious examination was going on in the minds of Ethel and her visitant, the conversation had not tarried. Edward had never been so far south, and the wonders of Naples were as new to him as to Ethel. Saville was eager to show them, and proposed going that very day to Pompeii. For, as he said, all their winter was not like the present day, so that it was best to seize the genial weather while it lasted. Was Mrs. Villiers too much fatigued? On the contrary, Ethel was quite on the alert; but first she asked whether Mrs. Saville would not accompany them.

"Clorinda," said Horatio, "promises herself much pleasure from your acquaintance, and intends calling on you to-day at twenty-four o'clock, that is, at the Ave Maria: how stupid I am," he continued, laughing, "I quite forget that you are not Italianized, as I am, and do not know the way in which the people here count their time. Clorinda will call late in the afternoon, the usual visiting hour at Naples, but she would find no pleasure in visiting a ruined city and fallen fragments. One house in the Chiaja is worth fifty Pompeiis in the eyes of a Neapolitan, and Clorinda is one, heart and soul. I hope you will be pleased with her, for she is an admirable specimen of her countrywomen, and they are wonderful and often sublime creatures in their way; but do not mistake her for an English woman, or you will be disappointed— she has not one atom of body, one particle of mind, that bears the least affinity to England. And now, is your carriage ordered?—there it is at the door; so, as I should say to one of my own dear sisters, put on your bonnet, Ethel, quickly, and do not keep us waiting; for though at Naples, days are short in December, and we have none of their light to lose."

When, after this explanation, Ethel first saw Clorinda, she was inclined to think that Saville had scarcely done his wife justice. Certainly she was entirely Italian, but she was very beautiful; her complexion was delicate, though dark and without much colour. Her hair silken and glossy as the raven's wing; her large bright black eyes resplendent; the perfect arch of her brows, and the marmoreal and harmonious grace of her forehead, such as is never seen in northern lands, except in sculpture imitated from the Greeks. The lower part of her face was not so good; her smile was deficient in sweetness, her voice wanted melody, and sounded loud to an English ear. Her gestures were expressive, but quick and wanting in grace. She was more agreeable when silent and could be regarded as a picture, than when called into action. She was complimentary in her conversation, and her manners were winning by their frankness and ease. She gesticulated too much, and her features were too much in motion,—too pantomimely expressive, so to speak, not to impress disagreeably one accustomed to the composure of the English. Still she was a beautiful creature; young, artless, desirous to please, and endowed, moreover, with the vivacious genius, the imaginative talent of her country. She spoke as if she were passionately attached to her husband; but when Ethel mentioned his English home and his relations, a cloud came over the lovely Neapolitan's countenance, and a tremor shook her frame. "Do not think hardly of me," she said, "I do not hate England, but I fear it. I am sure I should be disliked there—I should be censured, perhaps taunted, for a thousand habits and feelings as natural to me as the air I breathe. I am proud, and I should retort impertinence, and, displeasing my husband, become miserable beyond words. Stay with us; you I love, and should be wretched to part from. Stay and enjoy this paradise with us. Entreat his sisters, if they wish to see Horatio, to come over. I will be more than a sister to them; but let us all forget that such a place as that cold, distant England exists."

This was Clorinda's usual mode of speaking of her husband's native country: but once, when Ethel had urged her going there with more earnestness than usual, suddenly her countenance became disturbed; and with a lowering and stormy expression of face, that her English friend could never afterwards forget, she said, "Say not another word, I pray. Horatio loved—he loves an Englishwoman—it is torture enough for me to know this. I would rather be torn in quarters by wild horses, broken in pieces on the rack, than set foot in England. My cousin, as you have pity for me, and value the life of Horace, use your influence to prevent his only dreaming of a return to England. Methinks I could strike him dead, if I only knew that such a thought lived for a second in his heart."

These words said, Clorinda resumed her smiles, and was, more than usual, desirous of flattering and pleasing Ethel; so that she softened, though she could not erase, the impression her vehemence had made. However, there appeared no necessity for Ethel to exert her influence. Horace was equally averse to going to England. He loved to talk of it; he remembered, with yearning fondness, its verdant beauty, its pretty villages, its meandering streams, its embowered groves; the spots he had inhabited, the trivial incidents of his daily life, were recalled with affection: but he did not wish to return. Villiers attributed this somewhat to his unforgotten attachment to Lady Lodore; but it was more strange that he negatived the idea of one of his sisters visiting him:—"She would not like it," was all the explanation he gave.

Several months passed lightly over the heads of the new-married pair; while they, bee-like, sipped the honey of life, and, never cloyed, fed perpetually on sweets. Naples, its galleries, its classic and beautiful environs, offered an endless succession of occupation and amusement. The presence of Saville elevated their pleasures; for he added the living spirit of poetry to their sensations, and associated the treasures of human genius with the sublime beauty of nature. He had a tact, a delicacy, a kind of electric sympathy in his disposition, that endeared him to every one that approached him. His very singularities, by keeping alive an interest in him, added to the charm. Sometimes he was so abstracted as to do the most absent things in the world; and the quick alternations of his gaiety and seriousness were often ludicrous from their excess. There was one thing, indeed, to which Ethel found it difficult to accustom herself, which was his want of punctuality, which often caused hours to be lost, and their excursions spoiled. Nor did he ever furnish good excuses, but seemed annoyed at being questioned on the subject.

Clorinda never joined them in their drives and rides out of the city. She feared to trust herself to winds and waves; the heat, the breeze, the dust, annoyed her; and she found no pleasure in looking at mountains, which, after all, were only mountains; or ruins, which were only ruins—stones, fit for nothing but to be removed and thrown away. But Clorinda had an empire of her own, to which she gladly admitted her English relatives, and the delights of which they fully appreciated. Music, heard in such perfection at the glory of Naples, the theatre of San Carlo, and the heavenly strains which filled the churches with an atmosphere of sound more entrancing than incense—all these were hers; and her own voice, rich, full, and well-cultivated, made a temple of melody of her own home.

There was—it could not be called a wall—but there was certainly a paling, of separation between Ethel and Clorinda. The young English girl could not discover in what it consisted, or why she could not pass beyond. The more she saw of the Neapolitan, the more she believed that she liked her—certainly her admiration increased;—still she felt that on the first day that Clorinda had visited her, with her caressing manners and well-turned flatteries, she was quite as intimate with her as now, after several weeks. She had surely nothing to conceal; all was open in her conduct; yet often Ethel thought of her as a magician guarding a secret treasure. Something there was that she watched over and hid. There was often a look of anxiety about her which Ethel unconsciously dispelled by some chance word; or a cloud all at once dimmed her face, and her magnificent and dazzling eyes flashed sudden fire, without apparent cause. There was something in her manner that always said, "You are English, I am Italian; and there is natural war between my fire and your snow." But no word, no act, ever betrayed alienation of feeling. Thus a sort of mystery pervaded their intercourse, which, though it might excite curiosity, and was not unakin to admiration, kept the affections in check.

Sometimes Ethel thought that Clorinda feared to compromise her salvation, for she was a Catholic. During the revelries of the Carnival, this difference of religion was not so apparent; but when Lent began, it showed itself, and divided them, on various occasions, more than before. At last, Lent also was drawing to a close; and as Villiers and Ethel were anxious to see the ceremonies of Passion Week at Rome, it was arranged that they, and Mr. and Mrs. Saville, should visit the Eternal City together. Horatio manifested a distaste even to the short residence that it was agreed they should make together during the month they were to spend at Rome; but Clorinda showed herself particularly anxious for the fulfilment of this plan, and, the majority prevailing, the whole party left Naples together.

Full soon was the veil of mystery then withdrawn, and Villiers and his wife let into the arcana of their cousin's life. Horatio had yielded unwillingly to Clorinda's entreaties, and extracted many promises from her before he gave his consent; but all would not do—the natural, the uncontrollable violence of her disposition broke down every barrier; and in spite of his caution, and her struggles with herself, the reality opened fearfully upon the English pair. The lava torrent of Neapolitan blood flowed in her veins; and restraining it for some time, it at last poured itself forth with volcanic violence. It was at the inn at Terracina, on their way to Rome, that a scene took place, such as an English person must cross Alps and Apennines to behold. Ethel had seen that something was wrong. She saw the beauty of Clorinda vanished, changed, melted away and awfully transformed into actual ugliness: she saw tiger-like glances from her eyes, and her lips pale and quivering. Poor Saville strove, with gentle words, to allay the storm to which some jealous freak gave rise: perceiving that his endeavours were vain, he rose to quit the room. They were at dinner: she sprung on him with a knife in her hand: Edward seized her arm; and she sunk on the floor in convulsions. Ethel was scarcely less moved. Seeing her terrified beyond all expression, Horatio led her from the room. He was pale—his voice failed him. He left her; and sending Edward to her, returned to his wife.

The same evening he said to Villiers,—"Do not ask me to stay;—let me go without another word. You see how it is. With what Herculean labour I have concealed this sad truth so long, is scarcely conceivable. When Ethel's sweet smile has sometimes reproached my tardiness, I have escaped, but half alive, from a scene like the one you witnessed.

"In a few hours, it is true, Clorinda will be shocked—full of remorse—at my feet;—that is worse still. Her repentance is as violent as her rage; and both transform her from a woman into something too painful to dwell upon. She is generous, virtuous, full of power and talent; but this fatal vehemence more than neutralizes her good qualities. I can do nothing; I am chained to the oar. I have but one hope: time, reason, and steadiness of conduct on my part, may subdue her; and as she will at no distant period become a mother, softer feelings may develop themselves. Sometimes I am violently impelled to fly from her for ever. But she loves me, and I will not desert her. If she will permit me, I will do my duty to the end. Let us go back now. You will return to Naples next winter; and with this separation, which will gall her proud spirit to its core, as a lesson, I hope by that time that she will prove more worthy of Ethel's society."

Nothing could be said to this. Saville, though he asked, "Let us go back," had decreed, irrevocably, in his own mind, not to advance another step with his companions. The parting was melancholy and ominous. He would not permit Clorinda to appear again; for, as he said, he feared her repentance more than her violence, and would not expose Ethel as the witness of a scene of humiliation and shame. A thousand times over, his friends promised to return immediately to Naples, not deferring their visit till the following winter. He was to take a house for them, for the summer, at Castel à Mare, or Sorrento; and immediately after Easter they were to return. These kind promises were a balm to his disturbed mind. He watched their carriage from the inn at Terracina, as it skimmed along the level road of the Pontine Marshes, and could not despair while he expected its quick return. Turning his eyes away, he resumed his yoke again; and, melancholy beyond his wont, joined his remorseful wife. They were soon on their way back to Naples:—she less demonstrative in her repentance, because more internally and deeply touched, than she had ever been before.

• • •

CHAPTER XII

"Shall I compare thee to a summer's day?
Thou art more lovely and more temperate;
Rough winds do shake the darling buds of May,
And summer's lease hath all too short a date;
But thy eternal summer shall not fade."

—Shakespeare

❦

Parting thus sadly from their unfortunate cousin, Villiers and Ethel were drawn together yet nearer, and, if possible, with a deeper tenderness of affection than before. Here was an example before their eyes, that all their fellow-creatures were not equally fortunate in the lottery of life, and that worse than a blank befell many, while the ticket which they had drawn was a prize beyond all summing. Edward felt indeed disappointed at losing his cousin's society, as well as deeply grieved at the wretched fate which he had selected for himself. Ethel, on the contrary, was in her heart glad that he was absent. She had no place in that heart to spare away from her husband; and however much she liked Horatio, and worthy as he was of her friendship, she felt him as an encroacher. Now she delivered herself up to Edward, and to the thought of Edward solely, with fresh and genuine delight. No one stood between her and him—none called off his attention, or forced her to pass one second of time unoccupied by his idea. When she expressed these feelings to Villiers, he called her selfish and narrow-hearted, yet his pride and his affection were gratified; for he knew how true was every word she uttered, and how without flaw or blot was her faith and her attachment.

"And yet, my Ethel," he said, "I sometimes ask myself, how this boasted affection of yours will stand the trials which I fear are preparing for it."

"What trials?" she asked anxiously.

"Care, poverty; the want of all the luxuries, perhaps of the comforts of life."

Ethel smiled again. "That is your affair," she replied, "do you rouse your courage, if you look upon these as evils. I shall feel nothing of all this, while near you; care—poverty—want! as if I needed any thing except your love—you yourself—who are mine."

"Yes, dear," replied Villiers, "that is all very well at this moment; rolling along in a comfortable carriage—an hotel ready to receive us, with all its luxuries; but suppose us without any of these, Ethel—suppose yourself in a melancholy, little, dingy abode, without servants, without carriage, going out on foot."

"Not alone," replied his wife, laughing, and kissing his hand; "I shall have you to wait on me—to wait upon—"

"You take it very well now," said Edward; "I hope that you will never be put to the trial. I am far from anticipating this excess of wretchedness, of course, but I cannot help feeling, that the prospects of to-morrow are uncertain, and I am anxious for my long-delayed letters from England."

With Ethel's deep and warm affection, had she been ten or only five years older, she also must have participated in Edward's inquietude. But care is a word, not an emotion, for the very young. She was only seventeen. She had never attended to the disbursements of money—she was ignorant of the mechanism of giving and receiving, on which the course of our life depends. It was in vain that she sought in the interior of her mind for an image that should produce fear or regret, with regard to the absence or presence of money. No one reflection or association brought into being an idea on the subject. Again she kissed Edward's hand, and looked on him with her soft clear eyes, thinking only, "He is here—and Heaven has given me all I ask."

Left again to themselves, they were anxious to avoid acquaintances. Yet this was impossible during the Holy Week at Rome. Villiers found many persons whom he knew; women of high rank and fashion, men of wealth, or with the appearance of it, enjoying the present, and, while away from England, unencumbered by care. Mr. and Mrs. Villiers were among these, and of them; their rank and their style of living resembling theirs, associated them together. All this was necessary to Edward, for he had been accustomed to it—it was natural to Ethel, because, being wholly inexperienced, she did as others did, and as Villiers wished her to do, without reflection or forethought.

Yet each day added to Edward's careful thoughts. Easter was gone, and the period approached when they had talked of returning to Naples. The covey of English had taken flight towards the north; they were almost the only strangers in the ancient and silent city, whose every stone breathes of a world gone by—whose surpassing beauty crowns her still the glory of the world. The English pair, left to themselves, roamed through the ruins and loitered in the galleries, never weary of the very ocean of beauty and grandeur which they coursed over in their summer bark. The weather grew warm, for the month of May had commenced, and they took refuge in the vast churches from the heat; at twilight they sought the neighbouring gardens, or scrambled about the Coliseum, or the more ruined and weedgrown baths of Caracalla. The fire-flies came out, and the splashing of the many fountains reached their ears from afar, while the clear azure of the Roman sky bent over them in beauty and peace.

Ethel never alluded to their proposed return to Naples—she feared each day to hear Villiers mention it—she was so happy where she was, she shrunk from any change. The majesty, the simplicity, the quiet of Rome, were in unison with the holy stillness that dwelt in her soul, absorbed as it was by one unchanging image. She had reached the summit of human happiness—she had nothing more to ask; her full heart, not bursting, yet gently overflowing in its bliss, thanked Heaven, and drew nearer Edward, and was at peace.

"God help us!" exclaimed Villiers, "I wonder what on earth will become of us!"

They were sitting together on fragment of the Coliseum; they had clambered up its fallen wall, and reached a kind of weed-grown chasm whose depth, as it was moonlight, they could not measure by the eye; so they sat beside it on a small fragment, and Villiers held Ethel close to him lest she should fall. The heartfelt and innocent caress of two united in the sight of Heaven, wedded together for the endurance of the good and ills of life, hallowed the spot and hour; and then, even while Ethel nestled nearer to him in fondness, Edward made the exclamation that she heard with a wonder which mingled with, yet could not disturb, the calm joy which she felt.

"What but good can come of us, while we are thus?" she asked.

"You will not listen to me, nor understand me," replied her husband. "But I do assure you, that our position is more than critical. No remittances, no letters come from England; we are in debt here—in debt in Italy! A thousand miles from our resources! I grope in the dark and see no outlet—every day's post, with the nothing that it brings, adds to my anxiety."

"All will be well," replied Ethel gently; "no real evil will happen to us, be assured."

"I wish," said Villiers, "your experience, instead of your ignorance, suggested the assertion. I would rather die a thousand deaths than apply to dear Horace, who is ill enough off himself; but every day here adds to our difficulties. Our only hope is in our instant return to England—and, by heavens!—you kiss me, Ethel, as if we lived in fairy land, and that such were our food—have you no fears?"

"I am sorry to say, none," she answered in a soft voice; "I wish I could contrive some, because I appear unsympathizing to you—but

I cannot fear;—you are in health and near me. Heaven and my dear father's spirit will watch over us, and all will be well. This is the end and beginning of my anxiety; so dismiss yours, love—for, believe me, in a day or two, these forebodings of yours will be as a dream."

"It is very strange," replied Edward, "were you not so close to me, I should fancy you a spirit instead of a woman; you seem to have no touch of earthly solicitude. Well, I will do as you bid me, and hope for to-morrow. And now let us get down from this place before the moon sets and leaves us in darkness."

As if to confirm the auguries of Ethel, the following morning brought the long-expected letters. One contained a remittance, another was from Colonel Villiers, to say, that Edward's immediate presence was requisite in England to make the final arrangements before his marriage. With a glad heart Villiers turned his steps northward; while Ethel, if she could have regretted aught while with him, would have sighed to leave their lonely haunts in Rome. She well knew that whatever of sublime nature might display, or man might congregate of beautiful in art elsewhere, there was a calm majesty, a silent and awful repose in the ruins of Rome, joined to the delights of a southern climate, and the luxuriant vegetation of a sunny soil, more in unison with her single and devoted heart, than any other spot in the universe could boast. They would both have rejoiced to have seen Saville again; yet they were unacknowledgedly glad not to pursue their plan of domesticating near him at Naples. A remediless evil, which is for ever the source of fresh disquietude, is one that tasks human fortitude and human patience, more than those vaster misfortunes which elevate while they wound. The proud aspiring spirit of man craves something to raise him from the dust, and to adorn his insignificance; he seeks to strengthen his alliance with the lofty and the eternal, and shrinks from low-born cares, as being the fetters and bolts that link him to his baser origin. Saville, the slave of a violent woman's caprice, struggling with passions, at once so fiery and so feeble as to excite contempt, was a spectacle which they were glad to shun. Their own souls were in perfect harmony, and discord was peculiarly abhorrent to them.

They travelled by the beaten route of Mont Cenis, Lyons, and Calais, and in less than a month arrived in England. As the presence of Villiers was requisite in London, after staying a few days at an hotel in Brook Street, they took a furnished house in the same street for a short time. The London season had passed its zenith, but its decline was scarcely perceptible. Ethel had no wish to enter into its gaieties, and it had been Edward's plan to avoid them until they were richer. But here they were, placed by fate in the very midst of them; and as, when their affairs were settled, they intended again to return abroad, he could not refuse himself the pleasure of seeing Ethel, in the first flower of her loveliness, mingling with, and outshining, every other beauty of her country. It would have been difficult indeed, placed within the verge of the English aristocracy assembled in London, to avoid its engagements and pleasures—for he "also was an Arcadian," and made one of the self-enthroned "world." The next two months, therefore, while still every settlement was delayed by his father, they spent in the fashionable circles of London.

They did not indeed enter into its amusements with the zest and resolution of tyros. To Villiers the scene was not new, and therefore not exceedingly enticing; and Ethel's mind was not of the sort to be borne along in the stream of folly. They avoided going to crowded entertainments—they were always satisfied with one or two parties in the evening. Nay, once or twice in the week they usually remained at home, and not unseldom dined tête-à-tête. The serpent fang of pleasure, and the paltry ambition of society, had no power over Ethel. She often enjoyed herself, because she often met people of either sex, whose fame, or wit, or manners, interested and pleased her. But as little vanity as mortal woman ever had fell to her share. Very young, and (to use the phrase of the day) very new, flattery and admiration glanced harmlessly by her. Her personal vanity was satisfied when Villiers was pleased, and, for the rest, she was glad to improve her mind, and to she wishes, without hesitation or difficulty. Did she desire her lovely grown-up daughter to play a child's part towards her, she would soon contrive to bring it about. Lady Lodore is a woman of the world—she was nursed in its lessons, and piously adheres to its code; its ways are her's, and the objects of ambition which it holds out, are those which she desires to attain. She is talked of as admired and followed by the Earl of D——. You may spoil all, if you put yourself forward."

Ethel was not quite satisfied. The voice of nature was awake within, and she yearned to claim her mother's affection. Until now, she had regarded her more as a stranger; but at this time, a filial instinct stirred her heart, impelling her to some outward act—some demonstration of duty. Whenever she saw Lady Lodore, which was rarely, and at a distance, she gazed earnestly on her, and tried to read within her soul, whether Villiers was right, and her mother happy. The shining, uniform outside of a woman of fashion baffled her endeavours without convincing her. One evening at the Opera, she discerned Lady Lodore in the tier below her. Ethel drew back and shaded herself with the curtain of her box, so that she could not be perceived, while she watched her mother intently. A succession of visitors came into Lady Lodore's box, and she spoke to all with the animation of a heart at ease. There was an almost voluptuous repose in her manner and appearance, that contrasted with, while it adorned, the easy flow of her conversation, and the springtide of wit, which, to judge from the amusement of her auditors, flowed from her lips. Yet Ethel fancied that her smile was often forced, so suddenly did it displace an expression of listlessness and languor, which when she turned from the people in her box to the stage, came across her countenance like a shadow. It might be the gas, which shadows so unbecomingly the fair audience at the King's Theatre; it might be the consequences of raking, for Lady Lodore was out every night; but Ethel thought that she saw a change; she was less brilliant, her person thinner, and had lost some of its exquisite roundness. Still, as her daughter gazed, she thought, She is not happy. Yet what could she do? How pour sweetness into the bitter stream of life? As which had replied to Lord D——, said to her, "Your ear-ring is unfastened, Ethel; it will fall out." Ethel could not speak; she raised her hands, mechanically, to arrange the ornament; but her trembling fingers refused to perform the office. "Permit me," said the lady, drawing off her glove; and Ethel felt her mother's hand touch her cheek: her very life stood suspended; it was a bitter pain, yet a pleasure inconceivable; there was a suffocation in her throat, and the tears filled her eyes; but even the simple words, "I thank you," died on her lips—her voice could frame no sound. The world, and all within its sphere, might have passed away at that moment, and she been unconscious of any change. "Yes, she will love me!" was the idea that spoke audibly within; and a feeling of confidence, a flow of sympathy and enthusiastic affection, burst on her heart. As soon as she could recollect herself, she turned: Lady Lodore was no longer there; she had glided from her seat; and Ethel just caught a glimpse of her, as she contrived another for herself, behind a column, which afterwards so hid her, that her daughter could only see the waving of her plumes. On these she fixed her eyes until all was over; and then Lady Lodore went out hurriedly, with averted face, as if to escape her recognition. This put the seal on Ethel's dream. She believed that her mother obviously signified her desire that they should continue strangers to each other. It was hard, but she must submit. She had no longer that prejudice against Lady Lodore, that exaggerated notion of her demerits, which the long exile of her father, and the abhorrence of Mrs. Fitzhenry, had before instilled. Her mother was no longer a semi-gorgon, hid behind a deceptive mask—a Medea, without a touch of human pity. She was a lovely, soft-voiced, angelic-looking woman, whom she would have given worlds to be permitted to love and wait upon. She found excuses for her errors; she lavished admiration on all her attractions; she could do all but muster courage to vanquish the obstacles that existed to their intercourse. She fondly cherished her image, as an idol placed in the sanctuary of her heart, which she could regard with silent reverence and worship, but whose concealing veil she could not raise. Villiers smiled when she spoke in this way to him. He saw, in her enthusiasm, the overflowing of an affectionate heart, which longed to exhaust itself in loving. He kissed her, and bade her think any thing, so that she did nothing. The time for doing had indeed, for the present, passed away. Lady Lodore left town; and when mother and daughter met again, it was not destined to be beneath a palace roof, surrounded by the nobility of the land.

• • •

CHAPTER XIII

"I choose to comfort myself by considering, that even
while I am lamenting my present uneasiness, it is
passing away."

—*Horace Walpole*

An event occurred at this time, which considerably altered the plans of Mr. and Mrs. Villiers. They had been invited to spend some time at Maristow Castle, and were about to proceed thither with Lord Maristow and his daughters, when the sudden death of Mr. Saville changed every thing. He died of a malignant fever, leaving a young widow, and no child, to inherit his place in society.

Through this unlooked-for event, Horatio became the immediate heir of his father's title. He stept, from the slighted position of a younger son into the rank of the eldest; and thus became another being in all men's eyes—but chiefly in his father's.

Viscount Maristow had deeply regretted his son's foreign marriage, and argued against his choice of remaining abroad. He was a statesman, and conceived that Horatio's talents and eloquence would place him high among the legislators of St. Stephen's. The soundness of his understanding, and the flowing brilliancy of his language, were pledges of his success. But Saville was not ambitious. His imagination rose high above the empty honours of the world—to be useful was a better aim; but he did not conceive that his was a mind calculated to lead others in its train: its framework was too delicate, too finely strung, to sound in accord with the many. He wanted the desire to triumph; and was content to adore truth in the temple of his own mind, without defacing its worship by truckling to the many falsehoods and errors which demand subserviency in the world.

Lord Maristow had hitherto submitted to his disappointment, not without murmurs, but without making any great effort at victory. He had written many letters entreating his son to cast off the drowsy Neapolitan sloth;—he had besought Villiers, previous to his departure the preceding year, to bring his cousin back with him;—and this was all.

The death of his eldest son quickened him to exertion. He resolved to trust no longer to written arguments, but to go himself to Italy, and by force of paternal authority, or persuasions, to induce his son to come back to his native country, and to fill with honour the post to which fortune had advanced him. He did not doubt that Horatio would himself feel the force of his new duties; but it would be clenching his purpose, and paying an agreeable compliment to Clorinda, to make this journey, and to bring them back with him when he returned. Whatever Mrs. Saville's distaste to England might be, it must yield to the necessity that now drew her thither. Lord Maristow could not imagine any resistance so violent as to impede his wishes. The projected journey charmed his daughters, saddened as they were by their recent loss. Lucy was overjoyed at the prospect of seeing her beloved brother. She felt sure that Clorinda would be brought to reason and thus, with their hearts set upon one object, one idea, they bade adieu to Ethel and her husband, as if their career was to be as sunny and as prosperous as they doubted not that their own would be.

Lord Maristow alone guessed how things might stand. "Edward, my dear boy," he said, "give me credit for great anxiety on your account. I wish this marriage of yours had not taken place, then you might have roughed it as other young men do, and have been the better for a little tart experience. I do not like this shuffling on your father's part. I hear for a certainty that this marriage of his will come to nothing—

the friends of the young lady are against it, and she is very young, and only an heiress by courtesy—her father can give her as many tens of thousands as he pleases, but he has sworn not to give her a shilling if she marries without his consent; and he has forbidden Colonel Villiers his house. He still continues at Cheltenham, and assures every one that he is on safe ground; that the girl loves him, and that when once his, the father must yield. It is too ridiculous to see him playing a boy-lover's part at his time of life, trying to undermine a daughter's sense of duty—he, who may soon be a grandfather! The poor little thing, I am told, is quite fascinated by his dashing manners and station in society. We shall see how it will end—I fear ill; her father might pardon a runaway match with a lover of her own age; but he will never forgive the coldblooded villany, excuse me, of a man of three times her age; who for gain, and gain only, is seeking to steal her from him. Such is the sum of what I am told by a friend of mine, just arrived from Cheltenham. The whole thing is the farce of the day, and the stolen interviews of the lovers, and the loud, vulgarly-spoken denunciations of her father, vary the scene from a travestie of Romeo and Juliet to the comedies of Plautus or Molière. I beg your pardon, Edward, for my frankness, but I am angry. I have been used as a cat's-paw—I have been treated unfairly—I was told that the marriage wanted but your signature—my representations induced you to offer to Miss Fitzhenry, and now you are a ruined man. I am hampered by my own family, and cannot come forward to your assistance. My advice is, that you wait a little, and see what turn matters take; once decided, however they conclude, strong representations shall be made to your father, and he shall be forced to render proper assistance; then if politics take a better turn, I may do something for you—or you can live abroad till better times."

Villiers thanked Lord Maristow for his advice, and made no remarks either on his details or promises. He saw his own fate stretched drearily before him; but his pride made him strong to bear without any outward signs of wincing. He would suffer all, conceal all, and be pitied by none. The thought of Ethel alone made him weak. Were she sheltered during the storm which he saw gathering so darkly, he would have felt satisfied.

What was to be done? To go abroad, was to encounter beggary and famine. To remain, exposed him to a thousand insults and dangers from which there was no escape. Such were the whisperings of despair—but brighter hopes often visited him. All could not be so evil as it seemed. Fortune, so long his enemy, would yield at last one inch of ground—one inch to stand upon, where he might wait in patience for better days. Had he indeed done his utmost to avert the calamities he apprehended? Certainly not. Thus spoke his sanguine spirit: more could and should be done. His father might find means, he himself be enabled to arrange with his lawyer some mode of raising a sum of money which would at least enable him to go on the continent with his wife. He spent his thoughts in wishes for the attainment of this desirable conclusion to his adversity, till the very earnestness of his expectations seemed to promise their realization. It could not be that the worst would come. Absurd! Something must happen to assist them. Seeking for this unknown something which, in spite of all his efforts, would take no visible or tangible form, he spent weary days and sleepless nights, his brain spinning webs of thought, not like those of the spider, useful to their weaver—a tangled skein they were rather, where the clue was inextricably hid. He did not speak of these things to Ethel, but he grew sad, and she was anxious to go out of town, to have him all to herself, when she promised herself to dispel his gloom; and, as she darkly guessed at the source of his disquietude, by economy and a system of rigid privation, to show him how willing and able she was to meet the adversity which he so much dreaded.

• • •

CHAPTER XIV

"The pure, the open, prosperous love.
That pledged on earth, and sealed above.
Grows in the world's approving eyes.
   In friendship's smile and home's caress.
Collecting all the heart's sweet ties
   Into one knot of happiness."

—*Moore*, Lalla Rookh

Another month withered away in fruitless expectation. Villiers felt that he was following an ignis fatuus, yet knew not how to give up his pursuit. At length, he listened more docilely to Ethel's representations of the expediency of quitting town. She wished to pay her long-promised visit to her aunt, and Villiers at last consented to accompany her. They gave up their house, dispersed a tolerably numerous establishment, and left town for their sober and rural seclusion in Essex.

Taken from the immediate scene where care met him at every turn, Edward's spirits rose; and the very tranquillity and remoteness of Longfield became a relief and an enjoyment. It was bright October weather. The fields were green, the hedges yet in verdant trim. The air was so still that the dead leaves hung too lazy to fall, from the topmost boughs of the earlier trees. The oak was still dressed in a dark sober green—the fresh July shoot, having lost its summer

Ethel was especially delighted to renew her acquaintance with Longfield, her father's boyhood home, under such sunny circumstances. She had loved it before: with anguish in her heart, and heavy sadness weighing on her steps, she had loved it for his sake. But now that it became the home, the dedicated garden of love, it received additional beauty in her eyes from its association with the memory of Lord Lodore. All things conjoined; the season, calmed and brightened, as if for her especial enjoyment; remembrance of the past, and the undivided possession of her Edward's society, combined to steep her soul in happiness. Even he, whose more active and masculine spirit might have fretted in solitude and sloth, was subdued by care and uncertainty to look on the peace of the present moment as the dearest gift of the gods. Both so young, and the minds of both open as day to each other's eyes, no single blot obscured their intercourse. They never tired of each other, and the teeming spirit of youth filled the empty space of each hour as it came, with a new growth of sentiments and ideas. The long evening had its pleasures, with its close-drawn curtains and cheerful fire. Even whist with the white-haired parson, and Mrs. Fitzhenry in her spectacles, imparted pleasure. Could any thing duller have been devised, which would have been difficult, it had not been so to them; and a stranger coming in and seeing their animated looks, and hearing their cheerful tones and light-hearted laugh, must have envied the very Elysium of delight, which aunt Bessy's usually so sober drawing-room contained. Merely to see Ethel leaning on her husband's arm, and looking up in his face as he drew her yet closer, and, while his fingers were twined among her silken ringlets, kissed so fondly her fair brow, must have demonstrated to a worldling the irrefragable truth that happiness is born a twin, love being the parent.

The beauty of a pastoral picture has but short duration in this cloudy land,—and happiness, the sun of our moral existence, is yet more fitful in its visitations. Villiers and his young wife took their accustomed ride through shady lanes and copses, and through parks, where, though the magnificent features of nature were wanting, the eye was delighted by a various prospect of wood and lawny upland.

The soft though wild west wind drove along vast masses of snowy clouds, which displayed in their intervals the deep stainless azure of the boundless sky. The shadows of the clouds now darkened the pathway of our riders, and now they saw the sunlight advance from a distance, coming on with steps of light and air, till it reached them, and they felt the warmth and gladness of sunshine descend on them. The various coloured woods were now painted brightly in the beams, and now half lost in shadow. There was life and action everywhere—yet not the awakening activity of spring, but rather a vague, uneasy restlessness, allied to languor, and pregnant with melancholy.

Villiers was silent and sad. Ethel too well knew the cause wherefore he was dispirited. He had received letters that morning which stung him into a perception of the bitter realities which were gathering about them. One was to say that no communication had been received from his father, but that it was believed that he was somewhere in London—the other was from his banker, to remind him that he had overdrawn his credit—nearly the most disagreeable intelligence a man can hear when he possesses no immediate means of replenishing his drained purse. Ethel was grieved to see him pained, but she could not acutely feel these pecuniary distresses. She tried to divert his thoughts by conversation, and pointing out the changes which the advancing season made in the aspect of the country.

"Yes," said Villiers, "it is a beautiful world; poets tell us this, and religious men have drawn an argument for their creed from the wisdom and loveliness displayed in the external universe, which speaks to every heart and every understanding. The azure canopy fretted with golden lights, or, as now, curtained by wondrous shapes, which, though they are akin to earth, yet partake the glory of the sky—the green expanse, variegated by streams, teeming with life, and prolific of food to sustain that life, and that very food the chief cause of the beauty we enjoy— with such magnificence has the Creator set forth our table—all this, and the winds that fan us so balmily, and the flowers that enchant our sight—do not all these make earth a type of heaven?"

Ethel turned her eyes on him to read in his face the expression of the enthusiasm and enjoyment that seemed to dictate his words. But his countenance was gloomy, and as he continued to speak, his expressions took more the colour of his uneasy feelings. "How false and senseless all this really is!" he pursued. "Find a people who truly make earth, its woods and fells, and inclement sky, their unadorned dwelling-place, who pluck the spontaneous fruits of the soil, or slay the animals as they find them, attending neither to culture nor property, and we give them the name of barbarians and savages—untaught, uncivilized, miserable beings—and we, the wiser and more refined, hunt and exterminate them:—we, who spend so many words, either as preachers or philosophers, to vaunt that with which they are satisfied, we feel ourselves the greater, the wiser, the nobler, the more barriers we place between ourselves and nature, the more completely we cut ourselves off from her generous but simple munificence."

"But is this necessary?" asked the forest-bred girl: "when I lived in the wilds of the Illinois—the simplest abode, food and attire, were all I knew of human refinements, and I was satisfied."

Villiers did not appear to heed her remark, but continued the train of his own reflections. "The first desire of man is not for wealth nor luxury, but for sympathy and applause. He desires to remove to the furthest extremity of the world contempt and degradation; and according to the ideas of the society in which he is bred, so are his desires fashioned. We, the most civilized, high-bred, prosperous people in the world, make no account of nature, unless we add the ideas of possession, and of the labours of man. We rate each individual, (and we all desire to be rated as individuals, distinct from and superior to the mass,) not by himself, but by his house, his park, his income. This is a trite observation, yet it appears new when it comes home: what is lower, humbler, more despicable than a poor man? Give him learning, give him goodness—see him with manners acquired in poverty, habits dyed in the dusky hues of penury; and if we do not despise him, yet we do not admit him to our tables or society. Refinement may only be the varnish of the picture, yet it is necessary to make apparent to the vulgar eye even the beauties of Raphael."

"To the vulgar eye!" repeated Ethel, emphatically.

"And I seem one of those, by the way I speak," said Edward, smiling. "Yet, indeed, I do not despise any man for being poor, except myself. I can feel pride in showing honour where honour is due, even though clad in the uncouth and forbidding garb of plebeianism; but I cannot claim this for myself—I cannot demand the justice of men, which they would nickname pity. The Illinois would be preferable far."

"And the Illinois might be a paradise," said Ethel.

"We hope for a better—we hope for Italy. Do you remember Rome and the Coliseum, my love?—Naples, the Chiaja, and San Carlo?— these were better than the savannas of the west. Our hopes are good; it is the present only which is so thorny, so worse than barren: like the souls of Dante, we have a fiery pass to get through before we reach our place of bliss; that we have it in prospect will gift us with fortitude. Meanwhile I must string myself to my task. Ethel, dearest, I shall go to town to-morrow."

"And I with you, surely?"

"Do not ask it; this is your first lesson in the lore you were so ready to learn, of bearing all for me—"

"With you," interrupted his wife.

"With me—it shall soon be," replied Edward; "but to speak according to the ways of this world, my presence in London is necessary for a few days—for a very few days; a journey there and back for me is nothing, but it would be a real and useless expense if you went. Indeed, Ethel, you must submit to my going without you—I ask it of you, and you will not refuse."

"A few days, you say," answered Ethel— "a very few days? It is hard. But you will not be angry, if I should join you if your return is delayed?"

"You will not be so mad," said Villiers. "I go with a light heart, because I leave you in security and comfort. I will return—I need not protest— you know that I shall return the moment I can. I speak of a few days; it cannot be a week: let me go then, with what satisfaction I may, to the den of darkness and toil, and not be farther annoyed by the fear that you will not support my absence with cheerfulness. As you love me, wait for me with patience—remain with your aunt till I return."

"I will stay for a week, if it must be so," replied Ethel.

"Indeed, my love, it must—nor will I task you beyond—before a week is gone by, you shall see me."

Ethel looked wistfully at him, but said no more. She thought it hard—she did not think it right that he should go—that he should toil and suffer without her; but she had no words for argument or contention, so she yielded. The next morning—a cold but cheerful morning—at seven o'clock, she drove over with him in Mrs. Fitzhenry's little pony chaise to the town, four miles off, through which the stages passed. A first parting is a kind of landmark in life—a starting post whence we begin our career out of illusion and the land of dreams, into reality and endurance. They arrived not a moment too soon: she had yet a thousand things to say—one or two very particular things, which she had reserved for the last moment; there was no time, and she was forced to concentrate all her injunctions into one word, "Write!"

"Every day—and do you."

"It will be my only pleasure," replied his wife. "Take care of yourself."

He was on the top of the stage and gone; and Ethel felt that a blank loneliness had swallowed up the dearest joy of her life.

She drew her cloak round her—she gazed along the road—there were no traces of him—she gave herself up to thought, and as he was the object of all her thoughts, this was her best consolation. She reviewed the happy days they had spent together—she dwelt on the memory of his unalterable affection and endearing kindness, and then tears rushed into her eyes. "Will any ill ever befall him?" she thought. "O no, none ever can! he must be rewarded for his goodness and his love. How dear he ought to be to me! Did he not take the poor friendless girl from solitude and grief; and disdaining neither her poverty nor her orphan state, give her himself, his care, his affection? O, my Edward! what would Ethel have been without you? Her father was gone—her mother repulsed her—she was alone in the wide world, till you generously made her your own!"

With the true enthusiasm of passion, Ethel delighted to magnify the benefits she had received, and to make those which she herself conferred nothing, that gratitude and love might become yet stronger duties. In her heart, though she reproached herself for what she termed selfishness, she could not regret his poverty and difficulties, if thus she should acquire an opportunity of being useful to him; but she felt herself defrauded of her best privileges, of serving and consoling, by their separation.

Thus,—now congratulating herself on her husband's attachment, now repining at the fate that divided them,—agitated by various emotions too sweet and bitter for words, she returned to Longfield. Aunt Bessy was in her arm-chair, waiting for her to begin breakfast. Edward's seat was empty—his cup was not placed—he was omitted in the domestic arrangements;—tears rushed into her eyes; and in vain trying to calm herself, she sobbed aloud. Aunt Bessy was astonished; and when all the explanation she got was, "He is gone!" she congratulated herself, that her single state had spared her the endurance of these conjugal distresses.

• • •

CHAPTER XV

"How like a winter hath my absence been
From thee, the pleasure of the fleeting year!
What freezings have I felt, what dark days seen,
What old December's bareness every where!"

—*Shakespeare*

❧

E thel cheered herself to amuse her aunt; and, as in her days
of hopeless love, she tried to shorten the hours by occupation. It was difficult; for all her thoughts were employed in
conjectures as to where Edward was, what doing—in looking at her
watch, and following in her mind all his actions—or in meditating
how hereafter she might remedy any remissness on her part, (so tender
was her conscience,) and best contribute to his happiness. Such reveries beguiled many hours, and enabled her to endure with some show
of courage the pains of absence. Each day she heard from him—each
day she wrote, and this entire pouring out of herself on paper formed
the charm of her existence. She endeavoured to persuade him how
fortunate their lot might hereafter be—how many of his fears were
unfounded or misplaced.

"Remember, dearest love," she said, "that I have nothing of the fine
lady about me. I do not even feel the want of those luxuries so necessary
to most women. This I owe to my father. It was his first care, while he
brought me up in the most jealous retirement, to render me indepen-

dent of the services of others. Solitude is to me no evil, and the delight of my life would be to wait upon you. I am not therefore an object of pity, when fortunes deprives me of the appurtenances of wealth, which rather annoy than serve me. My devotion and sacrifice, as you are pleased to call the intense wish of my heart to contribute to your happiness, are nothing. I sacrifice all, when I give up one hour of your society—there is the sting—there the merit of my permitting you to go without me. I can ill bear it. I am impatient and weak; do not then, Edward dearest, task me too far—recall me to your side, if your return is delayed—recall your fond girl to the place near your heart, where she desires to remain for ever."

Villiers answered with few but expressive words of gratitude and fidelity. His letters breathed disappointment and anxiety. "It is too true," he said, "as I found it announced when I first came to town, my father is married. He got the banns published in an obscure church in London; he persuaded Miss Gregory to elope with him, and they are married. Her father is furious, he returns every letter unopened; his house and heart, he says, are still open to his daughter—but the—, I will not repeat his words, who stole her from him, shall never benefit by a shilling of his money—let her return, and all shall be pardoned— let her remain with her husband, and starve, he cares not. My father has spent much time and more money on this pursuit: in the hope of securing many thousands, he raised hundreds at a prodigal and ruin- ous interest, which must now be paid. He has not ten pounds in the world—so he says. My belief is, that he is going abroad to secure to himself the payment of the scanty remnant of his income. I have no hopes. I would beg at the corner of a street, rather than apply to a man who never has been a parent to me, and whose last act is that of a vil- lain. Excuse me; you will be angry that I speak thus of my father, but I know that he speaks of the poor girl he has deluded, with a bitter- ness and insult, which prove what his views were in marrying her. In this moment of absolute beggary, my only resource is to raise money. I believe I shall succeed; and the moment I have put things in train, with what heartfelt, what unspeakable joy, shall I leave this miserable place for my own Ethel's side, long to remain!"

Villiers's letters varied little, but yet they got more desponding; and Ethel grew very impatient to see him again. She had counted the days of her week—they were fulfilled, and her husband did not return. Every thing depended, he said, on his presence; and he must remain yet for another day or two. At first he implored her to be patient. He besought her, as she loved him, to endure their separation yet for a few more days. His letters were very short, but all in this style. They were imperative with his wife—she obeyed; yet she did so, she told him, against her will and against her sense of right. She ought to be at his side to cheer him under his difficulties. She had married him because she loved him, and because the first and only wish of her heart was to conduce to his happiness. To travel together, to enjoy society and the beauties of nature in each other's society, were indeed blessings, and she valued them; but there was another dearer still, of which she felt herself defrauded, and for which she yearned. "The aim of my life, and its only real joy," she said, "is to make your existence happier than it would have been without me. When I know and feel that such a moment or hour has been passed by you with sensations of pleasure, and that through me, I have fulfilled the purpose of my destiny. Deprived of the opportunity to accomplish this, I am bereft of that for which I breathe. You speak as if I were better off here than if I shared the inconveniences of your lot—is not this strange language, my own Edward? You talk of security and comfort; where can I be so secure as near you? And for comfort! what heart-elevating joy it would be to exchange this barren, meagre scene of absence, for the delight, the comfort of seeing you, of waiting on you! I do not ask you to hasten your return, so as to injure your prospects, but permit me to join you. Would not London itself, dismal as you describe it, become sunny and glad, if Ethel were with you?"

To these adjurations Villiers scarcely replied. Time crept on; three weeks had already elapsed. Now and then a day intervened, and he did not write, and his wife's anxiety grew to an intolerable pitch. She did not for an instant suspect his faith, but she feared that he must be utterly miserable, since he shrunk from communicating his feelings to her. His last letter was brief; "I have just come from my solicitor," he said, "and have but time to say, that I must go there again to-morrow, so I shall not be with you. O the heavy hours in this dark prison! You will reward me and make me forget them when I see you—but how shall I pass the time till then!"

These words made Ethel conceive the idea of joining him in town. He would not, he could not be angry? He could not bring his mind to ask her to share his discomforts—but ought she not to volunteer—to insist upon his permitting her to come? Permit! the same pride that prevented his asking, would induce him to refuse her request; but should she do wrong, if, without his express permission, she were to join him? A thrill, half fear, half transport, made her heart's blood stand still at the thought. The day after this last, she got no letter; the following day was Monday, and there would be no post from town. Her resolution was taken, and she told her aunt, that she should go up to London the following day. Mrs. Elizabeth knew little of the actual circumstances of the young pair. Villiers had made it an express condition, that she should not be informed of their difficulties, for he was resolute not to take from her little store, which, in the way she lived, was sufficient, yet barely so, for her wants. She did not question her niece as to her journey; she imagined that it was a thing arranged. But Ethel herself was full of perplexity; she remembered what Villiers had said of expense; she knew that he would be deeply hurt if she used a public conveyance, and yet to go post would consume the little money she had left, and she did not like to reach London pennyless. She began to talk to her aunt, and faltered out something about want of money for posting—the good lady's purse was instantly in her hand. Ethel had not the same horror as her husband of pecuniary obligation—she was too inexperienced to know its annoyances; and in the present instance, to receive a small sum from her aunt, appeared to her an affair that did not merit hesitation. She took twenty pounds for her journey, and felt her heart lighter.

There yet remained another question. Hitherto they had travelled in their own carriage, with a valet and lady's maid. Villiers had taken his servant to town with him. In a postscript to one of his letters, he said, "I was able to recommend Laurie to a good place, so I have parted with him, and I shall not take another servant at this moment." Laurie had been long and faithfully attached to her husband, who had never lived without an attendant, and who, from his careless habits, was peculiarly helpless. Ethel felt that this dismissal was a measure of economy, and that she ought to imitate it. Still as any measure to be taken always frightened her, she had not courage to discharge her maid, but resolved to go up to town without her. Aunt Bessy was shocked at her going alone, but Ethel was firm; nothing could happen to her, and she should prove to Edward her readiness to endure privation.

On Monday, at eleven in the forenoon, on the 28th of November, Ethel, having put together but a few things,—for she expected a speedy return,—stept into her travelling chariot, and began her journey to town. She was all delight at the idea of seeing Edward. She reproached herself for having so long delayed giving this proof of her earnest affection. She listened with beaming smiles to all her aunt's injunctions and cautions: and, the carriage once in motion, drawing her shawl round her, as she sat in the corner, looking on the despoiled yet clear prospect, her mind was filled with the most agreeable reveries—her heart soothed by the dearest anticipations.

To pay the post-horses—to gift the postillion herself, were all events for her: she felt proud. "Edward said, I must begin to learn the ways of the world; and this is my first lesson in economy and care," she thought, as she put into the post-boy's hand just double the sum he had ever received before. "And how good, and attentive, and willing every body is! I am sure women can very well travel alone. Every one is respectful, and desirous to serve," was her next internal remark, as she undrew her little silken purse, to give a waiter half-a-crown, who had brought her a glass of water, and whose extreme alacrity struck her as so very kind-hearted.

Her spirits flagged as the day advanced. In spite of herself, an uneasy feeling diffused itself through her mind, when, the sun going down, a misty, chilly twilight crept over the landscape. Had she done right? she asked herself; would Edward indeed be glad to see her? She felt half frightened at her temerity—alarmed at the length of her journey—timid when she thought of the vast London she was about to enter, without any certain bourn. She supposed that Villiers went each day to his club, and she knew that he lodged in Duke Street, St. James's; but she was ignorant of the number of the house, and the street itself was unknown to her; she did not remember ever to have been in it in her life.

Her carriage entered labyrinthine London by Blackwall, and threaded the wilds of Lothbury. A dense and ever-thickening mist, palpable, yellow, and impervious to the eye, enveloped the whole town. Ethel had heard of a November fog; but she had never witnessed one, and the idea of it did not occur to her memory: she was half-frightened, thinking that some strange phaenomena were going on, and fancying that her postillion was hurrying forward in terror. At last, in Cheapside, they stopped jammed up by carts and coaches; and then she contrived to make herself heard, asking what was the matter? The word "eclipse" hung upon her lips.

"Only, ma'am, the street has got blocked up like in the fog: we shall get on presently."

The word "fog" solved the mystery; and again her thoughts were with Villiers. What a horrible place for him to live in! And he had been enduring all this wretchedness, while she was breathing the pure atmosphere of the country. Again they proceeded through the "murky air," and through an infinitude of mischances;—the noise—the hubbub—the crowd, as she could distinguish it, as if veiled by dirty gauze, by the lights in the shops—all agitated and vexed her. Through Fleet Street and the Strand they went; and it seemed as if their progress would never come to an end. The whole previous journey from Longfield was short in comparison to this tedious procession: twenty times she longed to get out and walk. At last they got free, and with a quicker pace drove up to the door of the Union Club, in Charing Cross.

The post-boy called one of the waiters to the carriage door; and Ethel asked— "Is Mr. Villiers here?"

"Mr. Villiers, ma'am, has left town."

Ethel was aghast. She had watched assiduously along the road; yet she had felt certain that if he had meant to come, she would have seen him on Sunday; and till this moment, she had not entertained a real doubt but that she should find him. She asked, falteringly, "When did he go?"

"Last week, ma'am: last Thursday, I think it was."

Ethel breathed again: the man's information must be false. She was too inexperienced to be aware that servants and common people have a singular tact in selecting the most unpleasant intelligence, and being very alert in communicating it. "Do you know," she inquired, "where Mr. Villiers lodges?"

"Can't say, indeed, ma'am; but the porter knows;—here, Saunders!"

No Saunders answered. "The porter is not in the way; but if you can wait, ma'am, he'll be back presently."

The waiter disappeared: the post-boy came up—he touched his hat. "Wait," said Ethel;—"we must wait a little"; and he removed himself to the horses' heads. Ethel sat in her lonely corner, shrouded by fog and darkness, watching every face as it passed under the lamp near, fancying that Edward might appear among them. The ugly faces that haunt, in quick succession, the imagination of one oppressed by night-mare, might vie with those that passed successively in review before Ethel. Most of them hurried on, looking neither to the right nor left. Some entered the house; some glanced at her carriage: one or two, perceiving a bonnet, evidently questioned the waiter. He stood there for her own service, Ethel thought; and she watched his every movement—his successive disappearances and returns—the people he talked to. Once she signed to him to come; but— "No, ma'am, the porter is not come back yet,"—was all his answer. At last, after having stood, half whistling, for some five minutes, (it appeared to Ethel half-an-hour,) without having received any visible communication, he suddenly came up to the carriage door, saying, "The porter could not stay to speak to you, ma'am, he was in such a hurry. He says, Mr. Villiers lodges in Duke Street, St. James's: he should know the house, but has forgotten the number."

"Then I must wait till he comes back again. I knew all that before. Will he be long?"

"A long time, ma'am; two hours at least. He said that the woman of the house is a widow woman—Mrs. Derham."

Thus, as if by torture, (but, as with the whipping boys of old, her's was the torture, not the delinquent's,) Ethel extracted some information from the stupid, conceited fellow. On she went to Duke Street, to discover Mrs. Derham's residence. A few wrong doors were knocked at; and a beer-boy, at last, was the Mercury that brought the impatient, longing wife, to the threshold of her husband's residence. Happy beer-boy! She gave him a sovereign: he had never been so rich in his life before;—such chance-medleys do occur in this strange world!

• • •

CHAPTER XVI

"O my reviving joy! thy quickening presence
    Makes the sad night
    Sit like a youthful spring upon my blood.
    I cannot make thy welcome rich enough
    With all the wealth of words."

—*Middleton*

❦

The boy knocked at the door. A servant-girl opened it. "Does Mr. Villiers lodge here?" asked the postillion, from his horse. "Yes," said the girl.

"Open the door quickly, and let me out!" cried Ethel, as her heart beat fast and loud.

The door was opened—the steps let down—operations tedious beyond measures, as she thought. She got out, and was in the hall, going up stairs.

"Mr. Villiers is not at home," said the maid.

Through the low blinds of the parlour window, Mrs. Derham had been watching what was going on. She heard what her servant said, and now came out. "Mr. Villiers is not at home," she reiterated; "will you leave any message?"

"No; I will wait for him. Show me into his room."

"I am afraid that it is locked," answered Mrs. Derham repulsively: "perhaps you can call again. Who shall I say asked for him?"

"O no!" cried Ethel, "I must wait for him. Will you permit me to wait in your parlour? I am Mrs. Villiers."

"I beg pardon," said the good woman; "Mrs. Villiers is in the country."

"And so I am," replied Ethel—"at least, so I was this morning. Don't you see my travelling carriage?—look; you may be sure that I am Mrs. Villiers."

She took out of her little bag one of Edward's letters, with the perusal of which she had beguiled much of her way to town. Mrs. Derham looked at the direction—"The Honourable Mrs. Villiers";—her countenance brightened. Mrs. Derham was a little, plump, well-preserved woman of fifty-four or five. She was kind-hearted, and of course shared the worship for rank which possesses every heart born within the four seas. She was now all attention. Villiers's room was open; he was expected very soon:— "He is so seldom out in an evening: it is very unlucky; but he must be back directly," said Mrs. Derham, as she showed the way up the narrow staircase. Ethel reached the landing, and entered a room of tolerable dimensions, considerably encumbered with litter, which opened into a smaller room, with a tent bed. A little bit of fire glimmered in the grate. The whole place looked excessively forlorn and comfortless.

Mrs. Derham bustled about to bestow a little neatness on the room, saying something of the "untidiness of gentlemen," and "so many lodgers in the house." Ethel sat down she longed to be alone. There was the post-boy to be paid, and to be ordered to take the carriage to a coach-house; and then—Mrs. Derham asked her if she would not have something to eat: she herself was at tea, and offered a cup, which Ethel thankfully accepted, acknowledging that she had not eaten since the morning. Mrs. Derham was shocked. The rank, beauty, and sweet manners of Ethel had made a conquest, which her extreme youth redoubled. "So young a lady," she said, "to go about alone: she did not know how to take care of herself, she was sure. She must have some supper: a roast chicken should be ready in an hour—by the time Mr. Villiers came in."

"But the tea," said Ethel, smiling; "you will let me have that now?"

Mrs. Derham hurried away on this hint, and the young wife was left alone. She had been married a year; but there was still a freshness about her feelings, which gave zest to every change in her wedded life. "This is where he has been living without me," she thought; "Poor Edward! it does not look as if he were very comfortable."

She rose from her seat, and began to arrange the books and papers. A glove of her husband's lay on the table: she kissed it with a glad feeling of welcome. When the servant came in, she had the fire replenished—the hearth swept; and in a minute or two, the room had lost much of its disconsolate appearance. Then, with a continuation of her feminine love of order she arranged her own dress and hair; giving to her attire, as much as possible, an at-home appearance. She had just finished—just sat down, and begun to find the time long—when a quick, imperative knock at the door, which she recognized at once, made her heart beat, and her cheek grow pale. She heard a step—a voice—and Mrs. Derham answer— "Yes, sir; the fire is in—every thing comfortable";—and Ethel opened the door, as she spoke, and in an instant was clasped in her husband's arms.

It was not a moment whose joy could be expressed by words. He had been miserable during her absence, and had thought of sending for her; but he looked round his single room, remembered that he was in lodgings, and gave up his purpose with a bitter murmur: and here she was, uncalled for, but most welcome: she was here, in her youth, her loveliness, her sweetness: these were charms; but others more transcendent now attended on, and invested her;—the sacred tenderness of a wife had led her to his side; and love, in its most genuine and beautiful shape, shed an atmosphere of delight and worship about her. Not one circumstance could alloy the unspeakable bliss of their meeting. Poverty, and its humiliations, vanished from before the eyes of Villiers; he was overflowingly rich in the possession of her affections—her presence. Again and again he thanked her, in broken accents of expressive transport.

"Nothing in the whole world could make me unhappy now!" he cried; and Ethel, who had seen his face look elongated and gloomy at the moment he had entered, felt indeed that Medea, with all her potent herbs, was less of a magician than she, in the power of infusing the sparkling spirit of life into one human frame. It was long before either were coherent in their inquiries and replies. There was nothing, indeed, that either wished to know. Life, and its purposes, were fulfilled, rounded, complete, without a flaw. They loved, and were together—together, not for a transitory moment, but for the whole duration of the eternity of love, which never could be exhausted in their hearts.

After more than an hour spent in gradually becoming acquainted and familiar with the transporting change, from separate loneliness to mutual society and sympathy, the good-natured face of Mrs. Derham showed itself, to announce that Ethel's supper was ready. These words brought back to Edward's recollection his wife's journey, and consequent fatigues: he grew more desirous than Mrs. Derham to feed his poor famished bird, whose eyes, in spite of the joy that shone in them, began to look languid, and whose cheek was pale. The little supper-table was laid, and they sat down together.

Lady Mary Wortley Montagu has recorded the pleasure to be reaped

"When we meet with champagne and a chicken at last";

and perhaps social life contains no combination so full of enjoyment as a tête-à-tête supper. *Here* it was, with its highest zest. They feared no prying eyes—they knew no ill: it was not a scanty hour of joy snatched from an age of pain—a single spark illuminating a long blank night. It came after separation, and possessed, therefore, the charm of novelty; but it was the prelude to a long reunion—the seal set on their being once again joined, to go through together each hour of the livelong day. Full of unutterable thankfulness and gladness, as were the minds of each, there was, besides,

> "A sacred and home-felt delight,
> A sober certainty of waking bliss,"

which is the crown and fulfilment of perfect human happiness. "Imparadised" by each other's presence—no doubt—no fear of division on the morrow-no dread of untoward event, suspicion, or blame, clouded the balmy atmosphere which their hearts created around them. No. Eden was required to enhance their happiness; there needed no

> "Crisped brooks,
> Rolling on orient pearl and sands of gold";—

no

> "Happy, rural seat, with various view,"

decked with

> "Flowers of all hue,"
> "All trees of noblest kind for sight, smell, taste";—

nor "cool recess," nor

> "Vernal airs,
> Breathing the smell of field and grove."

In their narrow abode—their nook of a room, cut off from the world, redolent only of smoke and fog—their two fond hearts could build up bowers of delight, and store them with all of ecstasy which the soul of man can know, without any assistance of eye, or ear, or scent. So rich, and prodigal, and glorious, in its gifts, is faithful and true-hearted love,—when it knows the sacrifices which it must make to merit them, and consents willingly to forego vanity, selfishness, and the exactions of self-will, in unlimited and unregretted exchange.

Mutual esteem and gratitude sanctified the unreserved sympathy which made each so happy in the other. Did they love the less for not loving "in sin and fear?" Far from it. The certainty of being the cause of good to each other tended to foster the most delicate of all passions, more than the rougher ministrations of terror, and a knowledge that each was the occasion of injury to the other. A woman's heart is peculiarly unfitted to sustain this conflict. Her sensibility gives keenness to her imagination, and she magnifies every peril, and writhes beneath every sacrifice which tends to humiliate her in her own eyes. The natural pride of her sex struggles with her desire to confer happiness, and her peace is wrecked.

Far different was the happy Ethel's situation—far otherwise were her thoughts employed than in concealing the pangs of care and shame. The sense of right adorned the devotion of love. She read approbation in Edward's eyes, and drew near him in full consciousness of deserving it. They sat at their supper, and long after, by the cheerful fire, talking of a thousand things connected with the present and the future—the long, long future which they were to spend together; and every now and then their eyes sparkled with the gladness of renewed delight in seeing each other. "Mine, my own, for ever!"—And was this exultation in possession to be termed selfish? by no other reasoning surely, than that used by a cold and meaningless philosophy, which gives this name to generosity and truth, and all the nobler passions of the soul. They congratulated themselves on this mutual property, partly because it had been a free gift one to the other; partly because they looked forward to the right it ensured to each, of conferring mutual benefits; and partly through the instinctive love God has implanted for that which, being ours, is become the better part of ourselves. They were united for "better and worse," and there was a sacredness in the thought of the "worse" they might share, which gave a mysterious and celestial charm to the present "better."

* * *

CHAPTER XVII

"Do you not think yourself truly happy?
 You have the abstract of all sweetness by you,
 The precious wealth youth labours to arrive at.
 Nor is she less in honour than in beauty."

—Beaumont and Fletcher

The following day was one of pouring, unintermitting rain. Villiers and Ethel drew their chairs near their cheerful fire, and were happy. Edward could not quite conquer his repugnance to seeing his wife in lodgings, and in those also of so mean and narrow a description. But the spirit of Ethel was more disencumbered of earthly particles: that had found its rest in the very home of Love. The rosy light of the divinity invested all things for her. Cleopatra on the Cydnus, in the bark which—

> "Like a burnished throne
> Burnt on the water,"

borne along

> "By purple sails. . . .
> . . . . So perfumed, that
> The winds were love-sick with them";

was not more gorgeously attended than Ethel was to her own fancy, lapped and cradled in all that love has of tender, voluptuous, and confiding.

Several days past before Villiers could withdraw her from this blissful dream, to gaze upon the world as it was. He could not make her disgusted with her fortunes nor her abode, but he awakened anxiety on his own account. His father, as he had conjectured, was gone to Paris, leaving merely a message for his son, that he would willingly join him in any act for raising money, by mortgage or the absolute disposal of a part of the estate. Edward had consulted with his solicitor, who was to look over a vast variety of papers, to discover the most eligible mode of making some kind of sale. Delay, in all its various shapes, waited on these arrangements; and Villiers was very averse to leaving town till he held some clue to the labyrinth of obstacles which presented themselves at every turn. He talked of their taking a house in town; but Ethel would not hear of such extravagance. In the first place, their actual means were at a very low ebb, with little hope of a speedy supply. There was another circumstance, the annoyance of which he understood far better than Ethel could. He had raised money on annuities, the interest of which he was totally unable to pay; this exposed him to a personal risk of the most disagreeable kind, and he knew that his chief creditor was on the point of resorting to harsh measures against him. These things, dingy-visaged, dirty-handed realities as they were, made a strange contrast with Ethel's feeling of serene and elevated bliss; but she, with unshrinking heart, brought the same fortitude and love into the crooked and sordid ways of modern London, which had adorned heroines of old, as they wandered amidst trackless forests, and over barren mountains.

Several days passed, and the weather became clear, though cold. The young pair walked together in the parks at such morning hours as would prevent their meeting any acquaintances, for Edward was desirous that it should not be known that they were in town. Villiers also traced his daily, weary, disappointing way to his solicitor, where he found things look more blank and dismal each day. Then when evening came, and the curtains were drawn, they might have been at the top of Mount

Caucasus, instead of in the centre of London, so completely were they cut off from every thing except each other. They then felt absolutely happy: the lingering disgusts of Edward were washed clean away by the bounteous, everspringing love, that flowed, as waters from a fountain, from the heart of Ethel, in one perpetual tide.

In those hours of unchecked talk, she learned many things she had not known before—the love of Horatio Saville for Lady Lodore was revealed to her; but the story was not truly told, for the prejudices as well as the ignorance of Villiers rendered him blind to the sincerity of Cornelia's affection and regret. Ethel wondered, and in spite of the charm with which she delighted to invest the image of her mother, she could not help agreeing with her husband that she must be irrevocably wedded to the most despicable worldly feelings, so to have played with the heart of a man such as Horatio: a man, whose simplest word bore the stamp of truth and genius; one of those elected few whom nature elevates to her own high list of nobility and greatness. How could she, a simple girl, interest feelings which were not alive to Saville's merits? She could only hope that in some dazzling marriage Lady Lodore would find a compensation for the higher destiny which might have been hers, but that, like the "base Indian," she had thrown

> "A pearl away,
> Richer than all his tribe."

There was a peaceful quiet in their secluded and obscure life, which somewhat resembled the hours spent on board ship, when you long for, yet fear, the conclusion of the voyage, and shrink involuntarily from exchanging a state, whose chief blessing is an absence of every care, for the variety of pains and pleasures which chequer life. Ethel possessed her all—so near, so undivided, so entirely her own, that she could not enter into Villiers's impatience, nor quite sympathize with the disquietude he could not repress. After considerable delays, his solicitor informed him that his father had so entirely disposed of all his interest in the property, that his readiness to join in any act of sale would be useless. The next thing to be done was for Edward to sell a part of his expectations, and the lawyer promised to find a purchaser, and begged to see him three days hence, when no doubt he should have some proposal to communicate.

Whoever has known what such things are—whoever has waited on the demurs and objections, and suffered the alternations of total failure and suddenly renewed hopes, which are the Tantalus-food held to the lips of those under the circumstances of Villiers, can follow in imagination his various conferences with his solicitor, as day after day something new was discovered, still to drag on, or to impede, the tortoise pace of his negociations. It will be no matter of wonder to such, that a month instead of three days wasted away, and found him precisely in the same position, with hopes a little raised, though so frequently blasted, and nothing done.

In recording the annoyances, or rather the adversity which the young pair endured at this period, a risk is run, on the one hand, of being censured for bringing the reader into contact with degrading and sordid miseries; and on the other, of laying too much stress on circumstances which will appear to those in a lower sphere of life, as scarcely deserving the name of misfortune. It is very easy to embark on the wild ocean of romance, and to steer a danger-fraught passage, amidst giant perils,—the very words employed, excite the imagination, and give grace to the narrative. But all beautiful and fairy-like as was Ethel Villiers, in tracing her fortunes, it is necessary to descend from such altitudes, to employ terms of vulgar use, and to describe scenes of common-place and debasing interest; so that, if she herself, in her youth and feminine tenderness, does not shed light and holiness around her, we shall grope darkling, and fail utterly in the scope which we proposed to ourselves in selecting her history for the entertainment of the reader.

•••

CHAPTER XVIII

"I saw her upon nearer view,
A Spirit, yet a Woman too!
A Creature not too bright or good
For human nature's daily food;
For transient sorrows, simple wiles,
Praise, blame, love, kisses, tears, and smiles."

—Wordsworth

The end of December had come. New year's day found
and left them still in Duke Street. On the 4th of January
Villiers received a letter from his uncle, Lord Maristow,
entrusting a commission to him, which obliged him to go to the
neighbourhood of Egham. Not having a horse, he went by the stage.
He set out so late in the day that there was no chance of his returning the same night; and he promised to be back early on the morrow.
Ethel had letters to write to Italy and to her aunt; and with these
she tried to beguile the time. She felt lonely; the absence of Villiers
for so many hours engendered an anxiety, which she found some
difficulty in repressing. Accustomed to have him perpetually at her
side, and without any other companion or resource, she repined at
her solitude. There was his empty chair, and no hope that he would
occupy it; and she sat in her little room so near to thousands, and yet
so cut off from every one, with such a sense of desolation as Mungo

Park might have felt in central Africa, or a shipwrecked mariner on an uninhabited island.

Her pen was taken up, but she did not write. She could not command her thoughts to express any thing but the overflowing, devoted, all-engrossing affection of her heart, her adoration for her husband; that would not amuse Lucy,—she thought: and she had commenced another sheet with "My dearest Aunt," when the maid-servant ushered a man into her presence—a stranger, a working man. What could he want with her? He seemed confused, and stammered out, "Mr. Villiers is not in?"

"He will be at home to-morrow, if you want him; or have you any message that I can give?"

"You are Mrs. Villiers, ma'am?"

"Yes, my good man, I am Mrs. Villiers."

"If you please, ma'am, I am Saunders, one of the porters at the Union Club."

"I remember: has any message come there? or does Mr. Villiers owe you any money?" and her purse was in her hand.

"O no, ma'am. Mr. Villiers is a good gentleman; and he has been petiklar generous to me—and that is why I come, because I am afraid," continued the man, lowering his tone, "that he is in danger."

"Good heavens! Where? how?" cried Ethel, starting from her chair. "Tell me at once."

"Yes, ma'am, I will; so you must know that this evening—"

"Yes, this evening. What has happened? he left me at six o'clock—what is it?"

"Nothing, I hope, this evening, ma'am. I am only afraid for to-morrow morning. And I will tell you all I know, as quick as ever I can."

The man then proceeded to relate, that some one had been inquiring about Mr. Villiers at the Club House. One of the servants had told him that he lived in Duke Street, St. James's, and that was all he knew; but Saunders came up, and the man questioned him. He instantly recognized the fellow, and knew what his business must be. And he tried to deceive him, and declared that Mr. Villiers was gone out of town; but the fellow said that he knew better than that; and that he had been seen that very day in the Strand. He should look for him, no thanks to Saunders, in Duke Street. "And so, ma'am, you see they'll be sure to be here early to-morrow morning. So don't let Mr. Villiers stay here, on no account whatsomever."

"Why?" asked Ethel, simply; "they can't hurt him."

"I am sure, ma'am," said Saunders, his face brightening, "I am very glad to hear that—you know best. They will arrest him for sure, but—"

"Arrest him!"

"Yes, ma'am, for I've seen the tall one before. There were two of them—bailiffs."

Ethel now began to tremble violently; these were strange, cabalistic words to her, the more awful from their mystery. "What am I to do?" she exclaimed; "Mr. Villiers will be here in the morning, he sleeps at Egham, and will be here early; I must go to him directly."

"I am glad to hear he is so far," said Saunders; "and if I can be of any use you have but to say it; shall I go to Egham? there are night coaches that go through, and I might warn him."

Ethel thought—she feared to do any thing—she imagined that she should be watched, that all her endeavours would be of no avail. She looked at the man, honesty was written on his face; but there was no intelligence, nothing to tell her that his advice was good. The possibility of such an event as the present had never occurred to her. Villiers had been silent with regard to his fears on this head. She was suddenly transported into a strange sea, hemmed in by danger, without a pilot or knowledge of a passage. Again she looked at the man's face: "What is best to be done!" she exclaimed.

"I am sure, ma'am," he replied, as if she had asked him the question, "I think what I said is best, if you will tell me where I can find Mr. Villiers. I should think nothing of going, and he could send word by me what he wished you to do."

"Yes, that would indeed be a comfort. I will write three lines, and you shall take them." In a moment she had written. "Give this note into his own hand, he will sleep there—I have written the direction of the house—or at some inn, at Egham. Do not rest till you have given the letter, and here is for your trouble." She held out two sovereigns.

"Depend on me, ma'am; and I will bring an answer to you by nine in the morning. Mr. Villiers will pay me what he thinks fit—you may want your money. Only, ma'am, don't be frightened when them men come to-morrow—if the people here are good sort of folks, you had better give them a hint—it may save you trouble."

"Thank you: you are a good man, and I will remember you, and reward you. By nine to-morrow—you will be punctual?"

The man again assured her that he would use all diligence, and took his leave.

Ethel felt totally overwhelmed by these tidings. The unknown is always terrible, and the ideas of arrest, and prison, and bolts, and bars, and straw, floated before her imagination. Was Villiers safe even where he was? Would not the men make inquiries, learn where he had gone, and follow him, even if it were to the end of the world? She had heard of the activity employed to arrest criminals, and mingled every kind of story in her head, till she grew desperate from terror. Not knowing what else to do, she became eager for Mrs. Derham's advice, and hurried down stairs to ask it.

She had not seen much of the good lady since her first arrival. Every day, when Villiers went out, she came up, indeed, on the momentous question of "orders for dinner"; and then she bestowed the benefit of some five or ten minutes garrulity on her fair lodger. Ethel learnt that she had seen better days, and that were justice done her, she ought to be riding in her coach, instead of letting lodgings. She learnt that she had a married daughter living at Kennington: poor enough, but struggling on cheerfully with her mother's help. The best girl in the world she was, and a jewel of a wife, and had two of the most beautiful children that ever were beheld.

This was all that Ethel knew, except that once Mrs. Derham had brought her one of her grandchildren to be seen and admired. In all that the good woman said, there was so much kindness, such a cheerful endurance of the ills of life, and she had shown such a readiness to oblige, that the idea of applying to her for advice, relieved Ethel's mind of much of its load of anxiety.

She was too much agitated to think of ringing for the servant, to ask to see her; but hurried down stairs, and knocked at the parlour-door almost before she was aware of what she was doing. "Come in," said a feminine voice. Ethel entered, and started to see one she knew;—and yet again she doubted;—was it indeed Fanny Derham whom she beheld?

The recognition afforded mutual pleasure: checked a little on Ethel's part, by her anxieties; and on Fanny's, by a feeling that she had been neglected by her friend. A few letters had passed between them, when first Ethel had visited Longfield: since then their correspondence had been discontinued till after her return to England, from Italy, when Mrs. Villiers had wrote; but her letter was returned by the post-office, no such person being to be found according to the address.

The embarrassment of the moment passed away. Ethel forgot, or rather did not advert to, her friend's lowly destiny, in the joy of meeting her again. After a minute or two, also, they had become familiar with the change that time had operated in their youthful appearance, which was not much, and most in Ethel. Her marriage, and conversance with the world, had changed her into a woman, and endowed her with easy manners and self-possession. Fanny was still a mere girl; tall, beyond the middle height, yet her young, ingenuous countenance was unaltered, as well as that singular mixture of mildness and independence, in her manners, which had always characterized her. Her light blue eyes beamed with intelligence, and her smile expressed the complacency and condescension of a superior being. Her beauty was all intellectual: open, sincere, passionless, yet benignant, you approached her without fear of encountering any of the baser qualities of human beings,—their hypocrisy, or selfishness. Those who have seen the paintings of the calm-visaged, blue-eyed deities of the frescos of Pompeii, may form an idea of the serene beauty of Fanny Derham.

When Mrs. Villiers entered, she was reading earnestly—a large dictionary open before her. The book on which she was intent was in Greek characters. "You have not forgotten your old pursuits," said Ethel, smiling.

"Say rather I am more wedded to them than ever," she replied; "since, more than ever, I need them to give light and glory to a dingy world. But you, dear Ethel, if so I may call you,—you looked anxious as you entered: you wish to speak to my mother;—she is gone to Kennington, and will not return to-night. Can I be of any use?"

Her mother! how strange! and Mrs. Derham, while she had dilated with pride on her elder daughter, had never mentioned this pearl of price, which was her's also.

"Alas! I fear not!" replied Ethel; "it is experience I need—experience in things you can know nothing about, nor your mother either, probably; yet she may have heard of such things, and know how to advise me."

Mrs. Villiers then explained the sources of her disquietude. Fanny listened with looks of the kindest sympathy. "Even in such things," she said, "I have had experience. Adversity and I are become very close friends since I last saw you: we are intimate, and I know much good of her; so she is grateful, and repays me by prolonging her stay. Be composed: no ill will happen, I trust, to Mr. Villiers;—at least you need not be afraid of his being pursued. It the man you have sent be active and faithful, all will be well. I will see these troublesome people to-morrow, when they come, and prevent your being annoyed. If Saunders returns early, and brings tidings of Mr. Villiers, you will know what his wishes are. You can do nothing more to-night; and there is every probability that all will be well."

"Do you really think so?" cried Mrs. Villiers. "O that I had gone with him!—never will I again let him go any where without me."

Fanny entered into more minute explanations, and succeeded, to a great degree, in calming her friend. She accompanied her back to her own room, and sat with her long. She entered into the details of her own history:—the illness and death of her father; the insulting treatment her mother had met from his family; the kindness of a relation of her own, who had assisted them, and enabled them to pursue their present mode of life, which procured them a livelihood. Fanny spoke generally of these circumstances, and in a spirit that seemed to disdain that such things were; not because they were degrading in the eyes of others, but because they interfered with the philosophic leisure, and enjoyment of nature, which she so dearly prized. She thought nothing of privation, or the world's impertinence; but much of being immured in the midst of London, and being forced to consider the inglorious necessities of life. Her desire to be useful to her mother induced her often to spend precious time in "making the best of things," which she would readily have dispensed with altogether, as the easiest, as well as the wisest, way of freeing herself from their trammels. Her narration interested Ethel, and served to calm her mind. She thought—"Can I not bear those cares with equanimity for Edward's sake, which Fanny regards as so trivial, merely because Plato and Epictetus bid her do so? Will not the good God, who has implanted in her heart so cheerless a consolation, bring comfort to mine, which has no sorrow but for another's sake?"

These reflections tranquillized her, when she laid her head on her pillow at night. She resigned her being and destiny to a Power superior to any earthly authority, with a conviction, that its most benign influence would be extended over her.

• • •

VOLUME III

CHAPTER I

Т he still hours of darkness passed silently away, and morning
dawned, when

All rose to do the task, he set to each
Who shaped us to his ends, and not our own.

Ethel had slept peacefully through the livelong night; nor woke till
a knock at her door roused her. A rush of fear—a sense of ill, made
her heart palpitate as she opened her eyes to the light of day. While
she was striving to recall her thoughts, and to remember what the evil
was with which she was threatened, again the servant tapped at her
door, to say that Saunders had returned, and to deliver the letter he
had brought. She looked at her watch: it was past ten o'clock. She felt
glad that it had grown so late, and she not disturbed: yet as she took
the letter brought to her from her husband, all her tremor returned;

and she read it with agitation, as if it contained the announcement of her final doom.

"You send me disagreeable tidings, my sweet Ethel," wrote Villiers,—

> I hope unfounded; but caution is necessary: I shall not, therefore, come to Duke Street. Send me a few lines, by Saunders, to tell me if any thing has happened. If what he apprehended has really taken place, you must bear, my love, the separation of a day. You do not understand these things, and will wonder when I tell you, that when the clock strikes twelve on Saturday night, the magic spells and potent charms of Saunders's friends cease to have power: at that hour I shall be restored to you. Wait till then—and *then* we will consult for the future. Have patience, dearest love: you have wedded poverty, hardship, and annoyance; but, joined to these, is the fondest, the most faithful heart in the world;—a heart you deign to prize, so I will not repine at ill fortune. Adieu, till this evening;—and then, as Belvidera says, "Remember twelve!"
>
> "*Saturday Morning.*"

After reading these lines, Ethel dressed herself hastily. Fanny Derham had already asked permission to see her; and she found her waiting in her sitting-room. It was an unspeakable comfort to have one as intelligent and kind as Fanny, to communicate with, during Edward's absence. The soft, pleading eyes of Ethel asked her for comfort and counsel; and, in spite of her extreme youth, the benignant and intelligent expression of Fanny's countenance promised both.

"I am sorry to say," she said, "that Saunders's prognostics are too true. Such men as he describes have been here this morning. They were tolerably civil, and I convinced them, with greater ease than I had hoped, that Mr. Villiers was absent from the house; and I assured them, that after this visit of theirs, he was not likely to return."

"And do you really believe that they were"—Ethel faltered.

"Bailiffs? Assuredly," replied Fanny: "they told me that they had the power to search the house; but if they were 'strong,' they were also 'merciful.' And now, what do you do? Saunders tells me he is waiting to take back a letter to Mr. Villiers, at the London Coffee House. Write quickly, while I make your breakfast."

Ethel gladly obeyed. She wrote a few words to her husband. That it was already Saturday, cheered her: twelve at night would soon come.

After her note was dispatched, she addressed Fanny. "What trouble I give," she said: "what will your mother think of such degrading proceedings?"

"My mother," said Fanny, "is the kindest-hearted woman in the world. We have never exactly suffered this disaster; but we are in a rank of life which causes us to be brought into contact with such among our friends and relations; and she is familiar with trouble in almost all shapes. You are a great favourite of hers; and now that she can claim a sort of acquaintance, she will be heart and soul your friend."

"It is odd," observed Ethel, "that she never mentioned you to me. Had the name of Fanny been mentioned, I should have recollected who Mrs. Derham was."

"Perhaps not," said Fanny; "it would have required a great effort of the imagination to have fancied Mrs. Derham the wife of my father. You never knew him; but Lord Lodore made you familiar with his qualities: the most shrinking susceptibility to the world's scorn, joined to the most entire abstraction from all that is vulgar; a morbid sensibility and delicate health placed him in glaring contrast with my mother. They never in the least assimilated; and her character has gained in excellence since his loss. Before she was fretted and galled by his finer feelings—now she can be good in her own way. Nothing reminds her of his exalted sentiments, except myself; and she is willing enough to forget me."

"And you do not repine?" asked her friend.

"I do not: she is happy in and with Sarah. I should spoil their notions of comfort, did I mingle with them;—they would torture and destroy me, did they interfere with me. I lost my guide, preserver, my guardian angel, when my father died. Nothing remains but the philosophy which he taught me—the disdain of low-thoughted care which he sedulously cultivated: this, joined to my cherished independence, which my disposition renders necessary to me."

"And thus you foster sorrow, and waste your life in vain regrets?"

"Pardon me! I do not waste my life," replied Fanny, with her sunny smile;—"nor am I unhappy—far otherwise. An ardent thirst for knowledge, is as the air I breathe; and the acquisition of it, is pure and unalloyed happiness. I aspire to be useful to my fellow-creatures: but that is a consideration for the future, when fortune shall smile on me; now I have but one passion; it swallows up every other; it dwells with my darling books, and is fed by the treasures of beauty and wisdom which they contain."

Ethel could not understand. Fanny continued:—"I aspire to be useful;—sometimes I think I am—once I know I was. I was my father's almoner.

"We lived in a district where there was a great deal of distress, and a great deal of oppression. We had no money to give, but I soon found that determination and earnestness will do much. It was my father's lesson, that I should never fear any thing but myself. He taught me to penetrate, to anatomize, to purify my motives; but once assured of my own integrity, to be afraid of nothing. Words have more power than any one can guess; it is by words that the world's great fight, now in these civilized times, is carried on; I never hesitated to use them, when I fought any battle for the miserable and oppressed. People are so afraid to speak, it would seem as if half our fellow-creatures were born with deficient organs; like parrots they can repeat a lesson, but their voice fails them, when that alone is wanting to make the tyrant quail."

As Fanny spoke, her blue eyes brightened, and a smile irradiated her face; these were all the tokens of enthusiasm she displayed, yet her words moved Ethel strangely, and she looked on her with wonder as a superior being. Her youth gave grace to her sentiments, and were an assurance of their sincerity. She continued:—

"I am becoming flightly, as my mother calls it; but, as I spoke, many scenes of cottage distress passed through my memory, when, holding my father's hand, I witnessed his endeavours to relieve the poor. That is all over now—he is gone, and I have but one consolation—that of endeavouring to render myself worthy to rejoin him in a better world. It is this hope that impels me continually and without any flagging of spirit, to cultivate my understanding and to refine it. O what has this life to give, as worldlings describe it, worth one of those glorious emotions, which raise me from this petty sphere, into the sun-bright regions of mind, which my father inhabits! I am rewarded even here by the elevated feelings which the authors, whom I love so passionately, inspire; while I converse each day with Plato, and Cicero, and Epictetus, the world, as it is, passes from before me like a vain shadow."

These enthusiastic words were spoken with so calm a manner, and in so equable a voice, that there seemed nothing strange nor exaggerated in them. It is vanity and affectation that shock, or any manifestation of feeling not in accordance with the real character. But while we follow our natural bent, and only speak that which our minds spontaneously inspire, there is a harmony, which, however novel, is never grating. Fanny Derham spoke of things, which, to use her own expression, were to her as the air she breathed, and the simplicity of her manner entirely obviated the wonder which the energy of her expressions might occasion.

Such a woman as Fanny was more made to be loved by her own sex than by the opposite one. Superiority of intellect, joined to acquisitions beyond those usual even to men; and both announced with frankness, though without pretension, forms a kind of anomaly little in accord with masculine taste. Fanny could not be the rival of women, and, therefore, all her merits were appreciated by them. They love to look up to a superior being, to rest on a firmer support than their own minds can afford; and they are glad to find such in one of their own sex, and thus destitute of those dangers which usually attend any services conferred by men.

CHAPTER II

Marian. Could you so long be absent?
Robin. What a week?
   Was that so long?
Marian. How long are lovers' weeks,
   Do you think, Robin, when they are asunder?
   Are they not pris'ners' years?

—*Ben Jonson*

The day passed on more lightly than Ethel could have hoped; much of it indeed was gone before she opened her eyes to greet it. Night soon closed in, and she busied herself with arrangements for the welcome of her husband. Fanny loved solitude too well herself not to believe that others shared her taste. She retired therefore when evening commenced. No sooner was Ethel alone, than every image except Edward's passed out of her mind. Her heart was bursting with affection. Every other idea and thought, to use a chemical expression, was held in solution by that powerful feeling, which mingled and united with every particle of her soul. She could not write nor read; if she attempted, before she had finished the shortest sentence, she found that her understanding was wandering, and she re-read it with no better success. It was as if a spring, a gush from the fountain of love poured itself in, bearing away every object which she strove to throw upon the stream of thought, till its own sweet waters alone filled the channel through which it flowed. She gave herself up to the bewildering influence, and almost forgot to count the hours till Edward's expected arrival. At last it was ten o'clock, and then the sting of impatience and uncertainty was felt. It appeared to her as if a whole age had passed since she had seen or heard of him—as if countless events and incalculable changes might have taken place. She read again and again his note, to assure herself that she might really expect him: the minutes meanwhile stood still, or were told heavily by the distinct beating of her heart. The east wind bore to her ear the sound of the quarters of hours, as they chimed from various churches. At length eleven, half-past eleven was passed, and the hand of her watch began to climb slowly upwards toward the zenith, which she desired so ardently that it should reach. She gazed on the dial-plate, till she fancied that the pointers did not move; she placed her hands before her eyes resolutely, and would not look for a long long time; three minutes had not been travelled over when again she viewed it; she tried to count her pulse, as a measurement of time; her trembling fingers refused to press the fluttering artery. At length another quarter of an hour elapsed, and then the succeeding one hurried on more speedily. Clock after clock struck; they mingled their various tones, as the hour of twelve was tolled throughout London. It seemed as if they would never end. Silence came at last—a brief silence succeeded by a firm quick step in the street below, and a knock at the door. "Is he not too soon?" poor fearful Ethel asked herself. But no; and in a moment after, he was with her, safe in her glad embrace.

Perhaps of the two, Villiers showed himself the most enraptured at this meeting. He gazed on his sweet wife, followed every motion, and hung upon her voice, with all the delight of an exile, restored to his long-lost home. "What a transporting change," he said, "to find myself with you—to see you in the same room with me—to know again that, lovely and dear as you are, that you are mine—that I am again myself—not the miserable dog that has been wandering about all day—a body without a soul! For a few short hours, at least, Ethel will call me hers."

"Indeed, indeed, love," she replied, "we will not be separated again."

"We will not even think about that tonight," said Villiers. "The future is dark and blank, the present as radiant as your own sweet self can make it."

On the following day—and the following day did come, in spite of Ethel's wishes, which would have held back the progress of time: it came and passed away; hour after hour stealing along, till it dwindled to a mere point. On the following day, they consulted earnestly on what was to be done. Villiers was greatly averse to Ethel's leaving her present abode, where every one was so very kind and attentive to her, and he was sanguine in his hopes of obtaining in the course of the week, just commenced, a sum, sufficient to carry them to Paris or Brussels, were they could remain till his affairs were finally arranged, and the payment of his debts regulated in a way to satisfy his creditors. One week of absence; Villiers used all his persuasion to induce Ethel to submit to it. "Where you can be, I can be also," was her answer; and she listened unconvinced to the detail of the inconveniences which Villiers pointed out: at last he almost got angry. "I could call you unkind, Ethel," he said, "not to yield to me."

"I will yield to you," said Ethel, "but you are wrong to ask me."

"Never mind that," replied her husband, "do concede this point, dearest; if not because it is best that you should, then because I wish it, and ask it of you. You say that your first desire is to make me happy, and you pain me exceedingly by your—I had almost said perverseness."

Thus, not convinced, but obedient, Ethel agreed to allow him to depart alone. She bargained that she should be permitted to come each day in a hackney coach to a place where he might meet her, and they could spend an hour or two together. Edward did not like this plan at all, but there was no remedy. "You are at least resolved," he said, "to spur my endeavours; I will not rest day or night, till I am enabled to get away from this vast dungeon."

The hours stole on. Even Edward's buoyant spirits could not bear up against the sadness of watching the fleeting moments till the one should come, which must separate him from his wife. "This nice, dear room," he said, "I am sure I beg its pardon for having despised it so much formerly—it is not as lofty as a church, nor as grand as a palace, but it is very snug; and now you are in it, I discern even elegance in its exceedingly queer tables and chairs. When our carriage broke down on the Apennines, how glad we should have been if a room like this had risen, 'like an exhalation' for our shelter! Do you remember the barn of a place we got into there, and our droll bed of the leaves of Indian corn, which crackled all night long, and awoke us twenty times with the fear of robbers? Then, indeed, twelve o'clock was not to separate us!"

As he said this he sighed; the hour of eleven was indicated by Ethel's watch, and still he lingered; but she grew frightened for him, and forced him to go away, while he besought the delay of but a few minutes.

Ethel exerted herself to endure as well as she could the separation of the ensuing week. She was not of a repining disposition, yet she found it very hard to bear. The discomfort to which Villiers was exposed annoyed her, and the idea that she was not permitted to alleviate it added to her painful feelings. In her prospect of life every evil was neutralized when shared—now they were doubled, because the pain of absence from each other was superadded. She did not yield to her husband, in her opinion that this was wrong. She was willing to go anywhere with him, and where he was, she also could be. There could be no degradation in a wife waiting on the fallen fortunes of her husband. No debasement can arise from any services dictated by love. It is despicable to submit to hardship for unworthy and worldly objects, but every thing that is suffered for the sake of affection, is hallowed by the disinterested sentiment, and affords triumph and delight to the willing victim. Sometimes she tried in speech or on paper to express these feelings, and so by the force of irresistible reasoning to persuade Edward to permit her to join him; but all argument was weak; there was something beyond, that no words could express, which was stronger than any reason in her heart. Who can express the power of faithful and single-hearted love? As well attempt to define the laws of life, which occasions a continuity of feeling from the brain to the extremity of the frame, as try to explain how love can so unite two souls, as to make each feel maimed and half alive, while divided. A powerful impulse was perpetually urging Ethel to go—to place herself near Villiers—to refuse to depart. It was with the most violent struggles that she overcame the instigation.

She never could forget herself while away from him, or find the slightest alleviation to her disquietude, except while conversing with Fanny Derham, or rather while drawing her out, and listening to her, and wondering at a mechanism of mind so different from her own. Each had been the favourite daughter of men of superior qualities of mind. They had been educated by their several fathers with the most sedulous care, and nothing could be more opposite than the result, except that, indeed, both made duty the master motive of their actions. Ethel had received, so to speak, a sexual education. Lord Lodore had formed his ideal of what a woman ought to be, of what he had wished to find his wife, and sought to mould his daughter accordingly. Mr. Derham contemplated the duties and objects befitting an immortal soul, and had educated his child for the performance of them. The one fashioned his offspring to be the wife of a frail human being, and instructed her to be yielding, and to make it her duty to devote herself to his happiness, and to obey his will. The other sought to guard his from all weakness, to make her complete in herself, and to render her independent and self-sufficing. Born to poverty as Fanny was, it was thus only that she could find happiness in rising above her sphere; and, besides, a sense of pride, surviving his sense of injury, caused him to wish that his child should set her heart on higher things, than the distinctions and advantages of riches or rank; so that if ever brought into collision with his own family, she could look down with calm superiority on the "low ambition" of the wealthy. While Ethel made it her happiness and duty to give herself away with unreserved prodigality to him, whom she thought had every claim to her entire devotion; Fanny zealously guarded her individuality, and would have scorned herself could she have been brought to place the treasures of her soul at the disposal of any power, except those moral laws which it was her earnest endeavour never to transgress. Religion, reason, and justice—these were the landmarks of her life. She was kind-hearted, generous, and true—so also was Ethel; but the one was guided by the tenderness of her heart, while the other consulted her understanding, and would have died rather than have acted contrary to its dictates.

To guard Ethel from every contamination, Lord Lodore had secluded her from all society, and forestalled every circumstance that might bring her into conjunction with her fellow-creatures. He was equally careful to prevent her fostering any pride, except that of sex; and never spoke to her as if she were of an elevated rank: and the communication, however small, which she necessarily had with the Americans, made such ideas foreign to her mind. But she was exceedingly shy; tremblingly alive to the slightest repulse; and never perfectly fearless, (morally so, that is), except when under the shelter of another's care. Fanny's first principle was, that what she ought to do, that she could do, without hesitation or regard for obstacles. She had something Quixotic in her nature; or rather she would have had, if a clear head and some experience, even young as she was, had not stood in the way of her making any glaring mistakes; so that her enterprises were never ridiculous; and being usually successful, could not be called extravagant. For herself, she needed but her liberty and her books;—for others, she had her time, her thoughts, her decided and resolute modes of action, all at their command, whenever she was convinced that they had a just claim upon them.

It was singular that the resolute and unshrinking Fanny should be the daughter of Francis Derham; and the timid, retiring Ethel, of his bold and daring protector. But this is no uncommon case. We feel the evil results of our own faults, and endeavour to guard our children from them; forgetful that the opposite extreme has also its peculiar dangers. Lord Lodore attributed his early misfortunes to the too great freedom he had enjoyed, or rather to the unlimited scope given to his will, from his birth. Mr. Derham saw the unhappiness that had sprung from his own yielding and undecided disposition. The one brought up his child to dependence; the other taught his to disdain every support, except the applause of her own conscience. Lodore fostered all the sensibility, all the softness, of Ethel's feminine and delicat nature; while Fanny's father strove to harden and confirm a character, in itself singularly stedfast and upright.

In spite of the great contrast thus exhibited between Ethel and Fanny, one quality created a good deal of similarity between them. There was in both a total absence of every factitious sentiment. They acted from their own hearts—from their own sense of right, without the intervention of worldly considerations. A feeling of duty ruled all their actions; and, however excellent a person's dispositions may be, it yet requires considerable elevation of character never to deviate from the strict line of honour and integrity.

Fanny's society a little relieved Ethel's solitude: yet that did not weigh on her; and had she not been the child of her father's earliest friend, and the companion of past days, she would have been disinclined, at this period, to cultivate an intimacy with her. She needed no companion except the thought of Edward, which was never absent from her mind. But amidst all her affection for her husband, which gained strength, and, as it were, covered each day a larger portion of her being, any one associated with the name of Lodore—of her beloved father, had a magic power to call forth her warmest feelings of interest. Both ladies repeated to each other what they had heard from their several parents. Mr. Derham had,

CHAPTER III

"It does much trouble me to live without you:
Our loves and loving souls have been so used
To one household in us."

—*Beaumont and Fletcher*

The week passed on. It was the month of January, and very cold. A black frost bound up every thing with ice, and the piercing air congealed the very blood. Each day Ethel went to see her husband;—each day she had to encounter Mrs. Derham's entreaties not to go, and the reproaches of Villiers for coming. Both were unavailing to prevent the daily pilgrimage. Mrs. Derham sighed heavily when she saw her enter the ricketty hackney-coach, whose damp lining, gaping windows, and miserable straw, made it a *cold-bed* for catarrh—a very temple for the spirit of winter. Villiers each day besought her to have horses put to their chariot, if she must come; but Ethel remembered all he had ever said of expense, and his prognostications of how ill she would be able to endure the petty, yet galling annoyances of poverty; and she resolved to prove, that she could cheerfully bear every thing except separation from him. With this laudable motive to incite her, she tasked her strength too far. She kept up her spirits to meet him with a cheerful countenance; and she contrived to conceal the sufferings she endured while they were together. They got out and walked now and then; and this tended to keep up the vital warmth. Their course was generally taken over Blackfriars Bridge; and it was on their return across the river, on whose surface large masses of ice floated, while a bitter north-east wind swept up, bearing on its blasts the unthawed breath of the German Ocean, that she felt the cold enter her heart, and make her head feel dizzy. Still she could smile, and ask Villiers why he objected to her taking an exercise even necessary for her health; and repeat again and again, that, bred in America, an English winter was but a faint reflex of what she had encountered there, and insist upon being permitted to come on the following day. These were precious moments in her eyes, worth all the pain they occasioned,—well worth the struggle she made for the repetition. Edward's endearing attentions—the knowledge she had that she was loved—the swelling and earnest affection that warmed her own heart,—hallowed these hard-earned minutes, and gave her the sweet pleasure of knowing that she demonstrated, in some slight degree, the profound and all engrossing attachment which pervaded her entire being. They parted; and often she arrived nearly senseless at Duke Street, and once or twice fainted on entering the warm room: but it was not pain she felt then—the emotions of the soul conquered the sensation of her body, and pleasure, the intense pleasure of affection, was predominant through all.

Sunday came again, and brought Villiers to her home. Mrs. Derham took the opportunity to represent to him the injury that Ethel was doing herself; and begged him, as he cared for her health, to forbid her exposing herself to the inclement weather.

"You hear this, Ethel," said Villiers; "and yet you are obstinate. It this right? What can I urge, what can I do, to prevent this wrong-headed pertinacity?"

"You use such very hard words," replied Ethel, smiling, "that you frighten me into believing myself criminal. But so far am I from conceding, that you only give me courage to say, that I cannot any longer endure the sad and separate life we lead. It must be changed, dearest; we must be together."

Villiers was pacing the room impatiently: with an exclamation almost approaching to anger, he stopped before his wife, to remonstrate and to reproach. But as he gazed upon her upturned face, fixed so beseechingly and fondly on him, he fancied that he saw the hues of ill-health stealing across her cheeks, and thinness displacing the roundness of her form. A strange emotion flashed across him; a new fear, too terrible even to be acknowledged to himself, which passed, like the shadow of a storm, across his anticipations, and filled him with inquietude. His reprehension was changed to a caress, as he said, "You are right, my love, quite right; we must not live thus. You are unable to take care of yourself; and I am very wrong to give up my dearest privilege, of watching day and night over the welfare of my only treasure. We will be together, Ethel; if the worst come, it cannot be very bad, while we are true to each other."

Tears filled the poor girl's eyes—tears of joy and tenderness—at hearing Edward echo the sentiments she cherished as the most sacred in the world. For a few minutes, they forgot every thing in the affectionate kiss, which ratified, as it were, this new law; and then Edward considered how best he could carry it into effect.

"Gayland," he said, (he was his solicitor,) "has appointed to see me on Thursday morning, and has good hopes of definitively arranging the conditions for the loan of the five hundred pounds, which is to enable us to wait for better things. On Thursday evening, we will leave town. We will go to some pretty country inn, to wait till I have signed these papers; and trust to Providence that no ill will arise. We must not be more than fifteen or twenty miles from London; so that when I am obliged to go up, I can return again in a few hours. Tell me, sweet, does this scheme please you?"

Ethel expressed her warmest gratitude; and then Villiers insinuated his condition, that she should not come to see him in the interval, but remain, taking care of herself, till, on Thursday afternoon, at six o'clock, she came, with their chariot, to the northern side of St. Paul's Churchyard, where he would immediately join her. They might write, meanwhile: he promised letters as long as if they were to go to India;

and soothed her annoyance with every expression of thankfulness at her giving up this point. She did give it up, with all the readiness she could muster; and this increased, as he dwelt upon the enjoyment they would share, in exchanging foggy, smoky London, for the ever-pleasing aspect of nature, which, even during frost and snow, possesses her own charms—her own wonders; and can gratify our senses by a thousand forms of beauty, which have no existence in a dingy metropolis.

When the evening hour came for the young pair to separate, their hearts were cheered by the near prospect of re-union; and a belief that the, to them, trivial privations of poverty were the only ones they would have to endure. The thrill of fear which had crossed the mind of Villiers, as to the health and preservation of his wife, had served to dissipate the lingering sense of shame and degradation inspired by the penury of their situation. He felt that there was something better than wealth, and the attendance of his fellow-creatures; something worse than poverty, and the world's scorn. Within the fragile form of Ethel, there beat a heart of more worth than a king's ransom; and its pulsations were ruled by him. To lose her! What would all that earth can afford, of power or splendour, appear without her? He pressed her to his bosom, and knew that his arms encircled all life's worth for him. Never again could he forget the deep-felt appreciation of her value, which then took root in his mind; while she, become conscious, by force of sympathy, of the kind of revolution that was made in his sentiments, felt that the foundations of her life grew strong, and that her hopes in this world became stedfast and enduring. Before, a wall of separation, however slight, had divided them; they had followed a system of conduct independent of each other, and passed their censure upon the ideas of either. This was over now—they were one—one sense of right—one feeling of happiness; and when they parted that night, each felt that they truly possessed the other; and that by mingling every hope and wish, they had confirmed the marriage of their hearts.

•••

CHAPTER IV

"... Think but whither
Now you can go; what you can do to live;
How near you have barred all ports to your own
    succour.
Except this one that here I open, love."

—*Beaumont and Fletcher*

The most pleasing thoughts shed their balmy influence on Ethel's repose that night. Edward's scheme of a country inn, where the very freedom would make them more entirely dependent upon each other, was absolutely enchanting. Where we establish ourselves, and look forward to the passage of a long interval of time, we form ties with, and assume duties towards, many of our fellow-creatures, each of which must diminish the singleness of the soul's devotion towards the selected one. No doubt this is the fitting position for human beings to place themselves in, as affording a greater scope for utility: but for a brief space, to have no occupation but that of contributing to the happiness of him to whom her life was consecrated, appeared to Ethel a very heaven upon earth. It was not that she was narrow-hearted: so much affection demands a spacious mansion for its abode; but in their present position of struggle and difficulty, there was no possibility of extending her sphere of benevolence, and she gladly concentrated her endeavours in the one object whose happiness was in her hands.

All night, even in sleep, a peculiar sense of calm enjoyment soothed the mind of Ethel, and she awoke in the morning with buoyant spirits, and a soul all alive to its own pleasurable existence. She sat at her little solitary breakfast table, musing with still renewed delight upon the prospect opened before her, when suddenly she was startled by the vision of an empty purse. What could Villiers intend? She felt assured that his stock was very nearly exhausted, and for herself two sovereigns, which were not sufficient to meet the demands of the last week, was all that she possessed. She tried to recollect if Edward had said any thing that denoted any expectation of receiving money; on the contrary—diving into the recesses of her memory, she called to mind that he had said, "We shall receive your poor little dividend of a hundred pounds, in less than a fortnight, so we shall be able to live, even if Gayland should delay getting the other money—I suppose we have enough to get on till then."

He had said this inquiringly, and she knew that she had made a sign of assent, though at the time, she had no thought of the real purport of his question or of her answer. What was to be done? The obvious consequence of her reflections was at once to destroy the cherished scheme of going out of town with Villiers. This was a misfortune too great to bear, and she at last decided upon having again recourse to her aunt. Unused to every money transaction, she had not that terror of obligation, nor dislike of asking, which is so necessary to preserve our independence, and even our sense of justice, through life. Money had always been placed like counters in her hand; she had never known whence it came, and until her marriage, she had never disposed of more than very small sums. Subsequently Villiers had been the director of their expenses. This was the faulty part of her father's system of education. But Lodore's domestic habits were for a great part founded on experience in foreign countries, and he forgot that an English wife is usually the cashier—the sole controller of the disbursements of her family. It seemed as easy a thing for Ethel to ask for money from Mrs. Fitzhenry, as she knew it would be easy for her to give. In compliance, however, with Villiers's notions, she limited her request to ten pounds, and tried to word her letter so as to create no suspicion in her aunt's mind with regard to their resources. This task achieved, she dismissed every annoying thought, and when Fanny came to express her hope, that, bleak and snowy as was the day, she did not intend to make her accustomed pilgrimage, with a countenance beaming with delight, she dilated on their plan, and spoke as if on the much-desired Thursday, the gates of Elysium were to be thrown open for her.

There would have appeared something childish in her gladness to the abstracted and philosophic mind of Fanny, but that the real evils of her situation, and the fortitude, touching in its unconscious simplicity, with which she encountered them, commanded respect. Ethel, as well as her friend, was elevated above the common place of life; she also fostered a state of mind, "lofty and magnificent, fitted rather to command than to obey, not only suffering patiently, but even making light of all human cares; a grand and dignified self-possession, which fears nothing, yields to no one, and remains for ever unvanquished." When Fanny, in one of their conversations, while describing the uses of philosophy, had translated this eulogium of its effects from Cicero, Ethel had exclaimed, "This is love—it is love alone that divides us from sordid earthborn thoughts, and causes us to walk alone, girt by its own beauty and power."

Fanny smiled; yet while she saw slavery rather than a proud independence in the creed of Ethel, she admired the warmth of heart which could endow with so much brilliancy a state of privation and solitude. At the present moment, when Mrs. Villiers was rapturously announcing their scheme for leaving London, an expression of pain mantled over Fanny's features; her clear blue eyes became suffused, a large tear gathered on her lashes. "What is the matter?" asked Ethel anxiously.

"That I am a fool—but pardon me, for the folly is already passed away. For the first time you have made it hard for me to keep my soul firm in its own single existence. I have been debarred from all intercourse with those whose ideas rise above the soil on which they tread, except in my dear books, and I thought I should never be attached to any thing but them. Yet do not think me selfish, Mr. Villiers is quite right—it is much better that you should not be apart—I am delighted with his plan."

"Away or near, dear Fanny," said Ethel, in a caressing tone, "I never can forget your kindness—never cease to feel the warmest friendship for you. Remember, our fathers were friends, and their children ought to inherit the same faithful attachment."

Fanny smiled faintly. "You must not seduce me from my resolves," she said. "I know my fate in this world, and I am determined to be true to myself to the end. Yet I am not ungrateful to you, even while I declare, that I shall do my best to forget this brief interval, during which, I have no longer, like Demogorgon, lived alone in my own world, but become aware that there are ties of sympathy between me and my fellow-creatures, in whose existence I did not believe before."

Fanny's language, drawn from her books, not because she tried to imitate, but because conversing perpetually with them, it was natural that she should adopt their style, was always energetic and imaginative; but her quiet manner destroyed every idea of exaggeration of sentiment: it was necessary to hear her soft and low, but very distinct voice utter her lofty sentiments, to be conscious that the calm of deep waters was the element in which she dwelt—not the fretful breakers that spend themselves in sound.

The day seemed rather long to Ethel, who counted the hours until Thursday. Gladly she laid her head on the pillow at night, and bade adieu to the foregone hours. The first thing that awoke her in the morning, was the postman's knock; it brought, as she had been promised, a long, long letter from Edward. He had never before written with so much affection or with such an overflowing of tenderness, that made her the centre of his world—the calm fair lake to receive into its bosom the streams of thought and feeling which flowed from him, and yet which, after all, had their primal source in her. "I am a very happy girl," thought Ethel, as she kissed the beloved papers, and gazed on them in ecstasy; "more happy than I thought it was ever given us to be in this world."

She rose and began to dress; she delayed reading more than a line or two, that she might enjoy her dearest pleasure for a longer time—then again, unable to control her impatience, she sat half dressed, and finished all—and was beginning anew, when there was a tap at her door. It was Fanny. She looked disturbed and anxious, and Ethel's fears were in a moment awake.

"Something annoying has occurred," she said; "yet I do not think that there is any thing to dread, though there is a danger to prevent."

"Speak quickly," cried Ethel, "do not keep me in suspense."

"Be calm—it is nothing sudden, it is only a repetition of the old story. A boy has just been here—a boy you gave a sovereign to—do you remember?—the night of your arrival. It seems that he has vowed himself to your service ever since. Those two odious men, who were here once, are often at his master's place-an alehouse, you know. Well, yesterday night, he overheard them saying, that Mr. Villiers's resort at the London coffee-house, was discovered, or at least suspected, and that a writ was to be taken out against him in the city."

"What does that mean?" cried Ethel.

"That Mr. Villiers will probably be arrested to-day, or to-morrow, if he remains where he is."

"I will go directly to him," cried Ethel; "we must leave town at once. God grant that I am not too late!"

Seeing her extreme agitation, Fanny remained with her—forced her to take some breakfast, and then, fearing that if any thing had really taken place, she would be quite bewildered, asked her permission to accompany her. "Will you indeed come with me?" Ethel exclaimed, "How dear, how good you are! O yes, do come—I can never go through it all alone; I shall die, if I do not find him."

A hackney coach had been called, and they hastened with what speed they might, to their destination. A kind of panic seized upon Ethel, a tremor shook her limbs, so that when they at last stopped, she was unable to speak. Fanny was about to ask for Mr. Villiers, when an exclamation of joy from Ethel stopped her; Edward had seen them, and was at the coach door. The snow lay thick around on the roofs of the houses, and on every atom of vantage ground it could obtain; it was then snowing, and as the chilly fleece dropped through or was driven about in the dark atmosphere, it spread a most disconsolate appearance over every thing; and nothing could look more dreary than poor Ethel's jumbling vehicle, with its drooping animals, and the half-frozen driver. Villiers had made up his mind that he should never be mortified by seeing her again in this sort of equipage, and he hurried down, the words of reproach already on his lips, "Is this your promise?" he asked.

"Yes, dearest, it is. Come in, there is danger here.—Come in—we must go directly."

Seeing Fanny, Villiers became aware that there was some absolute cause for their journey, so he obeyed and quickly heard the danger that threatened him. "It would have been better," he said, "that you had come in the carriage, and that we had instantly left town."

"Impossible!" cried Ethel; "till to-morrow—that is quite impossible. We have no money until to-morrow."

"Well, my love, since it is so, we must arrange as well as we can. Do you return home immediately—this cold will kill you. I will take care of myself, and you can come for me on Thursday evening, as we proposed."

"Do not ask it of me, Edward," said Ethel; "I cannot leave you. I could never live through these two days away from you—you must not desire it—you will kill me."

Edward kissed her pale cheek. "You tremble," he said; "how violently you tremble! Good God! what can we do? What would you have me do?"

"Any thing, so that we remain together. It is of so little consequence where we pass the next twenty-four hours, so that we are together. There are many hotels in town."

"I must not venture to any of these; and then to take you in this miserable manner, without servants, or any thing to command attendance. But you shall have your own way; having deprived you of every other luxury, at least, you shall have your will; which, you know, compensates for every thing with your obstinate sex."

Ethel smiled, rejoicing to find him in so good and accommodating a humour. "Yes, pretty one," he continued, marking her feelings, "you shall be as wretched and uncomfortable as your heart can desire. We will play the incognito in such a style, that if our adventures were printed, they would compete with those of Don Quixote and the fair Dulcinea. But Miss Derham must not be admitted into our vagabondizing—we will not detain her."

"Yet she must know whither we are going, to bring us the letters that will confer freedom on us."

Villiers wrote hastily an address on a card. "You will find us there," he said. "Do not mention names when you come. We shall remain, I suppose, till Thursday."

"But we shall see you some time to-morrow, dear Fanny?" asked Ethel. Already she looked bright and happy; she esteemed herself fortunate to have gained so easily a point she had feared she must struggle for—or perhaps give up altogether. Fanny left them, and the coachman having received his directions, drove slowly on through the deep snow, which fell thickly on the road; while they, nestling close to each other, were so engrossed by the gladness of re-union, that had Cinderella's godmother transmuted their crazy vehicle for a golden coach, redolent of the perfumes of fairy land, they had scarcely been aware of the change. Their own hearts formed a more real fairy land, which accompanied them whithersoever they went, and could as easily spread its enchantments over the shattered machine in which they now jumbled along, as amidst the cloth of gold and marbles of an eastern palace.

•••

CHAPTER V

"Few people know how little is necessary to live.
What is called or thought *hardship* is nothing; *one*
unhappy feeling is worse than a thousand years of it."

—*Lord Edward Fitzgerald*

Uncertain what to do, Villiers had hastily determined that they should take up their abode at a little inn near Brixton, to wait till Thursday. He did not know the place except by having passed it, and observed a smart landlady at the door; so he trusted that it would be neat and clean. There was nothing imposing in the appearance of the young pair and their hackney coach, accordingly there was no bustling civility displayed to receive them. However, when the fire was once lighted, the old-fashioned sofa drawn near, and dinner ordered, they sat together and felt very happy; outcasts though they were, wanderers from civilized existence, shut out, through poverty, from the refinements and gilt elegancies of life.

One only cloud there was, when Villiers asked his wife an explanation about their resources, and inquired whence she expected to receive money on the following day. Ethel explained. Villiers looked disturbed. There was something almost of anger in his voice, when he said, "And so, Ethel, you feel no compunction in acting in exact opposition to my wishes, my principles, my resolves?"

"But, dear Edward, what can principles have to do with borrowing a few pounds from dear good Aunt Bessy? Besides, we can repay her."

"Be assured that we shall," replied Villiers; "and you will never again, I trust, behave so unjustly by me. There are certain things in which we must judge and act for ourselves, and the question of money transactions is one. I may suffer—and you, alas! may also, through poverty; though you have taken pains to persuade me, that you do not feel that struggles, which, for your sake chiefly, embitter my existence. Yet they are nothing in comparison with the loss of my independence—the sense of obligation—the knowledge that my kind friends can talk over my affairs, take me to task, and call me a burthen to them. Why am I as I am? I have friends and connexions who would readily assist me at this extremity, if I asked it, and I might turn their kind feelings into sterling gold if I would; but I have no desire to work this transmutation—I prefer their friendship."

"Do you mean," inquired his wife, "that your friends would not love you the better for having been of service to you?"

"If they could serve me without annoyance to themselves they might; but high in rank and wealthy as many of my relations are, there is not one among them, at least of those to whom I could have recourse, who do not dispose of their resources to the uttermost shilling, in their own way. I then come to interfere with and to disarrange their plans; at first, this might not be much—but presently they would weigh me against the gold I needed, and it might happen, that my scale would kick the beam.

"I speak for myself not for others; I may be too proud, too sensitive—but so I am. Ever since I knew what pecuniary obligations were, I resolved to lay under such to no man, and this resolve was stronger than my love for you; judge therefore of its force, and the violence you do me, when you would oblige me to act against it. Did I begin to borrow, a train of thoughts would enter the lender's mind; the consciousness of which, would haunt me like a crime. My actions would be scanned—I should be blamed for this, rebuked for that—even your name, my Ethel, which I would place, like a star in the sky, far above their mathematical measurements, would become stale in their mouths, and the propriety of our marriage canvassed: could you bear that?"

"I yield to all you say," she answered; "yet this is strange morality. Are generosity, benevolence, and gratitude, to be exploded among us? Is justice, which orders that the rich give of his superfluity to the poor, to be banished from the world?"

"You are eloquent," said Villiers; "but, my little wild American, this is philosophy for the back-woods only. We have got beyond the primeval simplicity of barter and exchange among gentlemen; and it is such if I give gratitude in return for fifty pounds: by-and-by my fellow-trader may grumble at the bargain. All this will become very clear to you hereafter, I fear—when knowledge of the world teaches you what sordid knaves we all are; it is to prevent your learning this lesson in a painful way, that I guard you so jealously from making a wrong step at this crisis."

"You speak of dreams," said Ethel, "as if dear aunt Bessy would feel any thing but pleasure in sending her mite to her own dear niece."

"I have told you what I wish," replied her husband, "my honour is in your hands; and I implore you, on this point, to preserve it in the way I desire. There is but one relationship that authorizes any thing like community of goods, it is that of parent and child; but we are orphans, dearest—step-children, who are not permitted to foster our filial senti-ments. My father is unworthy of his name—the animal who destroys its offspring at its birth is merciful in comparison with him: had he cast me off at once, I should have hardened my hands with labour, and earned my daily bread; but I was trained to "high-born necessities," and have all the "wide wants and narrow powers"* of the heir of wealth. But let us dismiss this ungrateful subject. I never willingly advert, even in my own mind, to my father's unpaternal conduct. Let us instead fancy, sweet love, that we were born to what we have—that we are cottag-ers, the children of mechanics, or wanderers in a barbarous country,

---

* The Cenci.

where money is not; and imagine that this repose, this cheerful fire, this shelter from the pelting snow without, is an unexpected blessing. Strip a man bare to what nature made him, and place him here, and what a hoard of luxury and wealth would not this room contain! In the Illinois, love, few mansions could compete with this."

This was speaking in a language which Ethel could easily comprehend; she had several times wished to express this very idea, but she feared to hurt the refined and exclusive feelings of her husband. A splendid dwelling, costly living, and many attendants, were with her the adjuncts, not the material, of life. If the stage on which she played her part was to be so decorated, it was well; if otherwise, the change did not merit her attention. Love scoffed at such idle trappings, and could build his tent of canvas, and sleep close nestled in her heart as softly, being only the more lovely and the more true, from the absence of every meretricious ornament.

This was another of Ethel's happy evenings, when she felt drawn close to him she loved, and found elysium in the intimate union of their thoughts. The dusky room showed them but half to each other; and the looks of each, beaming with tenderness, drank life from one another's gaze. The soft shadows thrown on their countenances, gave a lamp-like lustre to their eyes, in which the purest spirit of affection sat, weaving such unity of sentiment, such strong bonds of attachment, as made all life dwindle to a point, and freighted the passing minute with the hopes and fears of their entire existence. Not much was said, and their words were childish—words

Intellette dar loro soli ambedui,

which a listener would have judged to be meaningless. But the mystery of love gave a deep sense to each syllable. The hours flew lightly away. There was nothing to interrupt, nothing to disturb. Night came and the day was at an end; but Ethel looked forward to the next, with faith in its equal felicity, and did not regret the fleet passage of time.

They had been asked during the evening if they were going by any early coach on the following morning, and a simple negative was given. On that morning they sat at their breakfast, with some diminution of the sanguine hopes of the previous evening. For morning is the time for action, of looking forward, of expectation,—and they must spend this in waiting, cooped up in a little room, overlooking no cheering scene. A high road, thickly covered with snow, on which various vehicles were perpetually passing, was immediately before them. Opposite was a row of mean-looking houses, between which might be distinguished low fields buried in snow; and the dreary dark-looking sky bending over all, added to the forlorn aspect of nature. Villiers was very impatient to get away, yet another day must be passed here, and there was no help.

On the breakfast-table the waiter had placed the bill of the previous day; it remained unnoticed, and he left it on the table when the things were taken away. "I wonder when Fanny will come," said Ethel.

"Perhaps not at all to-day," observed Villiers, "she knows that we intend to remain till tomorrow here; and if your aunt's letter is delayed till then, I see no chance of her coming, nor any use in it."

"But Aunt Bessy will not delay; her answer is certain of arriving this morning."

"So you imagine, love. You know little of the various chances that wait upon borrowing."

Soon after, unable to bear confinement to the house, uneasy in his thoughts, and desirous a little to dissipate them by exercise, Villiers went out. Ethel, taking a small Shakespeare, which her husband had had with him at the coffee-house, occupied herself by reading, or turning from the written page to her own thoughts, gave herself up to reverie, dwelling on many an evanescent idea, and reverting delightedly to many scenes, which her memory recalled. She was one of those who "know the pleasures of solitude, when we hold commune alone with the tranquil solemnity of nature." The thought of her father, of the Illinois, and the measureless forest rose before her, and in her ear was the dashing of the stream which flowed near their abode. Her light feet again crossed the prairie, and a thousand appearances of sky and earth departed for ever, were retraced in her brain. "Would not Edward be happy there?" she thought: "why should we not go? We should miss dear Horatio; but what else could we regret that we leave behind? and perhaps he would join us, and then we should be quite happy." And then her fancy pictured her new home and all its delights, till her eyes were suffused with tender feeling, as her imagination sketched a variety of scenes—the pleasant labours of cultivation, the rides, the hunting, the boating, all common-place occurrences, which, attended on by love, were exalted into a perpetual gorgeous procession of beatified hours. And then again she allowed to herself that Europe or America could contain the same delights. She recollected Italy, and her feelings grew more solemn and blissful as she meditated on the wondrous beauty and changeful but deep interest of that land of memory.

Villiers did not return for some hours;—he also had indulged in reverie—long-drawn, but not quite so pleasant as that of his inexperienced wife. The realities of life were kneaded up too entirely with his prospects and schemes, for them to assume the fairy hues that adorned Ethel's. He could not see the end to his present struggle for the narrowest independence. Very slender hopes had been held out to him; and thus he was to drag out an embittered existence, spent upon sordid cares, till his father died—an ungrateful idea, from which he turned with a sigh. He walked speedily, on account of the cold; and as his blood began to circulate more cheerily in his frame, a change came over the tenor of his thoughts. From the midst of the desolation in which he was lost, a vision of happiness arose, that forced itself on his speculations, in spite, as he imagined, of his better reason. The image of an elegant home, here or in Italy, adorned by Ethel—cheered by the presence of friends, unshadowed by any cares, presented itself to his mind with strange distinctness and pertinacity. At no time had Villiers loved so passionately as now. The difficulties of their situation had exalted her, who shared them with such cheerful fortitude, into an angel of consolation. The pride of man in possessing the affections of this lovely and noble-minded creature, was blended with the tenderest desire of protecting and serving her. His heart glowed with honest joy at the reflection that her happiness depended upon him solely, and that he was ready to devote his life to secure it. Was there any action too arduous, any care too minute, to display his gratitude and his perfect affection? As his recollection came back, he found that he was at a considerable distance from her, so he swiftly turned his steps homeward, (that was his home where she was,) and scarcely felt that he trod earth as he recollected that each moment carried him nearer, and that he should soon meet the fond gaze of the kindest, sweetest eyes in the world.

Thus they met, with a renewed joy, after a short absence, each reaping, from their separate meditations, a fresh harvest of loving thoughts and interchange of grateful emotion. Great was the pity that such was their situation—that circumstances, all mean and trivial, drew them from their heaven-high elevation, to the more sordid cares of this dirty planet. Yet why name it pity? their pure natures could turn the grovelling substance presented to them, to ambrosial food for the sustenance of love.

• • •

CHAPTER VI

"There's a bliss beyond all that the minstrel has told,
When two that are linked in one heavenly tie,
With heart never changing, and brow never cold,
Love on through all ills, and love on till they die."

—*Moore*, Lalla Rookh

Villiers had not been returned long, when the waiter came in, and informed them, that his mistress declined serving their dinner, till her bill of the morning was paid; and then he left the room. The gentle pair looked at each other, and laughed. "We must wait till Fanny comes, I fear," said Ethel; "for my purse is literally empty."

"And if Miss Derham should not come?" remarked Villiers.

"But she will!—she has delayed, but I am perfectly certain that she will come in the course of the day: I do not feel the least doubt about it."

To quicken the passage of time, Ethel employed herself in netting a purse, (the inutility of which Villiers smilingly remarked,) while her husband read to her some of the scenes from Shakespeare's play of "Troilus and Cressida." The profound philosophy, and intense passion, of this drama, adorned by the most magnificent poetry that can even be found in the pages of this prince of poets, caused each to hang attentive and delighted upon their occupation. As it grew dark, Villiers stirred up the fire, and still went on; till having with difficulty decy-phered the lines—

> "She was beloved—she loved;—she is, and doth;
> But still sweet love is food for fortune's tooth,"—

he closed the book. "It is in vain," he said; "our liberator does not come; and these churls will not give us lights."

"It is early yet, dearest," replied Ethel;—"not yet four o'clock. Would Troilus and Cressida have repined at having been left darkling a few minutes? How much happier we are than all the heroes and hero-ines that ever lived or were imagined! they grasped at the mere shadow of the thing, whose substance we absolutely possess. Let us know and acknowledge our good fortune. God knows, I do, and am beyond words grateful!"

"It is much to be grateful for—sharing the fortunes of a ruined man!"

"You do not speak as Troilus does," replied Ethel smiling: "he knew better the worth of love compared with worldly trifles."

"You would have me protest, then," said Villiers;—

> "But, alas!
> I am as true as truth's simplicity,
> And simpler than the infancy of truth";

so that all I can say is, that you are a very ill-used little girl, to be mated as you are—so buried, with all your loveliness, in this obscurity—so bound, though akin to heaven, to the basest dross of earth."

"You are poetical, dearest, and I thank you. For my own part, I am in love with ill luck. I do not think we should have discovered how very dear we are to each other, had we sailed for ever on a sum-mer sea."

Such talk, a little prolonged, at length dwindled to silence. Edward drew her nearer to him; and as his arm encircled her waist, she placed her sweet head on his bosom, and they remained in silent reverie. He, as with his other hand he played with her shining ringlets, and parted them on her fair brow, was disturbed in thought, and saddened by a sense of degradation. Not to be able to defend the angelic creature, who depended on him, from the world's insults, galled his soul, and embittered even the heart's union that existed between them. She did not think—she did know of these things. After many minutes of silence, she said,—"I have been trying to discover why it is absolute pleasure to suffer pain for those we love."

"Pleasure in pain!—you speak riddles."

"I do," she replied, raising her head; "but I have divined this. The great pleasure of love is derived from sympathy—the feeling of union—of unity. Any thing that makes us alive to the sense of love—that imprints deeper on our plastic consciousness the knowledge of the existence of our affection, causes an increase of happiness. There are two things to which we are most sensitive—pleasure and pain. But habit can somewhat dull the first; and that which was in its newness, ecstasy—our being joined for ever—becomes, like the air we breathe, a thing we could not live without, but yet in which we are rather passively than actively happy. But when pain comes to awaken us to a true sense of how much we love—when we suffer for one another's dear sake—the consciousness of attachment swells our hearts: we are recalled from the forgetfulness engendered by custom; and the awakening and renewal of the sense of affection brings with it a joy, that sweetens to its dregs the bitterest cup."

"Encourage this philosophy, dear Ethel," replied Villiers; "you will need it: but it shames me to think that I am your teacher in this mournful truth." As he spoke, his whole frame was agitated by tenderness and grief. Ethel could see, by the dull fire-light, a tear gather on his eye-lashes: it fell upon her hand. She threw her arms round him, and pressed him to her heart with a passionate gush of weeping, occasioned partly by remorse at having so moved him, and partly by her heart's overflowing with the dear security of being loved.

They had but a little recovered from this scene, when the waiter, bringing in lights, announced Miss Derham. Her coming had been full of disasters. After many threatenings, and much time consumed in clumsy repairs, her hackney-coach had fairly broken down: she had walked the rest of the way; but they were much further from town than she expected; and thus she accounted for her delay. She brought no news; but held in her hand the letter that contained the means of freeing them from their awkward predicament.

"We will not stay another minute in this cursed place," said Villiers: "we will go immediately to Salt Hill, where I intended to take you to-morrow. I can return by one of the many stages which pass continually, to keep my appointment with Gayland; and be back with you again by night. So if these stupid people possess a post-chaise, we will be gone directly."

Ethel was well pleased with this arrangement; and it was put in execution immediately. The chaise and horses were easily procured. They set Fanny down in their way through town. Ethel tried to repay her kindness by heartfelt thanks; and she, in her placid way, showed clearly how pleased she was to serve them.

Leaving her in Piccadilly, not far from her own door, they pursued their way to Salt Hill; and it seemed as if, in this mere change of place, they had escaped from a kind of prison, to partake again in the immunities and comforts of civilized life. Ethel was considerably fatigued when she arrived; and her husband feared that he had tasked her strength too far. The falling and fallen snow clogged up the roads, and their journey had been long. She slept, indeed, the greater part of the way, her head resting on him; and her languor and physical suffering were soothed by emotions the most balmy and by the gladdening sense of confidence and security.

They arrived at Salt Hill late in the evening. The hours were precious; for early on the following day, Villiers was obliged to return to town. On inquiry, he found that his best mode was to go by a night-coach from Bath, which would pass at seven in the morning. They were awake half the night, talking of their hopes, their plans, their probable deliverance from their besetting annoyances. By this time Ethel had taught her own phraseology, and Villiers had learned to believe that whatever must happen would fall upon both, and that no separation could take place fraught with any good to either.

When Ethel awoke, late in the morning, Villiers was gone. Her watch told her, indeed, that it was near ten o'clock, and that he must have departed long before. She felt inclined to reproach him for leaving her, though only for a few hours, without an interchange of adieu. In truth, she was vexed that he was not there: the world appeared to her so blank, without his voice to welcome her back to it from out of the regions of sleep. While this slight cloud of ill-humour (may it be called?) was passing over her mind, she perceived a little note, left by her husband, lying on her pillow. Kissing it a thousand times, she read its contents, as if they possessed talismanic power. They breathed the most passionate tenderness: they besought her, as she loved him, to take care of herself, and to keep up her spirits until his return, which would be as speedy as the dove flies back to its nest, where its sweet mate fondly expects him. With these assurances and blessings to cheer her, Ethel arose. The sun poured its wintry yet cheering beams into the parlour, and the sparkling, snow-clad earth glittered beneath. She wrapped herself in her cloak, and walked into the garden of the hotel. Long immured in London, living as if its fogs were the universal vesture of all things, her spirits rose to exultation and delight, as she looked on the blue sky spread cloudlessly around. As the pure breeze freshened her cheek, a kind of transport seized her; her spirit took wings; she felt as if she could float on the bosom of the air—as if there was a sympathy in nature, whose child and nursling she was, to welcome her back to her haunts, and to reward her bounteously for coming. The trees, all leafless and snow-bedecked, were friends and intimates: she kissed their rough barks, and then laughed at her own folly at being so rapt. The snow-drop, as it peeped from the ground, was a thing of wonder and mystery; and the shapes of frost, beautiful forms to be worshipped. All sorrow—all care passed away, and left her mind as clear and bright as the unclouded heavens that bent over her.

• • •

CHAPTER VII

"Herein
Shall my captivity be made my happiness;
Since what I lose in freedom, I regain
With interest."

—Beaumont and Fletcher

T he glow of enthusiasm and gladness, thus kindled in her soul, faded slowly as the sun descended; and human tenderness returned in full tide upon her. She longed for Edward to speak to; when would he come back? She walked a little way on the London road; she returned: still her patience was not exhausted. The sun's orb grew red and dusky as it approached the horizon: she returned to the house. It was yet early: Edward could not be expected yet: he had promised to come as soon as possible; but he had prepared her for the likelihood of his arrival only by the mail at night. It was long since she had written to Saville. Cooped up in town, saddened by her separation from her husband, or enjoying the brief hours of reunion, she had felt disinclined to write. Her enlivened spirits now prompted her to pour out some of their overflowings to him. She did not allude to any of the circumstances of their situation, for Edward had forbidden that topic: still she had much to say; for her heart was full of benevolence to all mankind; besides her attachment to her husband, the prospect of becoming a mother within a few months, opened another source of tenderness; there seemed to be a superabundance of happiness within her, a portion of which she desired to impart to those she loved.

Daylight had long vanished, and Villiers did not return. She felt uneasy:—of course he would come by the mail; yet if he should not— what could prevent him? Conjectures would force themselves on her, unreasonable, she told herself; yet her doubts were painful, and she listened attentively each time that the sound of wheels grew, and again faded, upon her ear. If the vehicle stopped, she was in a state of excitation that approached alarm. She knew not what she feared; yet her disquiet increased into anxiety. "Shall I ever see him again?" were words that her lips did not utter, and yet which lingered in her heart, although unaccompanied by any precise idea to her understanding.

She had given a thousand messages to the servants;—and at last the mail arrived. She heard a step—it was the waiter:—"The gentleman is not come, ma'am," he said. "I knew it," she thought;—"yet why? why?" At one time she resolved to set off for town; yet whither to go—where to find him? An idea struck her, that he had missed the mail; but as he would not leave her a prey to uncertainty, he would come by some other conveyance. She got a little comfort from this notion, and resumed her occupation of waiting; though the vagueness of her expectations rendered her a thousand times more restless than before. And all was vain. The mail had arrived at eleven o'clock—at twelve she retired to her room. She read again and again his note: his injunction, that she should take care of herself, induced her to go to bed at a little after one; but sleep was still far from her. Till she could no longer expect—till it became certain that it must be morning before he could come, she did not close her eyes. As her last hope quitted her, she wept bitterly. Where was the joyousness of the morning?—the exuberant delight with which her veins had tingled, which had painted life as a blessing? She hid her face in her pillow, and gave herself up to tears, till sleep at last stole over her senses.

Early in the morning her door opened and her curtain was drawn aside. She awoke immediately, and saw Fanny Derham standing at her bed-side.

"Edward! where is he?" she exclaimed, starting up.

"Well, quite well," replied Fanny: "do not alarm yourself, dear Mrs. Villiers,—he has been arrested."

"I must go to him immediately. Leave me for a little while, dear Fanny,—I will dress and come to you; do you order the chaise meanwhile. I can hear every thing as we are going to town."

Ethel trembled violently—her speech was rapid but inarticulate; the paleness that overspread her face, blanching even her marble brow, and the sudden contraction of her features, alarmed Fanny. The words she had used in communicating her intelligence were cabalistic to Ethel, and her fears were the more intolerable because mysterious and undefined; the blood trickled cold in her veins, and a chilly moisture stood on her forehead. She exerted herself violently to conquer this weakness, but it shackled her powers, as bands of rope would her limbs, and after a few moments she sank back on her pillow almost bereft of life. Fanny sprang to the bell, then sprinkled her with water; some salts were procured from the landlady, and gradually the colour revisited her cheeks, and her frame resumed its functions—an hysteric fit, the first she had ever had, left her at last exhausted but more composed. She herself became frightened lest illness should keep her from Villiers; she exerted herself to become tranquil, and lay for some time without speaking or moving. A little refreshment contributed to restore her, and she turned to Fanny with a faint sweet smile, "You see," said she, "what a weak, foolish thing I am; but I am well now, quite rallied—there must be no more delay."

Her cheerful voice and lively manner gave her friend confidence. Fanny was one who believed much in the mastery of mind, and felt sure that nothing would be so prejudicial to Mrs. Villiers as contradiction, and obstacles put in the way of her attaining the object of her wishes. In spite therefore of the good people about, who insisted that the most disastrous consequences would ensue, she ordered the horses, and prepared for their immediate journey to town. Ethel repaid her cares with smiles, while she restrained her curiosity, laid as it were a check on her too impatient movements, and forced a calm of manner which gave her friend courage to proceed.

It was not until they were on their way that the object of their journey was mentioned. Fanny then spoke of the arrest as a trifling circumstance—mentioned bail, and twenty things, which Ethel only comprehended to be mysterious methods of setting him free; and then also she asked the history of what had happened. The tale was soon told. The moment Mr. Villiers had entered Piccadilly he had caused a coach to be called, but on passing to it from the stage, two men entered it with him, whose errand was too easily explained. He had driven first to his solicitor's, hoping to put every thing in train for his instant liberation. The day was consumed in these fruitless endeavours—he did not give up hope till past ten at night, when he sent to Fanny, asking her to go down to Mrs. Villiers as early as possible in the morning, and to bring her up to town. His wish was, he said, that Ethel should take up her abode at Mrs. Derham's till this affair could be arranged, and they were enabled to leave London. His note was hurried; he promised that another, more explicit, should await his wife on her arrival.

"You will tell the driver," said Ethel, when this story was finished, "to drive to Edward's prison. I would not stay away five minutes from him in his present situation to purchase the universe."

Any one but Miss Derham might have resisted Ethel's wish—have argued with her, and irritated her by the display of obstacles and inconveniences. It was not Fanny's method ever to oppose the desires of others. They knew best, she affirmed, their own sensations, and what was most fitting for them. What is best for me, habit, education, and a different texture of character, may render the worst for them. In the present instance, also, she saw that Ethel's feelings were almost too high wrought for her strength—that opposition, by making a further call on her powers, might upset them wholly. She had besides, the deepest respect for her attachment to her husband, and was willing to reward it by bringing her to him without delay. Having thus fortunately fallen into reasonable hands, guided by one who could understand her char-

even the black neglected grate, Villiers sat, reading. His first emotion was shame when he saw Ethel enter. There was no accord between her spotless loveliness and his squalid prison-room. Any one who has seen a sunbeam suddenly enter and light up a scene of housewifely neglect, and vulgar discomfort, and felt how obtrusive it rendered all that might be half-forgotten in the shade, can picture how the simple elegance of Ethel displayed yet more distinctly to her husband the worse than beggarly scene in which she found him. His cheeks flushed, and almost he would have turned away. He would have reproached, but a tenderness and an elevation of feeling animated her expressive countenance, which turned the current of his thoughts. Whether it were their fate to suffer the extremes of fortune in the savage wilderness, or in the more appalling privations of civilized life—love, and the poetry of love accompanied her, and gilded, and irradiated the commonest forms of penury. She looked at him, and her eyes then glanced to the barred windows. As Fanny and their conductor left them, she heard the key turn in the lock with an impertinent intrusive loudness. She felt pained for him, but for herself it was as if the world and all its cares were locked out, and as if in this near association with him, she reaped the reward of all her previous anxiety. There was no repining in her thoughts, no dejection in her manner; Villiers could read in her open countenance, as plainly as through the clearest crystal, the sentiments that were passing in her mind—it was something more satisfied than resignation, more contented than fortitude. It was a knowledge that whatever evil might attend her lot, the good so far outweighed it, that, for his sake only, could she advert to any feeling of distress. It was a consciousness of being in her place, and of fulfilling her duty, accompanied by a sort of rapture in remembering how thrice dear and hallowed that duty was. Angels could not feel as she did, for they cannot sacrifice to those they love; yet there was in her that absence of all self-emanating pain, which is the characteristic of what we are told of the angelic essences.

As when at night autumnal winds are howling, and vast masses of winged clouds are driven with indescribable speed across the sky—we note the islands of dark ether, built round by the white fleecy shapes; and as we mark the stars which gem their unfathomable depth, silence and sublime tranquillity appear to have found a home in that deep vault, and we love to dwell on the peace and beauty that live there, while the clouds still rush on, and the face of the lower heaven is more mutable than water. Thus the mind of Ethel, surrounded by the world's worst forms of adversity, showed clear and serene, entirely possessed by the repose of love. It was impossible but that, in spite of shame and regret, Villiers should not participate in these feelings. He gave himself up to the softening influence: he knew not how to repine on his own account; Ethel's affection demanded to stand in place of prosperity, and he could not refuse to admit so dear a claim.

The door had closed on them, and every outlet to liberty, or the enjoyment of life, was barred up. Edward drew Ethel towards him and kissed her fondly. Their eyes met, and the speechless tenderness that beamed from hers reached his heart and soothed every ruffled feeling. Sitting together, and interchanging a few words of comfort and hope, mingled with kind looks and affectionate caresses, they neither of them remembered indignity nor privation. The tedious mechanism of civilized life, and the odious interference of their fellow-creatures were forgotten, and they were happy.

•••

CHAPTER VIII

"Veggo purtroppo
Che favola è la vita,
E la favola mia non è compita."

—*Petrarca*

The darker months of winter had passed away, and the chilly, blighting English spring begun. Towards the end of March Lady Lodore came to town. She had long ago, in her days of wealth, fitted up a house in Park Lane, so she returned to it, as to a home—if home it might be called—where no one welcomed her—where none sat beside her at the domestic hearth.

For the first time she felt keenly this circumstance. During her mother's lifetime she had had her constantly for a companion, and afterwards as events pressed upon her, and while the anguish she felt upon Horatio Saville's marriage was still fresh, she had not reverted to her lonely position as the source of pain.

The haughty, the firm, the self-exalting soul of Cornelia had borne up long. She had often felt that she walked on the borders of a precipice, and that if once she admitted sentiments of regret, she should plunge without retrieve into a gulph, dark, portentous, inextricable. She had often repeated to herself that fate should not vanquish her, and that in spite of despair she would be happy: it is true that the misery occasioned by Saville's marriage was a canker at her heart, for which there was no cure, but she had recourse to dissipation that she might endeavour to forget it. A sad and ineffectual remedy. She was surrounded by admirers, whom she disdained, and by friends to whom she would have died rather than betray the naked misery of her soul. She had never planned nor thought of marriage. The report concerning the Earl of D—— was one of those which the world always makes current, when two persons of opposite sexes are, by any chance, thrown much together. His sister was Lady Lodore's friend, and she had chaperoned her, and been of assistance to her, during the courtship of the gentleman who was at present her husband. It was their house that Lady Lodore had just quitted on arriving in town. The new-born happiness of early wedded life had been a scene to call her back to thoughts which were the sources of the bitterest anguish. She abhorred herself that she could envy, that she could desire to exchange places with, any created being. She abridged her visit, and fancied that she should regain peace in the independence of her own home. But the enjoyment of liberty was cold in her heart, and loneliness added a freezing chilliness to her feeling.

The mind of Cornelia was much above the world she lived in, though she had sacrificed all to it; and, so to speak, much above herself. Take pride from her, and there was understanding, magnanimity, and great kindliness of disposition: but pride had been the wall of China to shut up all her better qualities, and to keep them from communicating with the world beyond;—pride, which grew strong by resistance, and towered above every aggressor;—pride, which crumbled away, when time and change were its sole assailants, till her inner being was left unprotected and bare.

She found herself alone in the world. She felt that her life was aimless, unprofitable, blank. She was humiliated and saddened by her relative position in the world. She did not think of her daughter as a resource; she was in the hands of her enemies, and no hope lay there. She entertained the belief that Mrs. Villiers was weak both in character and understanding; and that to make any attempt to interest herself in her, would end in disappointment, if not disgust. Imagining, as we are all apt to do, how we should act in another person's place, she had formed a notion of what she would have done, had she been Ethel; and as nothing was done, she almost despised, and quite pitied her. No! there was no help. She was alone;—none loved, none cared for her; and the flower of the field, which a child plucks and wears for an hour, and then casts aside, was of more worth than she.

Every amusement grew tedious—all society vacant and dull. When she came back from dinners or assemblies, to her luxurious but empty abode, the darkest thoughts, engendered by spleen, hung over its threshold, and welcomed her return. At such times, she would dismiss her attendant, and remain half the night by her fireside, encouraging sickly reveries, struggling with the fate that bound her, yet unable in any way to make an effort for freedom.

"Time"—thus would her thoughts fashion themselves— "yes, time rolls on, and what does it bring? I live in a desert; its barren sands feed my hour-glass, and they come out fruitless as they went in. Months change their names—years their cyphers: my brow is sadly trenched; the bloom of youth is faded: my mind gathers wrinkles. What will become of me?

"Hopes of my youth, where are ye?—my aspirations, my pride, my belief that I could grasp and possess all things? Alas! there is nothing of all this! My soul lies in the dust; and I look up to know that I have been playing with shadows, and that I am fallen for ever! What do I see around me? The tide of life is ebbing fast! I had fancied that pearls and gold would have been left by the retiring waves; and I find only barren, lonely sands! No voice reaches me from across the waters—no one stands beside me on the shore! Would—O would I could lay my head on the spray-sprinkled beach, and sleep for ever!

"This is madness!—these incoherent images that throng my brain are the ravings of insanity!—yet what greater madness, than to know that love, affection, the charities of life, the hopes of existence, are empty words for me. Am I indeed to have done with these? What is it that still moves up and down in my soul, making me feel as if something might yet be accomplished? Is it that the ardour of youth is not yet tamed? Alas! my youth has departed for ever. Yet wherefore these sighs, which wrap an eternity of wretchedness in their evanescent breath?—why these tears, that, flowing from the inmost fountains of the soul, endeavour to give passage to the flood of sorrow that deluges and overwhelms it? The husband of my youth!—the thought of him passes like a shadow across me! Had he borne with me a little longer—had I submitted to his control—how different my destiny had been! But I will not think of that—I do not! A mightier storm than any he could raise has swept across me since, and laid all waste. My soul has been set upon a hope, which has vanished, and desolation has come in its room. Could God, in his anger, bestow a bitterer curse on a condemned spirit, than that which weighs on me, when I reflect, that through my own fault I lost him, whom but to see was paradise? The thought haunts me like a crime; yet when is it absent from me?—it sleeps with me, rises with me—it is by me now, and I would willingly die only to dismiss it for ever.

"Miserable Cornelia! Thou hast been courted, lauded, waited on, loved!—it is all over! I am alone! My poor, poor mother!—my much reviled, my dearest mother!—by you, at least, I was valued! Ah! why are you gone, leaving your wretched child alone?

"O that I could take wings and rise from out of the abyss into which I am fallen! Can I not, myself being miserable, take pleasure in the pleasure of others; and by force of strong sympathy, forget my selfish woes? With whom can I sympathize? None desire my care, and all would repay my officiousness with ingratitude, perhaps with scorn. Once I could assist the poor; now I am poor myself: my limited means scarce suffice to keep me in that station in society, from which, did I once descend, I were indeed trampled upon and destroyed for ever. Tears rush from my eyes—my heart sinks within me, as I look forward.

Again the same cares, the same coil, the same bitter result. Hopes held out, only to be crushed; affections excited, only to be scattered to the winds. I blamed myself for struggling too much with fate, for rowing against wind and tide, for resolving to control the events that form existence: now I yield—I have long yielded—I have let myself drift, as I hoped, into a quiet creek, where indifference and peace ruled the hour; and lo! it is a whirlpool, to swallow all I had left of enjoyment upon earth!"

It was not until she had exhausted herself by these gloomy and restless reflections, that she laid her head upon her pillow, and tried to sleep. Morning usually dawned before she closed her eyes; and it was nearly noon before she rose, weary and unrefreshed. It was with a struggle that she commenced a new day—a day that was to be cheered by no event nor feeling capable of animating her to any sense of joy. She had never occupied herself by intellectual exertion: her employments had been the cultivation of what are called accomplishments merely; and when now she reverted to these, it was with bitterness. She remembered the interval when she had been inspirited by the delightful wish to please Horatio. Now none cared how the forlorn Cornelia passed her time;—no one would hang enraptured on her voice, or hail with gladness the developement of some new talent. "It is the same," she thought, "how I get rid of the heavy hours, so that they go. I have but to give myself up to the sluggish stream that bears me on to old age, not more bereft or unregarded than these wretched years."

Thus she lingered idly through the morning; her only enjoyment being, when she secured to herself a solitary drive, and reclining back in her carriage, felt herself safe from every intrusion, and yet enjoying a succession of objects, that a little varied the tenor of her thoughts. She had deserted the park, and sought unfrequented drives in the environs of London. Evening at last came, and with it her uninteresting engagements, which yet she found better than entire seclusion. Forced to rouse herself to adopt, as a mask, the smiling appearance which had been natural to her for many years, she often abhorred every one around her; and yet, hating herself more, took refuge among them, from her own society. Her chief care was to repress any manifestation of her despair, which too readily rose to her lips or in her eyes. The glorious hues of sunset—the subduing sounds of music—even the sight of a beautiful girl, resplendent with happiness and youth, moving gracefully in dance—had power to move her to tears: her blood seemed to curdle and grow thick, while gloomy shadows mantled over her features. Often, she could scarcely forbear expressing the bitterness of her feelings, and indulging in acrimonious remarks on the deceits of life, and the inanity of all things. It seemed to her, sometimes, that she must die if she did not give vent to the still increasing horror with which she regarded the whole system of the world.

Nor were her sufferings always thus negative. One evening, especially, a young travelled gentleman approached her, with all the satisfaction painted on his countenance, which he felt at having secured a topic for the entertainment of the fashionable Lady Lodore.

"You are intimate with the Misses Saville," he said; "what charming girls they are! I have just left them at Naples, where they have been spending the carnival. I saw them almost every day, and capitally we enjoyed ourselves. Their Italian sister-in-law spirited them up to mask, and to make a real carnival of it. A most lovely woman that. Did you ever see Mrs. Saville, Lady Lodore?"

"Never," replied his auditress.

"Such eyes! Gazelles, and stars, and suns, and the whole range of poetic imagery, might be sought in vain, to do justice to her large dark eyes. She is very young—scarcely twenty: and to see her with her child, is positively a finer tableau than any Raphael or Correggio in the world. She has a little girl, not a year old, with golden hair, and eyes as black as the mother's—the most beautiful little thing, and so intelligent. Saville doats on it: no wonder—he is not himself handsome, you know; though the lovely Clorinda would stab me if she heard me say so. She positively adores him. You should have seen them together."

Lady Lodore turned on him one of her sweetest smiles, and in her blandest tone, said, "If you could only get me an ice from that servant, who I see immovable behind those dear, wonderful dowagers, you would so oblige me."

He was gone in a minute; and on his return, Lady Lodore was so deeply engrossed in being persuaded to go to the next drawing room, by the young and new-married Countess of G——, that she could only reward him with another heavenly smile. He was obliged to take his carnival at Naples to some other listener.

Cornelia scarcely closed her eyes that night. The thought of the happy wife and lovely child of Saville, pierced her as with remorse. She had entirely broken off her acquaintance with his family, so that she was ignorant of Clorinda's disposition, and readily fancied that she was as happy as she believed that the wife of Horatio Saville must be. She would not acknowledge that she was wicked enough to repine at her felicity; but that he should be rendered happy by any other woman than herself—that any other woman should have become the sharer of his dearest affections, stung her to the core. Yet why should she regret? She were well exchanged for one so lovely and so young. At the age of thirty-four, which she had now reached, Cornelia persuaded herself, that the name of beauty was a mockery as applied to her—though her own glass might have told her otherwise; for time had dealt lightly with her, so that the extreme fascination of her manner, and the animation and intelligence of her countenance, made her compete with many younger beauties. She felt that she was deteriorated from the angelic being she had seemed when she first appeared as Lodore's bride; and this made all compliments show false and vain. Now she figured to herself the dark eyes of the Neapolitan; and easily believed that the memory of her would contrast, like a faded picture, with the rich hues of Clorinda's face; while her sad and withered feelings were in yet greater opposition to the vivacity she had heard described and praised—to the triumphant and glad feelings of a beloved wife. It seemed to her as if she must weep for ever, and yet that tears were unavailing to diminish in any degree the sorrow that weighed so heavily at her heart. These reflections sat like a night-mare on her pillow, troubling the repose she in vain courted. She arose in the morning, scarcely conscious that she had slept at all—languid from exhaustion—her sufferings blunted by their very excess.

• • •

CHAPTER IX

"O, where have I been all this time? How 'friended
That I should lose myself thus desp'rately.
And none for pity show me how I wandered!"

—*Beaumont and Fletcher*

❧

While it was yet too early for visitors, and before she had ordered herself to be denied to every one, as she intended to do, she was surprised by a double knock at the door, and she rang hastily to prevent any one being admitted. The servants, with contradictory orders, found it difficult to evade the earnest desire of the visitor to see their lady; and at last they brought up a card, on which was written, "Miss Derham wishes to be permitted to see Lady Lodore for Mrs. Villiers." *From* had first been written, erased, and *for* substituted. Lady Lodore was alarmed; and the ideas of danger and death instantly presenting themselves, she desired Miss Derham to be shown up. She met her with a face of anxiety, and with that frankness and kindness of manner which was the irresistible sceptre she wielded to subdue all hearts. Fanny had hitherto disliked Lady Lodore. She believed her to be cold, worldly, and selfish—now, in a moment, she was convinced, by the powerful influence of manner, that she was the contrary of all this; so that instead of the chilling address she meditated, she was impelled to throw off her reserve, and to tell her story with animation and detail. She spoke of what Mrs. Villiers had gone through previous to the arrest of her husband—and how constantly she had kept her resolve of remaining with him—though her situation day by day becoming more critical, demanded attentions and luxuries which she had no means of attaining. "Yet," said Fanny, "I should not have intruded on you even now, but that they cannot go on as they are; their resources are utterly exhausted,—and until next June I see no prospect for them."

"Why does not Mr. Villiers apply to his father? even if letters were of no avail, a personal appeal—"

"I am afraid that Colonel Villiers has nothing to give," replied Fanny, "and at all events, Mr. Villiers's imprisonment—"

"Prison!" cried Lady Lodore, "you do not mean—Ethel cannot be living in prison!"

"They live within the rules, if you understand that term. They rent a lodging close to the prison on the other side of the river."

"This must indeed be altered," said Lady Lodore, "this is far too shocking—poor Ethel, she must come here! Dear Miss Derham, will you tell her how much I desire to see her, and entreat her to make my house her home."

Fanny shook head. "She will not leave her husband—I should make your proposal in vain."

Lady Lodore looked incredulous. After a moment's thought she persuaded herself that Ethel's having refused to return to the house of Mrs. Derham, or having negatived some other proposed kindness originated this notion, and she believed that she had only to make her invitation in the most gracious possible way, not to have it refused. "I will go to Ethel myself," she said; "I will myself bring her here, and so smooth all difficulties."

Fanny did not object. Under her new favourable opinion of Lady Lodore, she felt that all would be well if the mother and daughter were brought together, though only for a few minutes. She wrote down Ethel's address, and took her leave, while at the same moment Lady Lodore ordered her carriage, and assured her that no time should be lost in removing Mrs. Villiers to a more suitable abode.

Lady Lodore's feelings on this occasion were not so smiling as her looks. She was grieved for her daughter, but she was exceedingly vexed for herself. She had desired some interest, some employment in life, but she recoiled from any that should link her with Ethel. She desired occupation, and not slavery; but to bring the young wife to her own house, and make it a home for her, was at once destructive of her own independence. She looked forward with repugnance to the familiarity that must thence ensue between her and Villiers. Even the first step was full of annoyance, and she was displeased that Fanny had given her the task of going to her daughter's habitation, and forced her to appear personally on so degrading a scene; there was however no help—she had undertaken it, and it must be done.

Every advance she made towards the wretched part of the town where Ethel lived, added to her ill-humour. She felt almost personally affronted by the necessity she was under of first coming in contact with her daughter under such disastrous circumstances. Her spleen against Lord Lodore revived: she viewed every evil that had ever befallen her, as arising from his machinations. If Ethel had been entrusted to her guardianship, she certainly had never become the wife of Edward Villiers—nor ever have tasted the dregs of opprobrious poverty.

At length, her carriage drew near a row of low, shabby houses; and as the name caught her eye she found that she had reached her destination. She resolved not to see Villiers, if it could possibly be avoided; and then making up her mind to perform her part with grace, and every show of kindness, she made an effort to smooth her brow and recall her smiles. The carriage stopped at a door—a servant-maid answered to the knock. She ordered Mr. Villiers to be asked for; he was not at home. One objection to her proceeding was removed by this answer. Mrs. Villiers was in the house, and she alighted and desired to be shown to her.

•••

CHAPTER X

"As flowers beneath May's footsteps waken
As stars from night's loose hair are shaken;
As waves arise when loud winds call,
Thoughts sprung where'er that step did fall."

—*Shelley*

Never before had the elegant and fastidious Lady Lodore entered such an abode, or ascended such stairs. The servant had told her to enter the room at the head of the first flight, so she made her way by herself, and knocked at the door. The voice that told her to come in, thrilled through her, she knew not why, and she became disturbed at finding that her self-possession was failing her. Slight things act powerfully on the subtle mechanism of the human mind. She had dressed with scrupulous plainness, yet her silks and furs were strangely contrasted with the room she entered, and she felt ashamed of all the adjuncts of wealth and luxury that attended her. She opened the door with an effort: Ethel was seated near the fire at work—no place or circumstance could deteriorate from her appearance—in her simple, unadorned morning-dress, she looked as elegant and as distinguished as she had done when her mother had last seen her in diamonds and plumes in the presence of royalty. There was a charm about both, strikingly in contrast, and yet equal in fascination—the polish of Lady Lodore, and the simplicity of Ethel were both manifestations of inward grace and dignity; and as they now met, it would have been difficult to say which had the advantage of the other. Ethel's extreme youth, by adding to the interest with which she must be regarded, was in her favour. Yet full of sensibility and loveliness as was her face, she had never been, nor was she even now, as strikingly beautiful as her mother.

Lady Lodore could not restrain the tear that started into her eye on beholding her daughter situated as she was. Ethel's feelings, on the contrary, were all gladness. She had no pride to allay her gratitude for her mother's kindness. "How very good of you to come!" she said, "how could you find out where we were?"

"How long have you been here?" asked Lady Lodore, looking round the wretched little room.

"Only a few weeks—I assure you it is not so bad as it seems. I should not much mind it, but that Edward feels it so deeply on my account."

"I do not wonder," said her mother, "he must be cut to the soul—but thank God it is over now. You shall come to me immediately, my house is quite large enough to accommodate you—I am come to fetch you."

"My own dearest mother!"—the words scarcely formed themselves on Ethel's lips; she half feared to offend the lovely woman before her by showing her a daughter's affection.

"Yes, call me mother," said Lady Lodore; "I may, at last, I hope, be allowed to prove myself one. Come then, dear Ethel, you will not refuse my request—you will come with me?"

"How gladly—but—will they let Edward go? I thought there was no hope of so much good fortune."

"I fear indeed," replied her mother, "that Mr. Villiers must endure the annoyance of remaining here a little longer; but I hope his affairs will soon be arranged."

Ethel bent her large eyes inquiringly on her mother, as if not understanding; and then, as her meaning opened on her, a smile diffused itself over her countenance as she said, "Your intentions are the kindest in the world—I am grateful, how far more grateful than I can at all express, for your goodness. That you have had the kindness to come to this odious place is more than I could ever dare expect."

"It is not worth your thanks, although I think I deserve your acquiescence to my proposal. You will come home with me?"

Ethel shook her head, smilingly. "All my wishes are accomplished," she said, "through this kind visit. I would not have you for the world come here again; but the wall between us is broken down, and we shall not become strangers again."

"My dearest Ethel," said Lady Lodore, seriously, "I see what you mean. I wish Mr. Villiers were here to advocate my cause. You must come with me—he will be much more at ease when you are no longer forced to share his annoyances. This is in every way an unfit place for you, especially at this time."

"I shall appear ungrateful, I fear," replied Ethel, "if I assure you how much better off I am here than I could be any where else in the world. This place appears miserable to you—so I dare say it is; to me it seems to possess every requisite for happiness, and were it not so, I would rather live in an actual dungeon with Edward, than in the most splendid mansion in England, away from him."

Her face was lighted up with such radiance as she spoke—there was so much fervour in her voice—such deep affection in her speaking eyes—such an earnest demonstration of heartfelt sincerity, that Lady Lodore was confounded and overcome. Swift, as if a map had been unrolled before her, the picture of her own passed life was retraced in her mind—its loneless and unmeaning pursuits—and the bitter disappointments that had blasted every hope of seeing better days. She burst into tears. Ethel was shocked and tried to soothe her by caresses and assurances of gratitude and affection. "And yet you will not come with me?" said Lady Lodore, making an effort to resume her self-command.

"I cannot. It is impossible for me voluntarily to separate myself from Edward—I am too weak, too great a coward."

"And is there no hope of liberation for him?" This question of Lady Lodore forced them back to matter-of-fact topics, and she became composed. Ethel related how ineffectual every endeavour had yet been to arrange his affairs, how large his debts, how inexorable his creditors, how neglectful his attorney.

"And his father?" inquired her mother.

"He seems to me to be kind-hearted," replied Ethel, "and to feel deeply his son's situation; but he has no means—he himself is in want."

"He is keeping a carriage at this moment in Paris," said Lady Lodore, "and giving parties—however, I allow that that is no proof of his having money. Still you must not stay here."

"Nor shall we always," replied Ethel; "something of course will happen to take us away, though as yet it is all hopeless enough."

"Aunt Bessy, Mrs. Elizabeth Fitzhenry, might give you assistance. Have you asked her?—has she refused?"

"Edward has exacted a promise from me not to reveal our perplexities to her—he is punctilious about money obligations, and I have given my word not to hurt his delicacy on that point."

"Then that, perhaps, is the reason why you refused my request to go home with me?" said Lady Lodore reproachfully.

"No," replied Ethel, "I do not think that he is so scrupulous as to prevent a mother from serving her child, but he shall answer for himself; I expect him back from his walk every minute."

"Then forgive me if I run away," said Lady Lodore; "I am not fit to see him now. Better times will come, dearest Ethel, and we shall meet again. God bless you, my child, as so much virtue and patience deserve to be blest. Remember me with kindness."

"Do not you forget me," replied Ethel, "or rather, do not think of me and my fortunes with too much disgust. We shall meet again, I hope?"

Lady Lodore kissed her, and hurried away. Scarcely was she in her carriage than she saw Villiers advancing: his prepossessing appearance, ingenuous countenance, and patrician figure, made more intelligible to her world-practised eyes the fond fidelity of his wife. She drew up the window that he might not see her, as she gave her directions for "home," and then retreating to the corner of her carriage, she tried to compose her thoughts, and to reflect calmly on what was to be done.

But the effort was vain. The further she was removed from the strange scene of the morning, the more powerfully did it act on, and agitate her mind. Her soul was in tumults. This was the being she had pitied, almost despised! Her eager imagination now exalted her into an angel. There was something heart-moving in the gentle patience, and unrepining contentment with which she bore her hard lot. She appeared in her eyes to be one of those rare examples sent upon earth to purify human nature, and to demonstrate how near akin to perfection we can become. Latent maternal pride might increase her admiration, and maternal tenderness add to its warmth. Her nature had acknowledged its affinity to her child, and she felt drawn towards her with inexpressible yearnings. A vehement desire to serve her sprung up—but all was confused and tumultuous. She pressed her hand on her forehead, as if so to restrain the strong current of thought. She compressed her lips, so to repress her tears.

Arrived at home, she found herself in prison within the walls of her chamber. She abhorred its gilding and luxury—she longed for Ethel's scant abode and glorious privations. To alleviate her restlessness, she again drove out, and directed her course through the Regent's Park, and along the new road to Hampstead, where she was least liable to meet any one she knew. It was one of the first fine days of spring. The green meadows, the dark boughs swelling and bursting into bud, the fresh enlivening air, the holiday of nature's birth—all this was lost on her, or but added to her agitation. Still her thoughts were with her child in her narrow abode; every lovely object served but to recall her image, and the wafting of the soft breeze seemed an emanation from her. It was dark before she came back, and sent a hurried note of excuse to the house where she was to have dined. "No more, O never more," she cried, "will I so waste my being, but learn from Ethel to be happy, and to love."

Many thoughts and many schemes thronged her brain. Something must be done, or her heart would burst. Pride, affection, repentance, all occupied the same channel, and increased the flood that swept away every idea but one. Her very love for Horatio, true and engrossing as it had been, the source of many tears and endless regrets, appeared as slight as the web of gossamer, compared to the chain that bound her to her daughter. She could not herself understand, nor did she wish to know, whence and why this enthusiasm had risen like an exhalation in her soul, covering and occupying its entire space. She only knew it was there, interpenetrating, paramount. Ethel's dark eyes and silken curls, her sweet voice and heavenly smile, formed a moving, speaking picture, which she felt that it were bliss to contemplate for ever. She retired at last to bed, but not to rest; and as she lay with open eyes, thinking not of sleep—alive in every pore—her brain working with ten thousand thoughts, one at last grew more importunate than the rest, and demanded all her attention. Her ideas became more consecutive, though not less rapid and imperious. She drew forth in prospect, as it were, a map of what was to be done, and the results. Her mind became fixed, and sensations of ineffable pleasure accompanied her reveries. She was resolved to sacrifice every thing to her daughter—to liberate Villiers, and to establish her in ease and comfort. The image of self-sacrifice, and of the ruin of her own fortunes, was attended with a kind of rapture. She felt as if, in securing Ethel's happiness, she could never feel sorrow more. This was something worth living for: the burden of life was gone—its darkness dissipated—a soft light invested all things, and angels' voices invited her to proceed. While indulging in these reveries, she sunk into a balmy sleep—such a one she had not enjoyed for many months—nay, her whole past life had never afforded her so sweet a joy. The thoughts of love, when she believed that she should be united to Saville, were not so blissful; for self-approbation, derived from a consciousness of virtue and well-doing, hallowed every thought.

•••

CHAPTER XI

"Like gentle rains on the dry plains,
 Making that green which late was grey;
Or like the sudden moon, that stains
 Some gloomy chamber's window panes,
With a broad light like day."

—*Shelley*

How mysterious a thing is the action of repentance in the human mind! We will not dive into the debasing secrets of remorse for guilt. Lady Lodore could accuse herself of none. Yet when she looked back, a new light shone on the tedious maze in which she had been lost; a light—and she blessed it—that showed her a pathway out of tempest and confusion into serenity and peace. She wondered at her previous blindness; it was as if she had closed her eyelids, and then fancied it was night. No fear that she should return to darkness; her heart felt so light, her spirit so clear and animated, that she could only wonder how it was she had missed happiness so long, when it needed only that she should stretch out her hand to take it.

Her first act on the morrow was to have an interview with her son-in-law's solicitor. Nothing could be more hopeless than Mr. Gayland's representation of his client's affairs. The various deeds of settlement and entail, through which he inherited his estate, were clogged in such a manner as to render an absolute sale of his reversionary prospects impossible, so that the raising of money on them could only be effected at an immense future sacrifice. Under these circumstances Gayland had been unwilling to proceed, and appeared lukewarm and dilatory, while he was impelled by that love for the preservation of property, which often finds place in the mind of a legal adviser.

Lady Lodore listened attentively to his statements. She asked the extent of Edward's debts, and somewhat started at the sum named as necessary to clear him. She then told Mr. Gayland that their ensuing conversation must continue under a pledge of secrecy on his part. He assented, and she proceeded to represent her intention of disposing of her jointure for the purpose of extricating Villiers from his embarrassments. She gave directions for its sale, and instructions for obtaining the necessary papers to effect it. Mr. Gayland's countenance brightened; yet he offered a few words of remonstrance against such unexampled generosity.

"The sacrifice," said Lady Lodore, "is not so great as you imagine. A variety of circumstances tend to compensate me for it. I do not depend upon this source of income alone; and be assured, that what I do, I consider, on the whole, as benefiting me even more than Mr. Villiers."

Mr. Gayland bowed; and Cornelia returned home with a light heart. For months she had not felt such an exhilaration of spirits. A warm joy thrilled through her frame, and involuntary smiles dimpled her cheeks. Dusky and dingy as was the day, the sunshine of her soul dissipated its shadows, and spread brightness over her path. She could scarcely control the expression of her delight; and when she sat down to write to Ethel, it was several minutes before she was able to collect her thoughts, so as to remember what she had intended to say. Two notes were destroyed before she had succeeded in imparting that sobriety to her expressions, which was needful to veil her purpose, which she had resolved to lock within her own breast for ever. At length she was obliged to satisfy herself with a few vague expressions. This was her letter:—

I cannot help believing, my dearest girl, that your trials are coming to a conclusion. I have seen Mr. Gayland; and it appears to me that energy and activity are chiefly wanting for the arrangement of your husband's affairs: I think I have in some degree inspired these. He has promised to write to Mr. Villiers, who, I trust, will find satisfaction in his views. Do you, my dearest Ethel, keep up your spirits, and take care of your precious health. We shall meet again in better days, when you will be rewarded for your sufferings and goodness. Believe me, I love as much as I admire you; so, in spite of the past, think of me with indulgence and affection.

Lady Lodore dressed to dine out, and for an evening assembly. She looked so radiant and so beautiful, that admiration and compliments were showered upon her. How vain and paltry they all seemed; and yet her feelings were wholly changed from that period, when she desired to reject and scoff at the courtesy of her fellow-creatures. The bitterness of spirit was gone, which had prompted her to pour out gall and sarcasm, and had made it her greatest pleasure to revel in the contempt and hate that filled her bosom towards herself and others. She was now at peace with the world, and disposed to view its follies charitably. Yet how immeasurably superior she felt herself to all those around her! not through vanity or supercilious egotism, but from the natural spring of inward joy and self-approbation, which a consciousness of doing well opened in her before dried-up heart. She somewhat contemned her friends, and wholly pitied them. But she could not dwell on any disagreeable sentiment. Her thoughts, while she reverted to the circumstances that so changed their tenor, were stained with the fairest hues, harmonized by the most delicious music. She had risen to a sphere above, beyond the ordinary soarings of mortals—a world without a cloud, without one ungenial breath. She wondered at herself. She looked back with mingled horror and surprise on the miserable state of despondence to which she had been reduced. Where were now her regrets?—where her ennui, her repinings, her despair? "In the deep bosom of the ocean buried!"—and she arose, as from a second birth, to new hopes, new prospects, new feelings; or rather to another state of being, which had no affinity to the former. For poverty was now her pursuit, obscurity her desire, ruin her hope; and she smiled on, and beckoned to these, as if life possessed no greater blessings.

Her impetuosity and pride served to sustain the high tone of her soul. She had none of that sloth of purpose, or weakness of feeling, that leads to hesitation and regret. To resolve with her had been, during the whole course of her life, to do; and what her mind was set upon she accomplished—it might be rashly, but still with that independence and energy, that gave dignity even to her more ambiguous actions. As before, when she cast off Lodore, she had never admitted a doubt that she was justified before God and her conscience for refusing to submit to the most insulting tyranny; so now, believing that she had acted ill in not demanding the guardianship of her daughter, and resolving to atone for the evils which were the consequence of this neglect of duty on her part, she had no misgivings as to the future, but rushed precipitately onwards. As a racer at the Olympic games, she panted to arrive at the goal, though it were only to expire at the moment of its attainment.

Meanwhile, Ethel had been enchanted by her mother's visit, and spoke of it to Villiers as a proof of the real goodness of her heart, insisting that she was judged harshly and falsely. Villiers smiled incredulously. "She gains your esteem at an easy rate," he observed; "cultivate it, if it makes you happier. It will need more than a mere act of ordinary courtesy—more than a slight invitation to her house, to persuade me that Lady Lodore is not—what she is—a worshipper of the world, a frivolous, unfeeling woman. Mark me whether she comes again."

Her letter, on the following day, strengthened his opinion. "This is even insulting," he said: "she takes care to inform you that she will not look again on your poverty, but will wait for *better days* to bring you together. The kindness of such an intimation is quite admirable. She has inspired Gayland with energy and activity!—O, then, she must be a Medea, in more senses than the more obvious one."

Ethel looked reproachfully. She saw that Villiers was deeply hurt that Lady Lodore had become acquainted with their distresses, and been a witness of the nakedness of the land. She could not inspire him with the tenderness that warmed her heart towards her mother, and the conviction she entertained, in spite of appearances, (for she was forced to confess to herself that Lady Lodore's letter was not exactly the one she expected,) that her heart was generous and affectionate. It was a comfort to her that Fanny Derham participated in her opinions. Fanny was quite sure that Lady Lodore would prove herself worthy of the esteem she had so suddenly conceived for her; and Ethel listened delightedly to her assertions—it was so soothing to think well of, to love, and praise her mother.

The solicitor's letter, which came, as Lady Lodore announced, somewhat surprised Villiers; yet, after a little reflection, he gave no heed to its contents. It said, that upon further consideration of particular points, Gayland perceived certain facilities; by improving upon which, he hoped soon to make a favourable arrangement, and to extricate Mr. Villiers from his involvements. Any thing so vague demanded explanation. Edward wrote earnestly, requesting one; but his letter remained unanswered. Perplexed and annoyed, he obtained permission to quit his bounds for a few hours, and called upon the man of law. Gayland was so busy, that he could not afford him more than five minutes' conversation. He said that he had hopes—even expectations; that a little time would show more; and he begged his client to be patient. Villiers returned in despair. The only circumstance that at all served to inspire him with any hope, was, that on the day succeeding to his visit, he received a remittance of an hundred pounds from Gayland, who begged to be considered as his banker till the present negociations should be concluded.

There was some humiliation in the knowledge of how welcome this supply had become, and Ethel used her gentle influence to mitigate the pain of such reflections. If she ever drooped, it was not for herself, but for Villiers; and she carefully hid even these disinterested repinings. Her own condition did not inspire her with any fears, and the anxiety that she experienced for her unborn child was untinctured by bitterness or despair. She felt assured that their present misfortunes would be of short duration; and instead of letting her thoughts dwell on the mortifications or shame that marked the passing hour, she loved to fill her mind with pleasing sensations, inspired by the tenderness of her husband, the kindness of poor Fanny, and the reliance she had in the reality of her mother's affection. In vain, she said, did the harsher elements of life try to disturb the serenity which the love of those around her produced in her soul. Her happiness was treasured in their hearts, and did not emanate from the furniture of a room, nor the comfort of an equipage. Her babe, if destined to open its eyes first on such a scene, would be still less acted upon by its apparent cheerlessness. Cradled in her arms, and nourished at her bosom, what more benign fate could await the little stranger? What was there in their destiny worthy of grief, while they remained true to each other?

With such arguments she tried to inspire Villiers with a portion of that fortitude and patience which was a natural growth in herself. They had but slender effect upon him. Their different educations had made her greatly his superior in these virtues; besides that she, with her simpler habits and unprejudiced mind, was less shocked by the concomitants of penury, than he, bred in high notions of aristocratic exclusiveness. She had spent her youth among settlers in a new country, and did not associate the idea of disgrace with want. Nakedness and gaunt hunger had often been the invaders of her forest home, scarcely to be repelled by her father's forethought and resources. How could she deem these shameful, when they had often assailed the most worthy and industrious, who were not the less regarded or esteemed on that account. She had acquired a practical philosophy, while inhabiting the western wilderness, and beholding the vast variety of life that it presents, which stood her in good stead under her European vicissitudes. The white inhabitants of America did not form her only school. The Red Indian and his squaw were also human beings, subject to the same necessities, moved, in the first instance, by the same impulses as herself. All that bore the human form were sanctified to her by the spirit of sympathy; and she could not, as Edward did, feel herself wholly outcast and under ban, while kindness, however humble, and intelligence, however lowly, attended upon her.

Villiers could not yield to her arguments, nor partake her wisdom; yet he was glad that she possessed any source of consolation, however unimaginable by himself. He buried within his heart the haughty sense of wrong. He uttered no complaint, though his whole being rebelled against the state of inaction to which he was reduced. It maddened him to feel that he could not stir a finger to help himself, even while he fancied that he saw his young wife withering before his eyes; and looked forward to the birth of his child, under circumstances, that rendered even the necessary attendance difficult, if not impracticable. The heaviest weight of slavery fell upon him, for it was he that was imprisoned, and forbidden to go beyond certain limits; and though Ethel religiously confined herself within yet narrower bounds than those allotted to him, he only saw, in this delicacy, another source of evil. Nor were these real tangible ills those which inflicted the greatest pain. Had these misfortunes visited him in the American wilderness, or in any part of the world where the majesty of nature had surrounded them, he fancied that he should have been less alive to their sinister influence. But here shame was conjoined with the perpetual spectacle of the least reputable class of the civilized community. Their walks were haunted by men who bore the stamp of profligacy and crime; and the very shelter of their dwelling was shared by the mean and vulgar. His aristocratic pride was sorely wounded at every turn;—not for himself so much, for he was manly enough to feel "that a man's a man for all that,"—but for Ethel's sake, whom he would have fondly placed apart from all that is deformed and unseemly, guarded even from the rougher airs of heaven, and surrounded by every thing most luxurious and beautiful in the world.

There was no help. Now and then he got a letter from his father, full of unmeaning apologies and unmanly complaints. The more irretrievable his poverty became, the firmer grew his resolve not to burden with his wants any more distant relation. He would readily give up every prospect of future wealth to purchase ease and comfort for Ethel; but he could not bend to any unworthy act; and the harder he felt pressed upon and injured by fortune, the more jealously he maintained his independence of feeling; on that he would lean to the last, though it proved a sword to pierce him.

He looked forward with despair, yet he tried to conceal his worst thoughts, which would still be brooding upon absolute want and starvation. He answered Ethel's cheering tones in accents of like cheer, and met the melting tenderness of her gaze with eyes that spoke of love only. He endeavoured to persuade her that he did not wholly shut his heart from the hopes she was continually presenting to him. Hopes, the very names of which were mockery. For they must necessarily be embodied in words and ideas—and his father or uncle were mentioned—the one had proved a curse, the other a temptation. He could trace his reverses as to the habits of expence and the false views of his resources, acquired under Lord Maristow's tutelage, as to the prodigality and neglect of his parent. Even the name of Horatio Saville produced bitterness. Why was he not here? He would not intrude his wants upon him in his Italian home; but had he been in England, they had been saved from these worst blows of fate.

The only luxury of Villiers was to steal some few hours of solitude, when he could indulge in his miserable reflections without restraint. The loveliness and love of Ethel were then before his imagination to drive him to despair. To suffer alone would have been nothing; but to see this child of beauty and tenderness, this fairest nursling of nature and liberty, droop and fade in their narrow, poverty-striken home, bred thoughts akin to madness. During each live-long night he was kept awake by the anguish of such reflections. Darker thoughts sometimes intruded themselves. He fancied that if he were dead, Ethel would be happier. Her mother, his relations, each and all would come forward to gift her with opulence and ease. The idea of self-destruction thus became soothing; and he pondered with a kind of savage pleasure on the means by which he should end the coil of misery that had wound round him.

At such times the knowledge of Ethel's devoted affection checked him. Or sometimes, as he gazed on her as she lay sleeping at his side, he felt that every sorrow was less than that which separation must produce; and that to share adversity with her was greater happiness than the enjoyment of prosperity apart from her. Once, when brought back from the gloomiest desperation by such a return of softer emotions, the words of Francesca da Rimini rushed upon his mind and completed the change. He recollected how she and her lover were consoled by their eternal companionship in the midst of the infernal whirlwind. "And do I love you less, my angel?" he thought; "are you not more dear to me than woman ever was to man, and would I divide myself from you because we suffer? Perish the thought! Whether for good or ill, let our existences still continue one, and from the sanctity and sympathy of our union, a sweet will be extracted, sufficient to destroy the bitterness of this hour. We prefer remaining together, mine own sweet love, for ever together, though it were for an eternity of pain. And these woes are finite. Your pure and exalted nature will be rewarded for its sufferings, and I, for your sake, shall be saved. I could not live without you in this world; and yet with insane purpose I would rush into the unknown, away from you, leaving you to seek comfort and support from other hands than mine. I was base and cowardly to entertain the thought, but for one moment—a traitor to my own affection, and the stabber of your peace. Ah, dearest Ethel, when in a few hours your eyes will open on the light, and seek me as the object most beloved by them, were I away, unable to return their fondness, incapable of the blessing of beholding them, what hell could be contrived to punish more severely my dereliction of duty?"

With this last thought another train of feeling was introduced, and he strung himself to more manly endurance. He saw that his post was assigned him in this world, and that he ought to fulfil its duties with courage and patience. Hope came hand in hand with such ideas— and the dawn of content on his soul was a proof that the exercise of virtue brought with it its own reward. He could not always keep his

CHAPTER XII

"The world had just begun to steal
Each hope that led me lightly on,
I felt not as I used to feel,
And life grew dark and love was gone."

—Thomas Moore

While the young pair were thus struggling with the severe visitation of adversity, Lady Lodore was earnestly engaged in her endeavours to extricate them from their difficulties. The ardour of her zeal had made her take the first steps in this undertaking, with a resolution that would not look behind, and a courage not to be dismayed by the dreary prospect which the future afforded. The scheme which she had planned, and was now proceeding to execute, was unbounded in generosity and self-sacrifice. It was not in her nature to stop short at half-measures, nor to pause when once she had fixed her purpose. If she ever trembled on looking forward to the utter ruin she was about to encounter, her second emotion was to despise herself for such pusillanimity, and to be roused to renewed energy. She intended to devote as much as was necessary of the money arising from the sale of her jointure, as fixed by her marriage settlement, for the liquidation of her son-in-law's debts. The remaining six hundred a-year, bequeathed to her in Lord Lodore's will, under circumstances of cruel insult, she resolved to give up to her daughter's use, for her future subsistence. She hoped to save enough from the sum produced by the disposal of her jointure, to procure the necessaries of life for a few years, and she did not look beyond. She would quit London for ever. She must leave her house, which she had bought during her days of prosperity, and which she had felt so much pride and delight in adorning with every luxury and comfort: to crown her good work, she intended to give it up to Ethel. And then with her scant means she would take refuge in the solitude where Lodore found her, and spend the residue of her days among the uncouth and lonely mountains of Wales, in poverty and seclusion. It was from no agreeable association with her early youth, that she selected the neighbourhood of Rhaider Gowy for her future residence; nor from a desire of renewing the recollections of the period spent there, nor of revisiting the scenes, where she had stepped beyond infancy into the paths of life. Her choice simply arose from being obliged to think of economy in its strictest sense, and she remembered this place as the cheapest in the world, and the most retired. Besides, that in fixing on a part of the country which she had before inhabited, and yet where she would be utterly unknown, the idea of her future home assumed distinctness, and a greater sense of practicability was imparted to her schemes, than could have been the case, had she been unable to form any image in her mind of the exact spot whither she was about to betake herself.

The first conception of this plan had dawned on her soul, as the design of some sublime poem or magnificent work of art may present itself to the contemplation of the poet and man of genius. She dwelt on it in its entire result, with a glow of joy; she entered into its details with childish eagerness. She pictured to herself the satisfaction of Villiers and Ethel at finding themselves suddenly, as by magic, restored to freedom and the pleasures of life. She figured their gladness in exchanging their miserable lodging for the luxury of her elegant dwelling; their pleasure in forgetting the long train of previous misfortunes, or remembering them only to enhance their prosperity, when pain and fear, disgrace and shame, should be exchanged for security and comfort. She repeated to herself, "I do all this—I, the despised Cornelia! I who was deemed unworthy to have the guardianship of my own child. I, who was sentenced to desertion and misery, because I was too worldly and selfish to be worthy of Horace Saville! How little through life has my genuine character been known, or its qualities appreciated! Nor will it be better understood now. My sacrifices will continue a mystery, and even the benefits I am forced to acknowledge to flow from me, I shall diminish in their eyes, by bestowing them with apparent indifference. Will they ever deign to discover the reality under the deceitful appearances which it will be my pride to exhibit? I care not; conscience will approve me—and when I am alone and unthought of, the knowledge that Ethel is happy through my means will make poverty a blessing."

It was not pride alone that induced Lady Lodore to resolve on concealing the extent of her benefits. All that she could give was not much if compared with the fortunes of the wealthy—but it was a competence, which would enable her daughter and her husband to expect better days with patience; but if they knew how greatly she was a sufferer for their good, they would insist at least upon her sharing their income—and what was scanty in its entireness, would be wholly insufficient when divided. Villiers also might dispute or reject her kindness, and deeply injured as she believed herself to have been by him—injured by his disesteem, and the influence he had used over Saville, in a manner so baneful to her happiness, she felt irrepressible exultation at the idea of heaping obligation on him,—and knowing herself to be deserving of his deepest gratitude. All these sentiments might be deemed fantastic, or at least extravagant. Yet her conclusions were reasonable, for it was perfectly true that Villiers would rather have returned to his prison, than have purchased freedom at the vast price she was about to pay for it. No, her design was faultless in its completeness, meagre and profitless if she stopt short of its full execution. Nor would she see Ethel again in the interim—partly fearful of not preserving her secret inviolate—partly because she felt so strongly drawn towards her, that she dreaded finding herself the slave of an affection—a passion, which, under her circumstances, she could not indulge. Without counsellor, without one friendly voice to encourage, she advanced in the path she had marked out, and drew from her own heart only the courage to proceed.

It required, however, all her force of character to carry her forward. A thousand difficulties were born at every minute, and the demands made were increased to such an extent as to make it possible that they would go beyond her means of satisfying them. She had not the assistance of one friend acquainted with the real state of things to direct her—her only adviser was a man of law, who did what he was directed—not indeed with passive obedience, but whose deviations from mere acquiescence, arose from technical objections and legal difficulties, at once unintelligible and tormenting.

Besides these more palpable annoyances, other clouds arose, natural to wavering humanity, which would sometimes shadow Cornelia's soul, so that she drooped from the height she had reached, with a timid and dejected spirit. At first she looked forward to ruin, exile, and privation, as to possessions which she coveted—but the further she proceeded, the more she lost view of the light and gladness which had attended on the dawn of her new visions. Futurity became enveloped in an appalling obscurity, while the present was sad and cheerless. The ties which she had formed in the world, which she had fancied it would be so easy to cut asunder, assumed strength; and she felt that she must endure many pangs in the act of renouncing them for ever. The scenes and persons which, a little while ago, she had regarded as uninteresting and frivolous—she was now forced to acknowledge to be too inextricably interwoven with her habits and pursuits, to be all at once quitted without severe pain. When the future was spoken of by others with joyous anticipation, her heart sunk within her, to think how her hereafter was to become disjointed and cast away from all that had preceded it. The mere pleasures of society grew into delights, when thought of as about to become unattainable; and slight partialities were regarded as if founded upon strong friendship and tender affection. She was not aware till now how habit and association will endear the otherwise indifferent, and how the human heart, prone to love, will entwine its ever-sprouting tendrils around any object, not absolutely repulsive, which is brought into near contact with it. When any of her favourites addressed her in cordial tones, when she met the glance of one she esteemed, directed towards her with an expression of kindliness and sympathy, her eyes grew dim, and a thrill of anguish passed through her frame. All that she had a little while ago scorned as false and empty, she now looked upon as the pleasant reality of life, which she was to exchange for she scarcely knew what—a living grave, a friendless desart—for silence and despair.

It is a hard trial at all times to begin the world anew, even when we exchange a mediocre station for one which our imagination paints as full of enjoyment and distinction. How much more difficult it was for Lady to despoil herself of every good, and voluntarily to encounter poverty in its most unadorned guise. As time advanced, she became fully aware of what she would have to go through, and her heroism was the greater, because, though the charm had vanished, and no hope of compensation or reward was held out, she did not shrink from accomplishing her task. She could not exactly say, like old Adam in the play,

> At seventeen years many their fortunes seek,
> But at fourscore it is too late a week.

Yet at her age it was perhaps more difficult to cast off the goods of this world, than at a more advanced one. Midway in life, we are not weaned from affections and pleasures—we still hope. We even demand more of solid advantages, because the romantic ideas of youth have disappeared, and yet we are not content to give up the game. We no longer set our hearts on ephemeral joys, but require to be enabled to put our trust in the continuance of any good offered to our choice. This desire of durability in our pleasures is equally felt by the young; but ardour of feeling and ductility of imagination is then at hand to bestow a quality, so dear and so unattainable to fragile humanity, on any object we desire should be so gifted. But at a riper age we pause, and seek that our reason may be convinced, and frequently prefer a state of prosperity less extatic and elevated, because its very sobriety satisfies us that it will not slip suddenly from our grasp.

The comforts of life, the esteem of friends—these are things which we then regard with the greatest satisfaction; and other feelings, less reasonable, yet not less keenly felt, may enter into the circle of sensations, which forms the existence of a beautiful woman. It is less easy for one who has been all her life admired and waited upon, to give up the few last years of such power, than it would have been to cast away the gift in earlier life. She has learned to doubt her influence, to know its value, and to prize it. In girlhood it may be matter of mere triumph—in after years it will be looked on as an inestimable quality by which she may more easily and firmly secure the benevolence of her fellow-creatures. All this depends upon the polish of the skin and the fire of the eye, which a few years will deface and quench—and while the opprobrious epithet of old woman approaches within view, she is glad to feel secure from its being applied to her, by perceiving the signs of the influence of her surviving attractions marked in the countenances of her admirers. Lady Lodore never felt so kindly inclined towards hers, as now that she was about to withdraw from them. Their admiration, for its own sake, she might contemn, but she valued it as the testimony that those charms were still hers, which once had subdued the soul of him she loved—and this was no disagreeable assurance to one who was on the eve of becoming a grandmother.

Her sensibility, awakened by the considerations forced on her by her new circumstances, caused her to make more progress in the knowledge of life, and in the philosophy of its laws, than love or ambition had ever done before. The last had rendered her proud from success, the first had caused her to feel dependent on one only; but now that she was about to abandon all, she found herself bound to all by stronger ties than she could have imagined. She became aware that any new connexion could never be adorned by the endearing recollections attending those she had already formed. The friends of her youth, her mere acquaintances, she regarded with peculiar partiality, as being the witnesses or sharers of her past joys and successes. Each familiar face was sanctified in her eyes by association; and she walked among those whom she had so lately scorned, as if they were saintly memorials to be approached with awe, and quitted with eternal regret. Her hopes and prospects had hinged upon them, but her life became out of joint when she quitted them. Her sensitive nature melted in unwonted tenderness while occupied by such contemplations, and they turned the path, she had so lately entered as one of triumph and gladness, to gloom and despondence.

Sometimes she pondered upon means for preserving her connexion with the world. But any scheme of that kind was fraught, on the one hand, with mortification to herself, on the other, with the overthrow of her designs, through the repugnance which Ethel and her husband would feel at occasioning such unmeasured sacrifices. She often regretted that there were no convents, to which she might retire with safety and dignity. Conduct, such as she contemplated pursuing, would, under the old regime in France, have been recompensed by praise and gratitude; while its irrevocability must prevent any resistance to her wishes. In giving up fortune and station, she would have placed herself under the guardianship of a community; and have found protection and security, to compensate for poverty and slavery. The very reverse of all this must now happen. Alone, friendless, unknown, and therefore despised, she must shift for herself, and rely on her own resources for prudence to insure safety, and courage to endure the evils of her lot. To one of another sex, the name of loneliness can never convey the idea of desolation and disregard, which gives it so painful a meaning in a woman's mind. They have not been taught always to look up to others, and to do nothing for themselves; so that business becomes a matter of heroism to a woman, when conducted in the most common-place way; but when it is accompanied by mystery, she feels herself transported from her fitting place, and as if about to encounter shame and contumely. Lady Lodore had never been conversant with any mode of life, except that of being waited on and watched over. In the poverty of her early girlhood, her mother had been constantly at her side. The necessity of so conducting herself as to prevent the shadow of slander from visiting her, had continued this state of dependence during all her married life. She had never stept across a street without attendance; nor put on her gloves, but as brought to her by a servant. Her look had commanded obedience, and her will had been law with those about her. This was now to be altered. She scarcely reverted in her mind to these minutiae; and when she did, it was to smile at herself for being able to give weight to such trifles. She was not aware how, hereafter, these small things would become the shapings and embodyings which desertion and penury would adopt, to sting her most severely. The new course she was about to enter, was too unknown to make her fears distinct. There was one vast blank before her, one gigantic and mishapen image of desertion, which filled her mind to the exclusion of every other, but whose parts were not made out, though this very indistinctness was the thing that often chiefly appalled her.

She said, with the noble exile[†],—

> "I am too old to fawn upon a nurse,
> Too far in years to be a pupil now."

It is true that she had not, like him, to lament that—

> "My native English, now I must forego";

but there is another language, even more natural than the mere dialect in which we have been educated. When our lips no longer utter the sentiments of our heart—when we are forced to exchange the spontaneous effusions of the soul for cramped and guarded phrases, which give no indication of the thought within,—then, indeed, may we say, that our tongue becomes

† Richard II.

.... "an unstringed viol, or a harp,

.... put into his hands,

That knows no touch to tune the harmony."

And this was to be Lady Lodore's position. Her only companions would be villagers; or, at best, a few Welsh gentry, with whom she could have no real communication. Sympathy, the charm of life, was dead for her, and her state of banishment would be far more complete than if mountains and seas only constituted its barriers.

Lady Lodore was often disturbed by these reflections, but she did not on that account waver in her purpose. The flesh might shrink, but the spirit was firm. Sometimes, indeed, she wondered how it was that she had first conceived the design, which had become the tyrant of her life. She had long known that she had a daughter, young, lovely, and interesting, without any great desire to become intimate with her. Sometimes pride, sometimes indignation, had checked her maternal feelings. The only time before, in which she had felt any emotion similar to that which now governed her, was on the day when she had spoken to her in the House of Lords. But instead of indulging it, she had fled from it as an enemy, and despised herself as a dupe, for being for one instant its subject. When her fingers then touched her daughter's cheek, she had not trembled like Ethel; yet an awful sensation passed through her frame, which for a moment stunned her, and she hastily retreated, to recover herself. Now, on the contrary, she longed to strain her child to her heart; she thought no sacrifice too great, which was to conduce to her advantage; and that she condemned herself never to see her more, appeared the hardest part of the lot she was to undergo. Why was this change? She could not tell—memory could not inform her. She only knew that since she had seen Ethel in her adversity, the stoniness of her heart had dissolved within her, that her whole being was subdued to tenderness, and that the world was changed from what it had been in her eyes. She felt that she could not endure life, unless for the sake of benefiting her child; and that this sentiment mastered her in spite of herself, so that every struggle with it was utterly vain.

Thus if she sometimes repined at the hard fate that drove her into exile, yet she never wavered in her intentions; and in the midst of regret, a kind of exultation was born, which calmed her pain. Smiles sat upon her features, and her voice was attuned to cheerfulness. The new-sprung tenderness of her soul imparted a fascination to her manner far more irresistible than that to which tact and polish had given rise. She was more kind and affectionate, and, above all, more sincere, and therefore more winning. Every one felt, though none could divine the cause of, this change. It was remarked that she was improved: some shrewdly suspected that she was in love. And so she was—with an object more enchanting than any earthly lover. For the first time she knew and loved the Spirit of good and beauty, an affinity to which affords the greatest bliss that our nature can receive.

...

CHAPTER XIII

"It is the same, for be it joy or sorrow.
The path of its departure still is free;
Man's yesterday can ne'er be like his morrow,
Nor aught endure save mutability."

—Shelley

The month of June had commenced. In spite of lawyer's delays and the difficulties attendant on all such negociations, they were at last concluded, and nothing remained but for Lady Lodore to sign the paper which was to consign her to comparative destitution. In all changes we feel most keenly the operation of small circumstances, and are chiefly depressed by the necessity of stooping to the direction of petty arrangements, and having to deal with subordinate persons. To complete her design, Lady Lodore had to make many arrangements, trivial yet imperative, which called for her attention, when she was least fitted to give it. She had met these demands on her patience without shrinking; and all was prepared for the finishing stroke about to be put to her plans. She dismissed those servants whom she did not intend to leave in the house for Ethel's use. She contrived to hasten the intended marriage of her own maid, so to disburthen herself wholly. The mode by which she was, solitary and unknown, to reach the mountains of Wales, without creating suspicion, or leaving room for conjecture, was no easy matter. In human life, one act is born of another, so that any one that disjoins itself from the rest, instantly gives rise to curiosity and inquiry. Lady Lodore, though fertile in expedients, was almost foiled: the eligibility of having one confidant pressed itself upon her. She thought of Fanny Derham; but her extreme youth, and her intimacy with Mrs. Villiers, which would have necessitated many falsehoods, so to preserve the secret, deterred her: she determined at last to trust to herself alone. She resolved to take with her one servant only, who had not been long in her service, and to dismiss him immediately after leaving London. Difficulties presented themselves on every side; but she believed that they could be best surmounted by obviating them in succession as they arose, and that any fixed artificial plan would only tend to embarrass, while a simple mode of proceeding would continue unquestioned.

Her chief art consisted in not appearing to be making any change at all. She talked of a visit of two or three months to Emms, and mentioned her intention of lending her house, during the interval, to her daughter. She thus secured to herself a certain period during which no curiosity would be excited; and after a month or two had passed away, she would be utterly forgotten:—thus she reasoned; and whether it were a real tomb that she entered, or the living grave which she anticipated, her name and memory would equally vanish from the earth, and she be thought of no more. If Ethel ever entertained a wish to see her, Villiers would be at hand to check and divert it. Who else was there to spend a thought upon her? Alone upon earth, no friendly eye, solicitous for her welfare, would seek to penetrate the mystery in which she was about to envelope herself.

The day came, it was the second of June, when every preliminary was accomplished. She had signed away all that she possessed—she had done it with a smile—and her voice was unfaltering. The sum which she had saved for herself consisted of but a few hundred pounds, on which she was to subsist for the future. Again she enforced his pledge of secrecy on Mr. Gayland; and glad that all was over, yet heavy at heart in spite of her gladness, she returned to her home, which in a few hours she was to quit for ever.

During all this time, her thoughts had seldom reverted to Saville. Hope was dead, and the regrets of love had vanished with it. That he would approve her conduct, was an idea that now and then flashed across her mind; but he would remain in eternal ignorance, and therefore it could not bring their thoughts into any communion. Whether he came to England, or remained at Naples, availed her nothing. No circumstance could add to, or diminish, the insuperable barrier which his marriage placed between them.

She returned home from her last interview with Mr. Gayland: it was four o'clock in the day; at six she had appointed Fanny Derham to call on her; and an hour afterwards, the horses were ordered to be at the door, which were to convey her away.

She became strangely agitated. She took herself to task for her weakness; but every moment disturbed yet more the calm she was so anxious to attain. She walked through the rooms of the house she had dwelt in for so many years. She looked on the scene presented from her windows. The drive in Hyde Park was beginning to fill with carriages and equestrians, to be thronged with her friends whom she was never again to see. Deep sadness crept over her mind. Her uncontrollable thoughts, by some association of ideas, which she could not disentangle—brought before her the image of Lodore, with more vividness than it had possessed for years. A kind of wish to cross the Atlantic, and to visit the scenes where he had dwelt so long, arose within her; and then again she felt a desire to visit Longfield, and to view the spot in which his mortal remains were laid. As her imagination pictured the grave of the husband of her youth, whom she had abandoned and forgotten, tears streamed from her eyes—the first she had shed, even in idea, beside it. "It is not to atone—for surely I was not guilty towards him"—such were Lady Lodore's reflections,—"yet, methinks, in this crisis of my fate, when about to imitate his abrupt and miserable act of self-banishment, my heart yearns for some communication with him; and it seems to me as if, approaching his cold, silent dust, he would hear me if I said, 'Be at peace! your child is happy through my means!'"

Again her reveries were attended by a gush of tears. "How strange a fate is mine, ever to be abandoned by, or to abandon, those towards whom I am naturally drawn into near contact. Fifteen years are flown since I parted from Lodore for ever! Then by inspiring one so high-minded, so richly gifted, as Saville, with love for me, fortune appeared ready to compensate for my previous sufferings; but the curse again operated, and I shall never see him more. Yet do I not forget thee, Saville, nor thy love!—nor can it be a crime to think of the past, which is as irretrievable as if the grave had closed over it. Through Saville it has been that I have not lived quite in vain—that I have known what love is; and might have even tasted of happiness, but for the poison which perpetually mingles with my cup. I never wish to see him more; but if I earnestly desire to visit Lodore's grave, how gladly would I make a far longer pilgrimage to see Saville's child, and to devote myself to one who owes its existence to him. Wretched Cornelia! what thoughts are these? Is it now, that you are a beggar and an outcast, that you first encourage unattainable desires?"

Still as she looked round, and remembered how often Saville had been beside her in that room, thoughts and regrets thronged faster and more thickly on her. She recollected the haughty self-will and capricious coquetry which had caused the destruction of her dearest hopes. She took down a miniature of herself, which her lover had so fruitlessly besought her to give him. It was on the belief that she had bestowed this picture on a rival that he had so suddenly come to the determination of quitting England. It seemed now in its smiles and youth to reproach her for having wasted both; and the sight of it agitated her bosom, and produced a tumult of regret and despair at his loss—till she threw it from her, as too dearly associated with one she must forget. And yet wherefore forget?—he had forgotten; but as a dead wife might in her grave, love her husband, though wedded to another, so might the lost, buried Cornelia remember him, though the husband of Clorinda. Self-compassion now moved her to tears, and she wept plentiful showers, which rather exhausted than relieved her.

With a strong effort she recalled her sense of what was actually going on, and struggling resolutely to calm herself, she sat down and began a letter to her daughter, which was necessary, as some sort of explanation, at once to allay wonder and baffle curiosity. Thus she wrote:

DEAREST ETHEL,

My hopes have not been deceived. Mr. Gayland has at last contrived means for the liberation of your husband; and to-morrow morning you will leave that shocking place. Perhaps I receive more pleasure from this piece of good fortune than you, for your sense of duty and sweet disposition so gild the vilest objects, that you live in a world of your own, as beautiful as yourself, and the accident of situation is immaterial to you.

It is not enough, however, that you should be free. I hope that the punctilious delicacy of Mr. Villiers will not cause you to reject the benefits of a mother. In this instance there is more of justice than generosity in my offer; and it may therefore be accepted without the smallest hesitation. My jointure ought to satisfy me, and the additional six hundred a year—which I may call the price of blood, since I bought it at the sacrifice of the dearest ties and duties,—is most freely at your service. It will delight me to get rid of it, as much as if thus I threw off the consciousness of a crime. It is yours by every law of equity, and will be hereafter paid into your banker's hands. Do not thank me, my dear child—be happy, that will be my best reward. Be happy, be prudent—this sum will not make you rich; and the only acknowledgment I ask of you is, that you make it suffice, and avoid debt and embarrassment.

By singular coincidence I am imperatively obliged to leave England at this moment. The horses are ordered to be here in half an hour—I am obliged therefore to forego the pleasure of seeing you until my return. Will you forgive me this apparent neglect, which is the result of necessity, and favour me by coming to my house to-morrow, on leaving your present abode, and making it your home until my return? Miss Derham has promised to call here this afternoon; I shall see her before I go, and through her you will learn how much you will make me your debtor by accepting my offers, and permitting me to be of some slight use to you.

Excuse the brevity and insufficiency of this letter, written at the moment of departure.—You will hear from me again, when I am able to send you my address, and I shall hope to have a letter from you. Meanwhile Heaven bless you, my angelic Ethel! Love your mother, and never, in spite of every thing, permit unkind thoughts of her to harbour in your mind. Make Mr. Villiers think as well of me as he can, and believe me that your welfare will always be the dearest wish of my heart. Adieu.

Ever affectionately yours,

C. LODORE

She folded and sealed this letter, and at the same moment there was a knock at the door of her house, which she knew announced the arrival of Fanny Derham. She was still much agitated, and trying to calm herself, she took up a newspaper, and cast her eyes down the columns; so, by one of the most common place of the actions of our life, to surmount the painful intensity of her thoughts. She read mechanically one or two paragraphs—she saw the announcements of births, marriages, and deaths. "My moral death will not be recorded here," she thought, "and yet, I shall be more dead than any of these." The thought in her mind remained as it were truncated; her eye was arrested—a paleness came over her—the pulses of her heart paused, and then beat tumultuously—how strange—how fatal were the words she read!—

"Died suddenly at the inn at the Mola di Gaeta, on her way from Naples, Clorinda, the wife of the honourable Horatio Saville, in the twenty-second year of her age."

Her drawing-room door was opened, the butler announced Miss Derham, while her eyes still were fixed on the paragraph: her head swam round—the world seemed to slide from under her. Fanny's calm clear voice recalled her. She conquered her agitation—she spoke as if she had not just crossed a gulf—not been transported to a new world; and, again, swifter than light, brought back to the old one. She conversed with Fanny for some time; giving some kind of explanation for not having been to see Ethel, begging her young friend to press her invitation, and speaking as if in autumn they should all meet again. Fanny, philosophic as she was, regarded Lady Lodore with a kind of idolatry. The same charm that had fascinated the unworldly and abstracted Saville, she exercised over the thoughtful and ingenuous mind of the fair young student. It was the attraction of engaging manners, added now to the sense of right, joined to the timid softness of a woman, who trembled on acting unsupported, even though her conscience approved her deeds. It was her loveliness which had gained in expression what it had lost in youth, and kindness of heart was the soul of the enchantment. Fanny ventured to remonstrate against her sudden departure. "O we shall soon meet again," said Cornelia; but her thoughts were more of heaven than earth, as the scene of meeting; for her heart was chilled—her head throbbed—the words she had read operated a revolution in her frame, more allied to sickness and death, than hope or triumph.

Fanny at length took her leave, and Lady Lodore was again alone. She took up the newspaper—hastily she read again the tidings; she sunk on the sofa, burying her face in the pillow, trying not to think, while she was indeed the prey to the wildest thoughts.

"Yes," thus ran her reflections, "he is free—he is no longer *married*! Fool, fool! he is still lost to you!—an outcast and a beggar, shall I solicit his love! which he believes that I rejected when prosperous. Rather never, never, let me see him again. My beauty is tarnished, my youth flown; he would only see me to wonder how he had ever loved me. Better hide beneath the mountains among which I am soon to find a home—better, far better, die, than see Saville and read no love in his eyes.

"Yet thus again I cast happiness from me. What then would I do? Unweave the web—implore Mr. Villiers to endure my presence—reveal my state of beggary—ask thanks for my generosity, and humbly wait for a kind glance from Saville, to raise me to wealth as well as to happiness.—Cornelia, awake!—be not subdued at the last—act not against your disposition, the pride of your soul—the determinations you have formed—do not learn to be humble in adversity—you, who were disdainful in happier days—no! if they need me—if they love me—if Saville still remembers the worship—the heart's entire sacrifice which once he made to me—will a few miles—the obscurity of my abode—or the silence and mystery that surrounds me, check his endeavours that we should once again meet?

"No!" she said, rising, "my destiny is in other and higher hands than my own. It were vain to endeavour to control it. Whatever I do, works against me; now let the thread be spun to the end, while I do nothing; I can but endure the worst patiently; and how much better to bear in silence, than to struggle vainly with the irrevocable decree! I submit. Let Providence work out its own ends, and God dispose of the being he has made—whether I reap the harvest in this world or in the next, my part is played, I will strive no more!"

She believed in her own singleness of purpose as she said this, and yet she was never more deceived. While she boasted of her resignation, she was yielding not to a high moral power, but to the pride of her soul. Her resolutions were in accordance with the haughtiness of her disposition, and she felt satisfied, not because she was making a noble sacrifice, but because she thus adorned more magnificently the idol she set up for worship, and believed herself to be more worthy of applause and love. Yet who could condemn even errors that led to such unbending and heroic forgetfulness of all the baser propensities of our nature. Nor was this feeling of triumph long-lived; the wounding and humiliating realities of life, soon degraded her from her pedestal, and made her feel, as it were, the disgrace and indignities of abdication.

Her travelling chariot drove up to the door, and, after a few moments' preparation, she was summoned. Again she looked round the room; her heart swelled high with impatience and repining, but again she conquered herself. She took up her miniature—*that* now she might possess—for she could remember without sin—she took up the news-paper, which did or did not contain the fiat of her fate; but this action appeared to militate against the state of resignation she had resolved to attain, so she threw it down: she walked down the stairs, and passed out from her house for the last time—she got into the carriage—the door was closed—the horses were in motion—all was over.

Her head felt sick and heavy; she leaned back in her carriage half stupified. When at last London and its suburbs were passed, the sight of the open country a little revived her—but she soon drooped again. Nothing presented itself to her thoughts with any clearness, and the exultation which had supported her vanished totally. She only knew that she was alone, poor, forgotten; these words hovered on her lips, mingled with others, by which she endeavoured to charm away her despondency. Fortitude and resignation for herself—freedom and happiness for Ethel. "O yes, she is free and happy—it matters not then what I am!" No tears flowed to soften this thought. The bright green country—the meadows mingled with unripe corn-fields—the tufted woods—the hedgerows full of flowers, could not attract her eye; pangs every now and then seized upon her heart—she had talked of resigna-tion, but she was delivered up to despair.

At length she sank into a kind of stupor. She was accompanied by one servant only; she had told him where she intended to remain that night. It was past eleven before they arrived at Reading; the night was chill, and she shivered while she felt as if it were impossible to move, even to draw up the glasses of her chariot. When she arrived at the inn where she was to pass the night, she felt keenly the discomfort of having no female attendant. It was new—she felt as if it were disgrace-ful, to find herself alone among strangers, to be obliged to give orders herself, and to prepare alone for her repose.

All night she could not sleep, and she became aware at last that she was ill. She burnt with fever—her whole frame was tormented by aches, by alternate hot and shivering fits, and by a feeling of sickness. When morning dawned, it was worse. She grew impatient—she rose. She had arranged that her servant should quit her at this place. He had been but a short time with her, and was easily dismissed under the idea, that she was to be joined by a man recommended by a friend, who was accustomed to the continent, whither it was supposed that she was going. She had dismissed him the night before, he was already gone, when on the morrow she ordered the horses.—She paid the bills herself—and had to answer questions about luggage; all these things are customary to the poor, and to the other sex. But take a high-born woman and place her in immediate contact with the rough material of the world, and see how like a sensitive plant she will shrink, close herself up and droop, and feel as if she had fallen from her native sphere into a spot unknown, ungenial, and full of storms.

The illness that oppressed Lady Lodore, made these natural feelings even more acute, till at last they were blunted by the same cause. She now wondered what it was that ailed her, and became terrified at the occasional wanderings that interrupted her torpor. Once or twice she wished to speak to the post-boy, but her voice failed her. At length they drove up to the inn at Newbury; fresh horses were called for, and the landlady came up to the door of the carriage, to ask whether the lady had breakfasted—whether she would take anything. There was something ghastly in Lady Lodore's appearance, which at once frightened the good woman, and excited her compassion. She renewed her questions, which Lady Lodore had not at first heard, adding, "You seem ill, ma'am; do take something—had you not better alight?"

"O yes, far better," said Cornelia, "for I think I must be very ill."

The change of posture and cessation of motion a little revived her, and she began to think that she was mistaken, and that it was all nothing, and that she was well. She was conducted into the parlour of the inn, and the landlady left her to order refreshment. "How foolish I am," she thought; "this is mere fancy; there is nothing the matter with me"; and she rose to ring the bell, and to order horses. When suddenly, without any previous warning, struck as by a bolt, she fainted, and fell on the floor, without any power of saving herself. The sound of her fall quickened the steps of the landlady, who was returning; all the chamber-maids were summoned, a doctor sent for, and when Lady Lodore opened her eyes she saw unknown faces about her, a strange place, and voices yet stranger. She did not speak, but tried to collect her thoughts, and to unravel the mystery, as it appeared, of her situation. But soon her thoughts wandered, and fever and weakness made her yield to the solicitations of those around. The doctor came, and could make out nothing but that she was in a high fever: he ordered her to be put to bed. And thus—Saville, and Ethel, and all hopes and fears, having vanished from her thoughts,—given up to delirium and suffering, poor Lady Lodore, alone, unknown, and unattended, remained for several weeks at a country inn—under the hands of a village doctor—to recover, if God pleased, if not, to sink, unmourned and unheard of, into an untimely grave.

•••

CHAPTER XIV

"But if for me thou dost forsake
Some other maid, and rudely break
Her worshipped image from its base,
To give to me the ruined place—

Then fare thee well—I'd rather make
My bower upon some icy lake,
When thawing suns begin to shine,
Than trust to love so false as thine!"

—*Moore*, Lalla Rookh

On the same day Mr. and Mrs. Villiers left their sad dwelling to take possession of Lady Lodore's house. The generosity and kindness of her mother, such as it appeared, though she knew but the smallest portion of it, charmed Ethel. Her heart, which had so long struggled to love her, was gladdened by the proofs given that she deserved her warmest affection. The truest delight beamed from her lovely countenance. Even she had felt the gloom and depression of adversity. The sight of misery or vice in those around her tarnished the holy fervour with which she would otherwise have made every sacrifice for Edward's sake. There is something in this world, which even while it gives an unknown grace to rough, and hard, and mean circumstances, contaminates the beauty and harmony of the noble and exalted. Ethel had been aware of this; she dreaded its sinister influence over Villiers, and in spite of herself she pined; she had felt with a shudder that in spite of love and fortitude, a sense, chilling and deponding, was creeping over her, making her feel the earth alien to her, and calling her away from the sadness of the scene around to a world bright and pure as herself. Her very despair thus dressed itself in the garb of religion; and though these visitations of melancholy only came during the absence of Villiers and were never indulged in, yet they were too natural a growth of their wretched abode to be easily or entirely dismissed. Even now that she was restored to the fairer scenes of life, compassion for the unfortunate beings she quitted haunted her, and her feelings were too keenly alive to the miseries which her fellow-creatures suffered, to permit her to be relieved from all pain by her own exemption. She turned from such reflections to the image of her dear kind mother with delight. The roof that sheltered her was hallowed as hers; all the blessings of life which she enjoyed came to her from the same source as life itself. She delighted to trace the current of feeling which had occasioned her to give up so much, and to imagine the sweetness of disposition, the vivacity of mind, the talents and accomplishments which her physiognomy expressed, and the taste manifested in her house, and all the things which she had collected around her, evinced.

In less than a month after their liberation, she gave birth to son. The mingled danger and rejoicing attendant on this event, imparted fresh strength to the attachment that united Edward to her; and the little stranger himself was a new object of tenderness and interest. Thus their days of mourning were exchanged for a happiness most natural and welcome to the human heart. At this time also Horatio Saville returned from Italy with his little girl. She was scarcely more than a year old, but displayed an intelligence to be equalled only by her extraordinary beauty. Her golden silken ringlets were even then profuse, her eyes were as dark and brilliant as her mother's, but her complexion was fair, and the same sweet smile flitted round her infant mouth, as gave the charm to her father's face. He idolized her, and tried by his tenderness and attention to appease, as it were, the manes of the unfortunate Clorinda.

She, poor girl, had been the victim of the violence of passion and ill-regulated feelings native to her country, excited into unnatural force by the singularity of her fate. When Saville saw her first in her convent, she was pining for liberty; she did not think of any joy beyond escaping the troublesome impertinence of the nuns and the monotonous tenor of monastic life, of associating with people she loved, and enjoying the common usages of life, unfettered by the restrictions that rendered her present existence a burthen. But though she desired no more, her disgust for the present, her longing for a change, was a powerful passion. She was adorned by talents, by genius; she was eloquent and beautiful, and full of enthusiasm and feeling. Saville pitied her; he lamented her future fate among her unworthy countrymen; he longed to cherish, to comfort, and to benefit her. His heart, so easily won to tenderness, gave her readily a brother's regard. Others, seeing the active benevolence and lively interest that this sentiment elicited, might have fancied him inspired by a warmer feeling; but he well knew the difference, he ardently desired her happiness, but did not seek his own in her.

He visited her frequently, he brought her books, he taught her English. They were allowed to meet daily in the parlour of the convent, in the presence of a female attendant; and his admiration of her talents, her imagination, her ardent comprehensive mind, increased on every interview. They talked of literature—the poets—the arts; Clorinda sang to him, and her fine voice, cultivated by the nicest art, was a source of deep pleasure and pain to her auditor. His sensibility was awakened by the tones of love and rapture—sensibility, not alas! for her who sang, but for the false and absent. While listening, his fancy recalled Lady Lodore's image; the hopes she had inspired, the rapture he had felt in her presence—the warm vivifying effect her voice and looks had on him were remembered, and his heart sank within him to think that all this sweetness was deceptive, fleeting, lost. Once, overcome by these thoughts, he resolved to return suddenly to England, to make one effort more to exchange unendurable wretchedness for the most transport-ing happiness;—absence from Cornelia, to the joy of pouring out the overflowing sentiments of his heart at her feet. While indulging in this idea, a letter from his sister Lucy caused a painful revulsion; she painted the woman of the world given up to ambition and fashion, rejoicing in his departure, and waiting only the moment when she might with decency become the wife of another. Saville was almost maddened—he did not visit Clorinda for three days. She received him, when at last he came, without reproach, but with transport; she saw that sadness, even sickness, dimmed his eye; she soothed him, she hung over him with fondness, she sung to him her sweetest, softest airs; his heart melted, a tear stole from his eye. Clorinda saw his emotion; it excited hers; her Neapolitan vivacity was not restrained by shame nor fear,—she spoke of her love for him with the vehemence she felt, and youth and beauty hal-lowed the frankness and energy of her expressions. Saville was touched and pleased,—he left her to meditate on this new state of things—for free from passion himself, he had never suspected the growth of it in her heart. He reflected on all her admirable qualities, and the pity it was that they should be cast at the feet of one of her own unrefined, uneducated countrymen, who would be incapable of appreciating her talents—even her love—so that at last she would herself become degraded, and sink into that system of depravity which makes a prey of all that is lovely or noble in our nature. He could save her—she loved him, and he could save her; lost as he was to real happiness, it were to approximate to it, if he consecrated his life to her welfare.

Yet he would not deceive her. The excess of love which she bestowed demanded a return which he could not give. She must choose whether, such as he was, he were worth accepting. Actuated by a sense of justice, he opened his heart to her without disguise: he told her of his ill-fated attachment to another—of his self-banishment, and misery—he declared his real and earnest affection for her—his desire to rescue her from her present fate, and to devote his life to her. Clorinda scarcely heard what he said,—she felt only that she might become his—that he would marry her; her rapture was undisguised, and he enjoyed the felicity of believing that one so lovely and excellent would at once owe every blessing of life to him, and that the knowledge of this must ensure his own content. The consent of her parents was easily yielded,—the Pope is always ready to grant a dispensation to a Catholic wife marrying a Protestant husband,—the wedding speedily took place—and Saville became her husband.

Their mutual torments now began. Horatio was a man of high and unshrinking principle. He never permitted himself to think of Lady Lodore, and the warmth and tenderness of his heart led him to attach himself truly and affectionately to his wife. But this did not suffice for the Neapolitan. Her marriage withdrew the veil of life—she imagined that she distinguished the real from the fictitious, but her new sense of discernment was the source of torture. She desired to be loved as she loved; she insisted that her rival should be hated—she was shaken by continual tempests of jealousy, and the violence of her temper, restrained by no reserve of disposition, displayed itself frightfully. Saville reasoned, reproached, reprehended, without any avail, except that when her violence had passed its crisis, she repented, and wept, and besought forgiveness. Ethel's visit had been a blow hard to bear. She was the daughter of her whom Saville loved—whom he regretted—on whom he expended that passion and idolatry, to attain which she would have endured the most dreadful tortures. These were the reflections, or rather, these were the ravings, of Clorinda. She had never been so furious in her jealousy, or so frequent in her fits of passion, as during the visit of the unconscious and gentle Ethel.

The birth of her child operated a beneficial change for a time; and except when Saville spoke of England, or she imagined that he was thinking of it, she ceased to torment him. He was glad; but the moment was passed when she could command his esteem, or excite his spontaneous sympathy. He pitied and he loved her; but it was almost as we may become attached to an unfortunate and lovely maniac; less than ever did he seek his happiness in her. He loved his infant daughter now better than any other earthly thing. Clorinda rejoiced in this tie, though she soon grew jealous even of her own child.

The arrival of Lord Maristow and his daughters was at first full of benefit to the discordant pair. Clorinda was really desirous of obtaining their esteem, and she exerted herself to please: when they talked of her return to England with them, it only excited her to try to render Italy so agreeable as to induce them to remain there. They were not like Ethel. They were good girls, but fashionable and fond of pleasure. Clorinda devised a thousand amusements—concerts, tableaux, the masquerades of the carnival, were all put in requisition. They carried their zeal for amusement so far as to take up their abode for a day or two at Pompeii, feigning to be its ancient inhabitants, and, bringing the *corps operatique* to their aid, got up Rossini's opera of the Ultimi Giorni di Pompeii among the ruins, ending their masquerade by a mimic eruption. These gaieties did not accord with the classic and refined tastes of Saville; but he was glad to find his wife and sisters agree so well, and under the blue sky, and in the laughing land of Naples, it was impossible not to find beauty and enjoyment even in extravagance and folly.

Still, like a funeral bell heard amidst a feast, the name of England, and the necessity of her going thither, struck on the ear and chilled the heart of the Neapolitan. She resolved never to go; but how could she refuse to accompany her husband's sisters? how resist the admonitions and commands of his father? She did not refuse therefore—she seemed to consent—while she said to Saville, "Poison, stab me—cast me down the crater of the mountain—exhaust your malice and hatred on me as you please here—but you shall never take me to England but as a corpse."

Saville replied, "As you will." He was tired of the struggle, and left the management of his departure to others.

One day his sisters described the delights of a London season, and strove to win Clorinda by the mention of its balls, parties, and opera; they spoke of Almack's, and the leaders of fashion; they mentioned

Lady Lodore. They were unaware that Clorinda knew any thing of their brother's attachment, and speaking of her as one of the most distinguished of their associates in the London world, made their sister-in-law aware, that when she made a part of it, she would come into perpetual contact with her rival. This allusion caused one of her most violent paroxysms of rage as soon as she found herself alone with her husband. So frantic did she seem, that Horatio spoke seriously to his father, and declared he knew of no argument nor power which could induce Clorinda to accompany them to England. "Then you must go without her," said Lord Maristow; "your career, your family, your country, must not be sacrificed to her unreasonable folly." And then, wholly unaware of the character of the person with whom he had to deal, he repeated the same thing to Clorinda. "You must choose," he said, "between Naples and your husband—he must go; do you prefer being left behind?"

Clorinda grew pale, even livid. She returned home. Horatio was not there; she raved through her house like a maniac; her servants even hid her child from her, and she rushed from room to room tearing her hair, and calling for Saville. At length he entered; her eyes were starting from her head, her frame working with convulsive violence; she strove to speak—to give utterance to the vehemence pent up within her. She darted towards him; when suddenly, as if shot to the heart, she fell on the marble pavement of her chamber, and a red stream poured from her lips—she had burst a blood-vessel.

For many days she was not allowed to speak nor move. Saville nursed her unremittingly—he watched by her at night—he tried to soothe her—he brought her child to her side—his sweetness, and gentleness, and real tenderness were all expended on her. Although violent, she was not ungenerous. She was touched by his attentions, and the undisguised solicitude of his manner. She resolved to conquer herself, and in a fit of heroism formed the determination to yield, and to go to England. Her first words, when permitted to speak, were to signify her assent. Saville kissed and thanked her. She had half imagined that he would imitate her generosity, and give up the journey. No such thought crossed his mind; her distaste was too unreasonable to elicit the smallest sympathy, and consequently any concession. He thanked her warmly, it is true; and looked delighted at this change, but without giving her time to retract, he hurried to communicate to his relations the agreeable tidings.

As she grew better she did not recede, but she felt miserable. The good spirits and ready preparations of Horatio were all acts of treason against her: sometimes she felt angry—but she checked herself. Like all Italians, Clorinda feared death excessively; besides that, to die was to yield the entire victory to her rival. She struggled therefore, and conquered herself; and neither expressed her angry jealousy nor her terrors. She had many causes of fear; she was again in a situation to increase her family within a few months; and while her safety depended on her being able to attain a state of calm, she feared a confinement in England, and believed that it was impossible that she should survive.

She was worn to a skeleton—her large eyes were sunk and ringed with black, while they burnt with unnatural brilliancy, for her vivacity did not desert her, and that deceived those around; they fancied that she was convalescent, and would soon recover strength and good looks, while she nourished a deep sense of wrong for the slight attention paid to her sufferings. She wept over herself and her friendless state. Her husband was not her friend, for he was not her countryman: and full as Saville was of generous sympathy and kindliness for all, the idea of returning to England, to his home and friends, to the stirring scenes of life, and the society of those who loved literature, and were endowed with the spirit of liberal inquiry and manly habits of thinking, so absorbed and delighted him, that he could only thank Clorinda again and again—caress her, and entreat her to get well, that she might share his pleasures. His words chilled her, and she shrunk from his caresses. "He is thinking of *her,* and of seeing *her* again," she thought. She did him the most flagrant injustice. Saville was a man of high and firm principle, and had he been aware of any latent weakness, of any emotion allied to the master-passion of his soul, he would have conquered it, or have fled from the temptation. He never thought less of Lady Lodore than now. The unwonted gentleness and concessions of his wife—his love for his child, and the presence of his father and dear sisters, dissipated his regrets,—his conscience was wholly at ease, and he was happy.

Clorinda dared not complain to her English relatives, but she listened to the lamentations of her Neapolitan friends with a luxury of woe. They mourned over her as if she were going to visit another sphere; they pointed out the little island on a map, and seated far off as it was amidst the northern sea, night and storms, they averred, perpetually brooded over it, while from the shape of the earth they absolutely proved that it was impossible to get there. It is true that Lord Maristow and his daughters, and Saville himself, had come thence—that was nothing—it was easy to come away. "You see," they said, "the earth slopes down, and the sun is before them; but when they have to go back, ah! it is quite another affair; the Alps rise, and the sea boils over, and they have to toil up the wall of the world itself into winter and darkness. It is tempting God to go there. O stay, Clorinda, stay in sunny Italy. Orazio will return: do not go to die in that miserable birthplace of night and frost."

Clorinda wept yet more bitterly over her hard fate, and the impossibility of yielding to their wishes. "Would to God," she thought, "I could abandon the ingrate, and let him go far from Italy and Clorinda, to die in his wretched country! Would I could forget, hate, desert him! Ah, why do I idolize one born in that chilly land, where love and passion are unknown or despised!"

At length the day arrived when they left Naples. It was the month of May, and very warm. No imagination could paint the glorious beauty of this country of enchantment, on the completion of spring, before the heats of summer had withered its freshness. The sparkling waves of the blue Mediterranean encircled the land, and contrasted with its hues: the rich foliage of the trees—the festooning of the luxuriant vines, and the abundant vegetation which sprung fresh from the soil, decorating the rocks, and mantling the earth with flowers and verdure, were all in the very prime and blossoming of beauty. The sisters of Saville expressed their admiration in warm and enthusiastic terms; the words trembled on poor Clorinda's lips; she was about to say, "Why then desert this land of bliss?" but Horatio spoke instead: "It is splendid, I own, and once I felt all that you express. Now a path along a grassy field—a hedge-row—a copse with a rill murmuring through it—a white cottage with simple palings enclosing a flower-garden—the spire of a country church rising from among a tuft of elms—the skies all shadowy with soft clouds—and the homesteads of a happy thriving peasantry—these are the things I sigh for. A true English home-scene seems to me a thousand times more beautiful, as it must be a thousand times dearer than the garish showy splendour of Naples."

Clorinda's thoughts crept back into her chilled heart; large teardrops rose in her eyes, but she concealed them, and shrinking into a corner of the carriage, she felt more lonely and deserted than she would have done among strangers who had loved Italy, and participated in her feelings.

They arrived at the inn called the Villa di Cicerone, at the Mola di Gaeta. All the beauty of the most beautiful part of the Peninsula seems concentered in that enchanting spot—the perfume of orange flowers filled the air—the sea was at their feet—the vine-clad hills around. All this excess of loveliness only added to the unutterable misery of the Neapolitan girl. Her companions talked and laughed, while she felt her frame convulsed by internal combats, and the unwonted command she exercised over her habitual vehemence. Horatio conversed gaily with his sisters, till catching a glimpse of the pale face of his wretched wife, her mournful eyes and wasted cheeks, he drew near her. "You are fatigued, dearest Clorinda," he said, "will you not go to rest?"

He said this in a tender caressing tone, but she felt, "He wants to send me away—to get rid even of the sight of me." But he sat down by her, and perceiving her dejection, and guessing partly at its cause, he soothed her, and talked of their return to her native land, and cheered her by expressions of gratitude for the sacrifice she was making. Her heart began to soften, and her tears to flow more freely, when a man entered, such as haunt the inns in Italy, and watch for the arrival of rich strangers to make profit in various ways out of them. This man had a small picture for sale, which he declared to be an original Carlo Dolce. It was the head of a seraph painted on copper—it was probably a copy, but it was beautifully executed; besides the depth of colour and grace of design, there was something singularly beautiful in the expression of the countenance portrayed,—it symbolized happiness and love; a beaming softness animated the whole face; a perfect joy, an ineffable radiance shone out of it. Clorinda took it in her hand—the representation of heart-felt gladness increased her self-pity; she was turning towards her husband with a reproachful look, thinking, "Such smiles you have banished from my face for ever,"—when Sophia Saville, who was looking over her shoulder, exclaimed, "What an extraordinary resemblance! there was never any thing so like."

"Who? what?" asked her sister.

"It is Lady Lodore herself," replied Sophia; "her eyes, her mouth, her very smile."

Lucy gave a quick glance towards her brother. Horatio involuntarily stepped forward to look, and then as hastily drew back. Clorinda saw it all—she put down the picture, and left the room—she could not stay—she could not speak—she knew not what she felt, but that a fiery torture was eating into her, and she must fly, she knew not whither. Saville was pained; he hesitated what to do or say—so he remained; supper was brought in, and Clorinda not appearing, it was supposed that she had retired to rest. In about an hour and a half after, Horatio went into her room, and to his horror beheld her stretched upon the cold bricks of the chamber, senseless; the moon-beams rested on her pale face, which bore the hues of death. In a moment the house was alarmed, the village doctor summoned, a courier dispatched to Naples for an English physician, and every possible aid afforded the wretched sufferer. She was placed on the bed,—she still lived; her faint pulse could not be felt, and no blood flowed when a vein was opened, but she groaned, and now and then opened her eyes with a ghastly stare, and closed them again as if mechanically. All was horror and despair—no help—no resource presented itself; they hung round her, they listened to her groans with terror, and yet they were the only signs of life that disturbed her death-like state. At last, soon after the dawn of day, she became convulsed, her pulse fluttered, and blood flowed from her wounded arm; in about an hour from this time she gave birth to a dead child. After this she grew calmer and fainter. The physician arrived, but she was past mortal cure,—she never opened her eyes more, nor spoke, nor gave any token of consciousness. By degrees her groans ceased, and she faded into death: the slender manifestations of lingering vitality gradually decreasing till all was still and cold. After an hour or two her face resumed its loveliness, pale and wasted as it was: she seemed to sleep, and none could regret that repose possessed that heart, which had been alive only to the deadliest throes of unhappy passion. Yet Saville did more than regret—he mourned her sincerely and deeply,—he accused himself of hard-heartedness,—he remembered what she was when he had first seen her;—how full of animation, beauty, and love. He did not remember that she had perished the victim of uncontrolled passion; he felt that she was his victim. He would have given worlds to restore her to life and enjoyment. What was a residence in England—the promises of ambition—the pleasures of his native land—all that he could feel or know, compared to the existence of one so young, so blessed with Heaven's choicest gifts of mind and person. She was his victim, and he could never forgive himself.

For his father's and sisters' sake he subdued the expression of his grief, for they also loved Clorinda, and were struck with sorrow at the sudden catastrophe. His strong mind, also, before long, mastered the false view he had taken of the cause of her death. He lamented her deeply, but he did not give way to unavailing remorse, which was founded on his sensibility, and not on any just cause for repentance.

CHAPTER XV

"The music
Of man's fair composition best accords,
When 'tis in consort, not in single strains:
My heart has been untuned these many months,
Wanting her presence, in whose equal love
True harmony consisted."

—*Ford*

At the beginning of September the whole party assembled at Maristow Castle. Even Mrs. Elizabeth Fitzhenry was among the guests. She had not visited Ethel in London, because she would not enter Lady Lodore's house, but she had the true spinster's desire of seeing the baby, and thus overcame her reluctance to quitting Longfield for a few weeks. Fanny Derham also accompanied them, unable to deny Ethel's affectionate entreaties. Fanny's situation had been beneficially changed. Sir Gilbert Derham, finding that his granddaughter associated with people *in the world*, and being applied to by Lord Maristow, was induced to withdraw Mrs. Derham from her mean situation, and to settle a small fortune on each of her children. Fanny was too young, and too wedded to her platonic notions of the supremacy of mind, to be fully aware of the invaluable advantages of pecuniary independence for a woman. She fancied that she could enter on the career—the only career permitted her sex—of servitude, and yet possess her soul in freedom and power. She had never, indeed, thought much of these things: life was, as it concerned herself, a system of words only. As always happens to the young, she only knew suffering through her affections, and the real chain of life—its necessities and cares—and the sinister influences exercised by the bad passions of our fellow-creatures—had not yet begun to fetter her aspiring thoughts. Beautiful in her freedom, in her enthusiasm, and even in her learning, but, above all, in the lively kindliness of her heart, she excited the wonder and commanded the affections of all. Saville had never seen any one like her—she brought to his recollection his own young feelings before experience had lifted "the painted veil which those who live call life," or passion and sorrow had tamed the ardour of his mind; he looked on her with admiration, and yet with compassion, wondering where and how the evil spirit of the world would show its power to torment, and conquer the free soul of the disciple of wisdom.

Yet Saville's own mind was rather rebuked than tamed: he knew what suffering was, yet he knew also how to endure it, and to turn it to advantage, deriving thence lessons of fortitude, of forbearance, and even of hope. It was not, however, till the seal on his lips was taken off, and the name of Cornelia mentioned, that he became aware that the same heart warmed his bosom, as had been the cause at once of such rapture and misery in former times. Yet even now he did not acknowledge to himself that he still loved, passionately, devotedly loved, Lady Lodore. The image of the pale Clorinda stretched on the pavement—his victim—still dwelt in his memory, and he made a sacrifice at her tomb of every living feeling of his own. He fancied, therefore, that he spoke coldly of Cornelia, with speculation only, while in fact, at the very mention of her name a revulsion took place in his being—his eyes brightened, his face beamed with animation, his very figure enlarged, his heart was on fire within him. Villiers saw and appreciated these tokens of passion; but Ethel only perceived an interest in her mother, shared with herself, and was half angry that he made no professions of the constancy of his attachment.

Still, day after day, and soon, all day long, they talked of Lady Lodore. None but a lover and a daughter could have adhered so pertinaciously to one subject; and thus Saville and Ethel were often left to themselves, or joined only by Fanny. Fanny was very mysterious and alarming in what she said of her beautiful and interesting favourite. While Ethel lamented her mother's love of the continent, conjectured concerning her return, and dwelt on the pleasures of their future intercourse, Fanny shook her head, and said, "It was strange, very strange, that not one letter had yet reached them from her." She was asked to explain, but she could only say, that when she last saw Lady Lodore, she was impressed by the idea that all was not as it seemed. She tried to appear as if acting according to the ordinary routine of life, and yet was evidently agitated by violent and irrepressible feeling. Her manner, she had herself fancied, to be calm, and yet it betrayed a wandering of thought, a fear of being scrutinized, manifested in her repetition of the same phrases, and in the earnestness with which she made assurances concerning matters of the most trivial import. This was all that Fanny could say, but she was intimately persuaded of the correctness of her observation, and lamented that she had not inquired further and discovered more. "For," she said, "the mystery, whatever it is, springs from the most honourable motives. There was nothing personal nor frivolous in the feelings that mastered her"; and Fanny feared that at that very moment she was sacrificing herself to some project—some determination, which, while it benefited others, was injuring herself. Ethel, with all her affection for her mother, was not persuaded of the justice of these suspicions, nor could be brought to acknowledge that the mystery of Lady Lodore's absence was induced by any motives as strange and forcible as those suggested by Fanny; but believed that her young friend was carried away by her own imagination and high-flown ideas. Saville was operated differently upon. He became uneasy, thoughtful, restless: a thousand times he was on the point of setting out to find a clue to the mystery, and to discover the abode of the runaway,—but he was restrained. It is usually supposed that women are always under the influence of one sentiment, and if Lady Lodore acted under the direction and for the sake of another, wherefore should Saville interfere? what right had he to investigate her secrets, and disturb her arrangements?

Several months passed. Mrs. Elizabeth Fitzhenry returned to Longfield, and still the mystery concerning Ethel's mother continued, and the wonder increased, Soon after Christmas Mr. Gayland, who was also Lord Maristow's solicitor, came down to the Castle for a few days. He made inquiries concerning Lady Lodore, and was somewhat surprised at her strange disappearance and protracted absence. He asked several questions, and seemed to form conclusions in his own mind; he excited the curiosity of all, yet restrained himself from satisfying it; he was evidently disquieted by her unbroken silence, yet feared to betray the origin of his uneasiness.

While he remained curiosity was dominant: when he went he requested Villiers to be good enough to let him know if any thing should be heard of Lady Lodore. He asked this more than once, and required an absolute promise. After his departure, his questions, his manner, and his last words recurred, exciting even more surprise than when he had been present. Fanny brought forward all he said to support her own conjectures; a shadow of disquiet crossed Ethel's mind; she asked Villiers to take some steps to discover where her mother was, and on his refusal argued earnestly, though vainly, to persuade him to comply. Villiers was actuated by the common-place maxim of not interfering with the actions and projects of others. "Lady Lodore is not a child," he said, "she knows what she is about—has she not always avoided you, Ethel? Why press yourself inopportunely upon her?"

But Ethel was not now to be convinced by the repetition of these arguments. She urged her mother's kindness and sacrifice;

her having given up her home to them; her house still unclaimed by her, still at their disposal, and which contained so many things which must have been endeared by long use and habit, and the relinquishing of which showed something extraordinary in her motives. This was a woman's feeling, and made little impression on Villiers—he was willing to praise and to thank Lady Lodore for her generosity and kindness, but he suspected nothing beyond her acknowledged acts.

Saville heard this disquisition; he wished Villiers to be convinced—he was persuaded that Ethel was right—he was angry at his cousin's obstinacy—he was miserable at the idea that Cornelia should feel herself treated with neglect—that she should need protection and not have it—that she should be alone, and not find assistance proffered, urged upon her. He mounted his horse and took a solitary ride, meditating on these things—his imagination became heated, his soul on fire. He pictured Lady Lodore in solitude and desertion, and his heart boiled within him. Was she sick, and none near her?—was she dead, and her grave unvisited and unknown? A lover's fancy is as creative as a poet's and when once it takes hold of any idea, it clings to it tenaciously. If it is thus even with ordinary minds, how much more with Saville, with all energy which was his characteristic, and the latent fire of love burning in his heart. His resolution was sudden, and acted on at once. He turned his horse's head towards London. On reaching the nearest town, he ordered a chaise and four post horses. He wrote a few hurried lines announcing an absence of two or three days, and with the rapidity that always attended the conception of his purposes and their execution, the next morning, having travelled all night, he was in Mr. Gayland's office, questioning that gentleman concerning Lady Lodore, and seeking from him all the light he could throw upon her long-continued and mysterious absence.

Mr. Gayland had promised Lady Lodore not to reveal her secret to Mr. or Mrs. Villiers; but he felt himself free to communicate it to any other person. He was very glad to get rid of the burden and even the responsibility of being her sole confidant. He related all he knew to Saville, and the truth flashed on the lover's mind. His imagination could not dupe him—he could conceive, and therefore believe in her generosity, her magnanimity. He had before, in some degree, divined the greatness of mind of which Lady Lodore was capable; though as far as regarded himself, her pride, and his modesty, had deceived him. Now he became at once aware that Cornelia had beggared herself for Ethel's sake. She had disposed of her jointure, given up the residue of her income, and wandered away, poor and alone, to avoid the discovery of the extent and consequences of her sacrifices. Saville left Mr. Gayland's office with a bursting and a burning heart. At once he paid a warm tribute of admiration to her virtues, and acknowledged to himself his own passionate love. It became a duty, in his eyes, to respect, revere, adore one so generous and noble. He was proud of the selection his heart had made, and of his constancy. "My own Cornelia," such was his reverie, "how express your merit and the admiration it deserves!—other people talk of generosity, and friendship, and parental affection—but you manifest a visible image of these things; and while others theorize, you embody in your actions all that can be imagined of glorious and angelic." He congratulated himself on being able to return to the genuine sentiments of his heart, and in finding reality give sanction to the idolatry of his soul.

He longed to pour out his feelings at her feet, and to plead the cause of his fidelity and affection, to read in her eyes whether she would see a reward for her sufferings in his attachment. Where was she, to receive his protestations and vows? He half forgot, in the fervour of his feelings, that he knew not whither she had retreated, nor possessed any clue whereby to find her. He returned to Mr. Gayland to inquire from him; but he could tell nothing; he went to her house and questioned the servants, they remembered nothings; at last he found her maid, and learnt from her, where she was accustomed to hire her post-horses; this was all the information at which he could arrive.

Going to Newman's, with some difficulty he found the post-boy, who remembered driving her. By his means he traced her to Reading, but here all clue was lost. The inn to which she had gone had passed into other hands, and no one knew any thing about the arrivals and departures of the preceding summer. He made various perquisitions, and lighted by chance on the servant she had taken with her to Reading, and there dismissed. From what he said, and a variety of other circumstances, he became convinced that she had gone abroad. He searched the foreign passport-office, and found that one had been taken out at the French Ambassador's in the month of April, by a Mrs. Fitzhenry. He persuaded himself that this was proof that she had gone to Paris. It was most probable that, impoverished as she was, and desirous of concealing her altered situation, that she should, as Lodore had formerly done, dismiss a title which would at once encumber and betray her. He immediately resolved to cross to France. And yet for a moment he hesitated, and reflected on what it was best to do.

He had given no intimation of his proceedings to his cousin, and they were unaware that his journey was connected with Lady Lodore. He had a lover's wish to find her himself—himself to be the only source of consolation—the only mediator to restore her to her daughter and to happiness. But his fruitless attempts at discovery made him see that his wishes were not to be effected easily. He felt that he ought to communicate all he knew to his cousins, and even to ensure their assistance in his researches. Before going abroad, therefore, he returned to Maristow Castle.

He arrived late in the evening. Lord Maristow and his daughters were gone out to dinner. The three persons whom Saville especially wished to see, alone occupied the drawing-room. Edward was writing to his father, who had advised him, now that he had a son, entirely to cut off the entail and mortgage a great part of the property: it was a distasteful task to answer the suggestions of unprincipled selfishness. While he was thus occupied, Ethel had taken from her desk her mother's last letter, and was reading it again and again, weighing every syllable, and endeavouring to discover a hidden meaning. She went over to the sofa on which Fanny was sitting, to communicate to her a new idea that had struck her. The studious girl had got into a corner with her Cicero, and was reading the Tusculan Questions, which she readily laid aside to enter on a subject so deeply interesting. Saville opened the door, and appeared most unexpectedly among them. His manner was eager and abrupt, and the first words he uttered were, "I am come to disturb you all, and to beg of you to return to London:— no time must be lost—can you go to-morrow?"

"Certainly," said Villiers, "if you wish it."

"But why?" asked Ethel.

"You have found Lady Lodore!" exclaimed Fanny.

"You are dreaming, Fanny," said Ethel; "you see Horace shakes his head. But if we go to-morrow, yet rest to-night. You are fatigued, pale, and ill, Horace—you have been exerting yourself too much—explain your wishes, but take repose and refreshment."

Saville was in too excited a state to think of either. He repelled Ethel's feminine offers, till he had related his story. His listeners heard him with amazement. Villiers's cheeks glowed with shame, partly at the injustice of his former conduct—partly at being the object of so much sacrifice and beneficence on the part of his mother-in-law. Fanny's colour also heightened; she clasped her hands in delight, mingling various exclamations with Saville's story. "Did I not say so? I was sure of it. If you had seen her when I did, on the day of her going away, you would have been as certain as I." Ethel wept in silence, her heart was touched to the core, "the remorse of love" awakened in it. How cold and ungrateful had been all her actions: engrossed by her love for her husband, she had bestowed no sympathy, made no demonstrations towards her mother. The false shame and Edward's oft-repeated arguments which had kept her back, vanished from her mind. She reproached herself bitterly for lukewarmness and neglect; she yearned to show her repentance—to seek forgiveness—to express, however feebly, her sense of her mother's angelic goodness. Her tears flowed to think of these things, and that her mother was away, poor and alone, believing herself wronged in all their thoughts, resenting perhaps their unkindness, mourning over the ingratitude of her child.

When the first burst of feeling was over, they discussed their future proceedings. Saville communicated his discoveries and his plan of crossing to France. Villiers was as eager as his cousin to exert himself actively in the pursuit. His ingenuous and feeling mind was struck by his injustice, and he was earnest in his wish to atone for the past, and to recompense her, if possible, for her sacrifices. As every one is apt to do with regard to the ideas of others, he was not satisfied with his cousin's efforts or conclusions; he thought more questions might be asked—more learnt at the inns on the route which Lady Lodore had taken. The passport Saville had imagined to be hers, was taken out for Dover. Reading was far removed from any road to Kent. They argued this. Horatio was not convinced; but while he was bent on proceeding to Paris, Edward resolved to visit Reading—to examine the neighbourhood—to requestion the servants—to put on foot a system of inquiry which must in the end assure them whether she was still in the kingdom. It was at once resolved, that on the morrow they should go to London.

Thither they accordingly went. They repaired to Lady Lodore's house. Saville on the next morning departed for France, and a letter soon reached them from him, saying, that he felt persuaded that the Mrs. Fitzhenry was Lady Lodore, and that he should pursue his way with all speed to Paris. It appeared, that the lady in question had crossed to Calais on the eleventh of June, and intimated her design of going to the Bagneres de Bigorre among the Pyrennees, passing through Paris on her way. The mention of the Bagneres de Bigorre clinched Saville's suspicions—it was such a place as one in Lady Lodore's position might select for her abode—distant, secluded, situated in sublime and beautiful scenery, singularly cheap, and seldom visited by strangers; yet the annual resort of the French from

Bordeaux and Lyons, civilized what otherwise had been too rude and wild for an English lady. It was a long journey thither—the less wonder that nothing was heard, or seen, or surmised concerning the absentee by her numerous acquaintances, many of whom were scattered on the continent. Saville represented all these things, and expressed his conviction that he should find her. His letter was brief, for he was hurried, and he felt that it were better to say nothing than to express imperfectly the conflicting emotions alive in his heart. "My life seems a dream," he said at the conclusion of his letter; "a long painful dream, since last I saw her. I awake, she is not here; I go to seek her—my actions have that single scope—my thoughts tend to that aim only; I go to find her—to restore her to Ethel. If I succeed in bestowing this happiness on her, I shall have my reward, and, whatever happens, no selfish regret shall tarnish my delight."

He urged Villiers, meanwhile, not to rely too entirely on the conviction so strong in himself, but to pursue his plan of discovery with vigour. Villiers needed no spur. His eagerness was fully alive; he could not rest till he had rescued his mother-in-law from solitude and obscurity. He visited Reading; he extended his inquiries to Newbury: here more light broke in on his researches. He heard of Lady Lodore's illness—of her having resided for several months at a villa in the neighbourhood, while slowly recovering from a fever by which for a long time her life had been endangered. He heard also of her departure, her return to London. Then again all was obscurity. The innkeepers and letters of post-horses in London, were all visited in vain—the mystery became as impenetrable as ever. It seemed most probable that she was living in some obscure part of the metropolis—Ethel's heart sunk within her at the thought.

Edward wrote to Saville to communicate this intelligence, which put an end to the idea of her being in France—but he was already gone on to Bagneres. He himself perambulated London and its outskirts, but all in vain. The very thought that she should be residing in a place so sad, nay, so humiliating, without one gilding circumstance to solace poverty and obscurity, was unspeakably painful both to Villiers and his wife. Ethel thought of her own abode in Duke Street during her husband's absence, and how miserable and forlorn it had been—she now wept bitterly over her mother's fate; even Fanny's philosophy could not afford consolation for these ideas.

An accident, however, gave a new turn to their conjectures. In the draw of a work-table, Ethel found an advertisement cut out of a newspaper, setting forth the merits of a cottage to be let near Rhaiyder Gowy in Radnorshire, and with this, a letter from the agent at Rhaiyder, dated the 13th of May, in answer to inquiries concerning the rent and particulars. The letter intimated, that if the account gave satisfaction, the writer would get the cottage prepared for the tenant immediately, and the lady might take possession at the time mentioned, on the 1st of June. The day after finding this letter, Villiers set out for Wales.

But first he persuaded Ethel to spend the interval of his absence at Longfield. She had lately fretted much concerning her mother, and as she was still nursing her baby, Edward became uneasy at her pale cheeks and thinness. Ethel was anxious to preserve her health for her child; she felt that her uneasiness and pining would be lessened by a removal into the country. She was useless in London, and there was something in her residence in her mother's house—in the aspect of the streets—in the memory of what she had suffered there, and the fear that Lady Lodore was enduring a worse repetition of the same evils, that agitated and preyed upon her. Her aunt had pressed her very much to come and see her, and she wrote to say, that she might be expected on the following day. She bade adieu to Villiers with more of hope with regard to his success than she had formerly felt. She became half convinced that her mother was not in London. Fanny supported her in these ideas; they talked continually of all they knew—of the illness of Lady Lodore—of her firmness of purpose in not sending for her daughter, or altering her plans in consequence; they comforted themselves that the air of Wales would restore her health, and the beauty of the scenery and the freedom of nature sooth her mind. They were full of hope—of more—of expectation. Ethel, indeed, had at one time proposed accompanying her husband, but she yielded to his entreaties, and to the fear suggested, that she might injure her child's health. Villiers's motions would be more prompt without her. They separated. Ethel wrote to Saville a letter to find him at Paris, containing an account of their new discoveries, and then prepared for her journey to Essex with Fanny, her baby, and the beautiful little Clorinda Saville, who had been left under her care, on the following day.

• • •

CHAPTER XVI

"I am not One who much or oft delights
To season my Friends with personal talk,—
Of Friends who live within an easy walk,
Or Neighbours, daily, weekly in my sight.
And, for my chance acquaintance, Ladies bright.
Sons, Mothers, Maidens withering on the stalk,
These all wear out of me, like Forms, with chalk
Painted on rich men's floors, for one feast-night."

—Wordsworth

Mrs. Elizabeth Fitzhenry returned to Longfield from Maristow Castle at the end of the month of November. She gladly came back, in all the dinginess and bleakness of that dismal season, to her beloved seclusion at Longfield. The weather was dreary, a black frost invested every thing with its icy chains, the landscape looked disconsolate, and now and then wintry blasts brought on snow-storms, and howled loudly through the long dark nights. The amiable spinster drew her chair close to the fire; with half-shut eyes she contemplated the glowing embers, and recalled many past winters just like this, when Lodore was alive and in America; or, diving yet deeper into memory, when the honoured chair she now occupied, had been dignified by her father, and she had tried to sooth his querulous complaints on the continued absence of her brother Henry. When, instead of these familiar thoughts, the novel ones of Ethel and Villiers intruded themselves, she rubbed her eyes to be quite sure that she did not dream. It was a lamentable change; and who the cause? Even she whose absence had been, she felt, wickedly lamented at Maristow Castle, Cornelia Santerre—she, who in an evil hour, had become Lady Lodore, and who would before God, answer for the disasters and untimely death of her ill-fated husband.

With any but Mrs. Fitzhenry, such accusations had, after the softening process of time, been changed to an admission, that, despite her errors, Lady Lodore had rather been misled and mistaken, than heinously faulty; and her last act, in sacrificing so much to her daughter, although the extent of her sacrifice was unknown to her sister-in-law, had cancelled her former delinquencies. But the prejudiced old lady was not so easily mollified; she was harsh alone towards her, but all the gall of her nature was collected and expended on the head of her brother's widow. Probably an instinctive feeling of her unreasonableness made her more violent. Her language was bitter whenever she alluded to her—she rejoiced at her absence, and instead of entering into Ethel's gratitude and impatience, she fervently prayed that she might never appear on the scene again.

Mrs. Elizabeth Fitzhenry was less of a gossip than any maiden lady who had ever lived singly in the centre of a little village. Her heart was full of the dead and the absent—of past events, and their long train of consequences, so that the history of the inhabitants of her village, possessed no charm for her. If any one among them suffered from misfortune she endeavoured to relieve them, and if any died, she lamented, moralized on the passage of time, and talked of Lodore's death; but the scandal, the marriages, the feuds, and wonderful things that came to pass at Longfield, appeared childish and contemptible, the flickering of earth-born tapers compared to the splendour, the obscuration, and final setting of the celestial luminary which had been the pole-star of her life.

It was from this reason that Mrs. Fitzhenry had not heard of the Lady who lodged at Dame Nixon's cottage, in the Vale of Bewling, till the time, when, after having exhausted the curiosity of Longfield, she was almost forgotten. The Lady, she was known by no other name, had arrived in the town during Mrs. Fitzhenry's visit to Maristow castle. She had arrived in her own chariot, unattended by any servant; the following day she had taken up her abode at Dame Nixon's cottage, saying, that she was only going to stay a week: she had continued there for more than three months.

Dame Nixon's cottage was situated about a mile and a half from Longfield. It stood alone in a little hollow embowered by trees; the ground behind rose to a slight upland, and a rill trickled through the garden. You got to it by a bye path, which no wheeled vehicle could traverse, though a horse might, and it was indeed the very dingle and cottage which Ethel had praised during her visit into Essex in the preceding year. The silence and seclusion were in summer tranquillizing and beautiful; in winter sad and drear; the fields were swampy in wet weather, and in snow and frost it seemed cut off from the rest of the world. Dame Nixon and her granddaughter lived there alone. The girl had been engaged to be married. Her lover jilted her, and wedded a richer bride. The story is so old, that it is to be wondered that women have not ceased to lament so common an occurrence. Poor Margaret was, on the contrary, struck to the heart—she despised herself for being unable to preserve her lover's affections, rather than the deceiver for his infidelity. She neglected her personal appearance, nor ever showed herself among her former companions, except to support her grandmother to church. Her false lover sat in the adjoining pew. She fixed her eyes on her Prayer-book during the service, and on the ground as she went away. She did not wish him to see the change which his faithlessness had wrought, for surely it would afflict him. Once there had not bloomed a fresher or gayer rose in the fields of Essex—now she had grown thin and pale—her young light step had become slow and heavy—sickness and sorrow made her eyes hollow, and her cheeks sunken. She avoided every one, devoting herself to attendance on her grandmother. Dame Nixon was nearly doting. Life was ebbing fast from her old frame; her best pleasure was to sun herself in the garden in summer, or to bask before the winter's fire. While enjoying these delights, her dimmed eyes brightened, and a smile wreathed her withered lips; she said, "Ah! this is comfortable"; while her broken-hearted grandchild envied a state of being which could content itself with mere animal enjoyment. They were very poor. Margaret had to work hard; but the thoughts of the head, or, at least, the feelings of the heart, need not wait on the labour of the hands. The Sunday visit to church kept alive her pain; her very prayers were bitter, breathed close to the deceiver and her who had usurped her happiness: the memory and anticipation haunted her through the week; she was often blinded by tears as she patiently pursued her household duties, or her toil in their little garden. Her hands were hardened with work, her throat, her face sunburnt; but exercise and occupation did not prevent her from wasting away, or her cheek from becoming sunk and wan.

Dame Nixon's cottage was poor but roomy; some years before, a gentleman from London had, in a freak, hired two rooms in it, and furnished them. Since then, she had sometimes let them, and now they were occupied by the stranger lady. At first all three of the inhabitants appeared each Sunday at church. The Lady was dressed in spotless and simple white, and so closely veiled, that no one could see her face; of course she was beautiful. Soon after Mrs. Elizabeth's return from Maristow Castle, it was discovered that first the lady stayed away, and soon, that the whole party absented themselves on Sunday; and as this defalcation demanded inquiry, it was discovered that a pony chaise took them three miles off to the church of the nearest village. This was a singular and yet a beneficial change. The false swain must rejoice at losing sight of the memento of his sin, and Margaret would certainly pray with a freer heart, when she no longer shrunk from his gaze and that of his wife.

It was not until the end of January that Mrs. Elizabeth heard of the Lady; it was not till the beginning of February that she asked a single question about her.

In January, passing the inn-yard, the curate's wife, who was walking with her, said, "There is the chariot belonging to the Lady who lodges at dame Nixon's cottage. I wonder who she is. The arms are painted out."

"Ah, dame Nixon has a lodger then; that is a good thing, it will help her through the winter. I have not seen her or her daughter at church lately."

"No," replied the other, "they go now to Bewling church."

"I am glad to hear it," said Mrs. Fitzhenry; "it is much better for poor Margaret not to come here."

The conversation went on, and the Lady was alluded to, but no questions were asked or curiosity excited. In February she heard from the doctor's wife, that the doctor had been to the cottage, and that the Lady was indisposed. She heard at the same time that this Lady had refused to receive the visits of the curate's lady and the doctor's lady—excusing herself, that she was going to leave Essex immediately. This had happened two months before. On hearing of her illness, Mrs. Elizabeth thought of calling on her, but this stopped her. "It is very odd," said the doctor's wife, "she came in her own carriage, and yet has no servants. She lives in as poor a way as can be, down in that cottage, yet my husband says she is more like the Queen of England in her looks and ways than any one he ever saw."

"Like the Queen of England?" said Mrs. Fitzhenry, "What queen?—Queen Charlotte?" who had been the queen of the greater part of the good lady's life.

"She is as young and beautiful as an angel," said the other, half angry; "it is very mysterious. She did not look downcast like, as if any thing was wrong, but was as cheerful and condescending as could be. 'Condescending, Doctor,' said I, for my husband used the word; 'you don't want condescension from a poor body lodging at dame Nixon's.'—'A poor body!' said he, in a huff, 'she is more of a lady, indeed more like the Queen of England than any rich body you ever saw.' And what is odd, no one knows her name—Dame Nixon and Margaret always call her Lady—the very marks are picked out from her pocket handkerchiefs. Yet I did hear that there was a coronet plain to be seen on one—a thing impossible unless she was a poor cast-away; and the doctor says he'd lay his life that she was nothing of that. He must know her name when he makes out her bill, and I told him to ask it plump, but he puts off, and puts off, till I am out of all patience."

A misty confused sense of discomfort stole over Mrs. Elizabeth when she heard of the coronet in the corner of the pocket handkerchief, but it passed away without suggesting any distinct idea to her mind. Nor did she feel curiosity about the stranger—she was too much accustomed to the astonishment, the conjectures, the gossip of Longfield, to suppose that there was any real foundation for surprise, because its wonder-loving inhabitants choose to build up a mystery out of every common occurrence of life.

This absence of inquisitiveness must long have kept Mrs. Fitzhenry in ignorance of who her neighbour was, and the inhabitants of Longfield would probably have discovered it before her, had not the truth been revealed even before she entertained a suspicion that there was any secret to be found out.

"I beg your pardon, ma'am," said her maid to her one evening, as she was superintending the couchée of the worthy spinster, "I think you ought to know, though I am afraid you may be angry."

The woman hesitated; her mistress encouraged her. "If it is any thing I ought to know, Wilmot, tell it at once, and don't be afraid. What has happened to you?"

"To me, ma'am,—la! nothing," replied the maid; "it's something about the Lady at dame Nixon's, only you commanded me never to speak the name of—"

And again the good woman stopped short. Mrs. Fitzhenry, a little surprised, and somewhat angry, bade her go on. At length, in plain words she was told:

"Why, ma'am, the Lady down in the Vale is no other than my lady—than Lady Lodore."

"Ridiculous—who told you so?"

"My own eyes, ma'am; I shouldn't have believed any thing else. I saw the Lady, and it was my Lady, as sure as I stand here."

"But how could you know her? it is years since you saw her."

"Yes, ma'am," said the woman, with a smile of superiority; "but it is not easy to forget Lady Lodore. See her yourself, ma'am,—you will know then that I am right."

Wilmot had lived twenty years with Mrs. Fitzhenry. She had visited town with her at the time of Ethel's christening. She had been kept in vexatious ignorance of subsequent events, till the period of the visit of her mistress and niece to London two years before, when she indemnified herself. Through the servants of Villiers, and of the Misses Saville, she had learnt a vast deal; and not satisfied with mere hearsay, she had seen Lady Lodore several times getting into her carriage at her own door, and had even been into her house: such energy is there in a liberal curiosity. The same disinterested feeling had caused her to go down to dame Nixon's with an offer from her mistress of service to the Lady, hearing she was ill. She went perfectly unsuspicious of the wonderful discovery she was about to make, and was thus rewarded beyond her most sanguine hopes, by being in possession of a secret, known to herself alone. The keeping of a secret is, however, a post of no honour if all knowledge be confined to the possessor alone. Mrs. Wilmot was tolerably faithful, with all her love of knowledge; she was sure it would vex her mistress if Lady Lodore's strange place of abode were known at Longfield, and Mrs. Fitzhenry was consequently the first person to whom she had hinted the fact. All this account she detailed with great volubility. Her mistress recommended discretion most earnestly; and at the same time expressed a doubt whether her information was correct.

"I wish you would go and judge for yourself, ma'am," said the maid.

"God forbid!" exclaimed Mrs. Fitzhenry. "God grant I never see Lady Lodore again! She will go soon. You tell me that dame Nixon says she is only staying till she is well. She will go soon, and it need never be known, except to ourselves, Wilmot, that she was ever here."

There was a dignity in this eternal mystery that somewhat compensated for the absence of wonder and fuss which the woman had anticipated with intense pleasure. She assured her mistress, over and over again, of her secrecy and discretion, and was dismissed with the exhortation to forget all she had learnt as quickly as possible.

"Wherefore did she come here? what can she be doing?" Mrs. Fitzhenry asked herself over and over again. She could not guess. It was strange, it was mysterious, and some mischief was at the bottom—but she would go soon—"would that she were already gone!"

It must be mentioned that Mrs. Elizabeth Fitzhenry had left Maristow Castle before the arrival of Mr. Gayland, and had therefore no knowledge of the still more mysterious cloud that enveloped Lady Lodore's absence. Ignorant of her self-destroying sacrifices and generosity, her pity was not excited, her feelings were all against her. She counted the days as they passed, and looked wistfully at Wilmot, hoping that she would quickly bring tidings of the Lady's departure. In vain; the doctor ceased to visit the cottage, but the Lady remained. All at once the doctor visited it again with greater assiduity than ever—not on account of his beautiful patient—but Dame Nixon had had a paralytic stroke, and the kind Lady had sent for him, and promised to defray all the expenses of the poor woman's illness.

All this was truly vexatious. Mrs. Fitzhenry fretted, and even asked Wilmot questions, but the unwelcome visitor was still there. Wherefore? What could have put so disagreeable a whim into her head? The good lady could think of no motive, while she considered her presence an insult. She was still more annoyed when she received a letter from Ethel. It had been proposed that Mr. and Mrs. Villiers should pay her a visit in the spring; but now Ethel wrote to say that she might be immediately expected. "I have strange things to tell you about my dear mother," wrote Ethel; "it is very uncertain where she is. Horatio can hear nothing of her at Paris, and will soon return. Edward is going to Wales, as there seems a great likelihood that she has secluded herself there. While he is away you may expect me. I shall not be able to stay long—he will come at the end of a week to fetch me."

Mrs. Fitzhenry shuddered. Her prejudices were stronger than ever. She experienced the utmost wretchedness from the idea that the residence of Lady Lodore would be discovered, and a family union effected. It seemed desecration to the memory of her brother, ruin to Ethel—the greatest misfortune that could befall any of them. Her feelings were exaggerated, but they were on that account the more powerful. How could she avert the evil?—a remedy must be sought, and she fixed on one—a desperate one, in truth, which appeared to her the sole mode of saving them all from the greatest disasters.

She resolved to visit Lady Lodore; to represent to her the impropriety and wickedness of her having any intercourse with her daughter, and to entreat her to depart before Ethel's arrival. Her violence might almost seem madness; but all people who live in solitude become to a certain degree insane. Their views of things are not corrected by comparing them with those of others; and the strangest want of proportion always reigns in their ideas and sentiments.

• • •

CHAPTER XVII

"So loth we part from all we love,
From all the links that bind us;
So turn our hearts, where'er we rove,
To those we've left behind us."

—*Thomas Moore*

O n the following morning Mrs. Elizabeth Fitzhenry drove to the Vale of Bewling. It was the last day of February. The March winds were hushed as yet; the breezes were balmy, the sunshine cheerful; a few soft clouds flecked the heavens, and the blue sky appeared between them calm and pure. Each passing air breathed life and happiness—it caressed the cheek—and the swelling buds of the trees felt its quickening influence. The almond-trees were in bloom—the pear blossoms began to whiten—the tender green of the young leaves showed themselves here and there among the hedges. The old lady felt the cheering influence, and would have become even gay, had not the idea of the errand she was on checked her spirits. Sometimes the remembrance that she was really going to see her sister-in-law absolutely startled her; once or twice she thought of turning back; she passed through the lanes, and then alighting from her carriage, walked by a raised foot-way, across some arable fields— and again through a little grove; the winding path made a turn, and dame Nixon's white, low-roofed cottage was before her. Every thing about it looked trim, but very humble: and it was unadorned during this early season by the luxury of flowers and plants, which usually give even an appearance of elegance to an English cottage. Mrs. Fitzhenry opened the little gate—her knees trembled as she walked through the scanty garden, which breathed of the new-sprung violets. The entrance to the cottage was by the kitchen: she entered this, and found Margaret occupied by a culinary preparation for her grandmother. Mrs. Fitzhenry asked after the old woman's health, and thus gained a little time. Margaret answered in her own former quiet yet cheerful voice; she was changed from what she had been a few weeks before. The bloom had not returned to her cheeks, but they no longer appeared streaked with deathly paleness; her motions had lost the heaviness that showed a mind ill at ease. Mrs. Elizabeth congratulated her on the restoration of her health.

"O yes," she replied, with a blush, "I am not the same creature I used to be, thank God, and the angel he has sent us here;—if my poor grandmother would but get well I should be quite happy; but that is asking too much at her time of life."

The old lady made no further observations: she did not wish to hear the praises of her sister-in-law. "Your lodger is still here?" at length she said.

"Yes, God be praised!" replied Margaret.

"Will you give her my compliments, and say I am here, and that I wish to see her."

"Yes, ma'am," said Margaret; "only the lady has refused to see any one, and she does not like being asked."

"I do not wish to be impertinent or intrusive," answered Mrs. Elizabeth; "only tell her my name, and if she makes any objection, of course she will do as she likes. Where is she?"

"She is sitting with my poor grandmother; the nurse—Heaven bless her! she would hire a nurse, to spare me, as she said—is lain down to sleep, and she said she would watch by grandmother while I got the gruel; but it's ready now, and I will go and tell her."

Away tripped Margaret, leaving her guest lost in wonder. Lady Lodore watching the sick-bed of an old cottager—Lady Lodore immured in a poverty-stricken abode, fit only for the poorer sort of country people. It was more than strange, it was miraculous. "Yet she refused to accompany poor Henry to America! there must be some strange mystery in all this, that does not tell well for her."

So bitterly uncharitable was the unforgiving old lady towards her brother's widow. She ruminated on these things for a minute or two, and then Margaret came to usher her into the wicked one's presence. The sitting-room destined for the lodger was neat, though very plain. The walls were wainscotted and painted white,—the windows small and latticed,—the furniture was old black, shining mahogany; the chairs high-backed and clumsy; the table heavy and incommodious; the fire-place large and airy; and the shelf of the mantel-piece almost as high as the low ceiling: there were a few things of a more modern construction; a comfortable sofa, a rose-wood bureau and large folding screen; near the fire was a large easy chair of Gillows's manufacture, two light cane ones, and two small tables; vases filled with hyacinths, jonquils, and other spring flowers stood on one, and an embroidery frame occupied the other. There was a perfume of fresh-gathered flowers in the room, which the open window rendered very agreeable. Lady Lodore was standing near the fire— (for Wilmot was not mistaken, and it was she indeed who now presented herself to Mrs. Fitzhenry's eyes)—she might be agitated—she did not show it—she came forward and held out her hand. "Dear Bessy," she said, "you are very kind to visit me; I thank you very much."

The poor recluse was overpowered. The cordiality of the greeting frightened her: she who had come full of bitter reproach and hard purposes, to be thanked with that sweet voice and smile. "I thought," at length she stammered out, "that you did not wish to be known. I am glad you are not offended, Cornelia."

"Offended by kindness? O no! It is true I did not wish—I do not wish that it should be known that I am here—but since, by some strange accident, you have discovered me, how can I help being grateful for your visit? I am indeed glad to see you; it is so long since I have heard any thing. Ah! dear Bessy, tell me, how is Ethel?"

Tears glistened in the mother's eyes: she asked many questions, and Mrs. Fitzhenry a little recovered her self-possession, as she answered them. She looked at Lady Lodore—she was changed—she could not fail of being changed after so many years,—she was no longer a beautiful girl, but she was a lovely woman. Despite the traces of years, which however lightly they impressed, yet might be discerned; expression so embellished her that it was impossible not to admire; brilliancy had given place to softness, animation to serenity; still she was fair—still her silken hair clustered on her brow, and her sweet eyes were full of fire; her smile had more than its former charm—it came from the heart.

Mrs. Fitzhenry was not, however, to be subdued by a little outward show. She was there, who had betrayed and deserted (such were the energetic words she was accustomed to employ) the noble, broken-hearted Lodore. The thought steeled her purpose, and she contrived at last to ask whether Lady Lodore was going to remain much longer in Essex?

"I have been going every day since I came here. In a few weeks I shall certainly be gone. Why do you ask?"

"Because I thought—that is—you have made a secret of your being here, and I expect Ethel in a day or two, and she would certainly discover you."

"Why should she not?" asked Lady Lodore. "Why should you be averse to my seeing Ethel?"

It is very difficult to say a disagreeable thing, especially to one unaccustomed to society, and who is quite ignorant of the art of concealing the sting of her intentions by flowery words. Mrs. Fitzhenry said something about her sister-in-law's own wishes, and the desire expressed by Lodore that there should be no intercourse between the mother and daughter.

Cornelia's eyes flashed fire—"Am I," she exclaimed, "to be always the sacrifice? Is my husband's vengeance to pursue me beyond his grave—even till I reach mine? Unjust as he was, he would not have desired this."

Mrs. Elizabeth coloured with anger. Lady Lodore continued—"Pardon me, Bessy, I do not wish to say any thing annoying to you or in blame of Lodore. God knows I did him great wrong—but—"

"O Cornelia," cried the old lady, "do you indeed acknowledge that you were to blame?"

Lady Lodore smiled, and said, "I were strangely blind to the defects of my own character, and to the consequences of my actions, were I not conscious of my errors; but retrospection is useless, and the punishment has been—is—sufficiently severe. Lodore himself would not have perpetuated his resentment, had he lived only a very little while longer. But I will speak frankly to you, Bessy, as frankly as I may, and you shall decide on my further stay here. From circumstances which it is immaterial to explain, I have resolved on retiring into absolute solitude. I shall never live in London again—never again see any of my old friends and acquaintances. The course of my life is entirely changed; and whether I live here or elsewhere, I shall live in obscurity and poverty. I do not wish Ethel to know this. She would wish to assist me, and she has scarcely enough for herself. I do not like being a burthen—I do not like being pitied—I do not like being argued with, or to have my actions commented upon. You know that my disposition was always independent."

Mrs. Elizabeth assented with a sigh, casting up her eyes to heaven.

Lady Lodore smiled, and went on. "You think this is a strange place for me to live in: whether here or elsewhere, I shall never live in any better: I shall be fortunate if I find myself as well off when I leave Essex, for the people here are good and honest, and the poor girl loves me,—it is always pleasant to be loved."

A tear again filled Cornelia's eyes—she tried to animate herself to smile. "I have nothing to love in all the wide world except Ethel; I do love her; every one must love her—she is so gentle—so kind—so warm-hearted and beautiful,—I love her more than my own heart's blood; she is my child—part of that blood—part of myself—the better part; I have seen little of her, but every look and word is engraved on my heart. I love her voice—her smiles—the pressure of her soft white hand. Pity me, dear Bessy, I am never to see any of these, which are all that I love on earth, again. This idea fills me with regret—with worse—with sorrow. There is a grave not far from here which contains one you loved beyond all others,—what would you not give to see him alive once again? To visit his tomb is a consolation to you. I must not seen even the walls within which my blessed child lives. You alone can help me—can be of comfort to me. Do not refuse—do not send me away. If I leave this place, I shall go to some secluded nook in Wales, and be quite—quite alone; the sun will shine, and the grass will grow at my feet, but my heart will be dead within me, and I shall pine and die. I have intended to do this; I have waited only till the sufferings of the poor woman here should be at an end, that I may be of service to Margaret, and then go. Your visit, which I fancied meant in kindness, has put other thoughts into my head.

"Do not object to my staying here; let me remain; and do yet more for me—come to me sometimes, and bring me tidings of my daughter—tell me what she says—how she looks,—tell me that she is at each moment well and happy. Ah! do this, dear Bessy, and I will bless you. I shall never see her—at least not for years; there are many things to prevent it: yet how could I drag out those years quite estranged from her? My heart has died within me each time I have thought of it. But I can live as I say; I shall expect you every now and then to come and talk to me of her; she need never know that I am so near—she comes so sel-dom to Essex. I shall soon be forgotten at Longfield. Will you consent? you will do a kind action, and God will bless you."

Mrs. Fitzhenry was one of those persons who always find it dif-ficult to say, No; and Lady Lodore asked with so much earnestness that she commanded; she felt that her request ought to be granted, and therefore it was impossible to refuse it. Before she well knew what she had said, the good lady had yielded her consent and received her sister-in-law's warm and heart-felt thanks.

Mrs. Fitzhenry looked round the room: "But how can you think of staying here, Cornelia?" she said; "this place is not fit for you. I should have thought that you could never have endured such homely rooms."

"Do you think them so bad?" replied the lady; "I think them very pleasant, for I have done with pride, and I find peace and comfort here. Look," she continued, throwing open a door that led into the garden, "is not that delightful? This garden is very pretty: that clear rivulet murmurs by with so lulling a sound;—and look at these violets, are they not beautiful? I have planted a great many flowers, and they will soon come up. Do you not know how pleasant it is to watch the shrubs we plant, and water, and rear ourselves?—to see the little green shoots peep out, and the leaves unfold, and then the flower blossom and expand, diffusing its delicious odour around,—all, as it were, created by oneself, by one's own nursing, out of a bit of stick or an ugly bulb? This place is very pretty, I assure you: when the leaves are on the trees they make a bower, and the grove behind the house is shady, and leads to lanes and fields more beautiful than any I ever saw. I have loitered for hours in this garden, and been quite happy. Now I shall be happier than ever, thanks to you. You will not forget me. Come as often as you can. You say that you expect Ethel soon?"

Lady Ladore walked with her sister-in-law to the garden-gate, and beyond, through the little copse, still talking of her daughter. "I cannot go further," she said, at last, "without a bonnet—so good-bye, dear Bessy. Come soon. Thank you—thank you for this visit."

She held out her hand: Mrs. Fitzhenry took it, pressed it, a half feeling came over her as if she were about to kiss the check of her offending relative, but her heart hardened, she blushed, and muttering a hasty good-bye, she hurried away. She was bewildered, and after walking a few steps, she turned round, and saw again the white dress of Cornelia, as a turn in the path hid her. The grand, the exclusive Lady Lodore—the haughty, fashionable, worldly-heartless wife thus metamorphosed into a tender-hearted mother—suing to her for crumbs of charitable love—and hiding all her boasted advantages in that low-roofed cottage! What could it all mean?

Mrs. Fitzhenry walked on. Again she thought, "How odd! I went there, determining to persuade her to go away, and miserable at the thoughts of seeing her only once; and now I have promised to visit her often, and agreed that she shall live here. Have I not done wrong? What would my poor brother say? Yet I could not refuse. Poor thing! how could I refuse, when she said that she had nothing else to live for? Besides, to go away and live alone in Wales—it would be too dreadful; and she thanked me as if she were so grateful. I hope I have not done wrong.

"But how strange it is that Henry's widow should have become so poor; she has given up a part of her income to Ethel, but a great deal remains. What can she have done with it? She is mysterious, and there is never any good in mystery. Who knows what she may have to conceal?" Mrs. Elizabeth got in her carriage, and each step of the horses took her farther from the web of enchantment which Cornelia had thrown over her. "She is always strange,"—thus ran her meditations; "and how am I to see her, and no one find it out? and what a story for Longfield, that Lady Lodore should be living in poverty in dame Nixon's cottage. I forgot to tell her that—I forgot to say so many things I meant to say—I don't know why, except that she talked so much, and I did not know how to bring in my objections. But it cannot be right: and Ethel in her long rambles and rides with Miss Derham or Mr. Villiers, will be sure to find her out. I wish I had not seen her—I will write and tell her I have changed my mind, and entreat her to go away."

As it occurs to all really good-natured persons, it was very disagreeable to Mrs. Fitzhenry to be angry, and she visited the ill-temper so engendered on the head of poor Cornelia. She disturbed herself by the idea of all the disagreeable things that might happen—of her sister-in-law's positive refusal to go; the very wording which she imagined for her intended letter puzzled and irritated her. She no longer felt the breath of spring as pleasant, but sat back in the chariot, "nursing her wrath to keep it warm." When she reached her home, Ethel's carriage was at her door.

The meeting, as ever, between aunt and niece was affectionate. Fanny was welcomed, the baby was kissed, and little Clorinda admired, but the theme nearest Ethel's heart was speedily introduced—her mother. The disquietudes she felt on her account—Mr. Saville's journey to Paris—the visit of Villiers to Wales to discover her place of concealment—the inutility of all their endeavours.

"But why are they so anxious?" asked her aunt; "I can understand you: you have some fantastic notion about your mother, but how can Mr. Villiers desire so very much to find her?"

"I could almost say," said Ethel, "that Edward is more eager than myself, though I should wrong my own affection and gratitude; but he was more unjust towards her, and thus he feels the weight of obligation more keenly; but, perhaps, dear aunt, you do not know all that my dearest mother has done for us—the unparalleled sacrifices she has made."

Then Ethel went on to tell her all that Mr. Gayland had communicated—the sale of her jointure—the very small residue of money she had kept for herself—the entire payment of Villiers's debts—and afterwards the surrender of the remainder of her income and of her house to them. Her eyes glistened as she spoke; her heart, overflowing with admiration and affection, shone in her beautiful face, her voice was pregnant with sensibility, and her expressions full of deep feeling.

Mrs. Elizabeth's heart was not of stone—far from it; it was, except in the one instance of her sister-in-law, made of pliable materials. She heard Ethel's story—she caught by sympathy the tenderness and pity she poured forth—she thought of Lady Lodore at the cottage, a dwelling so unlike any she had ever inhabited before—poverty-stricken and mean; she remembered her praises of it—her cheerfulness—the simplicity of taste which she displayed—the light-hearted content with which she spoke of every privation except the absence of Ethel. What before was mysterious wrong, was now manifest heroism. The loftiness and generosity of her mind rose upon the old lady unclouded; her own uncharitable deductions stung her with remorse; she continued to listen, and Ethel to narrate, and the big tears gathered in her eyes, and rolled down her venerable cheeks,—tears at once of repentance and admiration.

•••

CHAPTER XVIII

"Repentance is a tender sprite;
  If aught on earth have heavenly might,
  'Tis lodged within her silent tear."

—Wordsworth

Mrs. Elizabeth Fitzhenry was not herself aware of all that Lady Lodore had suffered, or the extent of her sacrifices. She guessed darkly at them, but it was the detail that rendered them so painful, and, but for their motive, humiliating to one nursed in luxury, and accustomed to all those intermediate servitors and circumstances, which stand between the rich and the bare outside of the working-day world. Cornelia shrunk from the address of those she did not know, and from the petty acts of daily life, which had gone on before without her entering into their detail.

Her illness at Newbury had been severe. She was attacked by the scarlet fever; the doctor had ordered her to be removed from the bustle of the inn, and a furnished villa had been taken for her, while she could only give a languid assent to propositions which she understood confusedly. She was a long time very ill—a long time weak and slowly convalescent. At length health dawned on her, accompanied by a disposition attuned to content and a wish for tranquillity. Her residence was retired, commodious, and pretty; she was pleased with it, she did not wish to remove, and was glad to procrastinate from day to day any consideration of the future. Thus it was a long time before the strength of her thoughts and purposes was renewed, or that she began to think seriously of where she was, and what she was going to do.

During the half delirium, the disturbed and uncontrollable, but not unmeaning reveries, of her fever, the idea of visiting Lodore's grave had haunted her pertinaciously. She had often dreamt of it: at one time the tomb seemed to rise in a lonely desert; and the dead slept peacefully beneath sunshine or starlight. At another, storms and howling winds were around, groans and sighs, mingled with the sound of the tempest, and menaces and reproaches against her were breathed from the cold marble. Now her imagination pictured it within the aisles of a magnificent cathedral; and now again the real scene—the rustic church of Longfield was vividly present to her mind. She saw the pathway through the green churchyard—the ruined ivy-mantled tower, which showed how much larger the edifice had been in former days, near which might be still discerned on high a niche containing the holy mother and divine child—the half-defaced porch on which rude monkish imagery was carved—the time-worn pews, and painted window. She had never entered this church but once, many, many years ago; and it was strange how in sleep and fever-troubled reverie, each portion of it presented itself distinctly and vividly to her imagination. During these perturbed visions, one other form and voice perpetually recurred. She heard Ethel continually repeat, "Come! come!" and often her figure flitted round the tomb or sat beside it. Once, on awakening from a dream, which impressed her deeply by the importunity and earnestness of her daughter's appeal, she was forcibly impelled to consider it her duty to obey, and she made a vow that on recovering from her illness, she would visit her husband's grave.

Now while pondering on the humiliations and cheerless necessities which darkened her future, and rousing herself to form some kind of resolution concerning them, this dream was repeated, and on awakening, the memory of her forgotten vow renewed itself in her. She dwelt on it with pleasure. Here was something to be done that was not mere wretchedness and lonely wandering—something that, connecting her with the past, took away the sense of desertion and solitude, so hard to bear. In the morning, at breakfast, it so chanced that she read in the Morning Herald a little paragraph announcing that Viscount Maristow was entertaining a party of friends at Maristow Castle, among whom were Mr. and Mrs. Villiers, and the Hon. Mrs. Elizabeth Fitzhenry. This was a fortunate coincidence. The dragon ceased for a moment to watch the garden, and she might avail herself of its absence to visit its treasure unnoticed and unknown. She put her project into immediate execution. She crossed the country, passing through London on her way to Longfield—she arrived. Without delay she fulfilled her purpose. She entered the church and viewed the tablet, inscribed simply with the name of Lodore, and the date of his birth and death. The words were few and common-place, but they were eloquent to her. They told her that the cold decaying shape lay beneath, which in the pride of life and love had clasped her in its arms as its own for evermore. Short-lived had been the possession. She had loosened the tie even while thought and feeling ruled the now insentient brain—he had been scarcely less dead to her while inhabiting the distant Illinois, than now that a stone placed above him, gave visible token of his material presence, and the eternal absence of his immortal part. Cornelia had never before felt so sensibly that she had been a wife neglecting her duties, despising a vow she had solemnly pledged, estranging herself from him, who by religious ordinance, and the laws of society, alone had privilege to protect and love her. Nor had she before felt so intimately the change—that she was a widow; that her lover, her husband, the father of her child, the forsaken, dead Lodore, was indeed no part of the tissue of life, action, and feeling to which she belonged.

Solitude and sickness had before awakened many thoughts in her mind, and she recalled them as she sat beside her dead husband's grave. She looked into her motives, tried to understand the deceits she had practised on herself, and to purify her conscience. She meditated on time, that law of the world, which is so mysterious, and so potent;

ruling us despotically, and yet wholly unappreciated till we think upon it. Petrarch says, that he was never so young, but that he knew that he was growing old. Lady Lodore had never thought of this till a few months back; it seemed to her, that she had never known it until now—that she felt that she was older—older than the vain and lovely bride of Lodore—than the haughty high-spirited friend of Casimir Lyzinski. And where was Casimir? She had never heard of him again, she had scarcely ever thought of him; he had grown older too—change, the effects of passion or of destiny, must have visited him also;—they were all embarked on one mighty stream—Lodore had gained a haven; but the living were still at the mercy of the vast torrent—whither would it hurry them?

There was a charm in these melancholy and speculative thoughts to the beautiful exile—for we may be indeed as easily exiled by a few roods of ground, as by mountains and seas. A strong decree of fate banished Cornelia from the familiar past, into an unknown and strange present. Still she clung to the recollection of bygone years, and for the first time gave way to reflections full of scenes and persons to be seen no more. The tomb beside which she lingered, was an outward sign of these past events, and she did not like to lose sight of it so soon. She heard that Mrs. Elizabeth Fitzhenry was to remain away for a month—so much time at least was hers. She inquired for lodgings, and was directed to Dame Nixon's cottage. She was somewhat dismayed at first by its penurious appearance, but "it would do for a few days"; and she found that what would serve for a few days, might serve for months.

> "Man wants but little here below,
> Nor wants that little long."

Most true for solitary man. It is society that increases his desires. If Lady Lodore had been visited in her humble dwelling by the least regarded among her acquaintances, she would have felt keenly its glaring deficiencies. But although used to luxury, Margaret's cuisine sufficed for herself alone; the low-roofed rooms were high enough, and the latticed windows which let in the light of heaven, fulfilled their purpose as well as the plate-glass and lofty embrasures of a palace.

Lady Lodore was obliged also to consider one other thing, which forms so large a portion of our meditations in real life—her purse. She found when settled in the cottage, in the Vale of Bewling, that her stock of money was reduced to one hundred pounds. She could not cross the country and establish herself at a distance from London with this sum only. She had before looked forward to selling her jewels and carriage as to a distant event, but now she felt that it was the *next* thing she must do. She shrunk from it naturally: the very idea of revisiting London— of seeing its busy shops and streets—once so full of life and its purposes to her, and in which she would now wander an alien, was inconceivably saddening; she was willing to put off the necessity as long as possible, and thus continued to procrastinate her departure from Essex.

Mrs. Fitzhenry returned; but she could neither know nor dream of the vicinity of her sister-in-law. We are apt to think, when we know nothing of any one, that no one knows any thing of us; experience can scarcely teach us, that the reverse of this is often the truth. Seeing only an old woman in her dotage—and a poor love-sick girl, who knew nothing beyond the one event which had blasted all her happiness—she never heard the inhabitants of Longfield mentioned, and believed that she was equally unheard of by them. Then her indisposition protracted her stay, and now the mortal illness of the poor woman. For she had become interested for Margaret and promised to befriend her; and in case of her grandmother's death, to take her from a spot where every association and appearance kept open the wounds inflicted by her unfaithful lover.

Time had thus passed on: now sad, now cheerful, she tried to banish every thought of the future, and to make the occurrences of each day fill and satisfy her mind. She lived obscurely and humbly, and perhaps as wisely as mortal may in this mysterious world, where hope is perpetually followed by disappointment, and action by repentance and regret. The days succeeded to each other in one unvaried tenor. The weather was cheerful, the breath of spring animating. She watched the swelling of the buds—the peeping heads of the crocuses—the opening of the anemones and wild wind-flowers, and at last, the sweet odour of the new-born violets, with all the interest created by novelty; not that she had not observed and watched these things before, with transitory pleasure, but now the operations of nature filled all her world; the earth was no longer merely the dwelling place of her acquaintance, the stage on which the business of society was carried on, but the mother of life—the temple of God—the beautiful and varied storehouse of bounteous nature.

Dwelling on these ideas, Cornelia often thought of Horatio Saville, whose conversations, now remembered, were the source whence she drew the knowledge and poetry of her present reveries. As solitude and nature grew lovely in her eyes, she yearned yet more fondly for the one who could embellish all she saw. Yet while her mind needed a companion so congenial to her present feelings, her heart was fuller of Ethel; her affection for Saville was a calm though deep-rooted sentiment, resulting from the conviction, that she should find entire happiness if united to him, and in an esteem or rather an enthusiastic admiration of his talents and virtues, that led her to dwell with complacency on the hope, that he still remembered and loved her: but the human heart is jealous, and with difficulty admits two emotions of equal force, and her love for her daughter was the master passion. The instinct of nature spoke audibly within her; the atoms of her frame seemed alive each one as she thought of her; often her tears flowed, often her eyes brightened with gladness when alone, and the beloved image of her beautiful daughter as she saw her last, smiling amidst penury and indignity, was her dearest companion by day and night. She alone made her present situation endurable, and yet separation from her was irksome beyond expression. Was she never to see or hear of her more? It was very hard: she implored Providence to change the harsh decree—she longed inexpressibly for one word that had reference to her—one event, however slight, which should make her existence palpable.

When Margaret announced Mrs. Fitzhenry, her heart bounded with joy. She could ask concerning Ethel—hear; her countenance was radiant with delight, and she really for a moment thought her sister-in-law's visit was meant in kindness, since so much pleasure was the result. This conviction had produced the very thing it anticipated. She had given poor Bessy no time to announce the actual intention with which she came; she had borne away her sullen mood by force of sweet smiles and sweeter words; and saw her depart with gladdened spirits, whispering to herself the fresh hopes and fond emotions which filled her bosom. She walked back to her little garden and stooped to gather some fresh violets, and to prop a drooping jonquil heavy with its burthen of sweet blooms. She inhaled the vernal odours with rapture. "Yes," she thought, "nature is the refuge and home for women: they have no public career—no aim nor end beyond their domestic circle; but they can extend that, and make all the creations of nature their own, to foster and do good to. We complain, when shut up in cities of the niggard rules of society, which gives us only the drawing-room or ball-room in which to display our talents, and which, for ever turning the sympathy of those around us into envy on the part of women, or what is called love on that of men, besets our path with dangers or sorrows. But throw aside all vanity, no longer seek to surpass your own sex, nor to inspire the other with feelings which are pregnant with disquiet or misery, and which seldom end in mutual benevolence, turn your steps to the habitation which God has given as befitting his creatures, contemplate the lovely ornaments with which he has blessed the earth;— here is no heart-burning nor calumny; it is better to love, to be of use to one of these flowers, than to be the admired of the many—the mere puppet of one's own vanity."

Lady Lodore entered the house; she asked concerning her poor hostess, and learnt that she slept. For a short time she employed herself with her embroidery; her thoughts were all awake; and as her fingers created likenesses of the flowers she loved, several times her eyes filled with tears as she thought of Ethel, and how happy she could be if her fate permitted her to cultivate her affection and enjoy her society.

"It is very sad," she thought; "only a few minutes ago my spirits were buoyant, gladdened as they were by Bessy's visit; but they flag again, when I think of my loneliness and the unreplying silence of this place. What is to become of me? I shall remain here: yes; I shall not banish myself to some inhospitable nook, where I should never hear her name. But am I not to see her again? Am I to be nothing to her? Is she satisfied with my absence—and are they all—to whom I am bound by ties of consanguinity or affection, indifferent to the knowledge of whether I exist or not? Nothing gives token to them of my life; it is as if the grave had closed abruptly over me—and had it closed, thus I should have been mourned, in coldness and neglect."

Again her eyes were suffused; but as she wiped away the blinding tears, she was recalled from her reflections by the bright rays of the sun which entered her little room. She threw open the door, stepped out into the garden—the sun was setting; the atmosphere was calm, and lighted up by golden beams; the few clouds were dyed in the same splendid hues, the birds sent forth a joyous song at intervals, and a band of rooks passed above the little wood, cawing loudly. The air was balmy, the indescribable freshness of spring was abroad, interpenetrating and cheerful. Cornelia's melancholy fled as she felt and gave way to its influence. "God blesses all things," she thought, "and he will also bless me. Much wrong have I done, but love pure and disinterested is in my heart, and I shall be repaid. My own sweet Ethel! I have sacrificed every thing except my life for your sake, and I would add my life to the gift, could it avail you. I ask but for you and your love. The world has many blessings, and I have asked for them before, with tears and anguish, but I give up all now, except you, my child. You are all the world to me! Will you not come, even now, as I implore Heaven to give you to me?"

She raised her eyes in prayer, and it seemed as if her wishes were to be accomplished—surely once in a life God will grant the earnest entreaty of a loving heart. Cornelia believed that he would, that happiness was near at hand, and life not all a blank. She heard a rustling among the trees, a light step;—was it Margaret? She had scarcely asked herself this question, when the dear object of her every thought and hope was before her—in her arms;—Ethel had entered from the wood, had seen her mother, had sprung forward and clasped her to her heart.

"My dear, dear child!"

"Dearest mother!" repeated Ethel, as her eyes were filled with tears of delight, "why did you go—why conceal yourself? You do not know the anxiety we have suffered, and how very unhappy your absence has made us. But I have found you—of all that have gone to seek you, I have found you; I deserve this reward, for I love you most of all."

Lady Lodore returned her daughter's caresses—and her tears flowed fast for very joy, and then she turned to Mrs. Fitzhenry, who followed Ethel, but who had been outspeeded by her in her eagerness. The old lady's face was beaming with happiness. "Ah, Bessy, you have betrayed me—traitress! I did not expect this—I do not deserve such excessive happiness."

"You deserve all, and much more than we can any of us bestow," cried Ethel, "except that your dear generous heart will repay you beyond any reward we can give, and you will be blest in the happiness we owe to you alone. Edward is gone far away into Wales in quest of you."

"An Angelica run after by the Paladins," said Lady Lodore, smiling through her tears.

"Paladins, worthy the name!" replied Ethel. "Horatio is even now on the salt seas for your sake—he is returning discomfited and hopeless from his journey of discovery to the Pyrenees—his zeal almost deserved the reward which I have found, yet who but she, for whom you sacrificed so much, ought to be the first to thank you? And while we all try to show you an inexpressible gratitude, ought not I to be the first to see, first to kiss, first—always the first—to love you?"

. . .

CONCLUSION

"None, I trust,
Repines at these delights, they are free and
    harmless:
After distress at sea, the dangers o'er,
Safety and welcomes better taste ashore."

—*Ford*

Thus the tale of "Lodore" is ended. The person who bore that title by right of descent, has long slept in peace in the church of his native village. Neither his own passions, nor those of others, can renew the pulsations of his heart. "The silver cord is loosed, and the pitcher broken at the fountain." His life had not been fruitless. The sedulous care and admirable education he had bestowed on Ethel, would, had he lived, have compensated to him for his many sufferings, and been a source of pure and unfading joy to the end. He was not destined in this world to reap the harvest of his virtues, though his errors had been punished severely. Still his memory is the presiding genius of his daughter's life, and the name of Lodore contains for her a spell that dignifies existence in her own eyes, and incites her to render all her thoughts and actions such as her beloved father would have approved. It was fated that the evil which he did should die with him—but the good out-lived him long, and was a blessing to those whom he loved far better than himself.

She who received the title on her marriage, henceforth continued her existence under another; and the wife of Saville, who soon after became Viscountess Maristow, loses her right to be chronicled in these pages. So few years indeed are passed since the period to which the last chapter brought us, that it may be safely announced that Cornelia Santerre possesses that happiness, through her generosity and devoted affection, which she had lost through pride and self-exaltation. She wonders at her past self—and laments the many opportunities she lost for benefiting others, and proving herself worthy of their attachment. Her pride is gone, or rather, her pride is now placed in redeeming her faults. She is humble, knowing how much she was deceived in herself—she is forgiving, for she feels that she needs forgiveness. She looks on the track of years she has passed over as wasted, and she wishes to retrieve their loss. She respects, admires, in some sense it may be said, that she adores her husband; but even while consenting to be his, and thus securing her own happiness, she told him that her first duties were towards Ethel—and that he took a divided heart, over the better part of which reigned maternal love. Saville, the least egoistic of human beings, smiled to hear her name that a defect, which was in his eyes her crowning virtue.

Edward Villiers learnt to prize worldly prosperity at its true value, and each day blesses the train of circumstances that led him to wed Ethel, even though poverty and suffering had followed close behind. Ethel herself might be said to have been always happy. She was incapable of being impressed by any sorrow, that did not touch her for another's sake: and while she exerted herself to alleviate the pain endured by those she loved, she passed on unhurt. Heaven spared her life's most cruel evils. Death had done its worst when she lost her father. Now, surrounded by dear friends, and the object of her husband's constant tenderness, she pursues a tranquil course: which for any one to consider the most blissful allotted to mortals, they must have a heart like her own—faithful, affectionate, and generous.

Mrs. Elizabeth Fitzhenry, kind and gentle aunt Bessy, always felt her heaven clouded while she indulged in her aversion to her sister-in-law. She is happy now that she is reconciled to Cornelia; strange to say, she loves her even more than she loves Ethel—she is more intimately connected in her mind with the memory of Lodore. She often visits her at Maristow Castle; in the neighbourhood of which Margaret is settled, being happily married. Colonel Villiers still lives in Paris. He is in a miserable state of poverty, difficulty, and ill-health. His wife has deserted him: he neglected and outraged her, and she in a fit of remorse left him, and returned to nurse her father during a lingering ill-ness, which is likely to continue to the end of his life, though he shows no symptoms of immediate decay. He is eager to lavish all his wealth on his child, if he can be sure that no portion of it is shared by her husband. With infinite difficulty, and at the cost of many privations, she, with a true woman's feeling, contrives to send him remittances now and then, though she receives in return neither thanks nor kind-ness. He pursues a course of dissipation in its most degraded form—a wretched hanger-on at resorts, misnamed of pleasure—gambling while he has any money to lose—trying to ruin others as he has been ruined.

Thus we have done our duty, in bringing under view, in a brief summary, the little that there is to tell of the personages who formed the drama of this tale. One only remains to be mentioned: but it is not in a few tame lines that we can revert to the varied fate of Fanny Der-ham. She continued for some time among her beloved friends, inno-cent and calm as she was beautiful and wise; circumstances at last led her away from them, and she has entered upon life. One who feels so deeply for others, and yet is so stern a censor over herself—at once so sensitive and so rigidly conscientious—so single-minded and upright, and yet open as day to charity and affection, cannot hope to pass from youth to age unharmed. Deceit, and selfishness, and the whole web of human passion must envelope her, and occasion her many sorrows; and the unworthiness of her fellow-creatures inflict infinite pain on her noble heart: still she cannot be contaminated—she will turn neither